TOURNAMENT OF SHADOWS

ANDREW WATTS

DALE M. NELSON

SEVERN RIVER
PUBLISHING

TOURNAMENT OF SHADOWS

Severn River Publishing
www.SevernRiverBooks.com

ISBN: 978-1-64875-390-9 (Paperback)

ALSO BY THE AUTHORS

The Firewall Spies

Firewall

Agent of Influence

A Future Spy

Tournament of Shadows

All Secrets Die

BY ANDREW WATTS

The War Planners Series

The War Planners

The War Stage

Pawns of the Pacific

The Elephant Game

Overwhelming Force

Global Strike

Max Fend Series

Glidepath

The Oshkosh Connection

Air Race

BY DALE M. NELSON

The Gentleman Jack Burdette Series

A Legitimate Businessman

The School of Turin

Once a Thief

Proper Villains

The Bad Shepherd

To join the reader list and find out more, visit

severnriverbooks.com/series/the-firewall-spies

1

Haifa, Israel

Colt missed the old days.

Not "missed" as in he lamented them gone, but "missed" in that he hadn't been there for them. In the old days, a cover was an easy thing to create and backstop with a few articles to support the legend. Now, a background can be checked instantly, a person's digital history dating back fifteen, twenty years verified. If someone didn't have those things, they stood out, they were the anomaly. Like, say, an identity created on the fly.

The Agency had software to forge those things, of course.

There were quiet agreements with social media companies which enabled CIA's analysts to fabricate digital profiles for their personnel and obfuscate the real ones. Colt maintained four covers, each serving a different purpose. More could be created, if the mission dictated, but the ones he had established verifiable habits, patterns of life—online and in the real world. They created connection and authenticity. This wasn't a common practice in the Agency. Most times, a legend was destroyed when the operation concluded. But there was a fear within Langley that their opposition, ever more sophisticated, might develop technology of their own to quickly unravel those AI-fabricated identities. So, Colt and some select other clandestine service officers maintained multiple covers and used them.

It was an experiment in the dangerous and unpredictable world of instant verification.

Today, he was Charles Reaves, an executive with a leading technology consulting practice recently contracted by a British shipping firm. He'd cultivated the Reaves legend over the last five years, and today, his credentials were augmented by additional documents supplied by Israeli intelligence.

Colt rode in the back of a small van as it drove the dusty frontage road between Haifa's airport and seaport.

The expansion and modernization of Haifa Bayport was a monumental undertaking, led by the Chinese construction firm responsible for the Port of Shanghai, regarded as the most modern and technologically advanced in the world. The detritus of rapid construction lay everywhere along the road. This would be landscaped eventually, Ava explained on the ride in, but now it was desert tan and the dusty gray of broken concrete.

They entered Haifa Bayport through the new gate on the road that ran next to the airport. The private security guard was thorough, and he scrutinized the identification documents provided and the papers Mossad created, identifying the two in the front seat as upper-level managers at the port and the two in the back as American IT contractors. The guard challenged them, aggressively, because he'd been trained to. Put them on their heels, get them to make a mistake. They did not. While he interrogated them, another guard walked around the van. Before they arrived, Ava explained that while they were parked at the gate, four different scanners drilled the vehicle looking for weapons, contraband, explosives.

The scanners were based on technology developed by the Israeli Defense Forces' Unit 8200, Israel's answer to the National Security Agency, in collaboration with Mossad.

It was some of the most advanced sensing equipment on earth, and Mossad knew just how to beat it. The gear—and the weapons they'd smuggled in—were safe.

Satisfied, the guard gruffly waved them through.

The man next to Colt McShane was nervous. He was a tech, and this was his first time in the field, first time using a cover. Colt knew the kid was edgy, but he hid it well and the guard didn't pick up on it.

They drove into the port. The two in the front were Mossad. This was a joint operation. Mossad wouldn't let a pair of CIA officers near the Israeli government's pet project without minders.

The driver took them down a short stretch to a concrete isthmus, passing a pair of security guards on foot patrol. On their right was an industrial district facing the water; the airport was directly behind it. On the left were cargo terminals and construction. Everything was the dun color of the desert and sandblasted concrete. There was landscaping, grass and palm trees, desert plants, but even those seemed the color of dirt.

Three Months Earlier

"Well, just because you're paranoid doesn't mean the Chinese aren't building a global electronic eavesdropping network to spy on everything," Fred Ford said, standing over a map of the Haifa Bayport. Ford, Colt, and Laura Weston, a liaison officer from CIA's Israel desk, stood around a conference table with a map of the newly constructed port, the target of their proposed operation.

Colt pointed to the map. "The Bayport is an extension on Haifa's existing port complex, fully automated and controlled by a sophisticated artificial intelligence designed to optimize port operations. It's built and managed by a Chinese firm as part of their Belt and Road Initiative, also called the Digital Silk Road."

Ford picked up the thread. "This is an investment of billions of dollars to connect Asia with Africa and Europe, physically and digitally, and create new economic zones for the Chinese. Chinese construction firms have built or modernized seaports from Jakarta to Istanbul. They carved out new, modern roads to reconnect Asia with Europe. The Soviets laid many of those existing roads, and they were as serviceable as one would expect.

Governments across the former Soviet Socialist Republics welcomed the investment and the interest. We go in during GWOT and just reconfigure Soviet airfields for us to stage out of, and they never hear from us again. Meanwhile, the Chinese promise to bring them into the twenty-first century. Chinese tech companies built data centers, 5G cell infrastructure, and high-speed internet conduits across continents, all supervised by an arm of the Chinese government called the Ministry of Technical Cooperation."

"Which is just a front for their foreign intelligence service?" Weston asked.

"The Ministry of State Security," Ford said, nodding. "Many of these partner nations are so hungry for renewal and economic rejuvenation they didn't pay attention to the real costs."

"I mean, the investment loans the Chinese government backed may keep some of those states in vassalage for decades," Colt said. "But every byte of traffic that crosses a Chinese-built server, every text or app used on one of these cell networks will be monitored by AI in Beijing. Data collected, parsed, sorted by Chinese computers, and rendered to analysts in the Ministry of State Security for consumption by the Chinese Communist Party."

They were creating a tool to spy on half the world and cloaking it in altruism.

"Okay," Ford said. "Young McShane, here, is going to walk us through the final ops plan. We'll give him the go/no-go after that. That work?"

"Let's do it," Weston said. This was the final operational checkout and the first time Colt presented the full plan to the Israel desk, who had the final say on whether the mission could go forward. It was the result of weeks of dedicated planning and several months of intense preparation.

"Right," Colt said. "We have two objectives here. First, the Israeli government has bankrolled multiple projects as part of this Belt and Road Initiative, but the Haifa Bayport is the largest one. This is a concern for us because of the amount of economic intelligence the Chinese government will be able to collect. As you know, we also use Haifa as a port of call for US Navy ships transiting the region. We must assume the Chinese have installed electronic intelligence capability and will target our ships."

Laura nodded. She had worked tirelessly over the last six months to convince their counterparts in Mossad of the threat, after Colt first briefed her.

"I met with Mossad's Washington Station Chief, Hiram Katz, whom I believe you two are both acquainted with. It took some convincing, but he eventually agreed to elevate it to his leadership in Tel Aviv. Your briefing material was really helpful, by the way. I showed them how this port management system would know every minute detail about every ship and every container of cargo that passed through this terminal. They would know the shipping manifests, the declared value of the contents and what markets they were destined for, where they were manufactured. That alone was economic intelligence of incredible value. The first time Katz bucked, I asked if the Israelis would be certain that there were no other electronic eavesdropping systems embedded in the RF signal transmitters used to communicate with the drones and autonomous vehicles that flitted about the port. And whether they'd be willing to risk our relationship because of it."

Mossad eventually came to view the situation as CIA did, but the Israeli government decided to continue with the project. Israel had a much more pragmatic view of espionage. They assumed everyone was already spying on everyone else and that it was the cost of doing business in an international system. They tended not to moralize it the way the Americans did. However, she had secured Mossad's support for their operation.

Colt continued. "We enter the port using the credentials provided by Mossad and access the server room, located in this facility." Colt pointed to a large structure on the map. "One of our technical officers will hack into the servers using a software exploit we developed. Once inside, he will deploy a program that will create a tunnel back here to Langley. We'll get to see everything the Chinese do."

"And that can't be done remotely?" Weston asked.

"No. Those servers are isolated from the internet and communicate with China on a closed-loop system. Doing it in person lets us create a back door. It shouldn't take us more than fifteen minutes to access the server, upload the exploit, and activate it. How are we doing on clearances?" Colt already knew the answer to that question because he'd been working with Ava Klein behind the scenes, so this was for show with the Israel desk.

"Mossad will supply credentials and escort you into the port. No way around that. They won't let us run around that port without adult supervision. They'll stick with you. The condition we agreed to is that we share any intel we gather with them once it's cleared for release."

"That was the plan," Ford said.

"Now, our second objective is to get eyes on Liu Che," Colt said. Liu was a Chinese intelligence officer wanted by the US government for running a spy he managed to put on the National Security Staff. "Thanks to Laura's sources in Mossad," Colt extended a hand across the table, "we have reason to believe Liu will be on hand to oversee the final implementation. We want to bring him in and make him answer for what he did."

Weston stood and folded her arms across her chest. "Mossad said they can slip a tracking device into his luggage as he's departing the country. See where he goes next."

Colt knew they couldn't capture Liu in Israel. It was too politically sensitive, given their Belt and Road investment and the country's increasing ties with the Chinese, but if they could figure out where his next stop was, they could try to put a capture plan in place.

"All right," Colt said. He'd spent nearly every waking moment in the last several months scouring the globe for Liu Che, who proved as effective at evading detection as he did running agents.

"Okay, Colt, what does success look like?" Weston said.

"Our tech installs the exploit on the server, and I can use a remote surveillance tool to image capture the Chinese in attendance. We verify Liu Che is with them, and Mossad slips a tracker into his bags. We're in and out in fifteen minutes."

"What does failure look like?"

Colt thought for a moment. "The Chinese identify the software vulnerability and patch it, which denies us access. There's no workaround for that in the field. If it happens, we walk away."

"I'm satisfied," Weston said. "I think it's a solid plan. So, what does NTCU hope to get out of this?"

"Well, the Belt and Road Initiative is hitting some speed bumps,"

Ford said. "The Chinese suffered several high-profile setbacks, and a lot of Western countries are questioning its efficacy and sustainability, if not its integrity. We've, ah, been helping there," Ford said, smirking. "The Italians have withdrawn their participation, along with other key European nations, after we convinced them of the surveillance and economic espionage risks. Ultimately, we want some solid intel that will convince people this thing is dangerous. Also, Israel is now a partner nation in the F-35 Joint Strike Fighter program, and we don't want the CHICOMMs getting any more information on that than they've already got."

"We also believe that the technology the Chinese are using to run these ports is based on intellectual property they stole from Jeff Kim," Colt said.

"The head of Pax AI?"

"The same," Colt said. "Getting under the hood can go a long way to proving that. Maybe once we can hold these guys accountable."

The driver parked the van in a lot in the shadow of a monolithic white building, and they got out. Each of them donned a hard hat and yellow vest, the port's only real uniform. The two Israelis had port badges; Colt and the tech had ones indicating "VISITOR." Golden light from a late afternoon sun fell across a blue-green sea. It had been many years since Colt was last in Haifa.

Colt had a complicated relationship with Israel. Ava almost died here. Had the dice landed just a little differently, Colt would have been caught in a terrorist's bomb not far from where he was right now. But this was also the place where he'd first truly *lived*. He met someone that gave his life meaning and purpose, more than the Navy ever had. Being back here, in Haifa, brought that stark distinction to him to blazing color, an overexposed picture that was too sharp in places, too dull in others.

The woman at the center of that division, Ava Klein, handed him his backpack.

The driver, a Mossad officer Colt knew only as "Ben," subtly motioned to a stretch along the western seawall populated with stubby white towers.

"That's the chemical terminal," he said, and Ava nodded. Ben checked his watch. "I'll run my search there. We'll meet back here in sixty minutes."

"Good luck," Ava said, and Ben left.

It seemed Colt wasn't the only one with a secondary objective.

Mossad had intel that a Palestinian terrorist group was planning something at the port, but they were lean on details. Israel invested billions in Belt and Road projects, including this port, city automation, data centers, and 5G wireless infrastructure. The Palestinian Authority either opted out or weren't invited to participate. Two months ago, a member of the Abu Ali Mustapha Brigades used a stolen ID to access the data center of a Tel Aviv telecom company and snuck a backpack bomb inside. The blast took out most of the building and knocked half of Tel Aviv offline for days. They were still recovering.

Palestinian terror groups mounted a lengthy rocket campaign, targeting locations of Belt and Road projects. The goal appeared to be chaos and fear, and it had the desired effect, particularly among the foreign workers here on infrastructure projects.

Disaffected Palestinians latched onto the growing anti-technologist movement with fierce vigor. That global rebellion against the inexorable march of progress. In other parts of the world, it was pipe bombs thrown at Apple stores; here it was Katyusha rockets launched into data centers and cell towers. Many Palestinians felt left out, left behind, and wanted payback. But the port was a little different. Israel and the Lebanese government—such as it was—had been embroiled in a maritime dispute for years. Israel feared one of the terrorist proxies was targeting Haifa because of it.

"We ready?" Ava asked.

Colt and Danny Harriman followed her to the massive building. They walked along a wide concrete path along the seawall, framed in green to indicate it was safe for humans to walk. The other flat surfaces were reserved for machines. Their forged credentials got them into the building easily.

From the ground floor to the fifth, the building was an enormous, open-air cargo bay. Rolling doors on either side opened at precisely the right time, allowing an autonomous cargo handling vehicle to enter, select or drop off its charge, and depart with minimal queue time. Far above them, they saw an observation window—a conference room that looked out over the bay. It was filled with a Chinese delegation and their Israeli counterparts. Ava's contact was in that group.

"The server farm is on the sixth floor," Ava said. "There are a few offices there, and a conference room, but this was designed to be run with a minimal staff."

"Why isn't it on the ground?" Danny asked.

"Because it's safer up there," she said curtly. "Let's take the stairs."

They didn't want to risk running into the delegation.

The building was so new, they could smell the tang of fresh paint in the wide stairwell as they climbed.

Colt, Ava, and Danny reached the sixth floor. The stairwell was in the corner of the building, with a long, windowed hallway running the length of either side. "The elevators are on the far side, so we should be good," Ava said. She checked her phone. "My contact is almost done. He'll meet us upstairs."

The door to the server room was halfway down the hallway extending to the left. They would need to backtrack to reach the stairs that would take them to the roof. Ava led them down the hallway. Late afternoon light fell in from outside, painting the walls in a dark orange. There was a sign on the door with "RESTRICTED AREA" written in Hebrew and again in, presumably, Mandarin beneath it. Ava produced a keycard from her pocket and badged into the room. Lights flickered on as they entered.

The room was cold, twenty or thirty degrees lower than the hallway. Long rows of black computer racks holding high-bandwidth CPUs and AI accelerators, specialized computers designed to speed up data-intensive operations. These extended from the front wall to the back; soft green light from their display panels illuminated the front. The room filled with the soft whirr of cooling fans. Ava handed Danny a small metal key. "This will open any of the lockers in here."

Danny took it. "Will you be watching the door?"

"No one is supposed to come by as long as there are no problems. This place is designed to run by itself."

Colt could tell Danny was apprehensive about being by himself.

"Danny, you're going to do fine," Colt said. Harriman's job was to access the system and clone several of the hard drives so NTCU analysts could study the code and look for vulnerabilities to exploit. Then, Danny would install software that would allow them to covertly watch the network and see exactly what data was transmitted back to Beijing. "If someone comes in here, just tell them it's part of the assessment."

"I got you," Danny said in an easy way. Colt had worked with him for about a year and knew he was in his element now that he was in the AI farm.

"We should go," Ava said, looking at her phone. She and Colt left. They moved quickly back down the hallway and past the stairwell they'd come up. The left side opened to the cargo bay, separated by a metal railing. The right had long windows facing the Mediterranean. They could see the now darkened conference room. The delegation had finished and was likely taking the elevators down to the main floor.

The stairs to the roof were across the hall from the conference room. They climbed those to a glass room. One door opened to the control center, windows on three sides with unobstructed views of the port, Haifa Bay, and the cargo yard. The control center was smaller than Colt expected, six workstations with four giant monitors at each. He couldn't read them in detail, but it looked like performance metrics and video feeds. The other door led to a break area and observation platform. They entered the control room with Ava's badge, and someone looked up. Colt's Hebrew was patchwork, at best, but he could pick out Ava explaining that he's part of the "ASE Maritime team" evaluating their system.

"He's not on the schedule," a man in a short-sleeved shirt said in English, not looking up from his console.

"This is a quality control visit," Ava replied in English. "We do unannounced drop-ins." She spoke with the vocal authority of upper management, and no one in the command center questioned her. "He's going to ask some questions, please show him around."

Normally, there would be Chinese technicians standing over the shoulders of the port operators, but they would be out with the delegation tonight. Wining and dining. Part of the reason Colt chose this window for the op.

"I need to clear this," the man said.

"I've got the authorization right here," Ava replied, impatient. She closed the distance between them, shoved the unfolded forged papers at him.

The man sighed and gave the documents back to Ava, who said she'd be back in a few minutes.

Ava stepped out of the room and out to the observation deck.

Mossad had an asset in the Ministry of Technical Cooperation. While he'd spill his guts to Ava, if she brought an American with her to the meet, it would be easy for him to guess the American was CIA. That's a detail the asset would find a way to slip to his bosses in the service, without letting on he was an Israeli spy.

Colt cast a quick glance to Ava. The observation deck was half of the roof. There were benches and tables along the wall with long rectangular rows of desert plants and grasses. There was another row of plants in the center and a third next to the outer wall. Colt saw a Chinese man in a light-colored, tropical-weight suit standing on the far side of the roof that faced the cargo yard. Colt was too far to read lips, but the body language and tightly screwed facial expression screamed tension. Colt turned back to the controllers, who ignored him with casual disinterest. Colt asked a few perfunctory questions.

"You're evaluating this system?" the man asked.

"That's right," Colt replied. Each operator was at a workstation with four UHD monitors, stacked two high. "We're thinking about installing something similar. What are you looking at?"

"Everything," he said. "The system manages all the cargo-handling equipment. Right now, we're loading a ship."

"This is the one bound for Southampton?"

"That's right," he said.

"My client is based there," Colt said. That should resolve any lingering skepticism. On the monitor, he saw the ship docked at one of the loading quays on the concrete isthmus that jutted out into the bay like a crooked finger. Automated cranes transferred cargo from the long line of stacked shipping containers, handing off from one crane to another, then to the ship. It was amazing to see in person. "So, the Chinese designed everything?"

"Yes, but we've added a few wrinkles."

Colt tried not to smile. One of the truisms of cooperating with the Israelis was that whatever you sold them, they were going to break down, reverse engineer, and redesign to suit their needs. The finished product was often better than the original. Colt asked him what they'd added.

"Integrated security system. We scan the crew manifest for every ship coming and going, see if anyone trips. The system looks at what they post online, what web traffic they access while on-ship. We also get a notice if the ship ever docked at a place designated as a known terror threat. The containers are scanned for explosives, chem, bio, and radiological material before being unloaded." He toggled a new view on one of his screens. "Between the drones and cameras, we see everything on the ship." One of the views switched to thermal imaging, showing crew members belowdecks.

Colt looked at Ava through the window. The Chinese man handed her something that looked like car keys.

Colt looked to another screen at a different station. There was not an inch of ground at this port uncovered by a camera or a drone.

"You don't run security out of here, do you?" he asked.

"No, but we see the same feeds. Or, most of them."

Colt turned his head and saw Ava alone. She nodded. Colt thanked the port controller for his time and joined Ava on the observation deck. The deck offered a staggering view of the harbor. On the opposite side of the small bay, there were two cargo terminals extending out into the water and another for cruise ships. Beyond that, separated by a seawall and docking facility, were the secured berths used by the Israeli and US Navies.

"Liu Che isn't here," she said flatly.

Colt swore. Ava knew that Liu was a senior intelligence officer from her time undercover in Jeff Kim's company, Pax AI, where she and Colt reconnected. She did not know that Liu had recently run a US Navy admiral as a spy for nearly three decades and that Colt had narrowly missed capturing him.

Colt's organization, the National Technical Counterintelligence Unit

(NTCU), discovered Liu's extensive espionage just before he exposed one of NTCU's own field operations and burned an undercover officer in the process. Liu escaped the dragnet, fleeing, they believed, to Canada. He resurfaced once in Geneva. Colt had been on his tail ever since.

"Our agent said Liu was here to inspect the port last week," Ava said.

That was fitting, Colt thought sourly, since Liu helped steal the technology that ran this place.

"That the delegation down there?" Colt asked, peering over the edge of the roof.

"Yeah. That's my guy running to catch up."

"Might as well find out who else is here," Colt said. He knelt down and dropped his backpack to the ground. "Cover me, will you?"

Ava moved to stand behind him. This would be difficult. There were cameras on the roof and a straight line of sight to the control center.

"They're not going to see that, are they?"

"Doubt it. It's about the size of a hummingbird. Lens is accurate to a hundred yards or so." Colt opened the backpack and the small box within it. In a few seconds, he'd assembled the micro drone, which resembled a ballpoint pen crossed with a quadcopter. Colt stood, keeping his back to the roof and any cameras. He powered the drone, the tiny rotors whirred to life, and it quickly disappeared into the evening sky. Colt zipped his backpack and shouldered it. He got out his phone, issued commands to the drone, and said to Ava, "Let's go get Danny."

A white Mercedes Sprinter pulled into the queue waiting for the signal to approach the port's security gate. Guards manned two of the four lanes. Security barriers blocked off the other two. The van waited behind a row of tractor trailers two-deep for their turn. After twenty minutes, a guard called them forward with an abrupt arm motion. The man in the passenger seat activated a tablet in a hardened case, opened an app, and then closed the cover. He set the tablet back in the bag next to the seat.

The device created an electromagnetic baffler around the vehicle that would scramble the sophisticated sensing equipment the port security used to scan for weapons, drugs, or explosives.

The driver, cool and easy, handed the guard his manifest and identification for everyone in the van. There were three others. Rear doors opened, and a guard with a submachine gun inspected the crates in the back, checked the customs tags and confirmed they were unbroken. It took another five minutes to clear before the guard lifted the red-and-white crossbar, waved them through.

The driver followed the road curving toward the water and the large white building. The two men in the back snipped the security seals on the transit cases, opened them, and popped the false bottoms, exposing AK-47s, pistols, tactical vests, and explosives.

2

Haifa, Israel

Colt and Ava left the observation deck and descended to the upper floor, Colt watching the drone feed on his phone. He'd programmed the device to orbit the Chinese delegation before they got into their waiting vans from a distance and to capture a photo of each of the faces. He saw the group walking, suits and grim smiles, China's answer to the Reservoir Dogs. A green bracket appeared around each face, blinking in rapid succession until it turned solid, capturing their image. NTCU analysts would run those photos against known images of Chinese intelligence officers and look for a match.

Colt and Ava hit the hallway in long strides, the sunlight outside the windows growing long and splashing burnt orange on the white walls. The cargo bay below was quiet but busy. Autonomous handling equipment, powered by electric motors, silently grabbed their assignments and loaded them onto vehicles to be carried out to wherever they were bound for. It was an elaborate, perfectly choreographed dance.

Colt looked down at his phone. The Chinese were in their vans and driving away.

But something wasn't right.

Through the drone's camera, he saw three men get out of a white van just outside the building. Colt directed the drone to get closer. From a distance, they looked...bulky. The image solidified as the camera flew nearer. Backpacks, AKs, and tactical vests.

Colt grabbed Ava's shoulder and showed her his phone.

"We've got a serious problem," Colt said.

No sooner had he gotten the words out, than the sound of sirens pierced the air. Muted by the walls, but still clear.

"That's a rocket alarm."

To Colt, it sounded like a tornado siren from his youth.

Ava tapped a button on her watch, activating the covert tactical radio that connected her with Ben, the other Mossad officer. She relayed the situation to him. "Whatever the Palestinians are doing, they timed it to start with the rocket attack," Ava said, voice hurried, drawing one of the pistols they'd smuggled through security. Mossad developed the scanning technology in conjunction with the Israeli Defense Forces and knew how to spoof it. Ava didn't admit as much, but Colt suspected that, too, was part of Mossad's test here today. They wanted to see what they could get through. "Get Danny, lock yourself in the server room."

Colt didn't like the idea of being trapped on the sixth floor of the largest building for blocks.

Colt drew his smuggled SIG Sauer P365 from a concealed holster under his shirt. He instructed the drone to follow them. The men were running now, running away from the drone's position.

Staccato blasts of gunfire.

Colt watched the guard building's door drop. The men were moving out of camera range.

"Ava, wait. They're almost inside. We have to hold them off until the response team gets here."

Ava shook her head. "No. You and Danny need to get clear. I'll cover for you and keep them busy."

"No way in hell."

Ava gave him a wry, knowing grin. "I'm a better shot than you. Besides, if two CIA officers get shot up here, there's going to be a lot of questions no one has good answers for. *And* you have whatever Danny scrubbed off those servers. We can't prove the Chinese are up to something if that bag gets blown up."

"I'm not leaving you."

"Then don't get yourself killed," Ava said with a wink. She handed him the key fob her agent gave her on the roof. "Just in case. Make sure this gets to the right people." She closed her hand around Colt's, leaned forward, and kissed him. Then, just as quickly, trotted off to the server room door and badged it open. Colt followed. The door opened, and Danny was standing there, pushing gear into his backpack and securing it with internal straps.

"I thought I just heard gunfire."

Colt said, "You did."

"We should probably get out of here, huh." Danny's voice was nonchalant, a complete change from his previous edginess. Colt shared the plan.

Ava in the lead, they ran along the nearest hallway. It was directly above the building's entry, so the terrorists wouldn't see them. There were two stairwells at opposite corners of the building, one directly behind them and the other at a diagonal. They reasoned the terrorists would take the closest one to the door. Colt directed the drone to follow the men. They'd blasted the door open, so it could fly through. There was an emergency exit on the ground floor, next to the stairwell.

"They're going for the servers or the control room," Colt said as they ran. "Probably both. They want to bring this place down, that's how to do it." Ava agreed. They rounded the corner at full speed, the now dark conference room was on the left. For a moment, they were shielded from the open bay. Colt and Danny made the stairwell. Ava kept going, crouching low.

"I'll see you," she said.

Colt and Danny raced down the stairs, taking them two at a time.

They had just hit the fifth floor when he heard a tight *pop-pop-pop*. A strangled cry. Shouting. A chainsaw rip of automatic fire.

Single shots rang out, terrible echoes in the stairwell.

Colt stopped when they reached the landing for the third floor, checking the drone feed on his phone. The tiny copter entered "sentry mode" when it lacked instructions, rotating for a panoramic view. One of the attackers was on the ground, clutching his leg. Ava knew about the tac vest from looking at the feed, knew to aim low. There were two more moving, fanned out to opposite sides of the bay. They were creating a cross-fire, hoping Ava would pop out of cover to hit one and get nailed by the other.

Colt had no way to warn her.

He motioned to Danny to keep moving. They hit the stairs again, pistol in one hand and phone in the other, backpack bouncing like a mad chimp jumping on his shoulders. They made the ground floor. Gunfire from a different spot, sounding farther away. Ava was mobile. They couldn't pin her yet.

Colt dropped the backpack and looked at the video feed. He only saw one of the attackers; that meant the other was behind the drone. It was trained to follow threats. If the camera picked up a weapon that wasn't tagged as a friendly, it kept eyes on it until directed otherwise. The drone also showed the cargo-handling equipment still moving about, carrying out its assignments. Autonomous forklifts and carts moving up and down rows, adding to the motion, the visual background noise.

Colt tried to orient his mind to the cargo bay floor, reconciling that with the image on the screen. If his mental geometry was correct, the target was about fifty feet in front of him. He motioned for Danny to wait, who nodded. Colt shoved the phone into his back pocket.

He and Danny could make the emergency exit, but they'd have to come out of hiding to do it. It would also mean leaving Ava to fend for herself. He wasn't going to do that.

There was no doorway in the stairwell—it just opened to the bay. Colt crouched low and moved out quickly, closing the distance between the stairwell and the first row of cargo stacked on metal rails. Red and white slanted stripes around the base told him he wasn't supposed to walk here. A cargo cart rounded the corner and stopped abruptly, right in front of him.

The vehicle must be trained to stop when it detected a person within a certain proximity.

Could he use that to his advantage?

Pop-pop-pop from above.

Return fire from below.

Colt rotated out of cover, sidestepping until he saw the man. He raised the pistol, sighted, and fired a three-shot burst.

The man must have seen Colt move in the corner of his eye, because he twisted just as Colt came into view, ducking behind a forklift idling in his row. Colt dove for cover just before the return fire.

The bay was organized into long rows, maybe fifty yards long, with three tiers of racks to store crates and pallets. Robotic arms moved along rails mounted on the racks to transfer cargo to a carrier. From his vantage point in the corner of the building, amplified by what he saw on the drone, Colt could see many of the arms still moving, carrying out their instructions to identify and transfer cargo to the appropriate carrier. Interestingly, these didn't cease operation after the missile alarm, suggesting it was not tied into the security system, or it was something the Chinese designers hadn't thought of.

Colt crouched behind the row and used the phone to send instructions to the drone. The little copter skimmed its row, lifting over the racks. Colt spotted the attacker by noticing the lack of mechanical movement around him. He was three rows deep, running away from Colt's position toward the center aisle that bisected the rows. He must not have hit him, or if he did, the tactical vest took the shot.

Colt ran down the rows, stopping at the third. He checked the screen before stowing it. The attacker fast-walked in a crouch, sneaking around to Colt's previous position for an ambush.

Colt whipped around the rack and came face-to-face with a cargo hauler. The vehicle stopped immediately, the tires screeching on the concrete. Colt jumped to the side and fired twice. Both shots were center mass, and the force knocked the terrorist down on his back. A shot cracked from above as he scrambled to his feet. The terrorist's head pulped, and his body dropped, lifeless. Colt couldn't see Ava to give her the all-clear without breaking cover, so he stayed where he was.

Colt instructed the drone to seek. The final adversary would be on the bay's far side. The drone picked him up immediately. Though, the AK burst did that too. He sent a long spray up to Ava's position. Colt heard several shots impact the concrete. Covering fire. The terrorist was bugging out. Probably hadn't expected a hard target.

Colt ran, sprinting for the last row. He wouldn't have time to check the feed, just needed to act.

He spun around the last row, pistol up.

There the attacker was, AK up and pivoting.

A crack of gunfire split the air, the terrorist's head snapped forward, and he dropped to the ground.

Ben emerged from the entryway.

The Mossad officer surged forward to check the body, spotted Colt, and brought his weapon around. Colt held up a hand and was recognized. "That's the last one," he shouted and trotted over.

Ava and Danny joined them.

Ben opened the terrorist's backpack. Inside were several bars of plastic explosives and additional magazines. He pulled the detonator out of the explosives and asked Ava to check the other body, the one she'd dropped. She ran over, opened the backpack, and found the same. She removed the detonators and brought the pack over. She and Ben consolidated the explosives into one pack and the detonators in the other.

They heard more gunfire outside.

The ground shook, and an explosion rocked the building.

It felt like an earthquake.

The building shuddered.

"Was that a rocket?" Colt asked, picking himself up from the floor.

"Doubtful," Ben said, skeptical. "Iron Dome is very effective. It must be something on the ground."

Silence, then sirens.

"We have to get out of here," Ava said. Colt pulled out his phone and directed the drone to return to him.

They found the third terrorist, the one Ava initially hit in the leg, lying just outside the entrance hallway. Ben had quietly resolved that problem on the way in.

Ben nodded and led them from the building. The entrance, decimated by gunfire, faced south. Beyond the edges of the port complex, they could see the city of Haifa rising into the rocky hills, bathed in the burnt orange of early evening. White streaks filled the otherwise cloudless sky, contrails terminating in gassy puffballs. Their eyes all pulled to the left, to the port's entrance and the rising column of greasy black smoke backlit by roiling flames. Did a rocket hit the gate? That seemed oddly precise.

Gunfire erupted behind them, perhaps coming from the direction of the ship. Then another burst from the three o'clock position, though in the middle distance, beyond the chemical terminal Ben had inspected.

"We're obviously not shooting our way out," Colt said. "What do you suggest?"

"Yeah, that would be a bad idea," Ben said. "We don't want port security to confuse us for those guys wearing disguises."

The bombed-out entry gate closed off their escape route. There was another gate to the west, coming off the Highway 22 exit and subsequent bridge over the channel, but the attackers might be trying to funnel evacuees through there so they could hit them with another bomb or ambush fire. The sounds of gunfire coming from that direction created other problems, however. They didn't want to survive one firefight just to have to run through a second one.

By now, the few workers in the building rushed down the stairs to evacuate. Colt heard their panicked shouts from the stairwell. Everyone stowed their weapons.

"Follow me," Ben said, taking off for their van. He and Ava tossed the confiscated backpacks in the back, and everyone piled in. "We're going to do a panicked evacuation, just like everyone else." The door was barely closed when Ben floored the accelerator, tires screeching beneath them.

They opted for the only real choice. Blast through an area they believed to be in another firefight and hope the combatants were too busy trying to kill each other to bother with them.

Could they hide somewhere and wait for Haifa police, port security, or the IDF or Shin Bet, Israel's counterintelligence service, to rescue them? Yes, but that would introduce questions that no one here wanted to answer. And the Israelis would confiscate the equipment the Americans had on them, which would force Mossad's hand and reveal the existence of the operation.

They fled and chanced crossfire.

Ben clearly aced Mossad's combat driving course.

He'd gotten them to the gate in record time. Security closed off the exit, but Ben hurriedly explained they were port workers and trying to escape. The guards let them through, and they blasted across the bridge as the responding vehicles surged across it in the opposite direction.

Ben brought them to a Mossad safe house in Tel Aviv not far from the water. The original plan was to recover to a different location, but until they knew what in the hell was going on, they would make it up as they went. A Mossad logistics team grabbed Colt's and Danny's things from their Haifa hotel and dropped them here.

Colt showered and changed into a pair of lightweight gray pants and navy short-sleeve button-down. He emerged from the bathroom to the amazing aromas of exotic spices, fresh pita, and sizzling lamb. Colt walked around to the kitchen and saw Ava simultaneously cooking and directing traffic, casually ordering a wide-eyed Danny and Ben about.

Israeli pragmatism never ceased to amaze. Three hours after surviving a terrorist attack and now they would feast.

But, he needed to check in with Jerusalem Station, let them know he and Danny were okay.

Ava, seemingly reading his mind, pointed at the bottle of wine on the dining room table without looking up from her work. She flipped what looked and smelled like lamb cubes in the small frying pan. "Pour, Colt," she said.

Colt grabbed the bottle of wine, a 2015 Pelter Shiraz, and poured a glass. Mossad did a hell of a job keeping their safe houses stocked. "The winery is in the Golan Heights, not far from the Lebanese border. The workers carry sidearms when they inspect the grapes." Colt took a sip. He didn't know much about wine, so wasn't quite sure what to look for, but it tasted good to him, if a bit spicy. He peeled off a hunk of steaming bread and dipped it in the bowl of hummus on the table.

Colt used an encrypted messaging system on his phone to inform CIA's Chief of Jerusalem Station he and Danny were okay. The CoS dispatched one of his officers to debrief them, and they should arrive within the hour. Mossad would be doing the same.

During dinner, Colt downloaded the photos the drone took to a tablet. He propped that on the table and turned it so that Ava and Ben could see. "In addition to the Chinese, I got a few shots of the attackers. We'll run this through our recognition programs, and once it's cleared for release, I'll make sure you get copies."

"I don't need that," Ben said.

He pointed at the screen. Still photos flipped through in a rotating carousel, starting from high and above, then close up. It was the terrorist Colt engaged with, the one Ava head-shot from the balcony. The man had Levantine features, hazel eyes, and dark hair cut low. He had a hawkbill nose and scars on his face. He looked like he could've been any of half a dozen nationalities. "Him, I know already," Ben said. "He was one of us."

"What, an asset?" Colt asked.

"No. He was Mossad."

3

The Old Man looked into the sky and decided aloud that today would be a hot one. Just like that. He walked around this place like he was Obi-Wan Kenobi or some shit, but Dave liked him. The Old Man had been here, along the riverbank, for as long as anyone knew and was what passed for the mayor of the homeless camp. Reminded him of the village elders they worked with in Iraq.

"Hot today," he said again. A pronouncement.

"Yeah, well, it isn't Yuma and it isn't Baghdad," Dave Reyes said. Weather here was predictable, which made living—if you could call it that—easier. Cool now but scorching by late afternoon, so he thought he'd get a quick swim in the river to wash up, clean his clothes. Dave walked down the gentle slope to the riverbank carrying his wash in a convenience store bag. He didn't have any soap but could at least get them soaked and bang 'em on a rock before hanging on a tree branch while a swam. Old school. The sun was up, he guessed it was about nine thirty, ten a.m. There were a couple kayakers on the water, but the American River was otherwise quiet.

Dave grew up in Yuma, Arizona, a fourth-generation farmer. He enlisted in the Army the second he was old enough to get away from that life. Of course, the Army sent him to Baghdad, which had pretty much the same climate as Yuma, just with a hell of a lot more mortars and the lettuce was shit. Two tours in Iraq and a third to Afghanistan. That was a different kind of worse.

After the Army, it was a string of jobs and apartments he couldn't hold onto. He bought camping gear with the last of his money, started walking. Eventually, he ended up here. The Old Man looked out for him when he found this place, showed him the ropes, how to find food and who the crazy ones were. Dave wasn't sure how long he'd been living like this. He'd lost track of the time. Maybe it was months, maybe it was years. Time loses its meaning when the next day is the same as the last day.

Being homeless was a lot like being deployed.

When he'd finished with his wash, Dave hung the clothes up on some branches and took off his shirt, shoes, and socks but left his shorts on. He'd learned the hard way not to skinny dip. "Going for a swim," he shouted up the bank, in the Old Man's direction. "Watch my stuff?"

The Old Man waved his hand, like he'd given some kind of permission, and Dave waded out into the cold water. It seemed deeper than he remembered from his swim the day before. Did rivers have tides, like the ocean did? He didn't know. He heard a rumble that sounded enough like thunder that he looked up to the sky, but it was clear.

So, Dave Reyes looked upstream and saw a wall of water coming his way.

Ted Harris banged on the keyboard and let out a string of obscenities. Stupid piece-of-shit computer was locked up. Again. Like, *again* again. Ted wasn't a fan of computers and had the distinct impression that the feeling was mutual. He shouted for Dixon and then put his cheaters on so he could read the message on the screen. He was locked out of his account and would need to speak to a system administrator.

Ted tried the password again, his daughter's birthday and name—he wasn't one of those idiots they talked about in the security briefings that just used "password1234" over and over. The red box told him, again, to contact his system admin.

"Dixon!" Ted shouted again. Dixon was probably on the can or smoking.

Ted got another cup of coffee. Got back to his station, everything looked the same as he left it.

Ted turned to see Hendrix, their shift super, running in and shouting his name.

"Where's the fire?" Ted asked, annoyed.

"What the hell is going on? The gates are open!"

"No, they're not," Ted said, incredulous. He pointed at the bank of monitors in front of him; everything read nominal. The camera feed was currently pointed at Lake Folsom, and he hadn't bothered to change it, because frankly that was a nicer view than looking at four giant floodgates that were always going to be closed this time of year.

"Look at the damned gauges," Hendrix said. Ted got up and walked over to the bank of gauges in the center console. These were analog but keyed to electronic sensors on the dam. All of those read nominal as well.

"That's all normal, too, chief," Ted said.

"Damn it, follow me. I was just outside, and all four gates are open and gushing water."

"You sure?" This was either a practical joke or a drill. Maybe it was one of those exercises security kept talking about, where they tried to get people to leave their posts or something. "Look, the gauges are all fine. I'd switch the cameras over, but I'm locked out of the system again and I can't find Dixon to open the damned thing back up."

Ted looked up at the screen and picture of Lake Folsom. The camera shot over the top of the dam so they could see if anything was moving toward the gates from the lake side. Now that he was looking at it, he could see that water was flowing. A lot of water.

Ted followed Hendrix in a flat run to the observation platform.

The sound outside was deafening. The control center and observation platform sat atop a concrete tower extending out from the front of the three-hundred-and-forty-foot-tall dam. Below them, all seven gates opened with water roaring from them in a torrent of liquid white fury. Already, water overtopped the sluice gates and emergency runoff channels built after the 1995 spill gate failure.

Over a hundred thousand cubic feet of water per second poured down from the floodgates. Waves crashed into the concrete walls of the power plant on the right side of the flow channel, lashing them with titanic and crushing force.

"Oh, holy God..."

"The governor will see you, Mr. Kim," the aide said.

Jeff stood, buttoned the jacket on his navy Brioni suit, and collected his small bag. "Thank you," he said to the governor's aide and followed her into the conference room with regal-blue carpet. She indicated the place at the long table that had been reserved for him.

"Could I get you a cup of coffee?" she asked. "The governor likes the good stuff."

"That would be great. Black, thank you," Jeff said. It seemed important to the aide that he take a cup.

Jeff sat and placed his bag next to him.

Jeff Kim didn't normally travel with an entourage. He disliked hangers-on and didn't need human assistants to manage his schedule or ensure he got where he needed to be on time. That was a problem better solved by machines, which he'd done. Rather, he brought trusted staff with him when the situation called for their specific expertise or there would be simultaneous breakout sessions.

The aide returned with the coffee and a small saucer, which she set down in front of him. Jeff thanked her, and she departed. Then, the door on the opposite side of the room opened, and the governor of California made his entrance. Jeff stood. The governor was tall, hair swept back to minimize the widow's peak and gray at the temples. His face already fixed in the camera-ready, thousand-watt smile showing whitewashed teeth. The governor extended a long arm for a handshake as he made fast strides around the table.

"Jeff Kim," he said, beaming. "It's really an honor to meet you. I've followed your career for some time. I'll try not to fanboy you too much."

"Thank you, Governor, for your time. I really appreciate it."

Practiced concern washed over the governor's face. "I hope you weren't waiting long. Beth got you coffee, I see."

"I'm good, thank you."

"Then let's get started." The governor sat and his people followed, occupying that side of the table and part of Jeff's. He introduced his team. There were reps from the state's Office of Information Technology within the Government Operations Agency, CalFire, and others. "Team," the governor said, placing his hands on the table. "Jeff Kim doesn't need an introduction, but I'm going to give one anyway. Not only is he a native son of California, was educated here and chose to keep his business here, Jeff's company, Pax AI, has led the way in artificial intelligence and robotics. As you've probably seen in the news, he's expanded into some groundbreaking virtual reality. And," the governor turned to face his people for effect, "he developed an artificial intelligence model to automate seaport operations, which he deployed at the Port of Long Beach as a proof of concept. We think that without Jeff's technology, we might still be digging out of the backlog the pandemic caused."

Jeff saw several head nods and smiles.

"But today," the governor's voice became serious, "we're talking about fire. Jeff, why don't you catch my team up on our conversation."

"Thank you, Governor." Jeff took a sip of coffee and stood. He walked over to a whiteboard and grabbed a marker. He'd learned early on that the person standing at the whiteboard controlled the room, it didn't matter who was in the audience. "As the CalFire team can attest, fire is the very definition of chaos and destruction. And we can't predict it. Where it will spread, how fast and how hot it will burn. But what if we could? Some of you may recall that a few years ago, I had a research lab in the Sierra Nevada. We used this for our company's most sensitive efforts. Three years ago, a small fire tore through that area and destroyed our facility. I was there at the time."

Jeff paused for the expected gasps. He took in the room, holding the marker like a wand and ensorcelled the audience. "As you can probably imagine, it was a profound experience for me. And I dedicated myself to finding a solution. I have the resources to rebuild, but not everyone does. What I spoke to the governor about was this."

Jeff explained how, given sufficient data, nearly anything could become predictable, even wildfires. He described in simple terms, amplified by whiteboard drawings, how AI could analyze current meteorological, environmental, and topographical data to produce a model and then incorporate information from other sources, such as aggregated climate information and satellite imagery, to create a predictive model for complex, dynamic systems. One that currently powered the CyberPort the governor mentioned in his introduction. Jeff said the key was rapid iteration, using evolving data to feed the model and inform decision loops in real time. They achieved this, in part, by deploying fleets of drones with thermographic and optical sensors.

"With this data, my AI can forecast the movement of wildfires with greater accuracy than any system deployed today."

"How much?" the head of CalFire asked, sounding dubious. "I mean, anything over what we can do today is an improvement, but I don't see—"

"My system is roughly a thousand times more accurate than any current models. I suspect that once deployed, we could provide advanced warning of a fire's trajectory with forty-eight to seventy-two hours' notice. Ultimately, prediction comes down to pattern analysis and mathematics. Until now, there were simply too many variables to combine, the dataset too large to reason over. I believe I have solved that problem."

Jeff spent the next ten minutes fielding technical questions from the governor's IT staff and practical ones from CalFire and Forestry. He was describing how the drones could also be used to feed real-time data to firefighters when the governor's aide rushed in and whispered to her boss. There was another man Jeff didn't recognize following close on her heels. The look on her face was unmistakable, and it transferred to the governor's as if by osmosis.

The governor paled and pushed himself back from his chair. When he stood, he said, "Ladies and gentlemen, I'm sorry I'm going to have to cut this short. We have a situation. Jeff, please accept my apologies. Talk with Magdalene, and she'll find a time for us to reconvene." The governor looked to the pair from the IT division. "Fiona, Ricardo, could you join me, please?" Baffled, the two stood. That got Jeff's attention.

"Sir, the system is completely unresponsive," the man who'd accompanied the governor's aide said.

"Governor," Jeff said, just as he was about leave the room. Everyone stopped their conversation and focused their attention on Kim. The governor looked concerned and irritated at the interruption.

"Jeff, I'm sorry, but it'll have to wait."

"That's not what I mean. I overheard your aide tell you that a system had locked its users out. Is that correct?"

The aide looked to the governor for authorization. He nodded. "That's correct," the man said. "It's the controls for the Folsom Dam. The operating system is completely locked out."

"Let me help, sir," Jeff said.

"I don't know, Jeff," the governor said, hedging.

"I have tools you don't."

The governor's staff quickly turned the conference room into a war room. The situation unfolded too quickly for them to make the drive to the state's Emergency Operations Center, but they patched into it by phone. The state's Director of Emergency Management briefed the governor on the situation. One of the staff brought a computer feed from the ops center into the conference room's wall screen.

The Folsom Dam, which held the nearly one billion cubic meters of water of Lake Folsom, had opened. All of the dam's gates simultaneously unlocked, but the spillways designed to manage excess flow were overwhelmed, sending a wall of water crashing down the American River below. None of the emergency dikes worked. Dam operators frantically reported that none of the controls responded to their commands. Even admin overrides resulted in error messages and prompts for users to "contact their system administrator." The operators reported that they'd even contacted the system's developer to see if there was a back door into it, but they were still trying to track down an engineer familiar with that particular operating system. Apparently, it was not only dated but had not been updated in quite some time.

"How long has the system been unresponsive?"

"At least five hours, sir."

"Five *hours*," the governor barked, incredulous.

"Yes, sir. It appears to have happened around shift change. That's when the gates opened, and there were electronic logs saying that it was a controlled release started on the previous shift. A supervisor thought that was strange since it wasn't mentioned in his turnover from the previous shift, so he called the night shift supe, and he didn't know anything about it. They tried to shut the gates and found they were locked out. The operations staff tried everything they could to get them back online, short of pulling the plug and doing a cold restart."

"Why didn't they try that?"

"It's an old system. They're worried it might not come back online."

"We've seen this before, right? This dam has flooded not too long ago," the governor said, forcing optimism into his voice. "We have fail-safes?"

"Yes, sir, that's true," the Director of Emergency Management said over the phone. "In '95. But we used the Nimbus Dam to relieve pressure on the river. We, ah, don't seem to have access to Nimbus right now."

"What do you mean?" the governor asked.

"Sir, as you probably know, the Nimbus Dam is downriver from Folsom." A cursor appeared on the onscreen map. "It acts as a runoff to further control the flow of the American River. But the controls aren't responding there either. We can't release the water coming into the river. If we can't get control of Folsom, we're going to overtop Nimbus in less than an hour. With that much pressure, the dam might fail entirely."

"Jesus Christ."

The Nimbus Dam was seven miles downstream from Folsom and approximately twenty miles northeast of Sacramento. Jeff remembered the '95 incident. He was in high school at the time in the East Bay suburb of Moraga. One of the floodgates broke, sending forty thousand cubic feet of water per second downstream. A quick-thinking dam operator raced by car the seven miles to Nimbus to open those gates and relieved the unexpected pressure on the lower dam. Though it took them several days to repair the damaged floodgate at Folsom, they were able to manage the flow of water downstream.

"What's your worst-case scenario?" the governor asked.

"Sir," the man said gravely. "This *is* the worst-case scenario. The Sacramento metro area has a million and a half residents. Six hundred thousand homes. If we lose Nimbus, we're going to have catastrophic flooding. Governor, downtown Sacramento could be under ten feet of water if we can't get control of this. It'll be like Katrina. There's nowhere for it to go."

A curtain of fear descended on the room, threatening to choke out everything else. Everyone in this room had a home somewhere nearby, and Jeff suspected most of them had families. The capitol grounds, where they now sat, were located in the center of the city.

The Director of Emergency Management continued, "Sir, we're estimating flooding in Folsom, Orangevale, and Nimbus within the hour. We've ordered the evacuation of the Rio Americano High School because it's right next to the river. We've already sent flash flood warnings out, and we've got CHP and Sacramento Sheriff helicopters in the air for river rescue. El Dorado and Placer Sheriffs both offered to help."

The governor steepled his fingers in front of his face. "What are we doing about Nimbus?"

"That's just it, sir. They are totally locked out of those computers. It's the same situation as Folsom. Admins can't get in to issue the override controls."

"How long do we have before Nimbus overtops?" the governor asked.

"Not long, sir. We've got a hundred thousand gallons a second coming out of Folsom."

"Governor," Jeff said, breaking in. "I think it is highly likely someone has gotten control of your systems and intentionally locked you out. I could explain the probability of experiencing two simultaneous failures on dependent systems during a crisis, but just trust me that it's a very low number."

"Tom," the governor said, "that's Jeff Kim speaking. We were in a meeting when this started, and he offered to help."

"Our people concluded this was probably a cyberattack, too. We've got calls into the FBI and the DHS cyber people, per the protocol, but, with respect, sir, that doesn't solve the damned problem."

"I have an idea, Governor. If you'd permit me to help."

"Sir, I need to urge caution here," a new voice said, a man in a suit standing in the back of the room. "With respect, Mr. Kim is a private citizen and not an employee of the State. We could be taking on liability here, especially if he's wrong."

The governor paused, for just a breath. Jeff doubted that anyone else in the room recognized it for what it was. The kind of in-the-moment, split-second decision making senior executives find themselves in every day.

"Carlos, I appreciate your concern, and your objection is noted. Please figure out how to make sure the State and Mr. Kim are covered from a liability standpoint." The man was about to object further, but the governor simply said, "That'll be all." He turned to Jeff. "What's your idea?"

"I might be able to get into those systems and unlock them."

"How?"

"We don't have time for a detailed explanation, but I think I can get into your system."

Several years ago, Jeff developed an AI that began as a natural language processor and evolved into an algorithm that could predict speech with surprising accuracy. The system taught itself about an individual's speech patterns, vocabulary, and perceived intellectual capacity and then rendered conversational responses to the individual. Jeff expanded the system's predictive capabilities to learn and automate certain tasks in his home and, later, expanded it as an operational testbed for AI concepts he was developing. Eventually, the system replaced his human assistants. Today, that AI was his research partner, an invaluable tool and collaborator. He named it "Saturn" after the Greek god of knowledge and the underworld.

Today, Saturn was the most sophisticated AI ever developed. Coupled with Kim's own quantum computing array, it could make short work of the dated security system ostensibly protecting the dam's OS.

"My AI can force its way in, lock out the hackers that corrupted your system, and restore control."

"What do you need from me?"

"Permission."

"You have it."

Jeff opened his phone. "Saturn?"

"Hello, Jeff. I've been advised of a flash flood warning in your area, and the Sacramento Airport has issued a Notice to Air Missions that will impact your flight home. I'm told your helicopter is relocating."

"That's what I'm calling about. I need you to do something for me." Jeff explained the situation to Saturn. He was conscious of the eye-rolling, the derisive looks and whispered words in the background. He knew what they were saying even if he couldn't hear them. Jeff was used to this.

"Governor, I'm not sure about this," the director said over the phone. "I agree with Carlos. Mr. Kim is a civilian. I'm also uncomfortable giving access to our systems over to him."

"With all due respect, sir, you don't *have* control of your systems," Jeff said to the speaker pod on the table.

"And we're not going to give them up to some guy off the street. For all we know, that's how we got into this situation. We've got the manufacturer working on getting us access to the systems *they* designed. Kim doesn't know anything about dam operating systems, Governor."

"I understand your point, Tom," the governor said. Jeff could see the governor wrestling with the decision.

"Sir, my system can teach itself everything everyone knows about that operating system in the time it'll take for us to argue about it. But I don't need to know what the systems do, I just need to know the language they are built in. My system will determine that quickly, if it hasn't already."

The governor glowered, and creases lined up on his brow like a newly risen mountain range. "I don't know. That seems a little farfetched to me."

"Sir," the director said, his voice stretched tight. "I have to object in the strongest possible terms. We've got the system's manufacturer trying to reset it. If we have someone else in there at the same time, it's just going to make it harder for the OEM to do their job. That's going to delay us getting control of the dam and probably cost us some lives."

The director's argument was so fundamentally asinine it almost defied logic. Jeff was used to people who didn't understand technology using it as a convenient excuse for why something wouldn't work. But to willfully ignore a possible solution to a crisis wasn't just stupid, it was criminally so.

"Mr. Director," Jeff said, "I don't think you understand how computers work. My AI trying to regain access is not going to affect anything the OEM is doing. Particularly if they can't get in themselves."

"We can't take this risk, Governor."

"The only risk is not doing anything," Jeff said.

The governor turned to face him. "Jeff, I have to make some tough decisions here. I appreciate your offer to help, but I think it'll be best if you leave. I'm going to evacuate the area. I think you need to get out while you can." The governor leaned back in his chair. "That goes for the rest of you. Emergency essential staff will report to the ops center immediately. Everyone else, please evacuate. This office will issue the formal order momentarily." The governor looked down at the phone. "Tom, I'm on my way. I'll have Ajit transfer you to my phone."

"Yes, sir."

"Governor, this is a mistake," Jeff said.

"Thanks, Jeff." And the governor was ushered out by a tide of aides.

Jeff opened the text interface he used to communicate with Saturn.

>>JEFF: Did you hear all of that?

>>SATURN: Yes, I did. Their logic is unfortunate.

>>JEFF: People are going to die b/c of this. How fast can you get in?

There was a pause.

Someone in the conference room had put a local news channel on. The group huddling together for support rather than evacuating. The banner on the screen proclaimed "FOLSOM FLOOD EMERGENCY" in bold red font. The scenes showed live helicopter footage of surging flood waters over the smaller Nimbus Dam, crashing against the concrete barrier and threatening to overtake it.

>>SATURN: I am in.

>>JEFF: Can you ID any malware?

>>SATURN: Yes.

>>JEFF: Quarantine but don't remove. Need for forensics. Lock out all users except you.

>>SATURN: There's traffic from an IP address in Bulgaria.

Jeff made fast strides for the door that communicated with the governor's office. He opened it.

"Governor, I'm in."

All eyes in the room turned to Jeff Kim.

"Excuse me?"

"Sir, we don't have time to argue this. Your director was wrong. He gave you bad advice."

"Sir," one of the aides said. "We're about to lose Nimbus."

"Everybody be quiet," the governor thundered. "Jeff, are you telling me you have access to the dam's operating system?"

"Yes, Governor. That's what I'm saying. I've also locked out any other users."

"That's the goddamned OEM!" the Director of Emergency Management shouted, practically vibrating the phone on the governor's desk.

"Not unless they were dialing in from Bulgaria," Jeff said.

No one spoke.

"What do we do, Jeff?"

"Put me in touch with the Folsom IT staff. I'll tell them what to do."

The Nimbus Dam suffered a partial collapse before they regained control of Folsom and reduced the flow of water. Communities on the lower northern side of the American River suffered the worst of the damage, with flooding up to ten feet in communities of Fair Oaks, Carmichael, La Riviera, and East Sacramento. There was flooding as far south as Clarksburg, Hood, and Merritt Island along the Sacramento River.

Initial estimates placed the damage in the hundreds of millions of dollars, with fifty thousand homes suffering flood damage, and many were lost. There were hundreds unaccounted for. Mostly, those were among hikers, swimmers, and kayakers in the recreation areas along the river when the flooding started, people out in the flood areas who couldn't receive the warnings or who got the EMS alert on their phone too late. The many homeless camps along the riverbanks were wiped out entirely.

Peak water flow was one hundred sixty thousand cubic feet per second.

Downtown Sacramento flooded completely, with water crashing onto the capitol grounds.

It looked like the southeast after a Category 5 hurricane, not central California.

"You saved a lot of people today, Jeff," the governor said over the phone. The governor had spent a lot of time behind a podium today, decked out in a California Office of Emergency Services polo. "I'm sorry we didn't listen to you sooner."

"I apologize for not consulting you first, but I felt we needed to act."

"No, no, Jeff. You were right. The state is in your debt. My people are going to send your media team a press release describing how the day unfolded. We were in a meeting, the crisis happened, and you offered your support." Jeff noted the governor did not mention the debate with his head of emergency services or the fact that Jeff did it anyway after being told not to.

"I'm happy to help any way I can."

"When the dust clears, let's restart our fires conversation. I'd also like to get your thoughts on infrastructure management. There's going to be a lot of rightful criticism that this happened, and we can't let it happen again."

Jeff told the governor he looked forward to that call.

Sacramento has three airports in the immediate area. Sacramento International, Sacramento Mather, and Sacramento McClellan, the latter two being former US Air Force bases that closed in the 1993 and 2001 Base Realignment and Closure rounds. The city also held the airfield used by the California Highway Patrol for its aviation academy. The Natomas area, which housed Sacramento International, suffered some of the deepest flooding in the region. All four airfields were either underwater or seriously damaged and were closed indefinitely. Jeff's helicopter evacuated twenty miles west to the airport on the University of California, Davis campus. Jeff got out of the city with the help of the National Guard on the governor's direction. They dropped him at a safe place to link up with his driver, who took him to Davis, and from there, he lifted off for the forty-nine-minute flight home.

Jeff took the governor's phone call from his home in Palo Alto.

Jeff paced for a long time, considering his options and the decision he had yet to make. He walked into his office with the two-hundred-and-seventy-degree view of the grounds and the mountains beyond. He opened a desk drawer and found a business card. The card bore the embossed emblem of the United States Department of Commerce and described the office symbol belonging to an economic analyst.

The phone number, Jeff knew, would not ring at a Commerce Department switchboard, but rather an answering service used by the Central Intelligence Agency. If he called that number, an anonymous voice would ask him to leave a message. There wasn't even the perfunctory promise of a return phone call.

It was one thirty in the morning in Washington.

Saturn determined, almost immediately, an external actor had disabled the dam's control software, any electronic overrides, and developer-built back doors. They used a combination of social engineering and targeted malware to gain access and, once inside, locked out the legitimate users. Once they had control, they opened the floodgates. Saturn told him the hackers attempted to block its attempts to regain control, but Saturn outmaneuvered and then overpowered them. No wonder the OEM's engineers could not. Had Jeff not been there, he wasn't sure that they'd have gotten control of the dam again, at least not for a long while.

This wasn't a simple hack. It was an overt attack few were capable of.

Jeff dialed Colt McShane's number.

4

Nadia's eyes followed Guy Hawkinson's footsteps as they traced the path from the curtained wings of the stage to the spotlight. Where, she noted ruefully, he felt most at home. Guy wore a five-thousand-dollar suit, shoes that were about half that, and a Rolex apparently favored by Army infantry officers.

Nadia knew the speech already—in fact, she'd helped write it. Guy addressed an international body of tech luminaries, academics, scientists, and representatives from a score of nongovernmental organizations. The forum, jokingly referred to in the press as "Davos for Nerds," was a body convened to discuss how emerging technologies could be used to solve the world's most critical challenges. As the president of the Geneva-based Hawk Technologies, now officially shortened to HawkTech, Guy represented an important voice on a number of the body's core issues. Hawk-Tech invested heavily in the developing world and launched partnerships with the United Nations and many of its technology-focused subsidiaries and had a research agreement with Cambridge University. Guy announced last week that HawkTech launched a new endeavor with Clean Water

Initiative, the pet project of a Hollywood film star, which Nadia was personally overseeing.

"...the challenge isn't that governments lack the resources or will or the expertise to solve these problems," Guy said. Nadia directed her attention back at her boss. "The challenge, friends, is that they lack the *ability*. We've each seen a government let promising initiatives wither and die because they simply lacked the know-how to fully realize them. Or, perhaps, the jurisdiction. I've come to believe that many of the solutions to the problems our global society faces, the things we have come here together to discuss, lie outside of government. What happens when the obvious solution stretches across national boundaries?" Nadia watched the reactions of the crowd. Solemn, knowing head nods and muffled words of assent.

"While there are many areas to choose from, I offer two examples of essential functions of government that we at HawkTech feel have grown beyond the traditional models. Further, the complexity of each is such that in the modern age, I would argue, government not only cannot provide these services, they *should* not. First, let's discuss election. This essential function is the core of liberal democracy and freedom-loving societies, but how many in the world have never experienced one? I can tell you as a former United States Army infantry officer, I have literally spilled blood to enshrine the right to vote in Iraq."

Nadia frowned. She knew for a fact Guy did not have a Purple Heart.

"The UN and other organizations work tirelessly to safeguard elections, but if the process itself is corrupt, how can we prove to the citizens risking their lives to cast a ballot that it's free and fair? In my own country, 'rigged elections' have become a talking point across the political spectrum whenever one side doesn't like the results. Here, technology provides a novel solution."

Guy paused and held up a finger to the audience, the wise technology rabbi.

"With our new voting system, deployed as a mobile app and also available on easily portable kiosks, users log in and their citizenship is verified using biometric data. Then, they cast their vote on the app. Their vote is stored in a quantum encrypted data vault in Geneva. HawkTech maintains this, but it can be audited by representatives from the Organization for

Security and Cooperation in Europe, the African Union, the United Nations Electoral Assistance Division, and the Carter Institute. Is any data truly secure, you ask? If anyone in the world understands this, it's this body. All data stored anywhere in the world is at risk. But that's true of physical documents, which can be stolen or forged, as it is of digital ones. The questions are how much integrity can we design into the system and how can we secure it? I think technology can solve this problem now, delivering a brighter, more accountable future for our world, and we can do this now."

Guy paused for applause.

"Education is the second focus of my talk tonight. AI, when paired with optical sensors—what people outside this room call 'cameras,'" a pause for laughter, "can detect the physiological indicators of comprehension, lack of attention or interest, or anxiety. This data is combined with daily progress assessments of the material. The AI can then tailor instructional blocks based on each student's individual needs. This allows the human teacher, which we do not propose to remove from the classroom, to accelerate or decelerate learning on a per-student basis."

Nadia knew the system he was talking about. It was a pivot from a tool he developed that used a computer to evaluate all of the known characteristics of deception. It was a lie detector. He'd used it on her once and she'd failed, miserably. Nadia shuddered to think what would have become of her had she not been able to convince Hawkinson that his tech was flawed.

She looked down at her phone. Guy would be reaching the closing points in his speech. "You want to get the car ready? He's just about done."

"I'm not a taxi service," the tall man lurking near her said. His suit was just a fraction less expensive than Guy's.

"I told you I could handle transpo, but you insisted. Don't be a dick when I'm giving you the timing cues."

"Fine, whatever," Matthew Kirby said. Kirby was Guy's lieutenant, confidant, and unofficial XO. He pulled his phone out and made the arrangements. Any trust Hawkinson had in her apparently had not translated to Kirby. He remained suspicious of her and derided her work, though she had yet to unearth why. Kirby and Hawkinson went back. They'd served in the Army together, went to Ranger school together, and were in Iraq together. Kirby, like many of the Army operators she'd met in her career, looked down on her for having been in the Air Force, viewing it as more of a country club with smart bombs than a branch of service. But there was something else that went beyond simple and convenient professional dislike.

Or, Kirby was just an asshole.

When they were within each other's circles, he loomed over her, reinforced his presence. Kirby was protective of his boss's time in the way lions were of food for their young. He didn't like the idea of Nadia reporting directly to Guy, allowing her to sidestep Kirby as the gatekeeper. Not that he could effectively filter. Kirby had no background in tech (not that Guy did either, but at least he knew what he was talking about).

Nadia looked up in time to see Guy striding confidently offstage, arm extended in a last wave to the crowd. Guy was skipping the typical closing ceremony cocktails and returning home. He'd been at HawkTech's new facility in Buenos Aires the week prior and was anxious to get off the road. They'd be returning to Geneva tonight.

Once Guy was offstage, his security detail of former Hawk Security Group executive protection heavies led the three of them through the concert hall where the keynote was to a rear entrance and the waiting Range Rovers. It was a short drive through the electric night of downtown London to London City Airport alongside the Thames.

Nadia used the ride to scroll through news feeds to see if she could learn anything new about the Folsom Dam tragedy. About a hundred people were confirmed dead. It was the tail end of summer, and there was a lot of recreational traffic on the river when it flooded, as well as being a popular location for homeless camps. Whole communities were leveled, homes just...gone. The city of Sacramento was still underwater. Worse, they needed the water from that reservoir for firefighting and irrigation; instead it was spilled all over the county, doubling up on an extant crisis.

The Range Rover drove through a security checkpoint, the vehicle precleared, and the driver took them right into the hangar. The driver and the security detail handled the bags. Nadia didn't have any, other than her backpack. She'd flown in that morning for the conference and to meet Guy. Everyone else had been in Argentina with Guy.

Nadia went on last so she could see where Guy was sitting. He chose a rear-facing seat, Kirby posted across from him. Nadia took one in the row behind them. She stowed her bag and set her phone on her lap.

The phone was her mission.

After that, she could go home.

Home was an abstract concept now. Nadia didn't know what to make of it anymore. Eighteen months ago she was a graduate student, recruited out of school by the Central Intelligence Agency and trained as a clandestine operations officer. They rushed into and through her training, ultimately pulled her out early and inserted her into a commercial company under-cover, because that's what the mission required. Colt McShane and Fred Ford were her teachers, her confidants, her confessor priests, and her only friends in this bizarre, surreal new existence. They continued her spy school at nights, on the weekends, on lunch breaks, whenever they could find time for a lesson in how to be a covert operator.

Nadia entered HawkTech as an AI expert and worked to enter Guy Hawkinson's confidences. She reported on everything he did, everything his company did. She knew from her Agency training that this was not normal. Most case officers ran agents, people they recruited in foreign governments or terrorist organizations or NGOs, anywhere the Agency might have an interest in keeping an eye. Rarely, if ever, did CIA operatives spend much time undercover.

Nadia had all the responsibilities of a case officer and all the gathering requirements of an asset.

A "normal" officer would go home at the end of the day, and the stresses of their responsibilities would still be with them. If they lived in a hostile country, they might be hounded or harassed, but they would have a home. They would have a safe place in the US Embassy. They would also have other CIA officers to commiserate with, to get support from, senior officers to ask questions of.

Nadia was on her own.

Every problem she had to solve, it was on her to puzzle it out. The nearest CIA officer, her local handler and only form of support, was two hours away. If Nadia got into trouble, she was her own backup. The lines between the job and her cover were so muddled, the divide was an inky smear.

But if she completed this job, it was over and she could go home.

CIA issued her a new phone earlier that year.

Well, it looked like a phone and did all the things an iPhone was supposed to. Except this had a device the Agency's tech wizards developed. It was called LONGBOW, and it used an infrared transmitter disguised as a camera lens to communicate with other phones. All it needed was to be able to "see" the optical sensor on another phone and LONGBOW would complete a digital handshake, connecting the two devices. From there, it would transmit an exploit known as a "jailbreak," something that unlocked a phone at the root level and gave Agency hackers access to everything on it. Nadia didn't know exactly how it worked, but she understood the technology well enough to know that, at some point, the Agency must have gotten access to the chip manufacturer.

They couldn't get onto the HawkTech computer network because electronic devices weren't permitted inside the building and they couldn't access the network from home. Work computers weren't permitted to leave the building, obsessive security masked as progressive corporate work/life balance policy.

LONGBOW was the only way CIA had to tunnel into the HawkTech network and get the conclusive proof of his treachery. It was still a long shot. The theory relied on Hawkinson ignoring his own security policy, but the Agency reasoned that was a good chance.

Unfortunately for her, it meant getting near Guy Hawkinson outside of work because it was the only place they would both have their phones. Nadia wasn't exactly in the CEO's social circle. But getting promoted onto his direct staff put her in a position to be with him outside the office. Long work went into setting up the conditions that resulted in that promotion. Ultimately, that is what put Nadia in a London tech conference and on the boss's private plane. This was the best chance she was going to get.

Nadia hunched over the phone, fumbling through apps in an effort to look distracted. She was looking for the app that would activate LONG-BOW. Anyone looking over her shoulder would think she was just taking a picture. A shadow appeared over her, and it took her a few moments to realize that one of the flight attendants was talking to her.

"Anything to drink, ma'am?"

Nadia looked up. Hawkinson and Kirby were speaking in low tones over scotch.

"What's the boss having?"

"Macallan twenty," she said.

Of course he is.

"Good enough for me," Nadia said. The flight attendant took her dinner selection and departed, returning with the scotch as the plane taxied. Nadia kept her face buried in her phone, pretending to look busy. She was seated diagonally from Hawkinson and facing him. She had a straight line of sight, if Kirby would just shut up a minute so Guy could pick up his phone.

The plane lifted off, and Nadia pressed back into her seat. Hawkinson's conversation with Kirby lasted until the plane reached a cruising altitude. Nadia had her earbuds in, which the tech guys rebuilt into directional microphones. Instead of cancelling sounds out, they vectored the input, allowing her listen in on targeted conversations around her. They also recorded everything she heard while they were on. Hawkinson and Kirby recapped the trip to Argentina and the formal opening of the new facility there.

HawkTech officially relocated to Geneva the year before but also had a small research facility in Greenland. Ostensibly, it was to use AI to model the impacts of climate change, but in truth it was just a place with a lot of open land and no neighbors where they could rebuild the massive quantum computing array the Russians destroyed when they wiped out Hawkinson's island. The Buenos Aires office was something different. Nadia knew from finding purchasing records that the new facility had both quantum and supercomputing capability, but she didn't know what it was *for*. Their conversation right now was mostly centered on housekeeping and logistics. They were talking about the deployment of servers.

Kirby got up from his seat and moved to the rear of the plane to use the lavatory. Nadia kept her head low, focused on the phone so Guy wouldn't use the break in conversation to start one up with her. She needed him to pull his damn phone out. Now, there was the problem of Kirby. He was behind her and in a position to see what was on her screen as he walked by. LONGBOW was a clandestine app, made to be used in the open. If someone happened to be looking at her screen, all they'd see was Nadia was taking a picture. Not that she'd have a good excuse for why she was taking a picture of Hawkinson using his cell phone at twenty thousand feet if Kirby caught her.

She had to wait until Kirby returned to his seat.

Nadia sensed a presence before the body stepped in front of the cabin light and threw its shadow over her.

She'd reclined the chair and turned it slightly so her back wasn't directly facing the rear of the aircraft. Kirby couldn't see her face from behind her, but she didn't have a line of sight on Hawkinson without being overt.

"What are you up to?" Kirby asked. Nadia reached for her scotch, took a sip, and returned it to the tray without looking up, pretending not to hear him. Then Kirby waved a hand in front of her face, and she knew he couldn't be avoided. Nadia took a fast glance at Guy. He had his phone up now and was in a perfect position.

Damn it, Kirby.

"Sorry," she said, disinterested. "What was that?" Hopefully, he'd interpret this as lingering annoyance from his behavior earlier.

"I asked what you were up to?"

What the hell is this?

"I'm having a drink and passing time until dinner," Nadia said, not looking up.

"So, I'm sorry for being a jerk earlier. You know how it is. Long flight from South America and all. Anyway, sorry."

That's awkward.

"So, what are you up to?" Kirby asked again. She'd answered this question once already.

Oh God, is he flirting?

"It's that stupid word game everyone is addicted to. A bunch of my friends back home are playing, and they got me hooked on it."

Nadia, normally hyperorganized with her devices, had the LONGBOW app on her phone screen in a cluster of other random apps so she could quickly shift to a different one if she needed to cover her activity. Kirby had moved to stand in front of her, interposing himself between her and Hawkinson. Nadia leaned back with the phone up. She had a straight line now. She looked up. Guy was leaning over and talking to one of his security detail sitting in the chair next to him. His phone rested on the tray in front of him, next to his drink.

Kirby was still talking.

Guy turned back around and picked up his glass, took a sip, and stared out the window.

Kirby was telling her how she wouldn't believe the food in Buenos Aires. Apparently, they don't butcher cows the way we do, and the cuts of meat were different. Fascinating. She'd have rolled her eyes out of her sockets if they hadn't been glued to the phone.

Guy picked up his phone.

Nadia thumbed the LONGBOW app, and Guy Hawkinson sitting in his chair on a private plane with a twenty-year-old glass of scotch appeared on her screen. A pair of red brackets framed his phone; they locked and turned green. The image dissolved. Did it work? She didn't actually know. Her training, like everything else with the Agency, it seemed, was rushed. Colt had handed her the box and said she'd had to figure it out. Wasn't his fault, they'd had about five minutes that day. Nadia made a note to talk to the tech guys about product design and how the feedback loop was important, especially for someone in a life-or-death situation using this thing.

She set the phone down. Kirby was still talking, and she pretended to be interested. She looked up and saw Guy Hawkinson's eyes on her, studying her. A cold jolt ran through her body. Did he know? Guy had some of the most advanced computing systems in the world at his disposal, including several recent and undisclosed strides in AI. It wasn't hard to believe that he could have something on his phone to detect a hack immediately.

And here Nadia was at twenty thousand feet with nowhere to go and everyone *but* her and the flight crew were trained killers.

Guy looked at her, held her gaze, and nodded.

The plane landed in Geneva just after ten. They exited the plane on the tarmac to find Hawkinson's black Mercedes G-Wagon in the glare of the airfield lighting. It was chilly, and Nadia wished she'd brought a heavier jacket. She heard Guy and Kirby exchange words but didn't know what they were. Kirby and the security detail got the bags loaded onto the G-Wagon, and Guy appeared at Nadia's side.

"Do you have a minute?" he asked.

"Of course," she said. *Here it comes.* She was caught.

"I'm having a follow-up meeting with our friend in the Chinese government, Liu Che, in a few days, and I'd like you to join this one. The Chinese still haven't disclosed what they mean by a partnership, and I'd like you to sit in again and help me puzzle that out."

Nadia didn't know if Hawkinson realized Liu Che's organization, the Ministry of Technical Cooperation, was a front for their foreign intelligence service. Figuring that out was one of her top intelligence targets. Whether or not Hawkinson knew he was meeting with the Chinese foreign intelligence service changed this operation entirely.

"Sure, yes, I'd love to." Nadia was stammering and stopped herself. She sounded like an idiot.

"Good," Guy said, nodding. "These guys really get off on the preamble of business." He rolled one of his hands in a dismissive gesture. "Five-thousand-year-old culture that guarantees they never get to the point in the first ten meetings, that kind of thing."

She wasn't sure if it was his nihilism or charisma, but Hawkinson had a preternatural ability to make the outlandish and the horrible sound reasonable. Like, *hey, I just designed a lethal bioweapon that targets people with their DNA*, and it sounds like a trip to the store for groceries.

"What would you like me to do?"

"I'd like you to run point on setting it up."

5

Langley, Virginia

Colt set the coffee down and thumbed through the report in his hand. It had long ago cooled to lukewarm and descended to levels of barely consumable. He'd only been back from Israel a few days and spent most of that in debriefing. They'd just gotten an update from Mossad, and while he'd skimmed it, Colt hadn't had time to fully digest it.

The Mossad officer, Ben, identified one of the Haifa attackers as a former Israeli operative. Now that they knew who he was, Colt thought he was lucky to be alive. According to the report in his hand, marked "EYES ONLY," Mossad recruited Zeev Yatom out of IDF special forces for a black hit squad known as "Kidon." Their job was to infiltrate Palestinian and Lebanese terrorist cells to conduct targeted assassinations. Yatom quit Mossad three years ago and disappeared. They assumed he, like many with his background, became a mercenary. Then he became a ghost. The Israelis also had no idea why he would be part of an attack team striking the port, disguised as Palestinian terrorists. Or how they'd known to coordinate their strike to coincide with a massive Hizballah rocket attack.

According to Mossad, three separate teams entered the port, each with small arms and explosives they'd smuggled through security and hid from their detectors. Neither Mossad nor the port security company figured out how they'd done it. Mossad insisted that the sensors could not be spoofed (except by them), though they neglected to provide proof of why. It seemed possible that these attackers, whoever they were, with their Mossad and IDF training, also figured out how to spoof the sensors. Something about that didn't ring true to Colt. That scanning tech was one of Israel's most tightly held secrets.

He read the report again and then locked it in the safe, left the dregs of the coffee in the cup on his desk, and went into the ops center for his shift as chief of watch.

One look at the board told him it was going to be a full day.

"There are too many shitstorms to keep track of," Colt muttered, looking at the board in the ops center. On a normal day, NTCU's role in the IC was to monitor foreign technical intelligence threats—from traditional hacking, like system intrusion, to more active measures, such as influencing public opinion on social media. Since the dam attack, the unit was using their specialized, expert systems to aid the digital forensics to help uncover the perpetrators.

"That's the truth, sir," the analyst, Annette Pierce, said.

"Can you bring me up to speed on the forensics effort?" Pierce was a senior analyst but relatively new on the NTCU team. They sourced personnel from across the intelligence community, with CIA, NSA, and FBI providing most. As NTCU's head of operations, one of Colt's many duties when he wasn't in the field was to train new personnel and check them out on unit systems.

"Sure thing," she said. Cyber forensics was a daunting practice that heavily favored the aggressor. Files that law enforcement or intelligence agencies might use to identify the source could be manipulated or deleted. Cyberspace was malleable in ways the physical world was not. However, thanks to Jeff Kim's AI, they at least had a place to start. Kim's system not only found evidence of malware, it also found an obfuscated IP address, the digital equivalent of someone trying to erase fingerprints. NTCU's hackers took it from there.

"This CERBERUS is really something," she said. "I'd need a team of people to do this, and it'd have taken us months."

NTCU launched CERBERUS the year before, and it was one of the most sophisticated artificial intelligences in use. CERBERUS aggregated and assessed massively distributed arrays of data, billions of discrete datapoints, made conclusions, and matched patterns. It taught itself from those conclusions and learned where to dig further, which increased its operational efficiency and speed. It also hooked into any networked US government computer system and a host of commercial ones who'd secretly consented to be monitored in the interests of national security.

CERBERUS was the world's preeminent digital detective.

"Okay, walk me through it," Colt said. This was as complicated as it got, which was saying something. Because the dam attack was part of US critical infrastructure, the Department of Homeland Security's Cyber and Infrastructure Security Agency (CISA) and National Infrastructure Coordinating Center (NICC) were supposed to be the lead agencies in identifying the attackers. However, because the intelligence community discovered, almost immediately, that the attack came from Eastern Europe, NTCU and the National Security Agency (NSA) jointly assumed responsibility for the investigation. Colt heard from NTCU's Director, Will Thorpe, that Homeland Security pitched a fit, but someone (who remained nameless in the retelling, but Colt suspected was Ford) reminded them that if they'd done their job in the first place, the enemy wouldn't have been able to do theirs.

Pierce exhaled heavily. "So, we start with the usual suspects. The leading candidates are Russia, China, North Korea, and Iran. They've all got the technical ability, more or less, and we can certainly check off the 'intent' box. Thing that surprised us all is that they actually *did* it."

And, Colt knew but didn't vocalize, that no one in the intelligence community saw it coming. Monitoring threats was incredibly difficult and, like forensics, heavily favored the aggressor. It was like living alone in a house in the woods with no lights on the outside and trying to stop a thousand burglars from breaking in.

Pierce continued, "Iran and the Russians have been inside our infrastructure for years. Iran hacked a dam in New York in 2012. That had the same operating system as Folsom, so that was actually our first guess. At the time—and I was around for that—we thought it was a test run for something bigger. Luckily, they got caught and we kicked them out. Next up, we look at DPRK."

"I'm familiar with their body of work," Colt said. "I've spent time in East Asia. They hacked Sony Pictures after they made a movie that made fun of Dear Leader."

"Yeah, those weirdos tend to stick with extortion, money laundering, and IP theft."

"Circumventing the sanctions," Colt said, finishing the thought.

"Yup," Pierce agreed. "You probably don't need the primer on China, then."

Colt chuckled. "Not really." Chinese intelligence collection primarily focused on technological and economic targets, though they admittedly took a vacuum-cleaner approach and pulled any minor detail they could get their hands on in the event it would become useful. "I don't see this as being PRC. They've got their eyes on taking back Taiwan and aren't going to provoke a war with us until they do it."

"That's what we thought too," she said in a direct tone. Colt hoped he hadn't come off as condescending. He knew too many ops officers that treated analysts like hired help. "That leaves the Russians. Their information warfare capabilities are scary good and run the gamut from extortion to social engineering. I swear, half of my day is spent doing whack-a-mole on Russian-made social media bots. They have a history of hacking USG networks. But it's a lot like what you said about China."

"How do you mean?"

"Well, their conventional forces are taking a beating in Ukraine. They attack us like this, that's basically an act of war. Why risk NATO calling to collect?"

"I can give you one good reason," Colt said. "They didn't think they'd get caught." Thanks to Jeff Kim's work, NTCU got ahold of the code, ripped it apart, and figured out how it was done.

"The attackers hid their source IP addresses, spoofed them to show a different origin. It's like when people like you slip through a border on another nation's passport." She said the latter with a slight, knowing smirk. "They deleted the executable files used to launch the attacks. Though, what was true in the physical world didn't necessarily hold true in cyberspace.

Given sufficient computing power, nothing deleted is ever truly gone. We got our big break yesterday. We were able to reconstruct the executables—those are the files they used to launch the code—and found that even though the hackers wrote the exploits in English to hide their hand, the execute commands were coded in Cyrillic. Give them credit," she said, "they hid them really well."

Fingerprints.

Even three years ago, identification and attribution this fast would have been impossible.

"Good work," Colt said. "Okay, so we think it's the Russians. What next?"

Pierce stood up from her workstation and cracked her neck. "The Russians like to do things through proxies," she said. "They train criminal gangs in Eastern Europe or even spinoffs from intelligence services. They provide the latest software exploits and digital intrusion technology and turn them loose on the West. They are free to do anything they want so long as they never target Russia."

"I think everyone agrees now that it's the Russians," Colt said, and folded his arms. "The whole intelligence community was just talking in circles about whether the Russians did it themselves or just gave the order."

"It was sophisticated. The attackers used a combination of techniques to gain access to the dam's control system. They targeted multiple personnel with emails spoofed to look like messages from the control system's manufacturer directing them to apply an urgent security patch. Once inside, they locked out the other users and opened the gates." Pierce shook her head slowly. "It's cold-blooded shit, what they did to those people." Colt didn't say anything, let her have the moment. "After we traced the files to a Russian origin, NSA fingered Russian military intelligence. We assume it's their Unit 74455."

"I know them," Colt said. "They call themselves 'Sandworm.'"

"Yeah, it's pretty lame when bad guys try to give themselves scary-sounding names."

Colt laughed. "Tell that to 'Cozy Bear.' Good job, Pierce," he said.

The dam control systems' manufacturer, which provided the management software for hundreds of dams across the country, scrambled to issue security patches and system upgrades across their enterprise. They were excoriated in the press for having deployed an "outdated" system. In truth, the state and municipal governments they counted as customers had not upgraded their systems, nor did they exercise what was known as "good hygiene" practices. Passwords were easily guessed and rarely changed, security patches not applied. Often, the operating systems themselves were years out of date.

Upgrading an enterprise IT system was costly and time-consuming. Rarely did it top the annual priorities for most bureaucracies.

The federal government wasn't scoring many points on its response, either. FEMA, in a rush to appear decisive, used a new electronic payment system designed to fast-track relief funds to flood victims. FEMA routed disaster relief payments to the wrong accounts, people with the same names as flood victims but in entirely different parts of the state paid by accident. Some people received their relief payments, but in laughably small amounts. NTCU watched the flood of social media traffic suggesting widespread fraud and people filing false claims to get relief payments. Many of these appeared to originate from bot accounts made to look like pundits.

Millions of dollars in relief payments were now tied up and unusable by anyone.

Once the news of the payment fiasco broke, NTCU began investigating whether it was possible someone hacked FEMA's electronic payment system. The Department of Homeland Security and Treasury both swooped in, argued that was their respective turf, and told NTCU to back off. They did.

NTCU had a cable news channel on one of the screens to help watch standers pass the time. Colt thought the news feeds were also useful in corroborating what they were seeing through intelligence channels. Open-source information was now as important as the secrets people like him stole from enemy governments. NTCU, as well as the Agency, subscribed to analysis feeds from private intelligence companies—Stratfor, GlobalWatch, ThreatSense, LTS4, the McKinnon Group, and the like, mostly to see what the private sector made of the same issues the IC chased. Unfortunately, rather than watching one of the webcasts from any of those firms, they were currently tuned to a cable news station featuring one Senator Preston Hawkinson, Guy Hawkinson's uncle and the current chair of the Senate Select Committee on Intelligence.

The senator was running for president and took every opportunity to point out the failures of the current administration. The election was still a year away and the senator faced strong primary challenges, which drove him farther to the fringe. Fist on a podium in a senate chamber empty but for the C-SPAN camera, Hawkinson demanded congressional inquiries into FEMA's handling of the response, the Department of the Interior's "botched" dam management strategy, and the current administration's inability to defend against cyber threats.

This was the same person who led a crusade against technology companies over the last few years. Appreciation of irony, it seemed, was still in short supply in Washington.

Colt's relief came in for shift change, and he walked the officer through what had happened that day. The wall-length monitors in the ops center showed a split between the latest Chinese Belt and Road infrastructure deployments, which now had CIA-designed digital sensors deployed on their network. The other half of the screen showed status reports related to the dam attack and any outstanding requests for information they owed other agencies that would need to be resolved in the upcoming shift.

Colt left the ops center after he'd finished the shift turnover briefing for his other full-time job, being an NTCU operations officer. He checked overseas cable traffic first and then reviewed the latest assessments from the Israel operation. These were mostly technical reports on the extent of the Chinese surveillance efforts. Colt made his recommendations for what should be shared with the Israelis, per their agreement. As NTCU feared, the Chinese intelligence-gathering operation was sweeping.

The port AI deployed allowed the Ministry of State Security to capture every single item that passed into or out of the parts of the Port of Haifa they controlled. They had the shipping manifests and ultimate destinations of all the cargo. They had the raw data on how long each action took to complete and under what conditions. That alone was incredibly useful to continually improve China's own seaport systems. Artificial intelligence needed raw data to learn from, to teach itself, and to self-optimize. With every bit they received, the system became smarter, faster, more efficient and able to handle more complex problems. Now, they had a digital sensor in the middle of a major Israeli port and one where US Navy ships often called.

That wasn't the true danger, though.

What Langley worried about with every Belt and Road deployment was that those countries put their infrastructure in China's hands. This could become a gun to the heads of those respective governments. If they chose not to acquiesce to Chinese pressure on a particular issue, say a UN vote or perhaps basing rights for the ever more expeditionary People's Liberation Army, China could simply decide to shut off whatever capability they deployed. That might be a port, that might be a country's entire access to the internet.

The worst part: few, if any, of those countries recognized the threat for what it was.

When he left Langley that day, Colt couldn't decide whether he was glad they now knew how deep the problem went. He drove home to his small house on a quiet street in Falls Church about seven miles from headquarters. He changed into his running gear and hit the pavement for about an hour to clear his head. Lately, running was a kind of meditation, something that gave his brain a place to go so that it wasn't focusing on tungsten projectiles falling from the sky or the tentacular reach of Chinese surveillance.

The nights were the hardest.

Colt had a few circles of friends outside of the Agency, but Washington's tyrannical traffic made getting together during the week difficult. To say nothing of his op tempo. He was at an age where his Navy buddies still on active duty were rotating through the Pentagon for staff tours, other government agencies, or the senior service schools, and they tried to meet up on occasion. It ended up being once or twice a year, in practice.

Colt dated occasionally, though that, too, was challenging. He, perhaps unfairly, compared every woman he met with Ava. There was also the simple matter of what to talk about. He was forbidden from telling them what his job was, who he worked for. Even if he dated someone else at Langley, they would still be walled off. They would just understand why.

When he did meet someone, it might last a few dates, but most of the time Colt would lose interest. He didn't like lying to them, saying he was a mid-level cubicle drone for the Commerce Department.

Bullshitting a foreign customs official was one thing, but Colt didn't like having to deceive people in regular life. It didn't feel fair to them. What kind of a relationship started off with a lie? Or perhaps they'd wonder what kind of a person was happy with a boring, bureaucratic job. Certainly not the kind of exciting, dynamic personality that made for interesting dates.

And none of them were Ava.

They'd spoken a little since he'd returned from Israel, but those were secure videoconferences between their respective agencies and they were just cast members in a larger play. Colt wasn't permitted to speak with her outside of official channels. Fred Ford knew about their history and reminded Colt every chance he got that he needed to stick to the rules. Ford was right, and Colt knew those reminders were coming from a place of genuine concern, but there was a part of him that was tired of hearing it. Colt understood a relationship with Ava was not just impossible logistically, it was illegal.

None of that helped him in the long, lonely hours between shifts when his restless mind looked for comfort.

Colt made himself a martini, another new hobby—though he *stirred* his —and passed the rest of the evening in silence on his patio.

When he arrived at Langley the next morning, Colt learned the malaise would be short-lived.

"Read this and follow me," Ford said, pressing a folder into one hand and a coffee into the other. Ford called him an hour ago and said he needed to head in, immediately. "Cable traffic from Nadia. There's a big info dump there, but I'll give you the highlights. Nadia reported last night that Hawk-Tech is meeting with the Ministry of Technical Cooperation again, and Liu Che will be there. In Geneva."

"Where are we going?"

"Ops center alerted Thorpe as soon as the cable came through. He's convened the principals, so ops officers from Euro Division and the China Mission Center. I told Thorpe we were ready to go to Geneva as soon as he green-lights the op."

"The principals" Ford referred to were the regional CIA divisions that NTCU liaised with on the Hawkinson case. Nadia was undercover at Hawkinson's headquarters in Geneva, and NTCU had far too few operations officers, so they leveraged the CIA staff at Bern Station for local support.

When NTCU led the hunt for the Chinese mole on the National Security Staff, they worked closely with the Agency's newly created China Mission Center and its head, Pete Pritchard. Pritchard was an old-school spook cut from the same cloth as Ford, though one who undoubtedly played politics far better.

Colt tried to review the document Ford gave him while matching his friend's long strides and not spilling his coffee.

"Oh shit," Colt said, reading the cable. "Who's briefing?"

"We are," Ford said. "And by 'we,' I mean 'you.'"

FBI Special Agent Will Thorpe, the NTCU Director, kicked the meeting off and facilitated the introductions. There was a new face this time, a case officer from the Argentina desk. Guy Hawkinson opened a HawkTech office in Buenos Aires earlier this year. The Argentina desk officer was here mostly to observe. They didn't know exactly what Hawkinson was doing in Buenos Aires, and Nadia was having a hard time finding out, but NTCU made it a matter of practice to involve the Argentina desk should the operation expand into their sphere.

"Good morning, I'm Colt McShane, head of operations for NTCU. This has been a long-running effort, and unlike most cases, it's not straightforward." A few of the officers around the table chuckled. Colt called up a slide, and the face of a middle-aged Chinese man appeared. "We're here to talk about Liu Che. Che is a Chinese foreign intelligence officer in their Ministry of State Security. Until June of this year, he ran what we believe is the most damaging spy in the post-Hanssen era. Liu is currently on the FBI's Top Ten Most Wanted List." Colt looked to Thorpe, who nodded.

"For the last two years, NTCU has been pursuing Guy Hawkinson as one of our top technical counterintelligence threats. Our investigation started when we suspected Guy Hawkinson of selling stolen technology to Russian intelligence. That relationship soured, or the SVR wanted to cut ties before the US found out about it, so they launched a space-borne kinetic weapon and wiped out Hawkinson's island research facility. Fred and I were there and escaped just before it blew."

Colt paused and scanned the room for questions. "We got little of intelligence value but were able to insert a covert operative into his organization, codenamed YELLOWCARD. Hawkinson relocates to Geneva and works on reputation laundering. He covers himself in good works, using his technology platforms to cozy up to the UN, NGOs, and prominent research organizations. He becomes a leader in artificial intelligence, mostly on the strength of what he stole and tried to sell to the Russians. At this time, he also starts developing a bioweapon that uses DNA targeting. This R&D is primarily done with AI supervised by a handful of human researchers, so it went undetected. YELLOWCARD reported HawkTech launched an AI-based hacking operation the likes of which had only previously been attempted by the Chinese, and they had about a million hackers trying to break into Western targets."

"To what end?" John Hoag, from the Euro Division, asked.

Colt thought about his answer for a moment.

He left out Hawkinson's connection with a terrorist organization made up of industrialists and scientists and government officials. He'd been chasing them for two years and still didn't know how to describe Archon. They didn't hide in caves and launch planes at buildings or blow themselves up on buses. They didn't demand changes from the world governments they opposed like every terror group before them. Archon didn't wait, and they weren't interested in governments bending to their will. They wanted to reshape the world order in their own image.

Colt gave the safest answer he could. The truth. Just not all of it. "We believe he was contracted to build the bioweapon by a third party who knew he had the capability to create it. As for their hacking operation, it was wide-ranging, a lot of collection targets, but the primary ones were private DNA labs. Shortly after this, Hawkinson contacted the Chinese government. We believe this is coincidence, not correlation. We do not think the Chinese are aware of the bioweapon. Still, if they end up working together, the risk is high that technology gets into Chinese hands. Our case officer thinks, superficially, Hawkinson is after financial investment and political cover.

"More importantly, he's interested in China's now global information network. AI needs data to self-learn and expand. When we're talking about the amount of data produced on nearly any subject, the Chinese are the world's unequivocal superpower. Hawkinson gets access to that and he's able to accelerate his research by orders of magnitude we don't have ways of measuring."

"What for? What does that get him?" Hoag asked.

"Artificial General Intelligence. At the risk of being reductive, it's a computer that can think and reason like humans do, can teach itself at an extraordinary rate." Colt held up his hands, seeing the skeptical looks on several faces. He knew bringing this up was a risk, as this was where it would introduce doubt into the skeptics' minds. "The top minds don't agree that AGI is even achievable, but if it is, Guy Hawkinson is not the person we want controlling it. In short, and at the risk of sounding hyperbolic, it renders every computer system in existence irrelevant. It's something that can reason and think and has the sum total of human knowledge available to it. An AGI could learn faster than we could keep up with. In the wrong hands, Christ, even in the *right* hands it's world-changing."

"But if it's not even possible...," said the officer from the Argentina desk.

"What matters is that the Chinese think it is, and Guy Hawkinson is one of their best bets to getting it," Pete Pritchard said. Pritchard was an old friend of Ford's. Those two went back. Tall and framed large, Pritchard had a full white beard and dark eyes. "Even if the Chinese don't achieve AGI, the pursuit of it can still unlock a technological arms race that has unfathomable consequences."

"Jeff Kim is the closest to getting there," Colt said. "And the Chinese and Guy Hawkinson have both stolen his technology. We think the Chinese are trying to get their hands on what Hawkinson acquired. Accelerate their work, fill in the gaps."

"Why now?" the Argentina desk officer asked. The Chinese significantly expanded their footprint in South America in recent years; this conversation doubtless had his interest.

Pritchard said, "Our analysts think China, as a global power, is peaking rather than ascending. We think that makes them dangerous and prone to risky action."

"What does that mean, exactly?" Thorpe asked.

"They can't sustain their current growth. More than that, there are some checks coming due, so to speak, and they don't have the cash on hand to cover them. China, today, is like an inverted pyramid. Without serious and immediate intervention, that period topples. Possibly by the 2030s. That has global consequences. But if they get a lock on potentially world-changing technology...well, that changes their trajectory considerably." He motioned to his younger officer who queued up the slides. "The Chinese military buildup and modernization effort is unprecedented in their history. We joked in the nineties that if they were going to invade Taiwan then, they'd have to swim there. Consider the fact that in 1999, the Chinese had a brown water navy, and they lacked the equipment or the know-how to move an army division from one part of the country to another. Even if they did, there was no infrastructure or road network to support it. That has all changed. There are some clear-eyed mil-to-mil analyses that suggest we'd lose this fight if it kicked off tomorrow. More than that, even, the Chinese Communist Party needs money to stay in power. Their whole system runs on graft. Bribes keep the PLA and the security services running and compliant."

"So this is Russia in the late eighties, then? We just spend them into collapse?" someone from Euro Division asked.

"Not exactly. All that buildup comes at a tremendous financial cost, that's true. The Chinese are more stable and have a broader economy than the Soviet Union did. They've expanded their industrial base and manufacture much of the world's goods. When the Belt and Road Initiative began, many of those early investments were because the Chinese overproduced in certain sectors and needed to get rid of the surplus. Their domestic economy is strained.

"They're becoming politically isolated because of hostility and unmasked intentions at regional hegemony. Some countries are starting to push back on the Belt and Road, seeing it for what it is. We, in the China Center, are doing everything we can to reinforce that message. It's one of the biggest political action campaigns the Agency has run, certainly since the end of the Cold War. We've got blogs and news articles running under aliases, front companies trying to undercut Chinese suppliers, quiet words to influential trade ministers in certain countries. We're hacking their digital 'Great Wall' and getting dissidents' VPNs so they can securely communicate. Whatever it takes. Starting to bear some fruit. Some influential companies, marquee names, are starting to look elsewhere."

Pritchard paused for questions, and seeing none, he continued. "Now, for those bills coming due that I mentioned. They've got an aging population that is about to enter retirement, and thanks to their one-child policy decades ago, there aren't enough workers to replace them or to generate the revenue basis to support them. It's one of the most top-heavy demographics we've ever seen."

"If they are peaking, as you say, does that make them less of a threat?"

He shook his head. "No, just the opposite. We expect they will take action on Taiwan soon, the next two to three years at most. They'll move before that pyramid I talked about starts to collapse. Taiwan makes ninety percent of the world's semiconductors, and that's not an industry you can just start up on a whim. They'll try to take that over before the world can respond."

"Thank you, Pete. We have a couple threads coalescing here," Colt said. "Liu Che is the Chinese intelligence officer liaising with Hawkinson. Che, until recently, was posted at the Chinese Embassy here in DC. He recruited and ran a US Navy officer for twenty-five years. We uncovered it when Admiral Glen Denney posted to the National Security Council. It's worth noting that Denney almost discovered and disclosed YELLOWCARD's identity. We believed Liu wanted to use that to get close to Hawkinson. Denney died before we could apprehend him, and Liu escaped. After his flight, Liu relocated to Geneva to manage Hawkinson's recruitment.

YELLOWCARD was present at their first meeting and just reported that there will be a follow-up next week. As far as we know, the cover is still in play."

"So, what's the next step?" John Hoag from Euro Division asked.

Colt scanned the table, taking each of the members in.

"We bag Liu Che."

6

Langley, Virginia

"You're proposing that we capture and exfiltrate a Chinese national from a neutral country?" the Euro Division head, John Hoag, said. "Team, I need to remind everyone that when the rendition program leaked, it did not go over well with the American people."

"We're not talking about black sites, John," Ford said. "Liu will be returned here to stand trial."

"Fine. If Hawkinson is the threat, why in the hell are we talking about this Liu?" Hoag wheeled on Thorpe. "What's the FBI doing about this?"

"It's not that simple, John," Thorpe said. "Because of Hawkinson's political connections, we can't just arrest him. They'll play it like the president is trying to take out a rival. So, we focus on the foreign intelligence threat and get them to kick. If a Chinese national says something about Guy Hawkinson in a FISA court, we neutralize the argument that this is a political hit job."

"Listen, if you were trying to tell me that Hawkinson's technology was what enabled the GRU to just open up Folsom Dam, I'd think—maybe—there was a reason for this conversation. What are we even doing here? Need I remind everyone that the Russians just committed an act of war?"

"The Chinese have almost all of our war plans for the Pacific theater," Colt said. "They have our entire strategy for the defense of Taiwan. They also have detailed intel on our submarine hunting capability, aircraft carriers, and fifth-gen aircraft."

"Which has jack shit to do with Russia!" Hoag thundered.

Pritchard cut in. "We should also assume they've shared most of that intel with the Russians or will. Unless we want to be fighting two wars, I strongly suggest we move forward with this and find out just how much damage was done."

"I don't know," Hoag said. "This is a steep escalation, and it breaks bad in a lot of horrible ways."

"For what it's worth," Pritchard said. "The China Center is behind it."

"But it blows up in *my* front yard if it goes poorly, Pete, not yours. And I've got my damned hands full already with this Russia hack. They launched it from my region, and we've got every available case officer trying to figure out who else is involved and whether there's another one coming." Hoag pushed back from the table and made to leave. "Sorry, but I don't have time for this cowboy bullshit."

Hoag's scared, Colt thought. The stations in his division were running all over Europe chasing ghosts. The dam attack came so far out of the blue, no one anticipated it. With everyone singularly focused on the Russians, damage assessment, and what to do about it, it was small wonder that the only support for bagging a Chinese intelligence officer came from the mission center.

"Sit down, Hoag," Ford said. While the forensics on every damaged relationship Ford had with senior clandestine service officers would take a very long time to puzzle out, Colt knew that Hoag and Ford had bad blood. "I know you're not suggesting that we pass up an opportunity to catch this guy. I appreciate your concern about not wanting this to blow up in our collective faces. So, we'll do it real quiet-like."

Hoag put his hands on the table and frowned. "Look, Hawkinson is your case. I can't stop you from doing it, but I can go to the deputy director and suggest now isn't the best time to go running and gunning all over Europe to kidnap a target. What if you get caught? What if he gets away?

That's all in my area, and it just raises the temp on an already boiling pot. Sorry, but that's my answer."

"Your team in Switzerland has been very helpful so far," Colt said, softening his tone. "We're grateful for their assistance. But, if you don't want them involved, we can go it alone. What we can't do is let Liu get away."

Colt wished he could walk back what he said about bagging Liu, but the words were in the air now. He should have approached this differently, built consensus for the mission privately among the principals before bringing it up here.

Liu was a mission priority for NTCU certainly and the China Mission Center, but the others at the table had real concerns elsewhere.

Hoag shook his head and stood. "Nope. I'm still out."

"I appreciate your position, John," Thorpe said in measured tones. "And I'll reiterate our gratitude for your division's assistance and support on this case. However, we have an authorization from the director to capture this man should the opportunity present itself. I'm speaking as a cop, not as a spook, now. Liu needs to answer for what he's done."

The conference room was silent.

A trace of red passed over Hoag's cheeks.

"What do you need," Hoag said wearily. It sounded like he'd just lost a judo match.

"SOG is supporting the grab," Colt said. "Chuck Harmon has been a huge help on this case. If he's available, we'd like him. I think that should do it." Harmon was a case officer assigned to Bern Station, two hours from Geneva, and acted as Nadia's local handler. He'd also saved her life.

Thorpe wrapped the meeting. "Once we get Liu and bring him back, we're going to turn him over to the China Mission Center to debrief, assisted by the Bureau. After that, he goes to trial, and then we put him in a cell in the center of the Earth."

Colt, Ford, and Thorpe returned to NTCU's offices in Langley's basement.

"How long before you can finalize the mission plan?" Thorpe asked.

"It's written. We knew Geneva was a high probability, so it was one of the main scenarios we planned for. I've rehearsed with the SOG guys." Colt nodded. "We're ready."

"Let me know when you're finished. I'm going to go brief the deputy director. Then, I need to tell *my* people over at the Bureau so they can be waiting when you land." Thorpe was halfway out the door when he turned back to them and said, "Gents, I'd be derelict in my duty if I didn't caution you here. Hoskins and the director are backing you, for now, but please be careful. This is a political time bomb. If you guys swing at Hawkinson and miss, careers are going to be ruined and not just yours."

Thorpe left, and Colt called Tony Ikeda.

The Special Operations Group was home to the Agency's paramilitary, covert action, and political active measures, the blackest of black operations. Covert actions were Agency-speak for those activities so sensitive that the president could deny their very existence if they failed. After Liu's escape, Colt immediately went to figuring out how to get him back. Ford made an introduction with people he knew in SOG. They kept their distance until the director's authorization came in, and the tone changed immediately.

Colt met Tony Ikeda, a covert action officer with a background in cyber warfare, to conduct the kind of hacking used in conjunction with covert ops —like shutting off all the power to a city block before a paramilitary team went in and took out a target, or spoofing an alarm system into thinking the tripped sensor was a routine operation. They spoke the same language and hit it off immediately. Ikeda was generous with his time and, over the course of several sessions, helped Colt plan exfiltration scenarios in the event they captured Liu.

By that afternoon, Colt, Ford, and Ikeda sat around a table in a secure room within NTCU. Maps, tablets, and notepads covered the surface. They finalized their plan to capture Liu Che and presented it to Thorpe early that evening. This was a major shift for NTCU, their first covert action and first direct operation against a foreign intelligence officer. Thorpe and Ford briefed the deputy director the next morning.

Ford wouldn't be going.

Denney had shot Ford during his escape with a nine-millimeter pistol. Ford was still recovering and not cleared for operational duty. Colt could tell Ford also wasn't itching to get out into the field. Two brushes with death in less than a year was enough for anyone.

The next day, Colt and Tony Ikeda were on a plane to Geneva.

———————

Colt, Tony, Nadia, and Chuck Harmon huddled in a safe house the Bern Station team set up in Montreux, on the opposite end of Lake Geneva.

"What's Hawkinson proposing?"

"He needs cash," Nadia said. "He sank millions into the island and hasn't gotten anything back from the insurance companies yet. It's still in arbitration. They're saying it's an act of war, which means they won't cover it."

Colt let out a cold, shallow laugh.

"Never thought an insurance company for multimillionaires would be one of the good guys," Colt quipped.

"He had to rebuild the quantum array in Geneva, which you knew. That cost a lot. This thing in Argentina, he's being really tight-lipped about. It's actually a carve-out, a subsidiary. Nobody outside the exec team is read in. I was able to get a look at some purchasing records, though." Nadia handed Colt her tablet.

"Crays? Supercomputers?"

"Purchased through a shell company, Infinity Global Services. That entity was set up during the Hawk Security Group days, which they used to buy weapons and equipment when they needed it off the books."

"And this all came from LONGBOW?"

Nadia nodded. "Guy is going to ask for investment in the near term. Longer term, he wants access to their data, like we've assessed. I think something else is at play, though."

"You mentioned political top cover in one of your earlier cables," Harmon said.

"I think that's part of the strategy, yeah. He's afraid of criminal prosecution from the US government, this is going back to the Jeff Kim stuff, plus the Russians. He's told me that himself. Then you add the fact that they assassinated a former MI6 officer." Nadia shrugged.

HawkTech, acting as the R&D arm of Archon, engineered a weapon using microscopic, biological robots that homed in on a target, aimed by that person's DNA, and then swarmed the heart, causing a fatal heart attack. They targeted a former MI6 officer turned member of Parliament and attacked him on the eve of his becoming the new head of the British Secret Intelligence Service.

If Archon's attack were ever attributed, it would be Hawkinson and not them.

Their hand, again, concealed.

Layers within layers.

NTCU didn't share the knowledge of that widely, even within the Agency. Archon was a little much for even the most open-minded intelligence officers to comprehend. Colt believed in his bones Archon was the dangerous new world of threats that would define intelligence work in the twenty-first century. It was too far removed from what most Agency personnel could grasp.

NTCU made the difficult decision not to share details of the attack with MI6. Either they'd either be laughed out of the room or, worse, their friends at Vauxhall Cross would take matters into their own hands. Guy Hawkinson belonged to CIA, to the National Technical Counterintelligence Unit and, most directly, to Colt.

"Okay, so Hawkinson is asking for investment and, later on, data to power his AI. What does he think the Chinese are interested in?"

"Well, he doesn't know that the Ministry of Technical Cooperation is a front for State Security, for one thing," Nadia said. "He thinks they want his open-source crawler. He knows the Chinese have a strong quantum computing game already but assumes they want to peek under HawkTech's hood anyway. As far as I know, he doesn't suspect they are after what he already stole from Kim."

NTCU's leading theory was that what the Chinese were really after with Hawkinson was the tech *he* stole from Jeff Kim. Together, that tech would set their own programs years ahead from where they were today.

"This is great work, Nadia. Really. Both of you," Colt said, looking to Harmon as well.

They walked through the primary extraction plan and each of the backups several times.

"The summit with MTC starts tomorrow, first thing." Nadia looked at her watch. It was late in the afternoon, and she'd need to leave soon in order to get back to Geneva by late night. It was only an hour drive under normal conditions, but Nadia would take a carefully planned route through the Swiss countryside designed to foil surveillance. It would take her several hours to execute. "Colt, can I get a minute?"

They walked up to the second-floor bedroom. The curtains were drawn back, showing clouds the color of spilled ink hanging low over Lake Geneva. The mountains on the other side were almost totally obscured.

"What's up?"

"LONGBOW is deployed," she said. "If you get Liu, what's next for me?"

Colt could hear the anxiety and tension in her voice. He knew from a career of running agents when one was reaching their limit. But Nadia was no agent, she was a trained clandestine officer. *Well, mostly*, Colt mused dourly. He'd rushed her through the CST course and then inserted her into HawkTech way before she was ready. Most clandestine services officers had a probationary tour at a CIA station where they were supervised by experienced case officers who taught them all of the things you didn't learn at the Farm.

The odds were that Nadia should have slipped up, been exposed, and left in a ditch somewhere. Yet, here she was. Without her work, they wouldn't have learned about Archon's bioweapon, HawkTech's expansion into South America, or their massive AI-powered hacking operation.

Nadia looked like a cog that was too close to being ground into a wheel.

"We need to find out what's going on in Argentina, why the move. I think LONGBOW is a great force multiplier, but it's no substitute for eyes and ears. The China thing, I don't know if this is a business move for Hawk-Tech or a play by Archon. We really need to know which one it is. Do you think you can hold on just a little longer?"

Colt recognized the hypocrisy for what it was. Hawkinson was an American citizen and protected by its laws. And the CIA wasn't a law enforcement organization. No matter what Guy did, Colt could never arrest him for it. Thorpe or one of the other FBI agents assigned to NTCU, perhaps, but they had to have evidence of a crime being committed. They all worried that evidence collected by an intelligence officer might well be thrown out.

So why keep Nadia in play?

Because everyone at NTCU believed Archon was an existential threat. They'd already demonstrated the ability to hold world leaders at risk. What if that was just their opening move?

"I can," she said slowly. "I just wanted to know what the game plan was."

Colt studied her. Nadia was holding back, he could tell that much. It was in her eyes. They looked as dark and obscured as the sky over the lake. He waited a beat, but she said nothing further.

The meeting dissolved.

Colt gave Nadia and Harmon a few minutes alone before they both departed.

When they'd left, Colt grabbed a pair of beers from the fridge for him and Ikeda. They'd stay at the safe house tonight and leave for Geneva in the morning.

"You good?" Ikeda asked when they were halfway through the beers and the small talk. He spoke with an easy way, the kind of casual only hard-earned confidence can bring. Ikeda had a way of packing a lot into two simple words.

Colt thought about his response.

"I'm good for the job we have to do."

Ikeda nodded and said nothing else.

They drove to Geneva, leaving just before sunrise. They had a shorter SDR planned because they didn't expect anyone knew they were here, but it was nonetheless a covert mission and they took no chances. They arrived in Geneva midmorning and went to the place Harmon set up. He was already there. It was an apartment in the city center, not as ideal as a private residence, but it had parking.

Nadia called at four thirty. Phones weren't allowed in the HawkTech building, so she must have found a way to step out.

"They're wrapping in thirty minutes. Liu said he has a dinner engagement at the Chinese Mission at seven." The Permanent Mission of China to the United Nations was at the northern end of the city, about two and a half miles from the HawkTech offices.

Colt hung up the phone and looked to Ikeda.

"We're on," he said.

Ikeda nodded and replied, "Let's roll."

7

Geneva, Switzerland

"This is an important meeting for us," Guy said.

Nadia watched the waves of rain rolling in from the lake, gray, dismal, dark. The HawkTech executive conference room on the building's top floor faced the water. On a clear day, they could see the mountains on the far side of it. It was just the two of them.

"Thanks for including me," Nadia said.

"Are you kidding? Of course, it's important for us to show off our rock stars. I'll do most of the talking during the meeting and Damien will lead the technical discussions, but what I want you to do is focus on Liu. Get to know him, become his friend."

"Want me to take him out for drinks? Show him around town?" Nadia quipped, a smirk on her face.

"If that's what it takes, yes," Guy said. If he knew she was joking, he didn't let on. Or was ignoring it. "These kinds of negotiations usually drag on for months, and we don't have that kind of time. Figure out what turns Liu's crank, and let's use that for leverage. Maybe it's closing the deal, might be something else. See what is going to get him promoted, and we'll figure out how to do that thing."

Jesus, he's talking about recruitment.

"I'm on it, boss," she said. "I'm sure you know this already, but I've spent a lot of time deep-diving on the requirements the CCP puts on foreign businesses. We'd have to allow them access to all our tech and basically hand over any data we collect in their country."

Guy smiled, and it was a grim, sly, loaded thing, like a gun that hadn't gone off yet.

"Good looking out," was all he said.

"I should get down to the lobby. They'll be arriving soon," Nadia said and headed downstairs.

Nadia met the Ministry of Technical Cooperation delegation and got them checked in to security. "You can store your phones in these lockers here," she said, waving to a bank of small lockers behind the security station. The guest lockers were painted in bright yellow. "It's a security precaution, I'm afraid. Employees are under the same restriction," she said. "We have time built into the schedule for you to check messages during breaks." Nadia watched their guests store their phones and retrieve the keys, noting where Liu stored his.

When they were finished, Nadia guided them to the elevator and from there, to the executive conference room.

Hawkinson, Kirby, and HawkTech's Chief Technology Officer, Damien, flitted between Liu and the members of his delegation. Nadia suspected all of Liu's team were actually Ministry of State Security technical analysts. Guy started guiding everyone to their seats. Nadia, purposefully, was the last to sit. She walked over to the buffet set up on the far wall and picked up a water pitcher, which she brought over to the table.

The HawkTech team occupied one side and the Chinese delegation the other.

Nadia wore a navy blazer over a white blouse and jeans. She had a lapel pin in the shape of the Air Force emblem—the "Buck Rogers wings." The pin contained a miniature camera. It could capture short snippets of high-def video about a minute long and would sync with a portable hard drive concealed in a glasses case, which was in her backpack. She'd upload the images and transmit them to Langley when she got back to her apartment tonight. NTCU analysts would run it through their image recognition software and see if they got hits on the suspected MSS officers. If not, they'd start a file with the aliases they used here.

Nadia took the water pitcher and filled up several glasses, setting them in front of people so that she could get a good face capture on each. As she stepped back, Nadia shifted her shoulders so that the camera panned from the Chinese to Guy in the same frame. She wanted to capture him with them in case they needed to turn this footage over to the Justice Department.

Guy thanked her for the waters, and Nadia took her seat, opening up a notebook as she did.

"Nadia, would you mind recording for us?" Guy said.

Way ahead of you, dude. "Sure thing," she replied.

Guy led the discussion, which was an in-depth look at each of Hawk-Tech's products. They talked about the secure voting initiative and the ed tech systems. Liu and his team seemed particularly interested in both. Guy gave Nadia an opportunity to discuss her work on their open-source information aggregator. As she spoke, she felt Liu's predatory eyes on her.

During their first extended break, several of Liu's people rode the elevators down to the lobby so they could retrieve their phones from the Faraday cages and check messages.

Nadia sensed him before she saw him in the corner of her eye.

Liu appeared at her side, holding a cup of coffee and a saucer. He was tall and thin, with a crisp suit that looked expensive and a dark tie that looked to her like a bruised eggplant. "Not a nice afternoon. I suppose I shall have to get my steps in on the treadmill," Liu said.

"Yeah," she said. "Normally it doesn't rain like this until later in the fall."

"Guy tells me you served in the Air Force," Liu said, and looked down at her pin.

"That's right. I was what we call a cyber operations officer, which was mostly managing technology programs. I did get into the field, though."

"Ah, interesting. Where did you serve? Not in Afghanistan, I hope."

"I had some operational time, yes."

"Of course, of course. I understand. Did you study computer science at university, then?"

"At the Air Force Academy, yes, and then graduate school at Cornell. My concentration in grad school was in AI." She could almost hear Colt in her head: *Feed him just enough crumbs to make him hungry.*

"What about you, Mr. Liu?"

"Che, please. I was educated at Tsinghua University in Beijing. My focus was electrical engineering."

"Did you start working for the Ministry straight out of university?"

"No, I was in industry for some time. Unfortunately, there is still some patronage required to secure positions in many of our ministries, and my family was not well connected within the party. However, I had the good fortune to study at the London School of Economics for my post-graduate work, and that afforded me an opportunity to get noticed by the Ministry." He turned to face the water. "How do you find the private sector as compared to the military?"

"I like having the freedom to make decisions here. I also connect with our mission. Technology can be democratizing, I think."

Nadia felt totally out of her depth.

Liu was a master spy. He'd recruited a naval officer and caused one of the costliest intelligence breaches ever, engineered the admiral's ascension to a position on the White House's National Security Staff, mere yards from the Oval Office. And she was supposed to go toe-to-toe with him?

The break ended, and they returned to the meeting. Liu asked how Guy expected to do business with the Ministry given the new restrictions the US government placed on trade with China. "I have a Swiss registered company we'll use for any collaboration. But even if the Commerce Department wanted to look into our arrangement, it will take them at least eighteen months to get it moving. By then, there will be another administration, and I suspect it will be less of an issue." Guy flashed his thousand-watt smile, the one he used to shine on his investors.

He was counting on his uncle to solve his legal problems.

That was something Liu could appreciate, given what turned the screws in his country.

Liu found her again on the next break, hoping to resume their earlier conversation. "Earlier, you were about to tell me about your impression on the difference between military life and corporate life," Liu said, prompting her. "I'd like to ask you more about that."

The hardest thing Nadia had ever done in her life was to be open to this conversation, because all she could think about when he spoke was, *You almost got me killed, you son of a bitch.* Of course, Liu hadn't gotten her name, just her CIA cryptonym and gender, but that had almost been enough.

"As I said, I have a lot more freedom here. More autonomy to make decisions. The military can be restrictive, even for officers."

"Indeed. I can appreciate that. They give us so little discretion, don't they?"

Where's he going with this, Nadia wondered.

"What do you hope to get from a partnership with HawkTech?" Nadia said, trying to retake the initiative.

"Certainly, there is much yet to work out, but I am optimistic about this venture," Liu said, still facing the water.

"We are as well," Nadia replied, sounding chipper.

"I hope this shows that China can partner well with Western companies, irrespective of the disagreements that our governments may have. Business transcends politics, as it were."

An interesting position for a communist to take, she thought.

"Hopefully, other businesses learn from HawkTech's example," Liu said.

"Do you think partnerships such as this are important to China's future?"

"I do," Liu said, though not immediately. "The world is changing rapidly around us. We must all do what we can to react favorably."

There's something in his tone, Nadia thought. *He's worried about China's footing. Or,* she mused, *he wants me to think he is.* China was ever more isolated, even within the region they believed they dominated. The Chinese struggled to regain their position after crippling backlogs to shipping from the earliest days of the pandemic. In response, several American tech companies developed algorithms to rapidly source commodities Americans and other countries used to buy from China from other manufacturers, loosening China's grip as the "world's manufacturer." The United States and Japan entered a mutual defense and technical collaboration pact recently. Jeff Kim had deployed his "seaport of the future" to Seoul last year, fully automating one of South Korea's major ports.

"AI is the great leveler," Nadia said. "I know your country has invested much in virtual reality as well. I tend to think virtualization is going to break barriers much faster than anything else."

"Yes," Liu said, exuberant.

Nadia looked over her shoulder. Guy returned to the table.

"Guess we should be getting back," she said.

"I should like to continue our discussion," Liu said. "You are quite insightful."

Nadia offered a practiced smile in response. "I would welcome that," she said, thinking she'd offered nothing particularly insightful. She returned to the table.

Nadia opened her laptop to resume taking notes, looked down at the screen, and then leaned over to Guy. "Someone on the open-source team just invented a new crisis," she said. "I need to go put this fire out. Can you spare me for ten?"

"Go," Guy said.

Nadia hit the elevator bank, rode it down to the lobby, and went straight for the lockers where employees stored their phones. She opened her locker, powered on the phone, and pretended to check it. She walked over to the guest lockers, still vamping being engrossed in her phone. That bank was right behind the security desk, but the guard faced monitors on his desk and an iPad below counter height, out of view from the front. He was watching a show.

Nadia produced a key that she'd lifted from the guard desk the week before and opened Liu's locker. She cast a look over her shoulder at the elevator bank, back to the security guard, and then opened the locker door a fraction of the way. It was a small space, large enough to accommodate a tablet or small laptop but little else. She grabbed Liu's phone and held it up, then toggled LONGBOW on her phone and hit it. Nadia returned Liu's phone to the locker, closed the door, and texted Colt.

Before going to Montreux, Colt and Tony came to Geneva to conduct recon. Ikeda suggested the easiest way to grab Liu was to spoof one of the Chinese government's diplomatic vehicles. They spent a few hours around the Chinese Permanent Mission to the United Nations, which was the formal name for the Chinese offices here in Geneva and their staff in various international organizations. The mission was a large chateau on Chemin de Surville in the Petit-Lancy neighborhood, about two miles from HawkTech's headquarters. The majority of vehicles they found, not just for the Chinese but for most missions, were German makes, except for the Americans, who shipped US-made vehicles over. The Bern Station team got them a pair of black Mercedes GLS SUVs with blacked-out windows, a vehicle commonly used by the Chinese.

Because they didn't know Liu's full schedule, they planned the capture for the HawkTech offices. The one place they knew he would be.

Ikeda said taking him from his state-furnished apartment would be too risky. There would be security, and the probability of discovery was high. But Liu wouldn't have a detail, which opened up the possibility of a street capture.

Challenging in a place like Geneva, but not impossible.

The HawkTech office occupied the end of a stubby row of buildings on a man-made island in the middle of the Rhône just as it emptied into Lake Geneva. A bridge connected it to either bank.

They pulled up in front of the HawkTech building in the SUVs after getting Nadia's signal and executed three-point turns on the narrow street to face the main road. There were removable metal pylons that prevented vehicle traffic on this part of the bridge, but Hawkinson must have made arrangements with the city for their removal. The drivers were both covert action officers from Ikeda's unit that flew over with them.

Both men wore inexpensive dark suits.

Colt intercepted the Chinese Mercedes sedan on the corner before it pulled up near the building. Covered by an umbrella, Colt leaned down and made the "roll the window down motion" with his free hand. The driver did so. "Hi, Joe Mitchell. I'm with HawkTech. They're running a little late. You know how it is. I need you to move the car, though. Mr. Hawkinson's Land Rover is going to be pulling up any minute, and I've got to get him to another event. There isn't enough room here for two cars." Colt motioned to the street, just wide enough for a car.

Colt wasn't sure how much the driver understood, but he seemed to pick up the gist. "Can you give us, maybe, fifteen minutes?"

"Fifteen minute?" the driver repeated in halting English.

"Yeah, that'd be great. Thanks, pal, appreciate it." Colt tapped the roof twice and returned to the sidewalk. The sedan pulled away. Colt walked quickly back to the HawkTech office, feeling the surge of nervous energy that flowed before an operation. He was grateful to have Tony Ikeda's expertise to plan this, but even more on the execution.

Colt walked over to stand near the first SUV.

Nadia escorted Liu and the Chinese delegation into the elevator, thumbed the lobby button, and waited the eternity for the doors to close. They were so close to the handoff. She thought about Colt's words, about needing to hang on just a little longer, to find out what was going on in Argentina. This was one step closer and she could go home.

Then she heard, "Hold the door," and her heart dropped to the floor.

Guy put his arm through the door to stop them from closing and stepped in.

"Wanted to ride down with you to see you off," he said to Liu.

Liu smiled.

Guy turned to Nadia.

"Did that situation resolve itself?"

"Yeah," she said, and they rode the rest of the way in silence.

Guy held the door for their guests and then made a show of guiding them to their phone lockers, as if they'd forgotten where they'd put them. Nadia needed to give Colt the no-go signal but couldn't do it with Hawkinson standing right here in the lobby. She couldn't go to her own locker, knowing Guy expected her to stay focused on the guests until they departed. He would also expect her upstairs for a debrief on the day's events as soon as they departed. Guy made small talk with Liu, asking about his event that night. Nadia put eyes on the door and the two SUVs idling out front. A man in a dark suit waited in front of each vehicle, holding an umbrella, ready to usher the occupants into their seats. She couldn't see their faces but prayed one of them was not Colt.

Guy had photos of Colt and Ford from their mission to the island.

"Gentlemen, thank you for a productive day," Guy said.

Nadia hadn't thought of the possibility of him riding down with them. Guy told her to do it. Her mind raced to find a way to get him the hell out of here so they could still pull this off.

Guy walked toward the door and made a comment about the rain.

Nadia had to act now.

She turned and moved over to her locker, opened it, and sent a text to Colt through their covert messaging app. A single letter *X*.

Colt's phone buzzed. He reached into his jacket and drew it out.

The office doors opened, and the Ministry of Technical Cooperation delegation poured out into the rain. The two covert action officers moved forward with umbrellas at the ready.

Colt looked down at his phone. There was a notification in the app he used to communicate with Nadia. It was designed to look like a social media application and actually pulled feeds in from real ones to help hide the actual messages in plain sight, though those were all encrypted and walled off from the public internet. He opened the app and saw Nadia's message...the no-go signal.

Colt, braced against the building so he wasn't immediately visible, stood with Ikeda. Harmon stood at the end of the block, on the bridge, beneath a covered platform for a light-rail stop.

The Chinese delegation left the building, rushing for the waiting vehicles. Guy saw Hawkinson follow them out.

Colt turned up the collar on his coat, giving their wave-off signal. Unfortunately, Ikeda's team would still have to chauffeur the Chinese delegation to their destination. It would raise too much suspicion if they just drove off now. Colt bowed his head against the rain and walked quickly for the end of the street.

They met at the new safe house an hour later. They'd moved from Montreux to Geneva that day for the operational phase. Water bottles and takeout boxes took over the counters.

Colt and Harmon both tried to reassure Nadia that none of this was her fault, but she was taking it hard. Colt sensed she was embarrassed in front of the covert action guys.

"Okay, on to Plan B," Ikeda said. "Thanks to Nadia, we now know where Liu is going to be."

Colt nodded to Ikeda, a gesture of thanks for supporting her.

"Yeah," she said, her voice still a little uneasy. "LONGBOW lets us see everything Liu sees on his phone. It's not like he's keeping a calendar, but it does give us access to his GPS data."

"Great. Where's he at right now?"

"He's at the PRC's Permanent Mission. There is some kind of official function tonight." Nadia pulled it up on her Agency-issued table and showed the group. It was about two miles south of where they were.

"He's staying at an apartment here in Old Town, though," Nadia said.

"So, we can expect that he'll leave there at some point this evening," Ikeda said. "I think our original ops plan still mostly works, right, we just need to change the setting." Ikeda went quiet, studying the map on the tablet.

"What's up?" Colt asked.

"Look here," he said, pointing. "These are one-way streets, easy to get bottlenecked, and we can expect heavy traffic. That's a problem if we need to move fast and can't. We get stuck, it's a problem. That's an affluent neighborhood."

"Security cameras on the houses," Nadia said. "There isn't a lot of idle time."

Ikeda nodded in agreement.

"That's going to limit the takedown options. And if he smells *anything*, we're in trouble, because there's nowhere to go fast, except on foot." Ikeda paused again, thinking through it. He looked over to Colt and Nadia. "You guys have anything to spoof cameras?"

Colt shook a negative. "Nothing we brought with us."

"In that case, this is what we'll do."

Colt, Ikeda, and Ricky Garcia, one of the covert action officers, got into one of the Mercedes SUVs and drove to the address on Chemin de Surville. The Petit-Lancy neighborhood was a wooded section of old money residences sandwiched between the Rhône and the industrial areas further southwest. Ikeda drove, with a chauffer's cap pulled low over his eyes. Ikeda learned Mandarin when he joined CIA, and he would bluff his way past the security checkpoint the mission staff set up on the road. Ikeda was a Japanese-American, but the large cap and the darkness would hide most of his face from the security guard. He also wore thick-framed glasses to further break up the profile.

Colt and Garcia sat in the back, both wearing suits.

When Ikeda pulled up to the checkpoint at the end of the street, he said in Mandarin, "Dropping off two and picking up one." Colt and Ricky carried on a meaningless conversation in the back seat in Swiss German. Ikeda held up his phone to the driver, showing the emblem of the rental car company the mission hired for the event. They'd gotten that from Liu's phone earlier.

The security guard shone a flashlight into the back seat, over Ikeda's shoulder, and verified what Ikeda told him. He waved a disinterested hand, and they drove through. There was a short line of cars, maybe four deep.

Once they were idling, Colt passed his phone up to Ikeda, who typed a text in Mandarin and sent it to Liu's phone via the LONGBOW instance on Colt's phone, informing him that his vehicle had arrived.

They waited in line about ten minutes.

The vehicle in front of them pulled away, and Ikeda drove up to the gate.

The Chinese Mission was a square, three-story mansion behind a stone and wrought iron fence with a line of trees behind it. A large white metal vehicle gate provided the only way in or out. Mission security staff flanked the open gate, checking attendee credentials on tablets. An equal number of guests were arriving and departing. It was good cover, lots of motion and activity.

"That's him," Colt said, seeing Liu exiting the mansion's front door. Colt turned in his seat to check behind them and saw the next car in line edging closer, almost to the bumper. "Watch the rear," Colt said.

"I see him," Tony replied. "That guy gets any closer and he's buying me dinner."

The problem was that now they couldn't reverse if they had to. The car in front hadn't cleared the way and was part of a line.

Colt opened the passenger door and slid out, vamping a party guest who was just dropped off. Garcia slid out the opposite door so Liu wouldn't see him in the vehicle when he stepped in. He walked back and looked down at the bumper, as though inspecting a fender bump. This earned him an indignant look from the driver in the car behind him.

Liu looked down at his phone, confirming he had the correct ride.

Colt kept his head down as Liu passed him and then turned. There was still a line of cars blocking their exit. Drivers were honking now, and Colt heard impatient shouts to get moving.

Ikeda stepped out and greeted Liu in Mandarin, opening the door for him.

Colt made eye contact with Ikeda. A line of cars blocked their exit route, and it was the only way out of the neighborhood. Even if the driver behind them wasn't kissing bumpers, there was a line just as long to the rear as the one to the front, and it was a single-lane drive.

Ikeda looked to Colt for the go/no-go signal.

If he waved off now, there might not be another chance at Liu. But if they couldn't leave quickly, there was always the risk they'd be discovered. They also didn't know what kind of surveillance equipment the Chinese had. A security camera that could see through tinted windows was table stakes at this level. Subduing Liu right in front of their mission might easily draw attention.

Colt patted himself, pretending to look for a phone, and then shook his head, swearing softly. He started off for the line of cars, nodding to Ikeda as he went.

It was worth the risk. Colt's job was to clear the path.

As Liu maneuvered into the vehicle, Ikeda quickly closed the door behind him. Garcia opened the rear driver's-side door and climbed in. Liu looked over at him, startled and confused. Garcia drew a taser, hidden under his suit jacket, and hit Liu with it just above the kidney. Liu jolted and collapsed to the floor of the vehicle. Ikeda returned to the driver's side. Garcia opened a small black case, assembled a syringe, and injected Liu. "Good night, Mr. Liu." The intelligence officer went silent.

They had maybe a minute if this had been captured on camera.

Colt moved along the line of cars in long, authoritative strides. It was three vehicles—all black SUVs or luxury sedans—to the corner, then a northward exit from the cul-de-sac. Colt walked on the driver's side in the street. There were streetlights, but the heavy foliage seemed to absorb the illumination. Colt turned and saw the problem. A Range Rover had rear-ended an Audi A8, and the drivers were in the street yelling at each other.

If cameras picked up the taser, Colt guessed they had forty seconds, probably thirty, until security responded and an outside chance local police might already be on the way.

"Hey," Colt shouted at the two drivers. "You need to move this along."

Both ignored him.

Colt closed the distance. "I said, you need to move this along. Now. *Verstehe*?" The arguing drivers turned now. "Get this out of here," Colt shouted, pointing at the collision. The passenger in the Range Rover stepped out and attempted to take control of the situation.

Colt turned to him. "Sir, you need to get back in your vehicle, *now*." The man did. Colt turned back to the two drivers. "You two are creating an unacceptable security situation here. I don't care who hit who, you can resolve it somewhere else. Pull out onto the main road, go wherever you want, but I need to get these cars moving. Right now."

The drivers looked at each other, as if trying to figure out what to do.

"*Now*, gentlemen," Colt said. They got into their respective cars, the Audi putting his hazards on, and slowly pulled forward. Colt started directing traffic, whistling loudly to get the other drivers' attention. He motioned for them to pull forward.

He saw Ikeda pull around the corner, and he slowed just enough for Colt to get in the front passenger door. "Don't save gas," Colt said.

Garcia removed a couple sets of zip ties, securing Liu's hands and feet. He pulled Liu upright in his seat, fastened the seat belt around him, and clicked it. Liu would be out for several hours.

Colt messaged Harmon and Nadia. **Picked up package.**

Garcia notified his partner, who was already on his way to the airfield in the other SUV with their personal gear and mission materials.

Ikeda drove to Payerne Air Base seventy miles north of Geneva, where a CIA aircraft waited to take them back to the United States. One of the Swiss Air Force's three remaining air bases, Payerne was home to two F/A-18 squadrons and another of the venerable F-5E Tiger IIs.

Ikeda showed his authorization paperwork from the Swiss government to the security guard, who'd already received instructions that an American would be coming through and not to ask questions. Liu was still unconscious in the back. They passed through another security cordon at the airfield and drove the vehicle up to the aircraft, a nondescript Gulfstream G5. The aircraft door opened at their approach, and Garcia's partner descended the steps to help with Liu. They opened the Mercedes's door, pulled Liu out, and carried him onto the aircraft.

Ikeda and Colt parked the SUV, retrieved their bags, and walked to the plane.

"You did good," Ikeda said.

"I really appreciate your help."

"What I'm here for."

Colt slung his bag over his shoulder and put a foot on the airplane step. He half turned to face Ikeda. "I know you already know how important Liu was to us, but I just wanted to tell you again how big a deal this was. That asshole did a lot of damage. We probably won't ever know how much."

Ikeda didn't say anything else, he just clapped Colt on the shoulder once and followed him into the airplane.

Colt notified Ford and Thorpe that the mission was successful.

It was an eight-hour, forty-one-minute flight to Virginia. They'd land at Dulles International Airport, where a squad of FBI agents would meet the plane, take Liu into custody, and shepherd him into the bowels of the earth. With the time change, they'd land around midday.

Colt changed out of his suit and into chinos and a dark blue dress shirt. He sat across the aisle from Liu, who was handcuffed to his seat.

Liu came to about an hour into the flight. He groggily looked around the cabin, disoriented and confused. Colt had to give the man credit, his composure was impeccable.

"Good evening, Mr. Liu. You are on a CIA aircraft bound for the United States. When we arrive, agents from our Federal Bureau of Investigation will meet us at the airfield, and they will arrest you for espionage. I suspect you will live out the rest of your life in solitary confinement in a maximum security prison. If there is anything you'd like to tell me before this becomes official, now would be the time."

"Are you the one who brings me coffee, or is that a different agency?"

Liu leaned back in his chair and fixed his gaze forward.

Colt ignored the jibe, decided Liu wasn't going to talk, and moved to the rear of the aircraft. He opened his laptop and worked for several hours, completing the first draft of his mission report while the events were still fresh. Then, he closed his laptop and went to sleep.

Ikeda woke Colt up.

"Colt, you need to go up to the cockpit," he said in a low voice. Colt blinked the sleep out and unbuckled.

"What's going on?"

Ikeda shook his head and indicated to the front of the plane where Liu was sitting. Colt went back to the galley to get himself a cup of coffee before going up to the cockpit. The sky outside the aircraft was lighter than he was expecting. They were supposed to land before dawn.

"What's up?"

The pilot handed controls over to the first officer and got out of his seat. "We've got a problem."

8

It started with Lufthansa Two-Four inbound to Dulles from Frankfurt.

"Wait a second," the Washington Center controller said, peering at his radar screen. He reconnected with New York Center and asked him to confirm Lufthansa Two-Four's position. The New York controller repeated what he'd previously told Washington. Washington then called the aircraft and asked the pilot to reverify his location. The pilot's reported location did not match the radar. In fact, Washington Center showed them at one hundred miles out and a different heading. Within moments, they received multiple warnings that flights across their airspace were deviating from their flight plans. Controllers scrambled to verify the locations of their planes. No one was where they were supposed to be.

The airspace on the Eastern Seaboard was the most congested in the United States, if not the world, and as of 11:14 a.m., ATC did not have positive control of it.

Sandra Rice—"Sandy" to her friends—had been an air traffic controller with the FAA for fifteen years and another eight with the US Air Force before that. Sandy grew up wanting to fly, but poor eyesight kept her on the ground. She found new love in controlling jets. It was solving a puzzle in three dimensions with pieces that were always moving. No day was ever the same. The weather, the number and compositions of the flights, all added to the dynamic.

She'd never seen anything like this in twenty-three years.

Every plane was in the wrong place.

The control center was laid out in two long rows on opposite ends of a narrow room. Each operator had a computer terminal with a large monitor. Above them, rows of backlit maps ran the length of the room. Each panel angled downward so the controller could look up at it. The room was dimly lit, beige carpet and black metal rails.

"Did we check that GPS is functioning?" Sandy knew that was an obvious question but needed to run the checklist.

"It's showing RAIM good," one of her controllers said. Receiver Autonomous Integrity Monitoring was a tool they used to assess the Global Positioning System's proper functioning in the event of an emergency. RAIM pinged a GPS satellite from the ground to verify that it was transmitting properly, that each satellite in the constellation was operational and reporting correct positioning.

How is it possible that everyone is in the wrong place? They drilled frequently, practicing various emergency scenarios. The constant drilling was a holdover from her military training. You practiced something until it was rote, until you knew it cold, until you could perform the steps calmly in a crisis.

She'd already called the towers at the three major airports in their region—Dulles, Reagan National, and Baltimore/Washington. All of them reported the same, that none of the aircraft were where they were supposed to be. "At least we're all wrong together," she said under her breath.

When it first started, they'd put Lufthansa Two-Four into a holding pattern. Of course, as a Boeing 777 on the tail end of an intercontinental flight, they didn't have a lot of loiter time. Aircraft started to stack up around their destinations, and several had declared in-flight emergencies for fuel.

She'd activated their own emergency procedures. Their IT people were trying to debug the systems without taking them offline, but so far, everything was checking out as normal. The diagnostics all showed that each system was working fine. Except that it wasn't.

They needed to get these planes on the ground and fast. Some of these jets were running low on fuel as it was; they couldn't loiter while the people on the ground tried to figure out what to do next. But, how to sequence aircraft for landing when you didn't know exactly who was where?

She instructed the towers at Dulles, Reagan, and BWI to land the aircraft based on their proximity to the field. Without radar to rely on, individual airfields needed to determine, locally, which flights were which and land them accordingly. It was the best plan they could come up with. The guard frequency, the emergency radio channel shared by all aircraft and controllers, erupted with pilots talking over each other, jockeying for position in the approach flow, each saying they needed to be the first on the ground. It was born, Sandy knew, out of the responsibility they each felt for their passengers' safety, but the chaos it caused only made their job harder.

Sandy asked her boss to call his counterpart at New York Center to see if they could take some of the overflow. They could at least divert the aircraft that had fuel and relieve the burden here. He came back about ten minutes after that, white-faced.

"New York Center is in the same situation we are," he said, his voice weak. Then he said, "And so is Boston."

Jesus holy Christ. The entire northeast corridor was...wrong.

The controller in her kicked in, spurred her into action.

They couldn't worry about New York or Boston right now, they had their own aircraft to get on the ground.

"Okay, everyone, this is the plan. We're prioritizing aircraft that are on reserve fuel. We need to get them on the ground ASAP. If they are within fifty miles of their original destination, they should proceed there and enter the approach flow. We'll hand them off to Approach Control, and then its towers' responsibility to land them. If the divert field on their flight plan is closer, instructions are to land there. Again, the priority is getting people safely on the ground as quickly as possible."

"What about municipal airfields?"

"Everything is on the table. Aircraft in fuel emergency situations should land at the closest available airfield that can accommodate their aircraft. Issue those instructions now, and let me know immediately if one of your jets does not have either option." Sandy turned to the center director. "We might need to use military airfields as divert locations for some of these heavies. Andrews Air Force Base can take wide-body aircraft. Can you call the wing commander there and grease it?" Washington Center handled all air traffic in the region, civilian and military alike, and they had the contact information for all of the military air bases in their sector.

"Sure thing. Anything specific you need to know?"

"How much ramp space do they have, and is there any reason they can't take civilians."

"I'm on it."

"Frank," she said. "Thank you."

"Hey, until this...whatever it is, is over, I work for you."

Sandy felt better now that they at least had a plan and a way to rack and stack. Her relief would prove to be premature and short-lived, because the situation got immeasurably worse.

At 12:31, Sandy made the hardest call of her life. "Attention all aircraft, this is Washington Center. ATC radar is down. Repeat: ATC radar is down."

They were now blind.

Within minutes, so was everyone else. The Global Navigation Satellite System was gone.

The pilot took his headphones off and set them on his lap, muttering that everyone was talking over each other anyway. The copilot said he'd continue to monitor the guard frequency.

"Let me guess, it somehow got worse?" Colt said.

The CIA pilot rubbed his eyes and nodded. He told Colt an hour ago that ATC put everyone in a holding pattern, saying that they had some kind of a computer malfunction and that the ATC system was incorrectly reporting aircraft locations. "ATC just issued an emergency notice that they lost radar."

"Oh shit," the copilot said. They both turned to look at him. "GNSS is out. I mean, we've still got our satnav, but ATC just reported that they no longer trust the data being reported in GNSS. It's giving false readings."

Colt understood the situation, at least notionally. He'd been a surface warfare officer in the Navy, a ship driver. Navigating an aircraft had much in common with driving a ship. They both used the Global Positioning System to pinpoint their specific location and used that to navigate according to the flight plan they filed with the FAA, or whatever the appropriate national authority. Originally, ATC informed them that their position was being falsely reported on their control system, but the aircraft at least knew where they were. Now, ATC was saying they had too many reports from individual aircraft that GPS positioning was wildly off from their Internal Navigation Systems and Radio Navigation Aids.

Now, ATC reported their remaining ground-based navigational beacons lost power. Without the Tactical Air Navigation (TACAN) system or the very high frequency omni-directional range (VOR), which gave short-range VHF positioning queues from ground beacons, pilots would have to rely on strictly visual cues and manual map references.

The CIA aircraft had its own navigation system that tied into an Agency satellite, so they at least knew where they were. But no one else did.

"We're about out of fuel," the pilot said. "We're going to have to put down fast or we're landing in a cornfield. Given who we have onboard, normally I'd have had you put a bag over his head and diverted to the Agency airfield in North Carolina, but we don't have gas for it. There are too many aircraft in the approach flow at Dulles for us to skip the line."

"What about Reagan?"

"Same boat. But Leesburg Executive Airport is only three miles away. That should make it easy for your FBI bubbas to get over from Dulles and pick that guy up. There won't be as many heavy diverts there because it's a smaller field. I'm declaring an emergency and heading over."

Colt clapped the pilot on the shoulder and said he'd tell everyone else to get ready for landing.

"Let me know where to send the scotch when we get on the ground."

"You got it," the pilot said.

They didn't "lose" the Global Navigation Support System in that the signals went down or that aircraft could no longer pick up the transmission from the satellites. In truth, it was so much worse. GNSS gave aircraft false reporting, just as the ATC system reported aircraft being miles away from their actual positions. Now, each plane had a conflict between what satellite positioning told them their location was and the flight management system, which had the flight plan.

The transmissions on the guard frequency were almost unintelligible.

Aircrew were talking over each other, everyone seemingly on the edge of panic, and it was nearly impossible to sort out which emergency situation was the most severe.

Sandy recalled a security briefing in the last year where ships passing through Russian waters reported GPS signals rendering incorrect or inconsistent positioning. Though ships traveled slow enough that they could spot other vessels before they collided, the real danger was navigating at night. The case study the briefer gave showed that one cargo ship almost ran aground in the Gulf of Finland at night because the navigation system reported their position as twenty miles different than what it actually was. The briefer went on to say that the Russians were incredibly adept at electronic warfare and that they could spoof GPS signals to give false reporting. As they lost one system after another, Sandy felt the cold realization that someone had taken ATC offline. There was no other explanation for losing control of *everything*.

They needed to get all aircraft on the ground as quickly as possible.

"Sandy," Frank, the center director, said behind her. He'd just finished up another call with his counterpart at New York Center. They were in the same situation. ATC did not have positive control of any aircraft on the Eastern Seaboard north of Washington, DC. "I just spoke with the administrator. We're executing SCATANA."

The Security Control of Air Traffic and Air Navigation Aids (SCATANA) was the FAA's emergency plan for landing in-flight aircraft. Frank handed her a binder with a red cover. She reviewed the checklist. While they practiced the emergency procedures periodically, SCATANA had only been implemented once since its creation in 1975, which was 9/11.

Sandy got on the guard frequency and transmitted the code word, which would direct all aircraft to land immediately at the closest airport. She then prepared a Notice to Air Missions (NOTAM) and entered it in the FAA database for transmission to aircraft and airfields.

FLIGHT RESTRICTIONS FOR WASHINGTON, DC

EFFECTIVE IMMEDIATELY UNTIL FURTHER NOTICE. PURSUANT TO 14 CFR SECTION 91.137(A)(1) TEMPORARY FLIGHT RESTRICTIONS ARE IN EFFECT DUE TO EXTRAORDINARY CIRCUMSTANCES AND FOR REASONS OF SAFETY. ATTENTION ALL AIRCRAFT OPERATORS, BY ORDER OF THE FEDERAL AVIATION COMMAND CENTER, ALL AIRPORTS/ AIRDROMES ARE NOT AUTHORIZED FOR TAKEOFF. ALL TRAFFIC INCLUDING AIRBORNE AIRCRAFT ARE DIRECTED TO LAND IMMEDIATELY.

Her controllers repeated the instructions every sixty seconds over guard frequency, VHF, and HF radios.

Sandy had never felt such helplessness in her life. She couldn't even watch the radar to see aircraft landing. The only thing they had to go by was reports from the airfields in their area calling out aircraft on the ground. Once they'd lost radar, she'd listed every aircraft in their airspace on a whiteboard in the control room. They marked each aircraft off when an airfield reported them having landed.

Reagan filled up first. It was a small airfield and couldn't accommodate large, international aircraft. Baltimore/Washington and Dulles both had a lot of ramp space. Dulles tower sent smaller aircraft to nearby Leesburg Executive to free up the traffic pattern for the incoming international flights that were low on fuel. Several aircraft were diverted to Dover Air Force Base in Delaware and Andrews Air Force Base in Maryland, both of which had very long runways designed for military cargo aircraft.

By late afternoon, the airspace was clear.

Aircraft entering Washington's, New York's, or Boston's airspace were diverted, returning to their point of origin if they had the fuel, or the closest airfield if they didn't.

Aircraft across the country were grounded until further notice. Tens of thousands of travelers were stranded in the wrong place. It would take weeks to sort this out, assuming they were cleared to start flying again. Out of the hundreds of aircraft they controlled that day, they didn't have current status on—miraculously—only fifteen. There were no reports of aircraft crashes, so they believed these planes just landed at uncontrolled airfields and had no way to report their locations.

They'd narrowly dodged the worst outcomes, but it would be a long, long time until air travel recovered.

Colt watched the black SUVs tear across the tarmac, lights flashing. They had the windows up so Liu could watch it happen. Colt didn't know what happened with the aircraft, but the pilot informed him that the FAA executed their emergency plan to immediately land all aircraft.

The copilot opened the aircraft door, and a swarm of dark-suited FBI agents washed onto the plane with Will Thorpe in the lead. Thorpe strode up to Liu's seat, a grim expression on his face. He produced his badge and credentials from a pocket. "Liu Che, I am Special Agent Will Thorpe of the Federal Bureau of Investigation, and it is my distinct pleasure to inform you that you are under arrest for espionage."

9

Washington, DC

Every aircraft in the United States was grounded, and the FAA would not resume any flights until they knew how someone got into their system and was certain they couldn't do it again.

Air travel across the globe was tangled in a Gordian knot as carriers tried to figure out how to route around the United States.

Colt's initial objective interrogating Liu Che was to understand exactly how much damage he'd done with his twenty-five-year case running Admiral Glen Denney. Colt also wanted to make damned sure Nadia's cover was safe.

That was before someone shut down air travel and injected enough fear into the system that it might not recover fully for years.

NTCU's analysts believed there were four nations and, perhaps, three or four terror groups capable of hacking into the air traffic control system—the same usual suspects investigated for the Folsom Dam crisis. That attack was expertly done, and if not for Jeff Kim's involvement, Russian involvement might not have been discovered. This time, there was no trace.

Speculation erupted that another actor viewed this as a target of opportunity, strike America while it was still reeling.

Colt's job was to determine if China was responsible.

Liu sat at a bare metal table in a small gray room. His feet and hands were shackled. He wore an orange jumpsuit. Thorpe and Colt sat across from him. Thorpe had a folio open in front of him, which contained a yellow legal pad and a dark brown folder filled with paper.

"Mr. Liu, the United States government is charging you with multiple counts of espionage, dating back to 2003. We are also charging you with the murder of Glen Denney. We've determined that your government used a security vulnerability in Admiral Denney's Tesla, overrode the autopilot function, and caused the car to refuse his commands. He crashed into a truck doing ninety miles an hour." Thorpe paused to let Liu speak, but the spymaster said nothing, remaining stone-faced and staring at the table. "Your wife is currently in federal custody, which you are no doubt aware of. She is awaiting trial for espionage herself."

They'd arrested her the night Liu escaped, hoping he'd return home for his family before he fled. She'd been in a federal holding facility awaiting trial ever since. "Your government does not acknowledge you or your work, so they will not be coming to your aid. Now, my colleague is going to ask you some questions. Your answers to those questions will allow us to assess your level of cooperation. If you are helpful, we may be able to work something out. At least for your wife. If you are not cooperative—" Thorpe stopped. "Look at me," he said.

Liu's gaze tracked upward, and their eyes met for the first time.

Colt saw only hate.

"If you choose not to cooperate with us, Mr. Liu, you will spend the rest of your life as far from the sun as I can make you."

"So much for due process?"

"You defied our laws for nearly thirty years, and now you want to hide behind them. That's rich. I just wanted you to fully appreciate the gravity of your situation, Mr. Liu."

Thorpe then spent the next hour unfolding the evidence they had against him in increasing levels of detail.

Because Denney was killed before law enforcement could interrogate him, NTCU, the FBI, and CIA's Counterintelligence Division had to start from scratch to assess the potential damage he did. They interviewed

Denney's wife several times, but that turned up little of use other than initial motive. Mrs. Denney suffered from a lifelong gambling addiction, and the admiral, apparently, began spying because he needed money to cover her losses.

She was completely unaware of her husband's spying.

"The late admiral alleges, Mr. Liu, that you were blackmailing him. You uncovered compromising information on him—Mrs. Denney's gambling addiction—and used that to coerce him into providing secrets to you."

"The admiral alleges this?" Liu said in dubious tones. "You've conjured up some way to commune with the dead?"

Thorpe paused a moment before responding, and Colt could tell he was enjoying himself considerably.

"Curiously," Thorpe said, his voice pleasant and conversational, "the admiral left what amounted to a confession, stored in a safe deposit box in an Arlington bank. He typed a comprehensive history of your, ah, collaboration, including the type of information he provided. Denney didn't say, specifically, what he gave you because that would be classified. You do have to appreciate the admiral's sense of irony. He admitted to providing technical specifications for several types of aircraft, weapons system design, and war plans. He went into considerable detail on his wife's gambling and the various places he had to hide money to pay off her debts. The admiral found it interesting that whenever Mrs. Denney seemed to have a clean period, a few years, she'd always find a way to slip back into the habit. Denney said, and I'm quoting him here, that he always felt like she'd been pushed."

"Addiction is a tragic disease," Liu deadpanned.

"And preying upon that is diabolical."

What they did not tell him was, courtesy of the worm that Jeff Kim helped them plant in the MSS's computer network, CIA knew exactly what Liu reported to his superiors in the Ministry going back several years. Chinese intelligence now had copies of US Indo-Pacific Command operations plans, schematics for the Navy and Marine Corps versions of the F-35, F/A-18, and P-8 aircraft. There were also volumes of intelligence reports and electronic message traffic transmitted by the National Military Command Center, which Denney at one time commanded.

CIA hackers used their back door into the Chinese intelligence network to secretly access and manipulate these files. Agency military analysts assumed the Chinese knew as much about the F-35 as Lockheed Martin. But to be able to subversively alter operations plans to reflect different deployment schedules, employment locations, and types and quantities of units and timing had extreme value for misinformation. To do it right under their enemy's noses was an intelligence masterstroke.

"Ask your questions, then," Liu said in a tired voice.

They began with rudimentary questions on Liu's service, where he'd been posted and what he'd done. CIA's interrogation training taught the first few hours were preamble, softening the subject. The real conversation wouldn't begin until much later. They assumed the Chinese operated the same way.

"What's your interest with Guy Hawkinson?" Colt asked in the beginning of the second hour.

He wouldn't ask about potential cyber warfare operations until he was sure Liu softened a little.

There was another reason for starting with Hawkinson, however. Both China and Hawkinson acquired some of the world's most advanced artificial intelligence technology from Jeff Kim. NTCU's analysts strongly suggested it could be weaponized.

Then there was China's interest in Hawkinson to consider. Colt kept thinking about what Pete Pritchard said in their principles meeting weeks ago, about the CCP being interested in HawkTech's voting technology. The Chinese "mentored" burgeoning dictatorships throughout the world, taught them the tradecraft of political subversion, surveillance, and making opposition disappear. It also created new markets for them to sell surveillance technology (which the Chinese no doubt would surreptitiously monitor). If they started exporting Hawkinson's voting tech, it could give dozens of repressive governments throughout the world the veneer of legitimacy.

All this, irrespective of their drive to be the first to AGI.

Before Liu would admit to anything, they first had to set the hook.

"I would think that should be obvious," Liu said. "He's made great strides in artificial intelligence. Such research is of value to my country."

"Is Hawkinson aware that you're an intelligence officer, or does he think the Ministry of Technical Cooperation is a legitimate organization?"

"The Ministry of Technical Cooperation's goal is to establish collaborations with like-minded organizations across the globe. We also look for new markets to sell excess capacity and excess hardware."

"We know the MTC is just a front for China's foreign intelligence service," Colt said.

"You do?" Liu countered. "They failed to inform *me* of this."

"So, you're denying that you spied on America for thirty years and are now running a case against Guy Hawkinson and his company, HawkTech?"

"I seem to recall Mr. Hawkinson running afoul of your government, or perhaps you simply fabricated charges to cause political difficulties for his uncle, the prominent senator. Mr. Hawkinson chose to relocate his business to a...more favorable climate. It shouldn't surprise you that there would be other suitors, but I don't know anything about a 'case.'"

The video camera in the upper corner of the room, as well as other concealed biological sensors in the room, monitored Liu's posture, his eye movement, and his vital signs. These were transmitted back to Langley, where a system broke them down and assessed them against all of the known indicators of deception, compiled by Agency psychologists and FBI profilers.

Colt didn't need any of that to know that Liu was lying to him.

"I've read some interesting analyses about your country recently. It seems that you're losing ground across the globe. Alliances are hard to come by. I guess people don't like being bullied."

"An interesting position for an American to take."

Colt ignored him. "China can't support the population it has now, let alone what happens when the current generation starts aging out. Then there's the extraordinary inefficiency," Colt said.

"We have development projects across the globe and the strongest economic engine on earth."

"Do you, though? It takes you three dollars to make one. And after that situation in Haifa a few weeks ago, I understand the Israelis are rethinking their investment in the Belt and Road Initiative. Other countries too. Afraid it will make them targets for countries that don't want the Belt and Road Initiative to succeed."

"An interesting position coming from a country that doesn't want the Belt and Road Initiative to succeed."

It was a deflection and nothing more, Colt knew he scored a point. Nadia's assessment of Liu was that he was worried about China's economic future and viewed the partnership with Hawkinson as strategic. That would be his way in.

"So, we find you, an MSS officer, meeting with Guy Hawkinson."

"I never said I worked for the MSS. You are the one who keeps bringing that up."

Colt looked to Thorpe.

"Special Agent Thorpe, would you show him the photos, please?"

"I'd like nothing more." Thorpe opened his folio and drew out several pieces of paper. There was a copy of the passport Liu used for his diplomatic cover to enter the US during his posting at the Chinese Embassy. The name was not "Liu Che." Thorpe then showed him photos taken from a drone that an FBI surveillance team used to capture Liu and Jeff Kim meeting earlier that year—first in Washington, DC, and then later near Kim's home in Palo Alto.

"According to Mr. Kim, he claimed to be meeting with a business development executive for a Hong Kong–based tech company called XZE Corporation looking to establish a presence in the US." Colt held back that he'd since turned Kim into a double agent, but he could use that if he needed.

"So, Mr. Liu, I think we can dispense with the fiction that you're a middle manager with the Ministry of Technical Cooperation. We also have a comprehensive document Admiral Denney wrote detailing his involvement with you and the extent of the information shared. Now, he claimed he was framed and blackmailed. No way to prove that, of course, because you murdered him."

Liu said nothing and was expressionless, save a minute pulsing in his lower jaw. The man's self-control was astounding.

"Now, you're meeting with Guy Hawkinson, shortly after having coerced Jeff Kim into handing over some of his most advanced R&D.

Virtual reality, seaport automation—which I see you've already put to good use. Guy, of course, has stolen from Jeff Kim already. You might not know this, but it's what he used to bootstrap HawkTech. Passed Jeff's IP off as his own." Colt shook his head slowly. "Hawkinson is also running one of the most sophisticated hacking operations we've ever seen. Government systems, private labs, news organizations, private security companies. You name it. You'd be amazed at some of the organizations he's penetrated." Colt shrugged. "Or, maybe you wouldn't. Personally, I think Guy is using this collaboration with your government to peek under the hood. The moment you exchange information with him, he's inside."

"It would be impossible for him to steal all of our research."

That was true. It's not as if the Chinese had a single digital vault with all of their R&D. But Hawkinson could tunnel into one of their government-funded research labs. His likely first move would be to hack into one of the networks controlled by the Chinese Communist Party to acquire their technology strategy and key players. From there, Hawkinson, or rather his AI, would know exactly where to look for what he was truly interested in.

"Unit 61486's existence was disclosed almost a decade ago. We know all about the PLA's usage of proxies to carry out officially deniable cyberattacks. And we know that since at least 2016, China has been using AI to hack Western targets. When I think about Hawkinson's AI advances and what he's using it for, coupled with his history of subverting governments, if not hacking them outright, that leads me to believe China's interest in him is more than commercial."

"Perhaps these are questions you should ask someone in the PLA. Or haven't you been able to kidnap any of them? I'd like to speak with my embassy now."

Colt looked down at his watch, the signal to Thorpe.

"Would you excuse us?" Thorpe said.

Colt and Thorpe stepped out of the room, telling Liu nothing further.

"It's not there today," Thorpe said.

Colt nodded. You couldn't force questioning, bad things could happen when you did. They'd let Liu sit for a night, give him time to marinate in the knowledge that the United States had securely identified him as a foreign intelligence officer and the implication of his meetings with Hawkinson.

They'd ignore his request to speak with his embassy.

They informed the guard they were done for the day and left. The guards kept Liu in the room for another thirty minutes, observing him on camera to see what he'd do.

Colt and Thorpe retrieved their phones, and both had urgent messages from the NTCU ops center to return at once. They raced back to Langley as quickly as DC traffic would allow.

Ford was still there when Colt and Thorpe arrived. The IC's unanimous agreement was someone highly capable hacked into the air traffic control network and devised a way to send false aircraft reporting from its navigation systems. Then, they spoofed the GNSS satellite feeds, adding more chaos, before shutting down ATC's radar in Washington, New York, and Boston, making them effectively blind in the northeast corridor. The FAA was deploying a new control system, called "NextGen," but it was behind schedule and only partially implemented. The current thinking was that the attacker found a vulnerability in the system, not surprising since it wasn't complete, and exploited it. Ford, with his usual sardonic wisdom, likened it to the second Death Star in *Return of the Jedi*.

The FAA, working with NSA, the United States Computer Emergency Response Team (US-CERT), and National Cybersecurity and Communications Integration Center (NCCIC), and multiple vendors were scrambling to patch the vulnerabilities. They couldn't launch aircraft until they did, leaving travelers stranded all over the country. Rental car companies, the bus and rail services were doing everything they could to route people to their destinations. Commercial supply chains and the US Postal Service, both of whom relied on air transportation, were left with millions of packages and letters stranded or misrouted.

Unlike the Folsom Dam attack, which left a trail of, albeit well hidden, digital breadcrumbs, there was nothing to point to in the air traffic control system, apart from the outcome. They found no obfuscated IP addresses, no deleted executable files. Someone in one of the endless briefings Colt sat through uttered, "Ghost in the machine."

Compared to the second, the first attack was inelegant, sloppy. It looked like a ham-fisted breaking-and-entering job pulled by an amateur burglar. The ATC attack was the work of a master thief.

Colt, Ford, and Thorpe met in Thorpe's office as soon as they returned from the FBI holding facility. Ford handed a printout to Colt and Thorpe for them each to read.

"We got this from the pinheads over at NSA today," Ford said as Colt scanned the document. It was an intelligence summary of a communications intercept, a phone call between the GRU and the Russian General Staff. The crux of the phone call was the General Staff demanding to know, on behalf of the Russian president, whether the GRU launched another cyberattack so soon after their successful run on the Folsom Dam.

Colt set the paper down.

"Holy shit."

"Yeah," Ford said. "This confirms Russian complicity. I mean, we basically proved it already, but still."

"But this suggests they were not behind the ATC attack," Thorpe said.

"Or, if they were, the GRU doesn't want anyone to know about it."

"Would they do that?"

Ford shrugged. "I'm not a Russia expert, but it does not seem likely to me. This is going in the PDB tomorrow." Thorpe nodded.

The President's Daily Brief was the summary of key intelligence for that day sourced from across the IC, with contextual assessments to inform decision making. CIA prepared and delivered it every morning.

"So," Thorpe said, "what we have is someone *else* that appears to be responsible for bringing down the air traffic control system?"

"Looks that way," Ford said, shrugging. "Unless the GRU or one of their client groups acted out of turn. Based on this," he tapped the paper on Thorpe's desk for emphasis, "if the Russians are involved, the Kremlin does not know about it. Deputy Director Hoskins came down right after this came through. He said to get ready to brief POTUS in the next couple of days."

"Super," Thorpe said.

"How'd it go with our new guest?" Ford asked.

"What an asshole," Colt said. "We played verbal judo for five hours before I called it. We learned very little about what his interest with Hawkinson is."

"I told Colt not to be too hard on himself," Thorpe said. "This guy is a pro. He's as tough as they come, and I've gone up against some of the best."

———

Colt and Thorpe went back to the FBI holding center the next day. Colt felt like he was trying to straddle two freight trains moving in opposite directions.

What was their goal here? If China was indeed involved, why strike at America so quickly after the Russians had?

Something about that didn't ring true to Colt. The US hadn't committed forces to fight the Russians, they weren't engaged in a war in Eastern Europe. If they were, an attack from the Chinese might make more sense.

The Agency knew perilously little about the inner workings of the Ministry of State Security. They didn't even know simple details like the organizational structure or job titles. Guessing motives was orders of magnitude more difficult.

Liu was only the second MSS officer the US had ever apprehended. American law enforcement agencies had rounded up many Chinese spies, but never their handlers. The only other MSS officer was nabbed in just the last five years, and they'd only gotten him because he'd become disgruntled and lazy. Liu Che was neither of those.

"Do you remember our flight into Washington?" Colt asked.

"It's not as though I've forgotten it," Liu said icily. "We spent considerable time in a holding pattern before landing. I also recall you running back and forth to the cockpit. I know what happened to your air traffic control system. They allow me an hour of recreation time each day, and there's a television there. The news is all that's on."

"Is your government responsible?" Colt asked.

Liu laughed. It was a cold, cruel sound.

"You're a fool."

Colt controlled his anger, but it was no easy thing. "I don't have a lot of time here, Liu. Someone attacked our country and could have killed thousands. That's an act of war, and there will be serious consequences. If your government did this, we will find out, no matter how long it takes. When we do, our response will be devastating."

A tired sigh issued from Liu's mouth. "Why do you think I would have any knowledge of this?"

"Three reasons. First, Jeff Kim. With what you've gotten from him, your engineers could easily repurpose his technology for offensive purposes. Two, your partnership with Guy Hawkinson. Hawkinson has also stolen a significant amount of technology from Mr. Kim." Yes, Colt was admitting things to Liu that he shouldn't, but this man was also not leaving federal custody, ever. "He's built an AI, using Kim's tech, that continually trolls the web for vulnerabilities and covertly tests those weaknesses in real time, which would be very attractive to your hackers. And three, Admiral Denney chaired the National Security Council's Technology Threat Working Group. He would have been in an ideal position to know exactly what the ATC vulnerabilities were and how they could be exploited. If I add those three things together, it seems highly likely the People's Republic just declared war on the United States."

Colt's eyes narrowed, and he folded his arms across his chest.

Liu said nothing, but Colt knew the calculations going on in his mind. He was tallying exactly what he could say.

"I do not believe we were involved in this, Mr. McShane," Liu finally said.

"Convince me."

"My service does not focus on information warfare, you must understand. The PLA's Second and Third Directorates, Intelligence and Operations, respectively, and their, ah, surrogates are primarily responsible for those activities. While it is *possible* they could have launched such a strike, and my service would know nothing about it, this seems contrary to the party's goals. I cannot imagine we would so overtly antagonize the West in this way. Consider this as well, though I am speculating. Were China to have done this and our hand exposed, war would be likely. But what would be certain is that America would shut off all economic ties between our countries. Thousands of Chinese nationals working in your companies, studying at your universities, would be immediately expelled. Those consequences would be far reaching."

A loaded statement if I've ever heard one, Colt mused.

"Would your government want to see the United States and the Russian Federation at war?" Thorpe asked.

"I cannot imagine that they would," Liu said. "We both know that only ends one way. The current regime in Moscow is favorable to us and our interests. Our president would not want to upset that. To the best of my abilities, gentlemen, I can tell you the People's Republic of China did not do this."

10

Washington, DC

Liu told them the Chinese didn't do it.

Did they believe him? Did they believe a cornered, captured intelligence officer with little left to lose? It troubled Colt to find that his instincts told him Liu was telling the truth.

Now, he had bigger problems. One of the other fires he was fighting was getting closer.

He was briefing the president.

Or rather, everyone else in the room was briefing the president, and Colt was there to be a subject matter expert, to speak only when asked exactly specific questions on which he had substantive and direct knowledge.

While intelligence officers often briefed policy makers, they were typically members of the senior intelligence service or members of the President's Daily Briefing team, not active operations officers and undercover. These, however, were extraordinary times, and it was Colt's source that helped the US identify the Russians' hand. He had knowledge no one else had, which might bear on a critical policy decision. Deputy Director

Hoskins made it clear on the way over that Colt was a bench player and only to speak if he was spoken to.

One thing that nearly every visitor to the Oval Office remarked on upon leaving was the gravity of the place. The density of history hung in the air, filled it like a physical presence. The same was true of the president. Whatever one might feel about the individual behind the Resolute Desk, their politics, or even their character, that was the most powerful person in the world, and the authority they commanded, their very presence, was as definite as gravity.

The other inescapable feeling Colt had was that he absolutely did not belong here.

He was the last one in the room. He followed Thorpe, who walked in behind the Deputy Director of the National Clandestine Service, Dwight Hoskins, and US Air Force General Julian Burgess, the dual-hatted Director of the National Security Agency and US Cyber Command. Burgess was a large man and tall, with a head that looked carved from petrified wood and polished to a sheen. His eyes were perpetually narrow slits, as though he disbelieved everything he saw until he could scrutinize it, pore over it like some seer of the ancient world. Burgess followed US Army General James Floyd, the Chairman of the Joint Chiefs of Staff. Floyd was a large, boxy presence, a defensive tackle past his prime.

This was an odd collection for a presidential briefing. Less than the full cabinet, not even the NatSec principals, just the cyber side of the military and CIA.

The president sat at the Resolute Desk with the National Security Advisor, Jamie Richter, standing next to him.

"Good morning, guys," the president said. "Please have a seat." The president motioned to the pair of cream-colored sofas facing each other in the center of the room, with a small table in the middle. Two chairs sat at each end, angled toward the sofas, with end tables between them and the end of couches. The president and the National Security Advisor took the chairs, Generals Floyd and Burgess one sofa; Hoskins, Thorpe, and Colt took the other. Colt sat as far from the president as he possibly could.

The National Security Advisor made introductions and informed the president that the Director of Central Intelligence was in London, meeting with the head of MI6, which was why he was not in the room.

"Mr. President, we're here today to discuss the cyberattack on our air traffic control system and what we're going to do about it."

"Okay, well, let's get started," the president said. He looked tired, ground down rather than worn out. His administration inherited an already dangerous world, but he'd had to steer the country through a series of unfathomable crises. Everyone in the room, Colt could tell just by reading the expressions, believed it was only the beginning. The president, most of all. Unlike many of his predecessors, this one did not play his cards close. For better or worse—and his tenure had seen sufficient doses of the latter —the president displayed his emotions the way the general displayed the ribbons on his service dress. Badges of office.

The president's face looked like skin stretched over gristle and willpower. "Now, I know these two gentlemen," he said, gesturing toward the generals. "But tell me about," the president looked down at the binder in his hand, "the N-T-C-U." He pronounced each letter individually.

Hoskins jumped in before Thorpe had an opportunity to speak. "Sir, the National Technical Counterintelligence Unit is a joint operation primarily staffed by Agency, NSA, and FBI personnel, with a dotted line to me. Their mission is to uncover and assess intelligence threats against the United States that use advanced technology, such as AI."

The president nodded, and he looked at Colt. "You're an intelligence officer, Mr. Daniels?"

It took Colt a moment to realize the president was addressing him.

"Mr. President," Hoskins said, "Daniels is an alias. We needed to provide a name for White House security, but Mr. McShane, here, is a clandestine service officer, so we needed to protect his cover. He's the chief of operations for NTCU."

"I see," the president said. He looked back to Colt. "I bet you didn't think you'd end up here today, did you?" he said, smiling.

"No, sir," Colt replied.

"I'd be shitting my pants, too, if I were in your shoes. Try not to let it get to you."

"Thank you, sir."

"Okay, Jamie, why are we here?"

The National Security Advisor leaned forward in his chair. "Thank you, Mr. President. The purpose of this meeting is for us to review the current intelligence as it relates to the Folsom Dam and air traffic control crises and determine what to do about it. We don't have the full national security team with us this morning, but we have the key players to discuss the situation and begin framing our response strategy. CIA, NSA, and NTCU agree that Russia hacked into the Folsom Dam, took it over, and forced it to flood. As you saw in the PDB earlier this week and again this morning, we believe this is in response to our supporting Ukraine. The ATC strike was different. Neither NSA nor CIA could trace the attack to its source."

"Julian?" the president said, turning to the head of the National Security Agency.

"Yes, sir. Yesterday, sir, we intercepted a phone call between General Valery Koskov, head of Russian military intelligence, and their primary cyber espionage group, Unit 74455. General Koskov demanded to know if they launched the attack against our air traffic control system. This is after the Kremlin called him to the carpet."

The president turned slightly to Hoskins. "Do we think someone is going rogue here, Dwight?"

"Sir, our assessment is that is unlikely. Frankly, looking at the execution, we believe the GRU didn't think they'd get caught. They covered their tracks exceedingly well, they just didn't count on NTCU and the NSA having the ability to conduct such rigorous digital forensics." Hoskins shifted in his seat. "Mr. President, as you're aware, we have a back channel with our counterparts in Russian intelligence."

Following the Cuban Missile Crisis, the US and Soviet governments, realizing how close they came to destroying the world, established a communications link between Washington and Moscow. Nicknamed "the Red Phone," the Washington-Moscow Hotline (known as "MOLINK" in military parlance) was an encrypted messaging system between the Pentagon's National Military Command Center (NMCC) and its corollary in Moscow.

CIA also established a reliable means of communicating with their counterparts in the KGB, which they maintained to this day. The purpose was simple. It was for one service to be able to ask of the other, "Are you guys *really* doing this?"

Hoskins said, "I've spoken, personally, with my opposite number in Moscow, Director Yuri Koslov. Russia's foreign intelligence service, the SVR, is adamant Russia did not hack our air traffic control system." Hoskins wouldn't admit it here, because he didn't trust the Pentagon not to leak it, or Burgess for that matter, but the SVR acknowledged Russia's complicity in the Folsom attack. They were not consulted. Apparently, the Russian president directed the GRU to do it and to blame a Bulgaria-based hacking collective well known to the West. After US intelligence so quickly determined their culpability, their president directed Russia's intelligence apparatus and their proxies to cease all attacks against the US until further notice.

The president looked to the National Security Advisor. "What do you think, Jamie?"

"Our policy is very clear on this. We treat cyberattacks the same way we do physical ones. We can consider Folsom an act of war. But we don't have a good answer for ATC, sir."

"Do we think someone else targeted us and wanted it to look like the Russians? Or is this just some other bad guy looking for a target of opportunity?" the president asked.

"ATC would be a dangerous escalation for the Russians. We assess they know a conventional fight against NATO is unwinnable," Hoskins said. "I should note that Director Koslov initiated the phone call the day of the ATC attack. They are already worried this is going to spin out of control and wanted us to know it wasn't them."

"And you believe him?" Burgess said.

Hoskins flicked an icy, sidelong glance to General Burgess and said nothing until he saw the same question in the president's eyes.

"Mr. President, I do believe him. This channel exists for a reason. It exists for times like this."

The Chairman of the Joint Chiefs added: "Russia is so heavily leveraged in Ukraine, they couldn't possibly handle another conflict."

"So, who do we think it is?"

"We're tracking increased activity from China," General Burgess said.

"The People's Liberation Army has a history of using proxies, the same way the Russians do, to conduct attacks against us, Japan, South Korea, Singapore, and the UK. Gives them deniability. The PLA has a large cyber espionage group and are highly effective."

"We are less bullish on that theory, sir," Hoskins said. "With all due respect to the NSA's analysis, our China Mission Center doesn't think PRC would try to provoke this."

"Of course they would," Burgess said, leaning forward in his seat. "They see a moment of weakness and a target of opportunity. One they could easily blame the Russians for."

"The Chinese don't want us fighting the Russians," Hoskins said. "Not when they're considering action over Taiwan."

"It's just the smokescreen they need to take attention away from their war planning. They don't think we can fight a war on two fronts."

"The Russians can't put up enough for a 'front,'" the Chairman of the Joint Chiefs said gruffly. "And the CHICOMMs know it."

Hoskins turned in his seat. "You think it's likely, General, that the Chinese are going to isolate a major ally by framing them for attacking us?"

Colt knew the Chinese had no intention of attacking the United States, not like this. He agreed completely with Hoskins's assessment, which were essentially the China Mission Center's talking points these last several months. Tensions between the US and the People's Republic had rarely been higher, but they weren't going to risk alienating the Russians, or worse, tricking America into going to war with them.

"No, I don't. We think it's far more likely that the Chinese are supporting their 'no limits' ally. They're trying to destabilize the West. If we get into a tussle with Russia, they're free to do whatever the hell they want in Taiwan knowing we can't cover both bases. Or, look at it this way, as we get ready to respond to the Russians, they give us another flank to worry about."

"Guys," the president said firmly, and everyone stopped talking. "We have to come up with a plan, here. The Russians *did* attack us, we all agree on that, and the American people expect a response. The first attack cost us a hundred lives and did billions of dollars in damage. But, this ATC thing, guys, we haven't begun to dig ourselves out from that. It took years to restore public confidence in air travel after 9/11. What I decide to do about that changes drastically if you tell me you're convinced the Russians are behind this too. I need better answers than what I'm getting."

Colt felt the room go cold.

"Mr. President, the NSA is firm in our position that the Chinese are the most likely culprits. The scenario I outlined is highly probable."

"The Chinese didn't do this. They also have *nothing* to gain by it," Colt said, and he didn't realize that he'd said that aloud until all sound in the Oval Office stopped.

No one spoke for a very long time.

"Say more," the president said slowly.

"Sir, what I believe Mr. McShane meant," Hoskins began, and the president cut him off.

"I asked *him* the question, Dwight."

"Sir, please forgive me for speaking out of turn, but the Chinese are not trying to provoke a war between the US and Russia, but maybe we are meant to think they are. We know the Russians believed they'd covered their tracks. The only reason for the ATC attack to follow so closely after Folsom Dam is someone wants us to think it *was* the Russians. With all due respect to General Burgess, the Chinese won't provoke us before they invade Taiwan."

Colt had a razor-thin line to walk here.

CIA had not cleared the intel from Liu's interrogation for release outside the Agency.

Colt also shared Hoskins's concerns about the Pentagon's porousness.

"About eight months ago, we successfully infiltrated the Chinese foreign intelligence service's information network. We deployed digital sensors—listening devices, if you will—without their knowledge. If China did it, that network would be lit up like a Christmas tree with traffic."

"Why didn't I know about this?" General Burgess demanded.

The president shot him a glare and held his hand up. "So who do you think it is, then?"

"Deputy Director Hoskins raised the potential of a non-state actor," Colt said, and he heard Thorpe suck in an anxious breath. A mistake, probably a severe one, but Colt was committed now. "Sir, for the last several years, NTCU has been tracking an organization we believe represents a kind of evolution in asymmetric information warfare." Colt always panned national security thrillers, especially on film, because people never spoke like that in the real world. But here, in the Oval Office briefing the president of the United States, he found himself drawing every twenty-dollar analyst word that came to mind without even thinking about it.

"This group has billions at their disposal and uses it to fund the most cutting-edge research in artificial intelligence and quantum computing to date. This group was initially allied with Russia, or at least with certain elements of their intelligence service, but that fell apart, and Russia tried covering their tracks by obliterating an island."

General Burgess broke in, "Mr. President, I've been in the Air Force for twenty-eight years. The idea that the Russians could take a design that we abandoned and make it work is preposterous. I've seen the DIA's report on the incident but, frankly, I'm not convinced."

"I was *there*, General," Colt said flatly. "I was on that island, and I saw it with my own eyes. *Arkhangel-2* worked. It didn't work perfectly, but enough of those rods hit their target. The Russian president was willing to risk a war with the US by destroying that island just to hit these people. That should tell you a little bit about their capability."

"What do these people want?"

"Mr. President, they want to upend the global order. They believe advanced technology gives them an opportunity to uproot governments and install themselves as benevolent dictators. What they're really seeking is a global oligarchy. What they want is a world in absolute chaos so that they can offer a more secure alternative. I agree with General Burgess on one thing, which is that I think the goal is to provoke the United States, the Russians, and the Chinese into a fight. That's as globally destabilizing as it gets."

Colt felt himself sinking. He was once again circling the inscrutability and believability of Archon's existence. A terrorist organization with nearly limitless resources that made no demands and whose membership consisted of members of governments, titans of industry, and some of the world's foremost intelligence services. And there was no tangible proof he could provide.

"This is that Trinity group?" the president asked skeptically. "The cult?"

"No, sir. Trinity are scientists, academics. They're researchers. This is a group of hard-line technocrats who split from them some time ago."

"Mr. President, are you listening to this?" General Burgess scoffed.

"Mr. President, we're looking at a spectrum of threats," Thorpe said quickly. "One of which, as Mr. McShane described, is a non-state actor. We're also investigating ISIS's so-called 'CyberCaliphate' and al-Qaeda. Both of whom would find our ATC network an attractive target, irrespective of the antecedent linkage to Russia."

"What I'm hearing, guys, is that we really don't know anything more than we did a day ago. And I don't have enough information for an appropriate response."

Burgess opened his mouth to protest, and Colt caught an unmistakable look from the National Security Advisor.

The outer door opened, and the president's chief of staff appeared in the doorway. "Mr. President," he prompted, the rest of the conversation unsaid.

The president swatted the air dismissively, saying, "Yeah, yeah." He stood, and everyone else stood as well.

"Thank you, Generals," the president said. "Dwight, why don't you and your people stay back. Jamie, you too." Perplexed, the National Security Agency Director left the room, but not before dropping a loaded glare right at Colt.

Colt's heart sank into oblivion. He was about to be dressed down by the president of the United States. His Agency career would be over before they got back to Langley. At least he wouldn't have to worry about the political fallout of *also* making an enemy out of the head of the NSA.

The president said, "Dwight, what's your assessment of Mr. McShane's theory?"

"The NTCU team briefed me on Archon last year when I took over as DCS. I admit, I was skeptical at first, but my predecessor, Jason Wilcox, believed them. I am convinced of their existence." Hoskins shifted his gaze to Colt. "But we still don't have *any* intelligence suggesting this organization was involved in ATC."

"You agree they're dangerous?"

"Yes, sir. We believe this organization has extended into bio-terrorism and they're responsible for the death of Sir Archibald Chalcroft last year. I'm not a cyber expert, sir, so I can't attest to what their capabilities are with regard to the ATC event. This was the first I'd heard of that theory."

Message received, Colt thought.

"Mr. President, if I may," Thorpe said. "Three days ago, Colt, here, executed an operation—himself—and captured a senior Chinese foreign intelligence officer. That man is currently in federal custody. Colt and I interrogated him. Colt, why don't you share what we learned."

"Well, sir," Colt said in a halting tone, thinking through what he could say. This was the president of the United States; this was not a hallway conversation. Colt wrestled with wanting to give the details he knew to be essential against just the conclusion those details let him make. "He made a convincing argument for why China wouldn't do this, sir. He said they would know we'd determine attribution. There would be crippling economic consequences on top of whatever military response we'd have. He knew we'd eject thousands of Chinese nationals from our country. I gathered the implication was it would effectively end their human intelligence program in the United States. We asked him specifically if China wanted to see us at war with the Russians, and he told us that was antithetical to the CCP's goals. We didn't bring this up earlier, sir, because this intel is less than twenty-four hours old, from a primary source. The Agency hasn't released it."

The president nodded but remained silent for some time.

"I owe the American people a response for both of these attacks, but I'm not getting duped into starting a war and certainly not with the wrong people. Find out if these other guys are responsible, and if they are, then I need you to give me some options. Jamie is going to draft a presidential finding for you. Get it done."

Colt was about to say, "Yes, sir," but Hoskins beat him to it.

The ride back to the Agency in Hoskins's SUV was quiet and tense. Colt well understood the gravity of what he'd done, understood that he was there to be called upon if needed, but he also couldn't sit idly by while Hoskins argued with General Burgess about phantom threats. Provoking a war with the wrong country was exactly the outcome Archon was looking for. Was he correct? Colt didn't know. But he knew he was *right*. For now, that would have to be enough.

"You're damned lucky he agreed with you," Hoskins said. He got out of the car and disappeared into headquarters with his security detail. One remained behind to park the car.

Ford grabbed Colt by the shoulders in a comic bear hug as soon as he stepped into NTCU. "You threw the NSA Director under the bus in front of the president *and* popped off without thinking." Ford barked a huge laugh and vamped wiping a tear from his eye. "I have nothing left to teach you, grasshopper."

Colt wished he felt as buoyant as his partner.

11

"NTCU thinks it is highly likely Archon executed the ATC attack," Colt said from the front of NTCU's small conference room. Ford, Thorpe, and Tony Ikeda sat around the table. They were the only unit members who were read in. "We're here today to talk about capturing a senior member of Archon's leadership element so that we can interrogate them and prove that theory. The president is under intense pressure to respond to the Russians, and our ability to determine whether Archon is responsible for the other attack might mean the difference between taking Moscow offline and going to war. We might be all that stands between it. This is our target," Colt said and pressed a button to advance the slide.

The face on the screen was an official photo of a woman with dark hair, dark eyes, and a smug, superior expression as though she were enjoying the punchline of a joke only she got.

Samantha Klein.

For Tony's benefit, Colt said, "This is Samantha Klein. She's ex-Mossad with over thirty years in operations, most of that in the field. Somewhere around 2002, she's recruited into Trinity. Klein does not have a scientific background, nor is she a computer specialist. But we know from a source that when she joined Archon, Trinity was trying to make inroads in Israel's tech industry."

"Sorry, Colt, I know you've briefed me on this before, but I'm still not clear on the Trinity-Archon thing," Tony said.

"No problem. This is something we need to make sure we get right," Colt replied. "And it's confusing as hell. Short version is, a group of scientists come out of the Manhattan Project having just seen what early computers can do. They're visionaries. Enrico Fermi, John von Neumann, and Edward Teller were the key figures. Von Neumann, in particular, was heavily influenced by Alan Turing, whom he'd met at Princeton in 1938. They believed in the possibility of 'thinking machines' and dedicated their lives to the fulfillment of that dream. But, having just seen what science can do, e.g., the atom bomb, they want to guard its development to ensure it only benefits mankind. They create this fellowship and name it 'Trinity,' after the site of the first atom bomb test. Fast-forward about fifty years. The organization has evolved significantly but still holds to that dream of ushering in thinking machines, what we now call 'Artificial General Intelligence.' They count among their number some of the leading scientists, academics, philosophers, and business leaders of the day. They drew heavily from NASA. They have also recruited members of government and the intelligence community—both ours and others."

"I get the scientists, but why the spooks?" Tony said.

"I've often wondered that myself," Thorpe said sardonically. "And this isn't the first time I've heard this story."

"Code-breaking is one of the biggest computing and mathematical challenges there is. The intelligence community has always been one of the largest consumers of advanced technology in the world, and we're also responsible for pushing the envelope on what computers can do, how small we can make them. That sort of thing. Plus, it was a way to keep tabs on the opposition. So, sometime in the late nineties, there starts to be some signs of division. Some of Trinity's members believe that the group isn't aggressive enough. They think they should be using their technology to combat real threats, take sides. They're also losing faith in government and their commitment to research. The eighties and nineties were what's known as the 'AI Winter' because very little progress was made. You also saw a huge consolidation of aerospace and defense companies at that time, fewer patents being filed, less innovation."

"Peace dividend?" Thorpe said.

"Yeah. By then, most of the original Trinity members are no longer alive. After 9/11, this faction argues that governments have outlived their effectiveness and that it needs to be reframed. There is a huge row, and the two sides can't come to agree, so they split. A few years after the split, the group that walked out formed their own coalition. They believed that they could use technology to reframe the idea of 'government,' correct the failures of the twentieth century. Eventually, they took to calling themselves 'Archon,' which is taken from the ancient Greek for 'to rule.' They align on the idea that an Artificial General Intelligence could more effectively manage all of the bureaucratic functions of government, it would just be guided by what they called a 'free-thinking elite,' the top minds."

"A ruling class?" Tony shook his head. "Man, we've seen that movie a hundred times. Ever notice how none of these assholes ever has an original idea?"

Colt laughed. "Sometime around 2006 or 2007, Samantha Klein becomes disillusioned with Trinity. This is a period of tremendous difficulty in Israel. The Palestinians are running a terror campaign that lasts almost a decade, there's bombings every week or so. Parents would send their children to school and not know if they would ever see them again. For many, reconciliation with the Palestinian Authority is now impossible. This event changes Israel forever."

"The Second Intifada," Ford said, his voice heavy.

"That's right. Klein is something of an ultra-nationalist. She's tired of seeing her countrymen die and the government unable to stop it. She radicalizes. She thinks a group like Archon could make terrorism obsolete, and she joins. Klein is capable and ambitious, she rises quickly." Colt leaves Ava, her father, and his death at Klein's direction out of his summary. Ford picks up on it but says nothing. "Our understanding of the current power structure in Archon is that Klein is a shot caller. We don't know exactly what their leadership element is, but we think it's a cellular organization with a ruling committee."

"Why *don't* we know that," Ford said, and Colt knew it was a loaded question. "We're talking to Trinity, right? They know who split, so why don't *we* know who split?"

"Trinity was always small. It was only about ten people that were in this hard-line faction that turned into Archon. We have their names, but we don't know who does what. Neither does Trinity."

"That's a huge fail," Ford said.

"They're scientists, Fred. From what I gather, most of Trinity either believes they can solve problems through technology, or they don't have the guile to understand how evil Archon actually is."

"Are there any Americans on the Archon list?" Thorpe asked.

"There are, yes. I'll get it for you."

"Thanks," Thorpe said. "And any Brits. I'll get this to MI5."

"I think Fred raises legitimate points, but it comes down to manpower. Until now, the Archon hunt has largely been the people in this room. We just haven't had the resources to look at everyone. And, for some pretty good reasons, we've focused our efforts on Guy Hawkinson. The best estimate is that HawkTech is Archon's R&D arm and weapons development—both cyber and biological."

"So, why Klein? Why not Hawkinson?" Tony asked.

"That's a good question," Thorpe said. "Right now, we still consider Hawkinson a hard target. And he's an American citizen with heavy political connections. If we get him, what do we do with him? We've got broad authority under FISA and the Espionage Act, but even with that, there isn't enough to charge him, and we don't want to swing at Hawkinson and miss. And with his senator uncle running for president in the opposition party, anything we do looks like a political hit job. Or at least it gets spun that way."

Ikeda nodded, satisfied, and Colt continued. "Thanks to Nadia, Klein has been pushed to the periphery. Klein was running a witch hunt inside HawkTech, looking for our asset and pushed too hard, almost got Archon exposed when she relied on an overzealous contractor. Nadia made sure Hawkinson was aware of this, and he suggested Klein step into the background for a bit."

"Do we know where she is right now?"

"We don't have a precise location but believe Western Europe is probable. We do have an asset that can help get the target into position."

Ford scoffed. "She better not hear you call *her* that."

Colt ignored the jab. "Even with LONGBOW letting us eavesdrop on Hawkinson's communications with Klein, we don't know where she is. Archon's OPSEC is very good. Even with the tools we've got available here, Klein is incredibly hard to find. We assume she's got tools to mask herself, even from us."

"We assume she has security?"

"Yes, though we don't know how much. If Hawkinson is an indication, assume she travels with two to four, armed and with military training."

"Mossad?"

"Or, ex–US SOF. They could be former Hawk Security Group."

"Christ," Tony mumbled. "Hope it's no one I know. Okay, I will start assembling my team. I can quietly make sure that no one has worked with HSG. We've got some in the unit who have. I can start planning extraction scenarios, but we really need more information before we can proceed. Location is obviously a key part of it. What kind of vehicle support do we have? I'm assuming we'll be using Air Branch for the exfil. I can coordinate that for you."

"I'm getting on a plane in four hours for a meeting that should get me answers to most of these questions."

Ikeda nodded, checking off items from a mental list. "You mentioned operational experience. Anything you can elaborate on?"

Colt pointed to the packet in front of Ikeda. "That's a dossier based on info from the Israel desk and two primary sources."

"How close?"

"One family, another a close friend. Klein conducted multiple snatch-and-grabs during her career. The Iranian IRGC general, Abbas Masoudi, that was her. She nabbed one of Bashar Assad's cousins in '98. There was also a string of PLO and HAMAS assassinations she's credited with following the Second Intifada."

"Okay, so she's a player. Solid tradecraft and will know what to look for during an attempted kidnapping."

"That's right," Colt said.

"I have enough to get started, though, again, I really need to know what location to plan for. Should I at least assume an urban setting in Western Europe?"

"I think that's a safe assumption. I'll get you the rest as soon as I have it."

Ikeda stood and left. Thorpe said, "I'll look forward to your trip report. Safe travels."

Air travel resumed earlier that week on a limited schedule. The FAA was reluctant, but there was too much pressure to get planes back in the air.

Colt took a red-eye to London, barely half full. The crew upgraded nearly everyone to business class for free. Everyone was tense, though the flight attendants did an exceptional job of trying to hide their nerves from the passengers. Once they landed, Colt rode a fifty-minute train ride to Cambridge. He stored his overnight bag in a rail station locker and found a café, where he got a walking breakfast and a coffee. Colt left the train station, stepping out into the damp cold. He wore a black Barbour Sapper jacket and a gray wool ball cap. He walked several blocks west of the station, doubling back a few times out of habit, and then made his way to the Cambridge University Botanic Garden across Hills Road. He found a footpath that led him beneath the tall, leafy trees, now in full fall colors, and walked, wet leaves squishing under his shoes.

Colt walked further into the gardens until he came to a large, circular pond with three fountains spurting water from the center. A concrete path ringed it, and there was a bench facing the water. A line of trees framed the distance with dark clouds looming above them. A woman in a red overcoat and blue scarf sat at the bench, contemplating the pond. She warmed her hands with a travel mug of tea, Colt could tell, by the tag hanging over the side. Colt took a seat next to her.

"You are an uncharacteristic three minutes late," she said.

Colt placed Ann in her early sixties. She'd graduated from Cambridge with a PhD in mathematics and was recruited into the Government Communications Headquarters, GCHQ, the British code-breaking agency

NSA was modeled on. Trinity recruited her in the mid-nineties and had, in turn, recruited Colt's CIA mentor, Jason Wilcox.

She'd also been a very close friend of Samantha Klein, which was why he was here.

"Probably could've saved you the trip, though," she said in somber tones.

"Let me guess," Colt said.

"Save you the trouble. Hard no."

"What's their excuse?" Colt asked. Ann was to meet with Trinity's leadership, such as it was, to get approval to release the information Colt was asking for. Trinity and the intelligence communities of the US and UK maintained an unacknowledged, highly curious, and legally questionable relationship.

"Don't want to get involved. They said that given the current state of things, escalation is in nobody's best interests."

Colt gave a terse laugh. "We're convinced that Archon took out our air traffic control system. There just aren't enough players who could do that so quickly and without any trace. We think they're trying to frame the Russians, provoke a conflict. Klein is our best lead."

"I don't disagree," she said. Colt hated that phrase, a conversational hedge against assent, an easy out against taking an uncomfortable position.

"You should know that America is going to respond. If the administration thinks Russia was behind both, it's going to be crippling. This is playing right into Archon's hand."

"Do you think this is payback for the island?" Guy Hawkinson acquired an unclaimed island in the US Virgin Island chain and tried to create a tech haven there, a sort of retreat for computer scientists. He used it to mask Archon's first R&D facility, largely built with Russian money. When it looked like Guy was growing beyond Russian control, they obliterated it with a space-based weapon they weren't supposed to have.

Colt shrugged. "Partially. We estimate that was a five-hundred-million-dollar investment. But it's something more. Their goal seems to be chaos for the sake of chaos. I think they're trying to cause so much instability that people turn to them as an alternative."

"Except they haven't offered anything yet."

"The world doesn't know who they are."

"What's your best guess, then?"

Colt sipped his coffee, thankful for the warmth. "They wait until the world is in complete shambles, people are terrified, willing to accept a solution, *any* solution, and then they come forward. That's how I'd do it."

"So," Ann said, "we're in violent agreement."

"Then why aren't you doing anything about it? I'll remind you, *your* organization tried to push me into action against them."

"Like I said, *they* don't want to escalate things further."

"But they're okay if we do? You people have been on the sidelines for seventy years. I think it's time you put some pads on and got in the game, no?"

"The committee thinks that the best way to counter Archon is by beating them to the punch, so to speak. Be the first to AGI. We do that and we can take Archon offline before they even get started."

Ann did not sound convinced.

From long conversations with Wilcox over the last several months, Colt knew that Trinity's members, now much thinner than when they'd founded, consisted primarily of scientists and academics. They now had just two operators in their ranks, both of whom were retired from active service in their respective intelligence agencies. Trinity had billions of dollars in investments accumulated since their inception. Their organization, in the form of a charitable trust with an innocuous title and mission, also held several lucrative patents, as did several of their members. They used this money to fund AI research around the globe—Cambridge University, MIT, Carnegie Mellon, and Stanford were the primary recipients, each receiving annual endowments in the tens of millions. They also operated a think tank, called the "Tomorrow Foundation," solely dedicated to AGI research, though only two members of the board of directors knew what the organization's actual mission was.

Colt shifted in his seat and turned to face Ann.

"I went out on a pretty big limb for you people. I've shared information that could've gotten me kicked out of the Agency, if not arrested. Not only that, I risked my officer's life so you could hack into Hawkinson's company."

"It's a watchdog, something of an early warning system."

"You said it was a weapon," Colt said, voice tight.

"He had just killed one of us," Ann said dourly. "We needed to make sure he didn't have anything else up his sleeve." It was only thanks to information Trinity gathered that Colt, and by extension the CIA, knew that Archon found a way to weaponize biologically engineered robots, called "xenobots." They used the subject's DNA to target them and deploy the payload, which was to swarm the subject's heart, causing a fatal heart attack. "I told you it was a way in, nothing more. There are payloads we can use it to deliver."

"You owe us," Colt said. It was the last plea he had.

"I know, dear boy, I know." Ann sounded tired. "I know the risks you've taken on my behalf. Wilcox and I, not surprisingly, don't believe we should be sitting this one out. But the committee is worried about what AI warfare would look like. Two superpowers beholden to no elected government duking it out across the digital world. You saw what an opening salvo looked like with your air traffic control system. Imagine what that fight is when the combatants aren't accountable to anyone. It gets bad quickly."

"How bad?"

"Conservative estimates are that we reset the clock to the fifties. Only with a bit more destruction. We start slugging it out, Archon goes after all of the countries Trinity calls home. What if they shut down *all* of the air traffic control systems and made it so you couldn't turn them back on? What about attacking the financial centers, stock exchanges in New York and London? What happens to currencies when people look up the exchange rates and see numbers that fluctuate exponentially every few seconds? The point, dear boy, is that they can hit us where it will hurt us the most, but there's little we can do in response. Could we wipe out Guy Hawkinson's company? Probably, and a few other organizations they own or are associated with. Is that worth a Chernobyl?" Ann shook her head slowly.

"The United States is going to counterattack. Whether that's a tactical retaliation or a full-scale war depends largely on you showing me where Samantha Klein is."

"You really think she'll talk?"

"I don't have the time to argue rhetoric."

Ann sighed and reached into her bag and drew out an envelope, which she handed to Colt. Colt broke the seal with this thumb and removed the contents. Surveillance photos, several of them. "Samantha has been living in the Italian lake country, in a city called Bellagio. Since April, she's been to Croatia four times and Greece, six. I'd concentrate my searches there."

"What do you think she's doing there?"

"Don't know precisely, but my guess is they realize that they have too many eggs in Hawkinson's basket. Athens is no Silicon Valley, but they are trying to catch up, modernize their economy. Someone like that might be very...pliable...for the right investment." Ann stood. "I'll be excommunicated if they find out I shared this with you, so please use them judiciously."

"Thank you," Colt said.

She'd spent their entire conversation explaining why Trinity wasn't going to help, only to give him, more or less, what he'd asked for. Perhaps she wanted him to understand what the risk to her was.

Trinity were among the smartest minds that ever were. They didn't think just in vague notions of futurism, or even how to make it a reality, but how to do it within the next five to ten years. Machines that could think and reason like humans. These same minds urged caution against Archon, worried that their involvement could provoke a response.

What did that fear say about Archon's capabilities?

12

Austin, Texas

"The question I'm most often asked is, what's the difference between artificial intelligence and artificial general intelligence? What's the thing that separates us from the state of the art today and the state of tomorrow?" Alana Howe paused on stage, shifting her posture slightly to one side and cocking her head as if considering the question. She was tall and slender, with chestnut hair that framed an oval face and danced above her shoulders when she moved. She'd just delivered eight minutes of her ten-minute keynote to close DecisionSpace, a leadership summit of the top companies in artificial intelligence.

Howe wore dark jeans, a white shirt, and black jacket.

"Certainly, that's the question we're all here to answer, right? Most of our talks this week and the work each of you does every day explores this topic in some way." She paused again, watching the knowing nods in the audience and hearing the mumbled sounds of agreement. "I think I can describe it best like this. The thing that separates the two is common sense." Howe folded her arms in mock annoyance. "If I ask a computer, 'Do I look fat in this outfit,' it's going to give me its objective opinion." A roll of laughter moved across the auditorium. "This machine probably has optical sensors and can factor in attributes like height, weight, build, and age to assess my appearance against that question. It will have access to the pictures of thousands of women my age—no, I'm not telling you what it is." Howe paused again to more chuckles. "And that machine will have been designed to reach an objective conclusion to that question. But should it give me the answer?" She shrugged. "It depends. And the state of play, today, is that a machine wouldn't know whether it's safe to answer that question. Because what is common sense? Most people would agree it's a set of informal principles, values, or attributes that we collectively agree to. It's based on shared, learned experience. Enough men have answered that question poorly that it's now burned into the collective consciousness of something you should either avoid or lie about. But a machine couldn't know that. It hasn't had the value of lived experience, social norms, or mistakes. We don't know, today, the particular alchemy required to get it there."

Howe paused again and walked across the stage. "I say 'alchemy' on purpose, because the set of things to get from state of the art to the state of tomorrow seems unknowable to us. The best and most optimistic estimates are that we can achieve this by 2030, not that far off. But the missing link between today and tomorrow, between AI and AGI, is still unknown to all of us." She smirked. "Or, one of you knows and isn't sharing." More laughter.

Howe was a futurist, an inventor. She'd formed, led, and sold a succession of highly successful companies. Alana Howe was on a short list of names to call when one wanted to know what the true state of the art was. She'd stepped aside from her last company a year ago to give herself more time for her boards and the speaking circuit. She could do more for the cause as a vocal champion than she could as an industrialist. Someone had to speak up, to speak out.

And it gave her more time to devote to Trinity.

Alana was what they called "fourth generation," meaning she was three links removed from one of the founding members. Howe, now in her mid-fifties, joined the group about fifteen years before. Today, she was Trinity's primary link to the American tech community. Her role on several influential boards, an angel investor and chair of research organizations, helped them steer development in the right direction. One of her chief goals, as evidenced, if not light-heartedly, in her keynote just now was ensuring that ethics were designed into the system. Of late, however, Howe was trying to shift Trinity's focus from pure research to more...what did the intelligence people call it? Active measures. This nascent anti-technologist movement, born out of a belief that tech was pushing whole sectors of the workforce into unemployment, took a dangerous and violent turn in recent years. Howe knew they had to do something about it.

No mere Luddites, this subculture had the feel of an organized movement. More than that, they were intensifying.

Alana believed Archon was behind it.

In the same way they'd tried to paint Trinity as a computer-worshipping techno-cult, Archon, through a comprehensive disinformation campaign, was convincing many that not only would their jobs be taken by computers, they themselves would be left behind. It tapped into that most primal human fear—obsolescence.

The most insidious tactic so far was doctoring a recent speech given by the US Treasury Secretary, who posited that thirty percent of jobs today would be outmoded by 2050, only they changed the clip to say 2030 and then targeted it to people in jobs he claimed would eventually be at risk.

What began as occasional riots turned into something more, something so much worse. Cities across the country were burning, with tech centers like here in Austin, Atlanta, New York City, Washington, DC, Seattle, and Silicon Valley bearing the worst. Rocks through Apple Store windows metastasized into firebombing tech companies, harassment of employees, and—in the case of a recent software CEO—an attempted murder.

"My friends, it's likely that if we achieve AGI, someone in this room will have been involved. One of you or one of the very smart people you hire and mentor and cultivate will have turned the common sense alchemy into an algorithm. I want to thank each of you for the work you do. It's so vital for our industry and our society. This has been an impactful couple of days for me and I hope you as well. I'll close with one question. By show of hands, who thinks I look fat in this?" Howe made another mock-serious face and scanned the crowd. Not a hand went up. "Exactly. Now figure out how to program *that*, and we'll have AGI."

Howe bowed slightly as the applause rose. She'd given this talk, or a version of it, several times now and found the absurdity in her definition of common sense was one of the more effective techniques for landing the message. Even among technologists, who fully understood the problem at hand. Though, to be fair to all concerned, it was a seemingly impossible problem to solve. How do you computationally equate lived experience?

Alchemy versus algorithm.

Alana genuinely didn't know if we could get there, if it was indeed a solvable problem. There were certainly days, like the air traffic control shutdown, when she wasn't sure that we even should. Would we be safer with a machine defending us, or would it open us to the kind of attacks that couldn't be defended? That, to her, was what Trinity *should* be about. Less pure research and more safeguarding humanity from the dangers of artificial intelligence without ethics.

Alana texted her assistant, said the talk went great and she would work from home the rest of the day. She climbed into her silver Mercedes AMG EQS parked in the reserved spot in front of the convention center. There was a nervous-looking valet standing in front of it, waving cars past on Trinity Street (Howe smiled at the irony).

Once she was moving, Alana dialed her husband. "Hey, babe," she said when he picked up. "I'm heading home."

"Not going back to the office? You clear that with Miranda first?" She could see the smile on his face and grinned herself.

"It's been a long week. I'm going to work from home for the rest of the day."

"Okay, I'll see you soon. Love you."

"Love you, too," and disconnected. She took West Cesar Chavez along the river as it turned into a variety of streets that all bore some homage to Stephen F. Austin. Alana crossed the river on Redbud Trail, heading toward home in Austin's Westlake neighborhood. Traffic thinned once she got out of downtown and could enjoy the drive through the winding, treelined streets. Alana planned to call Jeff Kim when she got home. She'd been wanting to pitch him on joining Trinity for some time, though the rest of the leadership committee shot her down. Jason Wilcox was the most vociferous, though he wouldn't explain why. She knew Trinity had a long and deep relationship with the intelligence community, but sometimes that cloak-and-dagger bullshit grated on her. Kim was an ideal candidate for their organization, and he was at the forefront of AI development. He also understood, better than most, what the threat was.

Archon, via Guy Hawkinson, stole much of his tech and repurposed it for themselves. That alone gave them a quantum leap in capability.

Alana stayed on Redbud as it climbed into the rolling hills her neighborhood was named for. She had the road to herself and decided to open the AMG's electric motor up. Zero to sixty in three seconds, though she admittedly had something of a head start.

Alana saw a flash of movement, and her eyes went to the rearview mirror, probably a bird dive-bombing past the car, but it was enough to draw her attention. Whatever it had been, it was gone now.

The Mercedes rounded a lazy corner, hugging a perfect line...and exploded.

The vehicle launched into the air with volcanic force, flipping over and —what little remained of it—landing on the roof with a wet, metallic crunch and shattering of glass.

The car was disintegrated up to the rear seats, everything else blasted by flash-fire.

Black scorch marks snaked out across the road's surface like shadowy tentacles. Smoke crawled up from the wreckage. There was nothing left.

Colt met Ford's Grand Cherokee outside the arrivals terminal at Dulles.

"I assume you saw the news?" Ford said as Colt climbed in.

He'd gotten the "breaking news" alert as soon as he landed, though these days a bad news banner was quite common. A tech executive in Austin had been killed when her vehicle exploded. Austin Police said only that an investigation was ongoing.

Almost immediately, social media was flooded with ghoulish anti-technologist messages saying that Alana Howe, driving an electric vehicle, had gotten what she'd asked for.

"Thorpe talked to some buddies in the Bureau. They're trying to keep this out of the press as long as they can, but they found bomb material in the wreckage. Expert job."

"I read she was killed on the road. Typically those things are attached to the starter, right?"

"Valet had the car the whole time she was in that conference. This would have to be remote detonated. Either they had a tracker on the car or had eyes on it. Our analysts are scrubbing the social media traffic, message boards, and some dark web sites as well."

As the so-called anti-technologist movement gained steam over the last few years, they became a target for NTCU's monitoring tools and intel analysts. They learned that Archon deployed message bots into some of these groups to amplify their messages and further stoke the fires. At one point, Archon had an entire disinformation campaign to paint Trinity as a techno-cult bent on creating a computer god to rule mankind. Internet crazies and conspiracy nuts latched onto that like it had actual magnetism and, like all good conspiracy theories, it took on an unnatural life of its own.

"It gets better," Ford said in a tone that indicated it wouldn't. "Do you remember the list that Nadia brought back?"

Colt did. Earlier that year, Nadia worked a source inside HawkTech's bio research division and accessed his computer. Inside, she found a list of names made to look like potential clients for a company biotech project. It was a list of targets. Colt shared the names with Ann, who confirmed every one of them was either a member of Trinity or benefited from the organization's covert investments.

Any of their deaths could easily be blamed on an anti-technologist assassin.

"Let me guess, Alana Howe's name was on it?"

Ford nodded.

13

Geneva, Switzerland

"This is a shitshow," Nadia mumbled, watching the BBC's continuing coverage of America's twin crises that morning before work.

Equally alarming was her most recent COVCOM message from Colt. He'd be in the field for some time, and Ford would be her main point of contact. Colt said in clipped shorthand that NTCU thought Archon could be responsible for the air traffic control shutdown. Nadia had to find out what was going on at the HawkTech Buenos Aires office.

Nadia read between the lines.

If Archon was responsible, they wouldn't launch the attack from Geneva.

But Nadia had been trying to get access to Argentina, and so far, nearly everything about that operation was walled off.

Guy, unfortunately, also took OPSEC seriously. There was nothing on the HawkTech Geneva network about the Buenos Aires operation. She'd asked about it once, trying to get some feelers out, see where to dig. Hawkinson told her that "HawkTech B.A." was a "wholly owned subsidiary" of the parent HawkTech corporation, a necessary inconvenience imposed on them by the Argentine government. Hawkinson explained that the lingering bad blood between the American and Argentine governments made it difficult for US companies to do business there. He had to completely wall the two organizations off from each other.

"It's the same with foreign-owned defense contractors doing business in the States," Hawkinson explained at the time.

That morning at work, Nadia trained the open-source intelligence aggregator on HawkTech B.A. The company's security system prevented employees from accessing the public internet, unless specifically authorized in advance, and that was monitored until shutdown. But Nadia ran the open-source project, HawkTech's system to seek out, aggregate, and parse all available data on whatever topic was the target of the search.

This tool, she knew, was secretly built on one of Jeff Kim's pattern-matching algorithms, and HawkTech engineers expanded its capability. It aggregated massive amounts of information and then rendered summaries for its human analysts to consume, like a virtual private eye. They'd recently inked a deal with two of Britain's leading private intelligence firms to deploy the system in their offices.

"Open source" was the term used to describe all publicly available information. It was every book, blog post, news article, and research paper ever written that had a digital copy. It was every speech ever given, and it was a person's résumé on a job site. It was court records, arrest warrants, aircraft call signs that airplane enthusiasts published to flight-tracking websites. It was weather reports and climate studies. It was the detailed assessments written by private intelligence companies for their high-paying clients. And it was social media. It was pictures, with date and time stamps, geolocation information embedded within the metadata that showed exactly where the subject was when it was taken and the name of the device that took the picture, along with its IP address. It was every photo taken by the multitude of corporate surveillance satellites now orbiting the earth. Open-source information would become as important as the secrets spies risked their lives to uncover, if it wasn't already.

The challenge with open-source information was that there was so *much* of it, and the quantity increased by orders of magnitude daily. Analysts of every stripe—intelligence, financial, law enforcement, sports and entertainment, real estate—used it to make conclusions every day.

Open-source was as simple as the unclassified research that one did. The difference between that and HawkTech's AI was that artificial intelligence had the ability to search for information and make connections at machine speed. Paired with the company's quantum computing array, the speed with which they could aggregate and assess data was mind-blowing. Her team could make conclusions that might take a human counterpart fifty years to come up with.

Society was not ready for the privacy implications of a publicly available tool like this. Every aspect of a person's life that had ever been digitized, whether they were aware of it or not, was available.

Their system would not unearth secrets, but it could fill in the gaps around them.

The tool could be used to spy on anyone with a cell phone, or effectively impersonate them online, because it had or could find all of the background details needed to become that person. All by following the patterns of data available in the public domain.

Guy tended not to talk about those parts in the interviews.

They called it "Delphi."

Using Delphi to unearth data on HawkTech B.A. was dangerous. There was no way for Nadia to mask her trail, no footprints to erase. HawkTech's security system would be following along because that's what it did. If she were questioned, Nadia would only say that she was testing the fences, so to speak, to make sure the company's adversaries couldn't glean anything Hawkinson didn't want them to know.

Hawkinson wouldn't launch an attack from a server he owned. But maybe he purchased equipment off the books?

LONGBOW allowed her to slip inside Guy's communication loop, to eavesdrop on his conversations with his Argentine team. They were guarded. They used innocuous phrasing, generic statements. One message said they "reviewed the balance sheet and found no anomalies." Another that their "first product beta was successful and user testing was ongoing."

She'd have ignored those messages entirely, dismissed them as noise, but Guy wasn't an especially hands-on CEO. He hired people for the detail work. Things like balance sheets. And it didn't seem likely that he'd be interested with something as low level as feedback from user testing.

Perhaps there was a way to correlate what she saw with LONGBOW and what she learned with Delphi.

These thoughts were on her mind when a message from the company's IM client popped up on her screen.

HawkActual: Hey—got a sec? Come up to my office pls.

Despite her nerves, Nadia mustered the effort not to eye-roll the message. She did it every time he pinged her. The guy actually used a play on his Army radio call sign as his IM handle.

Tool.

Nadia locked her system and headed up to the top floor. Guy's executive assistant, Tina, was expecting her and said she could go right in. Nadia did. Guy had his desk chair rotated a hundred and eighty degrees so it faced the window and the panoramic view of Lake Geneva. It felt staged.

Guy waited about three seconds, as though he was finishing a thought, and stood. "Thanks for coming," he said and motioned to the sofa and chair set up on the side of the office. He offered her coffee, water, or whatever lunatic energy drink was currently popular with the developers.

"I'm good, thank you. What's up?"

"I'm afraid our project with the Ministry of Technical Cooperation is going to be put on hold, at least for a little while."

"Why? What happened?" Nadia asked, doing her best to feign surprise. Once Liu was safely in custody, she'd used LONGBOW to spoof an email from Liu to Hawkinson saying he'd been called back to Beijing for an emergency but didn't elaborate what. She sent a follow-up saying that he would likely be delayed further, because air travel was so confused.

They were going to keep him on the hook, so to speak, for as long as they could. Nadia would keep her conversation, posing as Liu, with Hawkinson up as long as she could in hopes that it might net something. Hawkinson was too canny to reveal anything in an email that could later be discovered, but he might reveal something that pointed her in the right direction elsewhere.

"He's been called back to Beijing, apparently. No word yet on when he'll come back. I'll keep you posted."

"Roger that," she said, and moved to leave.

"Can I ask you a personal question?"

"Sure?"

"You getting enough sleep?" Guy asked. "I don't mean to pry. It's none of my business, of course, but you've seemed a little off. Tired."

She was definitely off. Four hours was a good night, and it usually wasn't four in a row.

"Not really," she said quickly, without thinking. "My, ah, sister is going through a tough time. Bad marriage. I'm trying to talk to her, but, you know the time change makes things complicated."

"I see. Where is she at?"

"Arizona."

Nadia was undercover, but because of the circumstances surrounding her recruitment and the speed with which they had to get her into place, she did not have a cover identity. She often wondered if she was the first officer in the history of the clandestine service to go undercover as herself. They hadn't expected it would be this long. One of the many logistical challenges that presented was that she had a social media and searchable internet presence long before her CIA recruitment.

Colt never admitted it, but Nadia often wondered if this was by design. Say her cover was "Jane Jones." Hawkinson's open-source AI could quickly troll and aggregate every picture of "Jane Jones" on the internet, only it would report back as "Nadia Blackmon." Not just on social media—she'd had numerous official photos from her eight years in uniform and four years at the academy before that, and all those identified her as Nadia Blackmon. She knew HawkTech security was doing exactly that when vetting new employees and prospective clients. Guy edged in on full paranoia ever since the Russians blew up his island. He took no chances.

Nadia did have a sister, who did live in Arizona. Like her, Patricia served in the Air Force but had stayed in. She'd married a pilot she'd met when they were lieutenants, and he was now an F-35A instructor pilot at Luke Air Force Base in Phoenix. But they were stupidly happy together, both of them now lieutenant colonels.

Lying on the fly was hard when anything you said could be verified in seconds.

"If you need to take time off," Guy said.

"No, I'm good. She's just having a rough patch."

"Intel officer, is that right? That what you told me?"

"She is, yes." Nadia had never mentioned that to Guy before.

Nadia took a deep breath but tried to mask it. Time to take the initiative. "So, when do I get a trip to Argentina? I hear the snowboarding in Patagonia is epic."

Guy laughed. "I've heard that too. For now, I have to keep you walled off from that. There are special provisions for me, because I'm an officer of the company."

"Just curious, is all. We haven't really talked about what we're doing there. I know they have a lot of tech talent, but it seems like an odd expansion."

"US time zones but not paying US labor rates is a big draw," Guy said. "I'm mostly using it for R&D, that's about what I can say, now, until I figure out the legal frameworks to better integrate the company. I invested in some supercomputers. I want to amplify our problem solving."

That's a non-answer if I ever heard one, Nadia thought.

"What are your thoughts about what's happened back home?" Hawkinson asked, abruptly changing the subject.

"Do you mean the air traffic control shutdown?"

Langley told her the government wanted to keep this one quiet, but information leaked almost immediately that it was caused by another hack.

Planes were flying now, but reports were that they were half full. People didn't trust air travel anymore.

Airlines were losing millions. The entire industry was on the verge of collapse.

Miraculously, none of the planes crashed that day, though several were forced to do emergency landings on airfields that couldn't handle them. Some runways were damaged so badly the aircraft couldn't take back off again. The planes had to be written off. The government was talking about another airline bailout to keep the airlines afloat, though it was incredibly unpopular at home. The proposal sparked some violent pushback against big business, out-of-control government spending. Nadia saw Hawkinson's uncle latch onto that point, arguing that if the administration had done its job in the first place, the ATC system couldn't have been hacked and shut down.

"This would never have happened if we ran air traffic control," Guy said confidently.

"You think we should take over the FAA?"

"The bureaucracy is the problem. They've known the system was vulnerable for twenty years and they haven't fixed it. It relies too heavily on people, who are fallible. With our quantum security, the system would be un-hackable. It would never need patching or downtime. The system would proactively find vulnerabilities and patch them *and* notify other systems that used those operating systems to do the same. An AI running traffic control could do this job so much better. It would self-optimize traffic patterns based on data, communicate with the aircraft themselves so it would have fuel status and the connecting information for every passenger on board. It would already be patched into expert meteorological systems from NOAA and the National Weather Service to factor that into the calculus. Even without GPS, an AI traffic controller gets every one of those planes on the ground safely."

Where is he going with this, she wondered.

"This is one example of a failure of government. The Folsom Dam is another. The operating system was designed in the *nineties*. The state, the Department of the Interior, presidential administrations going back thirty years are all culpable. Why do we continually give them the power to make bad decisions or, worse, make no decisions at all?"

Nadia said nothing. The air in the room suddenly felt charged.

"What's the alternative?" she asked.

"The problem is there *isn't* one. Our nation's operating system hasn't changed in two hundred and fifty years, and that was based, largely, on philosophies from ancient Greece and ancient Rome. We live in a world with problems the Founding Fathers couldn't have envisioned, yet we don't change our system of government to reflect those problems."

When he put it like that, Nadia couldn't help but agree with the logic.

If it wasn't coming from an unabashed sociopath.

"You know what Steve Jobs said when people asked him how he knew what products users wanted to see next?"

Of course she did. Every computer science professor she'd ever had opened their class with it.

"Yeah," Nadia said. "They'll know it when I show it to them."

Guy favored her with a slim, knowing smile.

Nadia checked her watch. She needed to be moving. She was due to meet with Chuck Harmon for their weekly check-in today, and her planned surveillance detection route would take about two and a half hours to execute.

She asked Guy if there was anything else, and he said that would be all.

Nadia returned to her desk, set her internal office calendar to show she had lunch and then a personal appointment, and left.

"It sounds to me," Harmon said, "like he's pitching *you*."

They walked through Parc de Montjoux on the far side of Lake Geneva.

"Man, that's not what I took from it."

"That's because you're keyed up. Nadia, you're so tense you're practically vibrating." Chuck stopped and turned to face her. He was wearing a black wool bomber jacket, jeans, and a gray ball cap. "You're clearly on edge, and I'm worried about you."

"Just need sleep, is all."

"Don't try to bullshit me. If you can't be honest with *me*, you can't be honest with anyone. Tell me what's on your mind."

"The AI we have at HawkTech are very, very good. Remember, just about everything Hawkinson did is based off tech he stole from Jeff Kim, and *he's* one of the smartest guys on the planet."

"Why are you telling me this?"

"Because I'm going to get *caught*, Chuck! Ever since I got LONGBOW on Guy's phone, I've been looking over both shoulders at the same time. I know our developers are good, but I am worried that they can't mask the app. They can't hide it from that goddamn Eye of Sauron that Hawkinson built."

"But this is the second hack you've put on Hawkinson's network. They didn't find the one that Trinity gave you, obviously."

"Didn't they? We don't know. That's the point. Every time I meet with him, every time he asks me some question, I know he's poking around at something. He *knows*."

"The conversation you repeated back to me," Chuck said evenly, "sounded like a recruitment pitch. I should know, I've made enough of them in my day. That Steve Jobs line? He's practically telegraphing."

"Why would he want to recruit me? I already work for him."

"Two immediate reasons come to mind. One, he recognizes the talent and he wants you part of Archon. Or, he knows who you really are and wants to make you a double agent."

"I think I'm going to throw up," Nadia said.

"No, you're going to do your job," Chuck replied. "You're going to continue collecting intelligence. But first, you need to find someone at the company that you can throw suspicion on to buy you some time."

"Why the hell would I want to do that?"

"Because, if Guy really is looking at you as a mole, you need to be able to make it look like someone else is. Throw him off your trail."

"I can't do that, Chuck. A lot of those people are my friends. Yeah, I'm getting intel from some, but I have relationships with them. They're the only people here that I know." Chuck couldn't appreciate how isolated Nadia felt. He was going to drive back to Bern and talk with the handful of other CIA officers at the station. Then he was going home to his wife. Nadia's only persistent human contact were the people she was spying on.

"You will do that," Chuck said, taking on a sterner tone. "Because that's the job. They're still teaching the history of our business, right?" Even now, in this park with no one around them, next to the gray lake, he talked around it.

"Yes," she said.

"During the Cold War, the Russians called this the 'Tournament of Shadows.' It's a black game, kid. We have to do some horrible things some-times, but we do them because there are people in this world—and you work for one of them—with the desire and the capability to cause great harm. You talked about how good HawkTech's AI is. I know Colt already thinks Archon is a leading candidate for the ATC attack. What if he's right? And I've read your reports, no one at HawkTech is innocent. They just don't know how guilty they are."

That night, Nadia sat in her apartment nursing a drink and listening to music.

Chuck Harmon's words tumbled over in her mind, over and over again. The conclusion was inescapable. She remembered thinking about a time when she'd first arrived here. Being undercover was exhilarating. She loved being on the street, in the action. Getting black. She flowed through the HawkTech offices, a predator, looking for acquisition targets. She cultivated assets, and she was *good* at it. Colt told her so. Colt was half a legend. Eight years in a non-official cover. Imagine living with *those* stakes. If you get caught, it's jail. Do not pass go, do not collect two hundred dollars.

Colt did eight years of that. Eight times what Nadia had and she was falling apart.

Chuck was right.

This *was* what she signed up for. This was the job, as much as ducking into the shadows was. As much as hacking Hawkinson's computer network was.

It was different, though. Setting someone up to take the fall for her was a far greater sin than getting them to tell you something they shouldn't. This would have real consequences if they were caught, life-altering ones.

Nadia took a drink and stared out at the old-world lights of Geneva. She could almost see the black blotch on the night, the abyssal smear that was the lake between buildings.

No one at HawkTech is innocent. They just don't know how guilty they are.

Words designed to ease her conscience.

Chuck was good. Recruiting her even though she was already in. Maybe you just never turned that skill off.

Nadia had two viable candidates that could be made to look like CIA officers. The first was Hawkinson's executive assistant, Tina Kiernan. Former Army commo officer, served with special forces units. Her going to the Agency after the Army would seem logical, even though she'd been with Hawkinson a long time.

The other was Tyler Gales. Tyler ran a team in the bio-sciences division. They'd seen each other socially, and Nadia liked him a lot. In fact, she was already attempting to recruit Gales as a source of information with the hopes of turning him into an asset. It was through him that she'd learned of the research that resulted in the bioweapon, though Nadia was convinced Gales didn't know anything about its ultimate weaponization. She'd used his credentials to get into his computer and find a list of names, which were coded, but Langley figured out it was a target list, they presumed, for the bioweapon Archon used to kill that British MP. Everyone on that list was a member of Trinity.

Gales didn't build the weapon. He just got them ninety percent of the way.

The bioweapon wasn't Archon's only foray into destabilizing governments, it was just the most terrifying. It was a sniper rifle for targeted assassination. In truth, they'd been at this game for a while, testing their concepts in the third world where no one would notice. Earlier that year, Nadia started investigating the countries where Hawkinson deployed his "secure voting technology." Liberia's 2017 presidential election, despite being monitored by multiple international watchdogs, showed significant irregularities and evidence of fraud. Eventually, their Supreme Court initiated a runoff, but a subsequent electoral commission found evidence of corruption and fraud. The opposition also launched legal challenges, questioning the process itself. NTCU found evidence of doctored articles from national media and a massive disinformation campaign on Facebook, which eighty-six percent of Liberians used regularly.

Now, HawkTech supplied the technology the Liberians would use for "free and fair" elections, all monitored and paid for by the UN. More importantly, they engineered the set of circumstances that had Liberians and the international observers doubting the process enough that they had to turn to a technological solution. NTCU's analysists concluded Archon didn't have any significant stake in the results of Liberia's elections, other than using it as a testbed for their process. That, and a way to get lucrative UN contracts to provide monitoring software.

But the bioweapon was the way to get her government to sit up and take notice.

Tyler Gales wasn't as good of an archetype as Kiernan to be the fake spy. He had the kind of knowledge that you couldn't fake and years of documented research to back it up. Of course, that's why Nadia was here herself. When Colt recruited her, it was because she was an expert in AI and only someone with that level of expertise could get through the door. She was a scientist they turned into a spy, not the other way around. Could that work with Gales?

Whiskey slow-burned on her tongue.

Warm guilt boiled up from her stomach to greet it.

14

Washington, DC

One last try, Colt thought.

He entered the holding facility and was escorted to the interview room where Liu Che was waiting for him. Thorpe stayed behind this time. There was too much going on at the unit for him to break away.

"Good morning," Colt said. "Sleep well?"

"No," Liu said flatly. "How much longer do we keep this up, Mr. McShane?"

"Keep what up?"

"This...this stupid dance. You asking me questions and my dodging them. At some point do you not have to charge me with a crime? Or would you rather that what I have to say not be made public?"

"Oh, I'm not worried about that, Mr. Liu. We have special courts for people like you. Nothing coming out of your mouth ever hits public ears, so we're not worried that you'll get on the stand and say something damaging. As for why we're here, it's for you to answer my questions. If you are helpful, that reflects positively on you and the judge takes that into account. If you're not, well, he takes that into account too. But this is the last time we do this. If you choose not to cooperate, I stop wasting my time with you and you're left with those consequences."

"I want to see my wife."

"Out of the question."

"I want to see her," Liu repeated, more firmly.

Now we're getting somewhere, Colt thought.

"Once I see my wife, I will consider answering your questions."

Colt gave a perfunctory chuckle. "It doesn't work that way. You give me something of value, and I consider whether I want to return the favor."

Liu exhaled. "Ask, then."

"Hawkinson has a new operation in Buenos Aires, which I'm sure you're aware of," Colt said. "He's installed a quantum computing array and supercomputers. He keeps this operation entirely firewalled from what's happening here. We want to know what's going on there."

"And your other asset inside Hawkinson's company cannot uncover what they're actually doing, so you want me to do it," Liu said, matter-of-factly. An eyebrow lifted up over the rim of his glasses. Liu knew NTCU had an asset inside HawkTech, that it was a woman and that her cryptonym was YELLOWCARD. But he didn't know Nadia's name. Colt feared Liu traded that knowledge to Hawkinson for access to him, to gain trust.

Colt ignored the jab and continued. "During your conversations with Hawkinson, did he mention Buenos Aires to you?"

"This is related to your recent cyberattacks, yes?"

"Yes, it is," Colt allowed. Sometimes, in interrogation, you had to give a little so that the subject felt some trust. And it wasn't as if Liu was going anywhere.

"You think Hawkinson is behind these?"

"We know HawkTech developed an AI that continually scours the internet and the dark web for vulnerabilities. We know he sells these vulnerabilities on the black market through an intermediary."

That was actually speculation, but Liu didn't need to know what was specifically true and what wasn't.

"But you don't believe that's what he's actually doing," Liu said, as a statement, not a question.

"You and I don't have a level of trust yet, so this is only going to go so far until you prove to me I can believe what you say. But, no, I don't think Hawkinson is doing something as basic as selling exploits to hackers...even the high-powered ones." Colt paused for a long moment, considering the other man. He'd told the president of the United States about Archon without blinking an eye, but somehow sharing that information with Liu Che seemed dangerous to him. "Guy Hawkinson is part of an organization. This group wants to undermine world governments and is using advanced technology to do it."

"That sounds highly dubious," Liu said.

Colt debated telling Liu about Archon. He and Ford role-played this exact conversation several times in their prep. Liu's reactions were largely what Ford portrayed them to be.

"We didn't believe it either, until we saw proof. I told you before that we think this group wants the US and the Russians to go to war. If we did, it would be more evidence for them to use to show that the existing world order needs to be reimagined."

"So you expect me to believe that Mr. Hawkinson is part of a worldwide techno-conspiracy on just your word?"

"Several prominent politicians in the United States and United Kingdom suffered debilitating scandals in recent years. The governor of California and prime minister of Great Britain were both exposed to violating their own government's COVID protocols. Meanwhile, the governor of New York weathered an initial allegation of sexual harassment, only to be bombarded by several more that ultimately forced him out of office," Colt said. "In the case of the first two, phone records and geolocation data from several photographs shared over the internet exposed the violation. The data existed in the public domain...more or less...one just needed to know where to look and have the capability to do it. In both instances, the reporters who broke those stories received anonymous emails from 'whistleblowers.' In the governor's case, the first allegation of misconduct proved to be true, but then journalists received multiple emails from—allegedly—anonymous officials and citizens exposing further impropriety and adding additional evidence of corruption. In these cases, they are engineering outcomes by looking for dirt and releasing it to undermine public confidence in their institutions."

"Sounds like an independent conscience to me," Liu said. "I believe your government wanted to prosecute WikiLeaks because they released classified and compromising information, not because it wasn't true."

"I wonder what the outcome would be if they turned their eyes on *your* government."

Liu shrugged.

"Political structures are undermined, sanctity of elections is questioned," Colt said. "The British vote to leave the European Union."

"That was the Russians," Liu said dryly.

"That was *mostly* the Russians," Colt countered. "Then, you have multiple cryptocurrencies crash, and the bottom falls out of that market. Lawsuits, allegations of fraud."

"Perhaps people shouldn't try to invent money."

Again, Colt ignored him. "The crypto markets were a first pass at undermining non-governmental institutions. The intent is to show people they don't have anywhere else to turn, that they can't solve the problem on their own, can't sidestep it. Scared people do foolish things, Mr. Liu. This is how dictators win elections. Hitler didn't seize power, the German people gave it to him."

Liu said, "Whether I believe you or not, conflict between you and the Russians does not further Chinese interests. I've told you this much already. If anything, it sets them back farther," Liu said.

"We think it likely this organization is responsible for one of the cyber-attacks against us. If America is a target, you should assume your country is as well. To force conflict, to cause chaos. To get the population to distrust their government. There is no evidence of their attack at HawkTech; there wouldn't be. So, I want to know what Hawkinson told you of his Argentine operation."

Liu's expression was inscrutable.

"Little," Liu said. "Just that he'd made a major investment there. Quantum and supercomputing. His most advanced AI research. He's very interested in a joint R&D effort, perhaps a HawkTech office in Zhongguan-cun. We were discussing the possibility of my taking a tour in his Buenos Aires office when I was...abducted. There's something there he wants me to see, but wouldn't elaborate."

Colt knew most of the substance of Liu's interactions with Hawkinson. Nadia was there for most of them, but there was a private dinner the two of them had, and that's what Colt was interested in.

"Did he ever discuss the context of those joint projects? Did he propose an objective?"

"You mean, did he say, 'Let's attack America together'?" Liu laughed. It was a haughty, arrogant sound that he seemed to take real joy in. "No. But he has expressed much interest in our Belt and Road Initiative. He suggested that his company could have a part to play." Liu halted his speech again. "Hawkinson was insistent that I visit his facility in Argentina. He did admit that he spent a considerable amount of money on what he called 'infrastructure investment.' I already know your follow-up question, and, no, he did not elaborate. Just to say that he was spreading investment around. He mentioned a think tank he intended to start." Liu steepled his fingers beneath his chin. The chains connecting his wrist restraints to the chair clinking against the table as he did. "Now, I have a question for you."

"Yeah, I'll see about getting visitation with your wife."

"Not, it is not that. You know I am aware of the operative you have in the Hawkinson organization, from Glen's files. YELLOWCARD was the code name, I believe, yes?"

"We terminated that operation when Denney exposed it."

"Right," Liu said, drawing the word out, like someone picking apart a spiderweb. "It could only be Ms. Blackmon. She's capable, but not as good as she thinks she is."

"That's a fantastic theory," Colt said. "I hope you don't intend to ruin the career of an innocent person with wild speculation."

"Of course not," Liu replied. "But consider the timeline of her recruitment into the company. Consider also that the questions you've asked me today could only have come from a highly placed source. I don't believe it could be anyone else. Perhaps it is as you say, wild speculation. This is why I haven't shared my theory with my service."

"Why are you telling me this?"

"I find it always useful to have a few cards left in my hand. Ask yourself this. If I could figure this out in a few hours, what do you think Guy

Hawkinson could do with several months?" Liu paused, as if pondering something. Then he said, "Or perhaps she works for Hawkinson."

Colt returned to Langley.

He found Thorpe and Ford in the ops center, watching the board and the status reports of both field ops and cyberspace ops coming up on the screens.

NTCU operators covertly intruded on adversary systems across the world, digging for clues on who might be responsible and whether another strike was on the horizon.

On top of the two crises NTCU followed on the threat board, they'd uncovered falsified news reports and some emails targeting the pilots, aircrew, and families of Air Force and Marine CV-22 Ospreys. The "reports," mostly appearing on Facebook and Twitter feeds, alleged that the tilt rotor aircraft were failing at a staggering rate, were unsafe to fly, and the government DID NOT WANT YOU TO KNOW ABOUT IT. This was not a campaign designed to cause widespread panic, just to get a few key people to question whether their aircraft were actually safe. NTCU analysts thought the PLA's intelligence division was responsible and that it was just another of the regular disinformation campaigns they ran.

Colt walked to Thorpe's station at the back of the room.

"How's our party guest?" Ford asked.

"Surprisingly talkative," Colt said. He filled them in on the discussion. "I have an idea. It's a little crazy, but hear me out."

"Like, 'regular Colt crazy,' or is this a new, specially formulated crazy that's designed to really get under my skin?" Ford asked.

"Just hear me out," Colt repeated. "Liu wasn't giving on anything today. I think he realizes that we've got him over a barrel. If he cooperates, *maybe* he gets a reduced sentence, but he knows he's not going home."

"Okay," Ford said, drawing it out.

"So, maybe we don't prosecute him."

"Then what *do* we do with the guy?" Thorpe asked.

Colt said: "We recruit him."

"Absolutely not!"

"Out of the goddamn question."

"Are you out of your mind?"

Their rebuttals came so swift and so furious, Colt could only tell them apart because of Ford's choice of words.

"Colt, Liu is only the second Chinese intelligence officer we've ever caught. His value to us is inestimable," Thorpe said. "We're turning him over to the China Mission Center and then the Bureau's CI team. I appreciate your initiative, but even if I were inclined to go along with this—and for the record, I am not—the litany of people that would have to sign off on this now would never go for it. Pritchard's folks, Hoskins, CIA counterintelligence, the Bureau, the Justice Department, they are all going to tell you that this is entirely too risky."

"I—" Colt started to say, and then let it drop.

Thorpe said, "Don't you have a flight to catch?"

Back home, Tony Ikeda was working up the capture plan for Samantha Klein with his team members from SOG's Ground Branch. This would be a tougher go than with Liu. First, Klein would know to look for opposition on an instinctual level. Chinese intelligence, typically, didn't pull people off the street. They only did that at home and used their state police to do the job. Their focus was still economic intelligence, military and industrial secrets. They plied their trade differently than Mossad.

Klein would know what to look for because she'd done it.

She would also have security with her.

Ikeda and his team planned for an urban extraction scenario and assumed a hard target.

Colt hoped Ava could shed some light on this, though he had reservations. He knew now that without Ava's help, they could never find Samantha Klein in time. But Colt couldn't guess her reaction. Samantha was the only family Ava had left. Would she turn on her? Would she believe him? They'd made the decision *not* to tell the Israel desk or Mossad. This was an extraordinary circumstance, and in such a situation, there would be certain professional courtesy paid. No one ever truly retired from an intelligence service, unless it was in disgrace or they quit over a moral objection. Samantha Klein would still have ties to Mossad, might even be contracted with them.

But NTCU and the Agency agreed a mission this sensitive needed to be completely black.

Outside of Ford and Thorpe, the deputy director...no one knew about it.

If they couldn't find Klein, however, Colt's last remaining option was to involve Ava. Of course, that would involve a conversation that he was not prepared to have.

Colt knew the truth about Samantha Klein. Ava did not.

NTCU also had CERBERUS engaged on the problem. Ford headed that up while Colt flew to Europe. He wanted to check in on Nadia first before continuing on to Greece. Chuck Harmon's last cable said she was edgy and he was worried about her. Chuck bluntly said they needed to make plans to pull her out and relocate her to the States.

Colt landed in Munich and took the rail to Zurich, where he stayed for several hours to make sure he was clear. He wore glasses with clear lenses but made with a photoreflective coating that would render his eyes indistinguishable on cameras. He selected large, aviator-style lenses because they'd also help obscure his face. His brown hair, grown longer, was streaked with blond from a dye job. Colt wore a tweed blazer, padded to give the appearance of an extra ten pounds, over a brown sweater and blue shirt. He looked a bit like Redford in *Three Days of the Condor*. Klein had an operative in Swiss intelligence, a small but highly capable service with a strong electronic surveillance capability—with help from Colt's own service to help the Swiss track terror suspects seeking safe harbor. He had to assume that if Klein had one, there would be others.

Colt met Chuck Harmon at a coffee shop in Évian-les-Bains on the eastern side of Lake Geneva.

Harmon handed Colt a coffee in a to-go cup when he walked in.

"Thanks," Colt said.

"Have we gotten anything useful out of Liu?" Chuck said as they stepped out onto the street.

"He's adamant that China didn't take down the air traffic control network. Said it would be contrary to their goals. Acknowledged that we'd kick thousands of Chinese nationals out of the country."

"Pretty significant brain drain for them," Harmon said. "Not to mention losing God knows how many sleepers."

"Yep," Colt agreed. "He guessed Nadia," Colt said. "Narrowed it down based on what he knows. Shouldn't be surprised, really."

"We going to pull her?"

"Not yet. I don't think he told Hawkinson yet. I gathered he was holding that one back. If China and Russia didn't do ATC, I think Archon is the only one who could. But we can't prove it. Nadia has been all over Hawkinson's Geneva files, there's nothing here to point to it."

"So, you're thinking they are launching it out of Argentina somehow?"

"I don't *know*, and that's the problem."

Chuck stopped and turned to face Colt, putting a hand on his shoulder. "Colt, I said this in the cable, but maybe you need to hear it in person. She's coming apart. She needs to come off the line for a bit. If it were up to me, I'd insert her back into the training program at the point you yanked her out." Chuck held up a hand. "I'm not criticizing the decision. I'd have made the same one. I'm just saying she makes mistakes."

"Heard and acknowledged," Colt said slowly.

Chuck likely knew how Liu puzzled out Nadia was the Agency plant, so he didn't waste precious time asking.

"He told me something else," Colt said. "He said he *didn't* tell Beijing that he figured out Nadia is ours. I told him we shut it down already, but I could tell he didn't believe me."

"Why not?"

"That's the part I can't figure. It felt like a card game and he wanted me to know what was in his hand. He knows that he can't tell Beijing now, or Hawkinson. He's not getting out of that cell except for trial and prison. Trial will be in a FISA court, no one will see it. He knows there's no chance we don't convict him."

"Think he told you to buy some good will?" Harmon ventured.

"Maybe. Every time I talk to that guy, it's like I'm in the opening move of a chess game he started ten moves ago." Colt shook his head, frustrated. "I wanted to see Nadia, but I don't dare get close to Geneva, and we have to be careful about her missing too much work. Tell her I was here and am checking in on her. And, that she's doing incredible work. I mean that. We all do."

"Will do," Harmon said.

"One last thing. If Nadia can't get the info we need on Argentina, do you think Liu could? I pitched Thorpe on turning him into an asset, and they shot me down."

Harmon let out a soft whistle. "That's playing with fire. You'd want to let him out after all the trouble you went through to grab him?"

"There's always a chance that Klein doesn't talk. Just, hypothetically, do you think Nadia could run him?"

"Colt, I think Nadia will do anything and everything you ask of her. That's exactly what worries me about her. She hasn't learned yet where the lines begin and where they end."

15

Athens, Greece

Colt walked across the mosaic tile of Monastiraki Square, reds, blues, and yellows a patchwork blur under his feet. Beyond the monastery on the square's opposite side, Colt saw the Acropolis perched upon its rocky hill like a god of the ancient world peering down upon his subjects.

Colt wore an olive green, short-sleeve shirt over tan pants and Randolph aviators. He had a beige linen blazer folded in the crook of his arm. And, unfortunately, still sporting the highlights from his dye job.

He spotted Ava immediately. She wore a white sundress with a blue shawl made of some gauzy, local fabric across her shoulders. She wore large sunglasses, which he knew she preferred for the unobstructed field of view. Ava stood near a fruit cart, as agreed, casually inspecting its wares. She set the lemon down when he approached and gave him a slight smile when she saw him.

They were guarded in public.

Always act like someone was watching.

They left the square, walking up Areos in the direction of the Acropolis. They passed the domed monastery, angling toward the park of ruins beyond it.

"Thanks for coming," Colt said.

"Of course. I'm surprised you could get away."

"Never stops," he said through a heavy exhale.

"I like the Sun-In," she quipped.

Colt frowned and said nothing.

"I'm very sorry about what happened in California."

"Thanks. It's...it's...terrible," Colt said, at a loss for words. "Terrible" was reductive, it minimized the magnitude of human suffering, the utter destruction of lives to an adjective. He didn't know what else to say.

"Interesting that Jeff was there, no?"

After their abrupt separation following the death of her parents in the bombing, Colt and Ava were thrust together again, seemingly by fate, when both were undercover infiltrating Jeff Kim's company. Ava was hired as Pax AI's head of public affairs, Colt an external consultant from a prominent venture capital firm, ostensibly to advise Jeff on a funding round. Neither Colt nor Ava knew at the time the other was an officer in their nation's intelligence service. America and Israel both had a vested interest in Kim's artificial intelligence and quantum computing research, seemingly years ahead of anyone else.

They each developed an affinity for the laconic, quirky, and reclusive genius.

"Yes and no," Colt said. "He was pitching the State of California on the wildfire predictor that he'd developed when we were both working with him. Lucky for us that he was. He helped shut the attack off before it got worse and shared what he knew with us. Saved a lot of time."

"Yes, I didn't mean to imply anything," Ava said. "Just that it *was* lucky he was there."

There is a saying: There are friendly nations, there are no friendly intelligence services. Working with another service was always complicated. Both might share a common goal, but each held information back and tried to come out of the engagement knowing more than the other. Working with Ava exponentially amplified the complication.

"None of this is official, of course," he said.

"Of course," Ava replied with that sly smile of hers.

"I think this is all related. The Russians launch the dam attack, and then our air traffic control network goes down. Someone wanted it to look like the Russians. No attribution on the second attack, but it has the feel of it being the same actor. I think the second one was Archon. They want us and the Russians to start swinging."

"That fits what we know about Archon's motives of driving global instability, but why?"

Colt shrugged. "That's the part we can't puzzle out. We think they're trying to undermine the current world order, nations, international organizations and the like, but to what end? It's not like they're offering an alternative. Still, chaos for the sake of chaos doesn't seem like their MO."

"So, you believe, now?"

Colt and Ava learned about Archon together in that fateful meeting in a Vienna hotel room. Ann told them, and Colt hadn't wanted to believe. It was too farfetched for him. Colt was a traditionalist. He thought it fantastical and farcical that a cabal of Trinity offshoots could be an existential threat to the world order.

He was wrong.

"When I got back from Vienna, I met with Wilcox. He told me it was all true." Ava knew Jason Wilcox, Colt's friend and mentor and formerly the youngest head of the National Clandestine Service. Wilcox "recruited" Ava into the operation against Hawkinson and the Russian SVR before knowing she was a Mossad officer. She had a fatherly fondness for the spymaster and regretted his politically forced retirement. "Wilcox is a member of Trinity," Colt said.

They stopped among the ancient columns.

"Huh," was all Ava said.

"Ann brought him in. They were old colleagues, apparently. Posted together in Eastern Europe during the Cold War. He and Ann are the only two that are members of an intelligence service. At least that they've told me. Though, I gather the group is significantly less aggressive than when your father was in."

Colt did not know how to say what would need to come next. He'd been dreading it for weeks, ever since he'd concocted this plan. But they couldn't do it without Ava.

"I'm not surprised, somehow. So, why are we here? I know you too well to know that you're seeing me in an unofficial capacity." Ava put a hand on Colt's chest, and he felt an electric bolt shoot through him.

"They are meeting us, Wilcox and Ann. I didn't want you to feel ambushed, but I was worried about telling you before. Security. I'm still not sure how to handle all of this."

"Colt, it's fine. And I agree. You did the right thing."

"We need to talk about what to do next. First, we eat." Colt guided her across the field of ancient Greek ruins, columns jutting up from the ground, and broken, two-thousand-year-old stonework. They took a jagged route through the streets and alleys into the Plaka neighborhood, doubling back several times to ensure they weren't followed. Their destination was the Electra Palace Hotel. It was a white stucco, neoclassical building with gold trim. Colt slipped his jacket on and took them to the rooftop garden restaurant. He gave the name "Bennet Blake" to the receptionist. A hostess guided them through a modern restaurant of cream-colored tile and brown wood with floor-to-ceiling sliding glass windows, most of which were open. They were shown to their table on the patio that wrapped around the restaurant, with a staggering view of the Parthenon, now lit from below, glowing in evening sky. Colt saw Ava's questioning expression when the hostess did not remove the additional place settings. The surrounding tables were empty and all bore placards in Greek script that presumably indicated they were reserved.

Colt set his phone on the table and thumbed an app, an NTCU addition to his phone that would make electronic eavesdropping difficult. Colt ordered a bottle of a local Syrah.

The server reappeared with their wine, poured two glasses, and disappeared.

"Is your government changing its stance?" Ava asked.

Colt gave a curt laugh behind his wineglass. "No. You and I meeting is on the books. Officially, this is a follow-up from what happened in Haifa, seeing if you'd uncovered anything new. Only Thorpe and Ford know about it."

"So, what's this about?"

"We're moving on Archon. We think Archon took down our air traffic control network. We know who Archon's operational leader is and are going to take them down. We need your help to do it. It's the only way we can find out what's next. Ava, it isn't just the attacks on our infrastructure. They've gone after politicians, and we think they were behind the assassination of Alana Howe."

"The tech exec?"

"And Trinity member."

"No shit," she said at length. "What do you need me for?"

"Ava, it's your aunt. Samantha Klein is Archon's operational leader."

"No," she said, resolute. "No, she isn't."

"Wilcox told me. Ann also knows, but she didn't want to tell you. Said it wasn't her place."

"And I suppose it's yours?" Tears rimmed her eyes, held in place by force of will.

"If you were going to hear about it from someone, wouldn't you rather it was me?"

"How could you? Samantha is the only family I have left, and now you're trying to take that away from me too? What if you're wrong? Didn't it ever occur to you that maybe that's what they want you to think, to turn allies on each other? Their whole game is misdirection, Colt!"

"I'm afraid he's right," Jason Wilcox said, appearing at the table. Wilcox wore an off-white suit and navy shirt, open collar, with a blue-and-pink pocket silk peeking just above the edge of the breast pocket. He was tan, hair longer than the last time Colt had seen him, and a closely trimmed salt-and-pepper beard. Retirement looked good on him.

Colt stood and shook his hand. "Good to see you, boss."

"Colt."

Ann stepped out from behind the former head of CIA's clandestine service, black pants and red jacket. "Hello, dear," she said, placing a hand on Ava's shoulder.

"What the hell is this," Ava whispered.

"Well," Wilcox began as he poured Ann a glass and then another for himself. "Colt was worried you might not believe him, so he asked us to provide a little assistance. He's not lying to you, Ava. Your aunt is involved in Archon and highly placed. We are quite confident she's their head of operations."

"That's impossible."

"She's working with Hawkinson," Colt said flatly. "She almost exposed my undercover."

"She told me all about that," Ava snapped. "She needed to get closer to Hawkinson, so she decided to sell out your agent. I shouldn't even be telling you this." Ava pushed her chair back. "I'm sorry, I just...I cannot do this. I cannot *listen* to this."

"Ava, I've known your aunt for a long time," Ann said in mellow tones. "I didn't want to believe it either. I thought she was my friend. We know she was behind your father's death."

"No!" Ava slapped the table, and the wineglasses shook.

"We traced the funds," Ann said gravely. "We have the tools that you do not. That's the only way we could prove it. She paid a Hizballah faction through an intermediary. We unwound the shell corporations she used and followed that back to a fund that Trinity originally established, one she co-opted after she left."

"I don't believe you," Ava said in a voice that at once lacked conviction but held force. As though that alone would turn reality around.

"Ava, it won't surprise you to know that your father was a fighter," Wilcox said. "He recognized Archon for what it was and said we needed to act. The others just didn't want to listen. Samantha had him killed to silence him and send a message to the rest. And, unfortunately, it worked. Instead of galvanizing them, they retreated into their shells. Ann and I, a few others, almost quit over it. The only reason we didn't was we thought a further fracturing of the group would only further Archon's ends."

Ava was quiet for a long time. Then she stood. "I need some air."

Colt rose from his chair, but Wilcox put a hand up. "Let her go. It's a lot to take in." Wilcox held up his wineglass. "Colt, let's talk."

They walked out to the garden on the terrace.

"Can you do this without her?" Wilcox said.

"Klein went to ground after Nadia outed her. We find everyone...eventually," Colt said, "but do we have that long to wait? If we can't convince POTUS that the Russians aren't behind both attacks, he's going to war."

"Yeah, that's a tricky spot," Wilcox said nonchalantly. "Nice work with him, by the way. Though you do need to learn to watch your mouth. That is *not* the place to speculate."

"How did you hear about that?"

Wilcox lifted an eyebrow. "It's not like I used to run a spy service or anything."

"I thought Hoskins was going to pull my spine out through my nose. I appreciate your help with him. If you hadn't talked to him, we wouldn't be here."

"He's not entirely on board. But he's at least willing to listen. I had to tell him that I only knew about it because of a case I started working years ago that led me to Trinity. It was mostly true."

"Ava will come around," Colt said. "I think she knows we're right, but she doesn't want to believe it. Can't say that I blame her." Colt gave his mentor a hard stare. "I'll get Klein, and hopefully we get her to talk. But, Jason, you guys need to get off the fucking bench."

"Excuse me?"

"Your group can go back to being benevolent nerds once Guy Hawkinson isn't trying to start World War Three."

"It's not that simple, Colt."

"Maybe this time it is. Ann told me their reasons. I'm risking my career, maybe more, even talking to you. I can't be the only one with a stake in the game."

"You have to understand, these people..." Wilcox's voice trailed off, and he looked up to the spotlit Parthenon on the hill above them and drank. "They aren't warriors, Colt. They don't necessarily see the world in terms of sides or even in a 'fight.' Many of them tend to believe that science wins. If they discover AGI, that'll be the end of this."

"Yeah, just not the way they hope."

"Do you remember that South Korean engineer I had you recruit?"

"I do," Colt said.

The first eight years of Colt's Agency career was undercover inside a venture capital firm that gave him unique insight into the global technology trade. For most of that time, only Jason Wilcox, then the Chief of Station in Vancouver, knew Colt was a clandestine services officer. On the assignment in question, Wilcox wanted a closer look at a South Korean tech company building advanced avionics for use in the F-15 and F-16 variants the US sold them. CIA feared someone was leaking the blueprints to a source north of the DMZ and that DPRK was getting insight into the Republic of Korea's Air Force capability. Colt was to recruit the company's head of engineering. Colt cultivated the man for about six months before making the pitch, and when he did, the man turned him down. He said it wasn't his fight. CIA and their counterparts in the Korean National Intelligence Service already investigated and cleared him as the mole. The guy just didn't want to get involved.

"That's a good example of where Trinity is at," Wilcox said.

"That's not good enough," Colt said. "Not this time. They're coming for you. They have a *list*, Jason. They have targets. They'd already gotten Archibald Chalcroft and now Alana Howe. Who's next? Our Korean engineer could afford to sit out. He was correct, it wasn't his fight. But this *is* yours." Colt paused, searching for words. "I'll say it this way, Jason. You know that I'd go to the ends of the earth for you. I have. I can justify risking my career, and my life, to pursue Archon. I can't say the same about supporting Trinity. You guys give us intel when it suits your aims but drag your feet when it doesn't. You guys had me risk my life and one of my officers to hack Hawkinson's network but won't tell me why or what it was for. Why should I keep putting myself in danger for you people?"

"Colt, Trinity was formed out of the most destructive event of the twentieth century. They saw what technology could do and wanted to ensure it was used to benefit humanity, not destroy it. They believed that thinking machines, what we now call AGI, could bring about a new era of human prosperity. They also wanted to inspire by their example. To strive for something greater. To create beneficial technologies for the betterment of everyone. I think they've largely succeeded in that. They—we—are the good guys."

"I need more than that. The people who call the shots certainly do. You guys keep playing fast and loose with the law and the sides you take. And then try to justify it by saying you just want to do science and hope for rainbows."

Hard lines appeared around Wilcox's jaw. Colt could see him struggling

—over what, though, he couldn't tell. He didn't understand what Wilcox was holding back or why.

"Trinity invests hundreds of millions every year funding research initiatives across the globe. Most of them directly related to AGI, but some are in corollary areas, like quantum computing and materials science. I'm also pushing them to get political. We're funding an advanced technology think tank now and are going to start lobbying governments. We need leaders to sit up and take notice. That's not going to happen from within the bureaucracy."

Colt crossed his arms, not even bothering to hide his frustration. Was Wilcox serious? He was supposed to risk his life for lobbyists?

"Do better," Colt said flatly. "Or I walk." Colt was surprised with how forcefully he spoke, he hadn't intended to. He was also tired of being everyone's pawn and only ever getting half the story, if that.

"I hadn't wanted to tell you this, for reasons that will become obvious," Wilcox said softly. "I don't want to put you in a position where you feel like you're choosing between loyalty to me and to your agency. If you don't want me to continue, tell me now." Wilcox leveled his gaze on Colt and waited for a response.

"Tell me," Colt said.

Wilcox paused, as if thinking through whether to keep speaking. After several long breaths, he said, "I'm telling you this because I know I can trust you. You're exactly right, we need to get off the bench, as you so eloquently put it. So, I'm pushing us into a more operational space. Alana Howe and I disagreed on a lot of things and battled quite a bit, but she was as much in favor of getting us involved as I am. I suspect that was why she was targeted. Archon doesn't respect laws or borders or conventions. Maybe we've reached the point where we shouldn't either. Or, at least, not feel as constrained by them. What happens when they put one of their pawns in the White House, or at Ten Downing? We're dangerously close to that as it is, with Preston Hawkinson. I don't want to wait around to find out. It doesn't matter if Trinity develops AGI first if Archon is able to truly weaponize this technology and does something terrible with it." Wilcox looked off into the distance. "Any more than they already have. I just need time to get it into place."

"What, you're creating your own intelligence agency? A dirty tricks outfit to fill in the gaps?"

"Hardly," Wilcox said, clearly not amused at the quip. "And you've been spending too much time around Ford. He's starting to rub off on you. What I have in mind is more of the bright reflection of what Archon sees in the mirror. We counter them where we can. Maybe that is providing people like you and Thorpe with intelligence and tools. Maybe it means direct action. The internet is the Wild West. I don't know what the legality of attacking a disinformation campaign is, but I doubt the FBI is going to come after me for it."

"And what if your response requires something a little more kinetic?"

"You really think the world is a better place with Guy Hawkinson in it? I don't know that it will ever come to that, and I still very much believe in the rule of law. But I am also not going to sit by while bad people act faster than our governments do. We knew about bin Laden before 9/11, and we didn't act. We know what Guy Hawkinson has already done..." Wilcox's voice trailed off. "Your instinct to go after Klein is right. She is their shot caller, but don't lose sight of Hawkinson. He's the research arm. My guess is that he's using his operations in Argentina as a screen for Archon's warfare activities." Wilcox turned. "We should be getting back," he said.

Colt walked back to their table. Ava had returned.

That was not the conversation he was expecting.

Wilcox was making Trinity "operational." He was a good man, just, with unassailable integrity. Archon—acting through Senator Preston Hawkinson—ended Wilcox's career at CIA just after he was named the head of the National Clandestine Service. Perhaps the finest man to ever hold that position. Had that changed him, darkened his perspective? Or maybe Wilcox understood that the West was facing a threat it was totally unprepared for and was acting accordingly, willing to risk his ethics, his reputation, his own moral code to counter it.

Colt did not know the answer to that.

Colt sat back down to find another bottle of wine and a table full of aromatic Mediterranean food that he suddenly had no appetite for.

"Colt told me that he thinks Archon is trying to push the US into a conflict with the Russians," Ava said. "Is that your assessment as well?"

Wilcox rejoined them.

"I don't know that the organization entirely agrees with it," Ann said. "But I do."

"What do they have to gain?"

Ann and Wilcox traded a look and held each other's gaze for a time, but said nothing immediately.

Wilcox poured himself another glass of wine and swirled it, like he was stalling for time. "We don't really know. Like a terrorist group, they have first demonstrated capability to show they are serious. But unlike a terrorist group, Archon hasn't asked for anything, hasn't demanded anyone do anything. They haven't even claimed responsibility."

"And you're sure it's them?" Ava asked.

Colt considered his answer carefully. He was, again, in dangerous territory. Any information shared with a foreign intelligence service had to be vetted and cleared first. Even though Wilcox was retired CIA and still consulting for them on certain issues, Colt was not authorized to talk about the attacks with him and certainly not Ann.

"We are," he said. "We've ruled out everyone else. At least, NTCU has." Colt regretted adding that last part, as it suggested the American intelligence community was not unified in this assessment.

"You believe it," Ava said, looking at Colt. "Or you wouldn't be here."

Ava leaned over and put a hand on top of Colt's. "I'll do it," she said in low tones. "I'll help you find my aunt. On one condition." Colt was about to agree, but Ava spoke over him anyway. "I get to meet with her first. You don't act until I give the signal. I want to talk to her myself. If I'm not convinced, you don't go in. Are we clear?"

"Perfectly," Colt said.

"Colt, if you're lying to me, I will never forgive you, and I will never speak to you again."

"I understand."

16

The voice in Jeff's earpiece tried to sound calm, but it came across as forced. Jeff could tell the newscaster was edgy.

Jeff could hardly blame her.

The newscaster continued her intro, piped into Jeff's ear. "Disruptions to transportation and travel continue across the country in the wake of the unprecedented shutdown of multiple oil and gas refineries. Americans are now reeling from gas shortages, fueling long lines at the pump and short tempers."

Jeff, watching along on a muted television in his office, saw the footage of people waiting in long lines in cold weather for precious fuel. The footage cut to scenes of violence at some gas stations with angry patrons taking their frustration out on gas station proprietors. Many service stations were closed, boarded up against vandalism, with signs saying they'd be shut down until further notice.

The newscaster continued: "Compounding the situation, the shortage is disrupting supply chains for many major retailers ahead of the busy holiday season. Our guest tonight is innovator and entrepreneur, Jeff Kim. Jeff is the founder and CEO of Pax AI and also helped the government uncover the source behind last summer's cyberattack on Sacramento's Folsom Dam. Jeff, good evening."

"Thank you, Brianna. It's good to be with you."

It happened a week ago.

Eight oil refineries from Texas to New Jersey went offline. They just shut down, as though someone pulled a plug. In a situation eerily similar to the Folsom Dam, controllers found themselves locked out of the computers used to run the refineries, and production simply...stopped.

The worst, however, was the refinery in Baton Rouge, Louisiana. The fifth largest in the United States, thirteenth in the world, was responsible for over half a million barrels a year. Shortly after operators realized they no longer had control of their plant, several of the production facilities reported heat alarms, apparently unable to vent the excess gases built up in the refining process. The resulting explosions could be heard for miles. Crews contained the fires before the damage became catastrophic and, amazingly, there were no serious injuries reported.

The problems didn't stop there. Gas production dropped by forty percent overnight. Much of the fuel that was already in distribution became trapped as pipelines also shut down, seemingly at random, locking the fuel in transit to distribution hubs. Oil companies couldn't get access to their systems to restart the refineries, distributors didn't have control of their pipelines.

The gas supply was already strained as many Americans opted for traveling by car, not trusting air travel following the earlier shutdown of the air traffic control system.

Americans couldn't get gas for their cars.

Shipping companies couldn't get diesel for their trucks.

Supply chains across the country ground to a halt, froze up.

Then, retailers complained that many of the shipments they *could* get were going to the wrong location. Produce, meat, and dairy shipments showed up at industrial warehouses, offices, and box stores. The supply chain systems supposedly feeding the locations to satisfy deliveries routed shipments to the wrong locations, reported incorrect inventory levels, which hampered restocking efforts. Worse, all of those misrouted shipments used precious fuel that was now in scarce supply.

All this just two weeks before the holiday travel and shopping boom.

"Jeff, what do you make of all this? The Department of Homeland Security said, without question, that this was the result of a cyberattack against our petroleum infrastructure."

"I'm not an information security specialist, so I need to caveat my answers, but yes, I would agree with that assessment."

"So, Jeff, how is this possible? Aren't there protections against this sort of thing?"

"There are, of course, but people have to use them. Think of the internet as the most dangerous neighborhood in the largest city in the world. You'd be crazy to walk down that street at night by yourself. And yet, that's exactly what millions of private citizens and businesses do every day. I was on the ground when the Folsom Dam disaster happened, saw it first-hand. That software hadn't been updated in *years*. I am not as close to the refinery crisis as I was to Folsom Dam, but I'd be willing to bet that if we looked at the operating systems of those plants, we'd find out-of-date passwords, infrequently patched systems, and generally outdated software. We can't expect to walk down dangerous streets, unprotected, and not expect bad outcomes. My company, Pax AI, invests heavily in information security, and we still see hundreds of dedicated attempts to breach our systems every day."

"Do you think we're too connected, Jeff, too integrated? Is technology itself the problem?"

Jeff felt the anger rise at the inanity of her question, but he could hear the words of his media coach in his ears telling him to pause, reflect, and then answer calmly. Part of Jeff's personal rebranding was hiring a top-tier (and very quiet) PR firm to help change his and his firm's reputation.

"No, Brianna, I don't. Respectfully, I think we should be cautious about saying 'technology' is the problem. It's also important to note that 'technology' is a broad term. Networked computer systems, automation, artificial intelligence, these are just tools. Advanced ones, to be sure, but tools just the same."

"There are some who argue the tools are the problem, though. That perhaps we're too reliant on them. This is a major focus of Senator Hawkinson's presidential campaign."

Jeff forced himself not to eye-roll that comment.

"Well, that's an ironic position given how much money the senator has made from the tech sector. His nephew runs an AI research firm. Again, the problem isn't the tool, it's the application of the tool. You can't build a house without using a hammer to nail together the frame. But that same hammer can just as easily be used to smash a window to steal what's inside that house."

"That's an interesting point. Let's talk about intent for a moment, Jeff. I'll go back to the question that I led the interview with. What do you make of all this? Do you think the Russian government did this?"

"I don't think I'm in a position to speculate. There's enough of that already."

"You did help the government uncover a Russian attack, though."

"That's true. But I also have some of the most advanced computer systems in the world at my disposal. All I did was be in a position to point the proper authorities in the right direction. They concluded it was the Russian government. I should note that since then, we've seen a three-hundred-percent increase in intrusion attempts on Pax AI networks. Some of those, our security experts believe, have come from the Russians."

"Have any gotten through?"

Jeff gave a curt laugh. "No."

"In your estimation, Jeff, where do we go from here?"

"Well, I think it's going to be a difficult holiday season for many and, unfortunately, a cold winter. But Americans will do what we always do and come together in a crisis. We'll put aside our differences and help. You may know that Pax AI piloted an autonomous vehicle fleet two years ago. These are all electric vehicles, largely solar powered. I've already deployed these, free of charge, to help get goods moving. I've also offered a version of the system we used to operate the Port of Long Beach to help rebuild our supply chains. This we're also doing free of charge. Our citizens need food and clothing. Pax AI will use every tool at its disposal to help."

The reporter was asking her follow-up when she cut herself off, announcing breaking news. The connection broke, and the producer's voice in his earpiece said they had to cut the interview short. Then he dropped as well. Jeff, in his home office, turned on the television and tuned to the news channel he was just on. The anchor's concerned expression hovered over an alarming red banner.

The video feed cut to an image of the president in a White House conference room with congressional members of his party and several cabinet secretaries seated at the long table covered in open binders. The president leaned over and appeared to have a private conversation with the Speaker of the House. The reporter's voice continued over the video. "The president was caught on an apparent hot mic during a White House meeting today on the current oil crisis." Audio cut to the president's voice. "I've had it with this guy. We have war plans ready to go for retaliatory strikes. And, I'll tell you, regime change is on the table. We're already talking with people on the inside who can take over."

17

Athens, Greece

"Okay, let's run it again," Colt said.

Ava, Colt, and Tony were alone in the safe house. The rest of Ikeda's team was conducting recon of the mission site, a beachside restaurant near Kalamakion. Colt, Tony, and his team arrived three days ago to prep. Though Ground Branch relied heavily on contractors for many of its operations, given the sensitivity of this mission, they'd run it entirely in-house. They exhaustively vetted any team member to confirm they'd never worked with Hawk Security Group or served with Hawkinson in the Army.

The team flew in on a CIA Gulfstream like the one Colt and Tony took to Geneva. They left as soon as Ava confirmed she'd set up a meeting with her aunt. It had been three weeks since the meeting with Wilcox and Ann. In that time, NTCU concluded that the president's alleged "hot mic" where he surreptitiously told the Speaker of the House that "regime change was on the table" was a deepfake, an AI-manipulated video made to look and sound like a real person.

Deepfakes were gaining ground among cybercriminals who used them to falsify compromising situations to be exploited through blackmail. Hollywood used a version of the technology to authentically render younger versions of actors. But to create a convincing replication of the president of the United States? That would take serious computing power.

Unfortunately, for a president with a history of off-the-cuff gaffes and making policy on the fly, the statement was plausible enough that people wouldn't be utterly shocked when they learned about it. Or, rather, shocked by the statement and not that it had been made. NTCU shared their evidence with the White House, who shared it with the American people, but the damage was done.

The White House's explanation sounded to most like dissembling or, at worst, "Washington spin" and buck passing, trying to blame a phantom computer for a politician getting caught.

The Russians responded in a statement saying it was "dangerously provocative" and executed their largest naval mobilization since the Cold War, scrambled aircraft in combat air patrols, and put all of their forces on alert.

Athens Station provided the safe house and staging area; they didn't know what for and knew not to ask. It was a two-story apartment with ground-floor access and street parking in Glyfada a few miles east of the airport and just blocks from the A113, a six-lane road that would take them into Athens proper.

Once they had Klein, the plan was to bring her to a site outside Athens for interrogation. It was a black site the Agency used during the GWOT days to question terrorists captured in the region. There was an inter-rogator on standby.

Athens Station was used to the requests by now. This place had always been the Wild West and usually on the front lines of *something*.

Ava was to meet her aunt at the restaurant that evening for dinner. The team would be positioned in, around, and behind the restaurant. Colt would remain at the safe house, as Klein could identify him. Plan A was to grab her as she went to the restroom, spiriting her out a nearby service entrance. Plan B was to get her leaving the restaurant.

Assuming Ava gave them the go-ahead signal.

To do that, she had to be convinced, in the moment, that her aunt, a master spy in her own right, was a member of Archon's leadership team. Colt knew Ava would never give her aunt up, even if she suspected her of something shady, unless she believed Samantha had direct knowledge of Archon's operations against Trinity *and* the United States.

Ava's bargain was she had to catch her aunt in a lie. Ava would get her to acknowledge information Nadia had uncovered that could only have come from Archon. Samantha told Ava once that she was still loyal to Israel, that she was working on the outside to protect her country's interests.

That would be the test.

Clearing a member of a foreign intelligence service to have access to original source HUMINT took a little convincing. In fact, Thorpe cautioned Colt against this, practically begged him to find another way. If this leaked, not only would it end their campaign against Hawkinson, it would put Nadia's life in imminent danger and open NTCU up to retribution from within the US government. If Senator Hawkinson learned the intelligence community was investigating his nephew, he'd turn this into a political firestorm.

The senator would say the president was using his own deep state to attack a political rival because he couldn't defeat him in the tournament of ideas.

That narrative would catch fire so quickly and furiously, the administration couldn't possibly defend against it.

This was the sort of thing that brought presidencies down.

In ways Colt couldn't explain to Thorpe, he implicitly trusted Ava to protect his source. Ava *knew* Nadia. She'd already risked her own life protecting Nadia's cover. That mattered to Colt, even if it didn't matter to his government.

Colt played this as safe as he possibly could and selected information Ava already knew for their "blue dye."

The assassination of Archibald Chalcroft.

The setup, which Ava once explained to Colt was her very real fear, was that someone could use a weapon like this to wipe her people out, finish the work the Nazis started and that the Iranian government hoped to complete.

"She's not coming," Ava said, hanging up the phone.

"Where is she?" Colt asked.

"Kavala," Ava said. "It's about four hundred miles northeast of here. Past Thessaloniki."

Less familiar with Athens, Colt pulled it up on his phone. Sure enough. Kavala was practically in Bulgaria and not far from the Turkish border.

"We can make this work," Ikeda said. "As it is, we didn't have a target location to plan around until we got here. Any chance you can set a location now?"

"I'm sure I can. I told her that I needed to see if I could get a rail ticket first. She'll be expecting a call back."

"Any chance she suspects something?" Colt asked. A last-minute pivot was an ideal way to shake surveillance.

"Impossible," Ava said stiffly. "I'd know."

Colt and Ikeda traded a look.

Ikeda opened his Agency laptop, a Toughbook, and pulled up a map of Kavala.

"Jesus," he said slowly. "Streets in this place are about a foot wide. Crazy-ass geometry." After another few moments of study, he leaned back and looked to Colt. "Beach town, some tourism, but this isn't the high season. Looks to be mostly residential traffic. Still, if we have to bug out in a hurry, it could be messy. Those roads around the castle are narrow, and none of them are straight."

"Are you saying we shouldn't?"

"Your call, Colt, but I've worked in worse places. We can make this work. I just need to point out the complication."

"Thanks, Tony. Any suggestions on where to go?"

"I think Kavala Castle is a good spot. Easy for us to cover the entrance. It's a tourist spot, the kind of landmark someone from out of town would suggest. This is outdoors, walkable, fits the profile. Our team can blend in as tourists."

"How does this break badly?" Colt asked.

Tony thought about the answer. "She makes a scene leaving or, worse, decides to go down swinging. There's bound to be people there to see it. Could be difficult to covertly get the sedative in her."

"I cover for that by saying she's fainted," Ava said. "We carry her out before anyone can call for an ambulance, say we're taking her to a hospital."

"Medical emergencies tend to make people uncomfortable," Tony said. "Eye wits want it to go away. They won't say anything."

"Okay," Ava said. "I'll set it up."

⸻

They cleared out of the safe house within the hour.

Colt notified the interrogator of the change in location. Athens Station gave them a fresh set of license plates for their vehicles so they would appear to be registered in Kavala. It was a small detail and perhaps an unimportant one, but it was the type of detail their target would notice. Once noticed, she may just start to wonder, an anomaly since Ava would be traveling by train.

The team rode in a van with their weapons and equipment. Colt and Ikeda drove separately in a sedan.

It took them six and a half hours on the A1 highway. They stopped at a roadside diner outside Thessaloniki for an early dinner and continued on to Kavala, arriving around seven p.m. local time.

Unfortunately, Athens Station didn't have a support asset in Kavala that could arrange a safe house on short notice, so the team opted for a hotel near city center. Colt told the hotel staff they were a documentary film crew shooting a new special on Alexander the Great and Macedonia. They'd likely be coming and going at odd hours and would have equipment cases with them. The hotel manager, beaming with pride about his home, asked if there was anything they needed and even identified a few locations on the map he was sure that only a local would know about.

The group retired to their room. Colt and Ikeda brought up takeout, pita, souvlaki, fries, and a few six-packs of ice-cold Mythos. Colt remembered the beer fondly from his many Greek port calls in the Navy.

Ava texted him using an app called Wormhole, an anonymized and encrypted messaging app that stored no data on any server and automatically deleted exchanges after transmission. She was using a new phone, and Colt's iPhone was heavily modified by NTCU's tech wizards.

They communicated as securely as possible given the circumstances.

But, with Archon involved, who really knew?

Ava said she'd gotten a ticket on the Athens-Alexandroupoli overnight train, which would arrive at 0600. She would be in Kavala by mid-morning.

The team pulled up maps of the area around Kavala Castle on Toughbooks and tablets.

The castle stood atop a steep, shark-tooth-shaped peninsula jutting into the Gulf of Kavala. Red-tiled homes, seemingly stacked upon each other, surrounded the castle. If they didn't make the capture immediately, they would be looking at a furious chase through crowded, labyrinthine streets.

"Holy shit," one of the Ground Branch men said. "You guys seeing this?"

They had CNN International on in the room to mask their conversation. Everyone stopped what they were doing and looked at the television.

US Air Force F-35s, F-22s, and F-15s flew combat air patrols over the Baltic and around the airspace of the surrounding NATO countries. Each nation provided their own fighters for the effort, but the American air force had the largest presence. The reporter said that Russian aircraft, MiG-35s and the fifth-generation Su-57s, increasingly pressed into Baltic airspace (not yet officially designated a no-fly zone). Today, two Su-57s charged a US Navy destroyer in the Baltic in a pattern indicating an attack run. The US Air Force scrambled a pair of F-35s to intercept. They did, and the Russians broke off, but the military analysts interviewed speculated the provocative maneuver looked to be a test run for an attack with anti-ship missiles and certainly testing NATO's response time.

The Russian president ordered their nuclear forces to alert status. Washington responded by declaring DEFCON 2.

18

The city reminded Ava of her own Jerusalem. Not in its geography or its size, but in how the ancient world and the modern one coexisted, like two pictures developed together. Like her homeland, Kavala changed hands numerous times throughout its history and was known by nearly as many names. Founded in the seventh century BCE as Neapolis, or "New City," by the fourth century, it was an important trade center for Macedonia. The Romans conquered Neapolis first and held it until the Byzantine Empire took it. By then, the city was known as Christopolis. The newly formed Ottoman Empire conquered the city in one of their first conquests to expand their borders in 1387, and it stayed under Turkish control—except for a short tune under the tenure of the Republic of Venice—until the Greeks finally liberated the city during the Second Balkan War in 1913.

Ava entered the castle a little after noon. It was a warm day, and a late autumn sun lit the sky. She wore a blazer, a light tan sweater, and jeans. She had a 9mm Jericho 941F in a holster at the small of her back under the sweater. The weapon was clean and one of the major firearms Israel exported to the Greeks, so if it was somehow recovered here, it would not raise any eyebrows due to its country of origin. Not that she expected to use it.

Colt's story of Samantha trying to expose a CIA operative in Hawkinson's organization and her supposed use of a Swiss intelligence officer to do it still echoed in Ava's mind. CIA's version was that this Swiss, Bastian Stager, lurked around HawkTech headquarters following their female employees...because their lead was that the spy was woman. This Stager assaulted and chased Nadia and might have killed her if her Agency handler hadn't shown up at exactly the right moment. He shot Stager, who was subsequently arrested and hospitalized and then quietly dismissed from the Swiss Federal Intelligence Service.

If that was indeed Samantha, and Ava was not yet ready to admit that it was, there would certainly be a reason. Using a contract agent was a common practice of the world's intelligence agencies, and it fit with the work her aunt was now doing. And sometimes, contractors went off their leashes...a problem her American friends were all too familiar with.

She paid her ticket and entered the castle.

The Kavala Acropolis began as a simple defensive fortification erected in the fifth century BCE, and a succession of Roman emperors and generals modified and expanded the fortification through the year 926. The Byzantines extended the walls in 1307 from the shore to the top of the hill where the castle perched. They also added a seventy-five-meter-tall aqueduct to carry fresh water to the fortress. The aqueduct, which ran through the center of the old city, still stood. Turks destroyed the castle during a siege in 1391, resulting in the capture of the city. They rebuilt the fortification in 1425, and it remained largely intact and unchanged since.

The castle was a gray stone rectangle of walls and towers atop the hill, with a wedge-shaped enclosure that formed the northern wall. From above, it looked like a lazily drawn L. There was a structure, originally a guard house, on the southern side facing the water. The fortification had a single cylindrical tower rising from the center, which afforded an unobstructed view of the surrounding city. A long, low building ran along the outer wall that served as the castle's arsenal. Though, in later years, the storage was converted to a prison.

It was the off season, and there were few tourists here. Ava stood near the northwest gate, in the large wedge-shaped area that now held a stage and stadium seating climbing up the low hill. Ava looked up and saw Samantha seated at the café atop the hill, beneath a canvas umbrella. She didn't make a show of seeing her aunt or seek her attention but casually walked across the lawn to the stone steps leading to the café.

Samantha wore jeans, a light black leather jacket, and a black blouse. She also wore sunglasses. Her hair was shorter than Ava remembered, curling back toward her ears. There was a glass of white wine in front of her and a bottle in an ice bucket.

Samantha stood as Ava approached. Ava noted she wore fashionable white leather tennis shoes, but ones she could run in if necessary.

They embraced, and Samantha motioned for her to sit.

"I'm sorry for the last-minute change in plans. I'm meeting with a prospective client today. All this disruption so that I can have a fifteen-minute meeting on his yacht." Samantha smiled, shook her head, and took a drink.

"It's no problem. I took an overnight train, which I haven't done since college. It was nice," Ava said. "And good to have a few hours to myself."

"I understand that."

Samantha claimed to be a security consultant for the kinds of clients who measured wealth in numbers resembling GDP.

After a few minutes of small talk, Samantha asked, "So, dear, why are you really here? We could've caught up on the phone."

"The Institute has questions, and they're hoping you can answer them," Ava said. How many times had she been in this position in her career, pulling information out of a collection target. And yet, she had to fight to keep her voice from quavering. She didn't pick up her wineglass for fear of Samantha seeing it shake.

"Of course. They thought I'd be more receptive if they sent you?"

"No, I volunteered. Katz assumed you wouldn't take his phone call and asked me if I would be willing to broker a meeting. I told them to just send me."

Samantha gave a strange smile, her expression indecipherable behind those glasses.

"Well, ask away."

"It has to do with Guy Hawkinson," Ava said. She let a little bit of the nervousness seep through for effect.

Samantha set her wineglass down and put her hands in her lap.

"Katz did not want this in a cable to me at headquarters. Or in any of the other methods they have to communicate with you."

"I understand. He wouldn't trust anyone else with this, either. Seeing as how you know Guy," Samantha said.

"Exactly. The question is about Archibald Chalcroft. He died the night before he was to be confirmed as the head of MI6. The British believe he was assassinated. We learned from a source in MI5 that they think it was a bioweapon. Used a DNA sample to target Chalcroft."

Samantha nodded slowly, as though completing an equation in her head. "If true, that would explain why his sons were also killed but the wife survived." Samantha spoke in clinical tones.

"That's the theory, yes. Katz believes that apart from certain governments, only Hawkinson's organization, Archon, would have the capability to create such a weapon."

The first test was Samantha's reaction to the statement that Archon was Guy's doing. Her expression remained blank.

"And Katz thinks I can confirm this?"

"Yes. They, we, are worried that Hawkinson might sell this to Iran."

Samantha picked her glass back up and sipped.

With the question hanging in the air between them, Ava wondered if she was just here because she let Colt talk her into this. Did she let her feelings for him cloud her operational judgment? Her aunt was a dedicated servant of Israel, an avenging angel if ever there was one. Her field career canonized into Mossad's mythology. She was a legend.

Yes, Ava wondered why Samantha allowed herself to become so close to Hawkinson. But she believed, and still did, that it was to act as a final line of defense. Official or not, Samantha Klein would not allow a group like Archon to threaten their home, their very existence.

Colt was wrong. There was no other explanation.

"Well, I don't think that's very likely. Guy doesn't have a very high opinion of the ayatollahs. And the IRGC was responsible for a lot of American deaths in Iraq. But he did kill Archie Chalcroft."

Holy shit, Colt thought.

The audio on Ava's button mic was crisp, perfect. Colt sat in a small café a block outside and below the castle's southern wall. He was watching the video feed on his phone from the micro drone hovering above the castle wall and listening in through his earbuds. Thorpe and Ford would also be listening in at the NTCU ops center, along with the National Security Advisor, who had authorization to terminate this operation at any point. After hearing that, Colt couldn't imagine that he would.

Colt keyed the radio. "Watch for the jacket," he said. The team members deployed in and around the castle rogered.

Ava removing her jacket was the "go" signal.

"Hawkinson trusts me," Samantha said. "Or at least, he did. Now, I was always on the outside, of course. But he confided in me. Probably more than that group of his would've liked."

"Archon?" Ava asked.

Samantha nodded in response. Then picked up her wineglass, considering the contents for a moment before drinking again.

"What do you know about them?"

"About the same as you, I'm afraid," Samantha said. "Businessmen, politicians, and some scientists with a strange view of what constitutes 'research.' Think they can use AI to replace governments."

"Why did Hawkinson confide in you?"

"My background," Samantha said, in a way that suggested the answer was obvious.

"And he admitted they made this weapon?"

"Oh, he can't *help* himself. Hawkinson isn't a scientist, he isn't a general, he's only 'elite' because of his money, and even then it's family money. It's not as if he'd earned it. He wanted me to know how clever he is, developing this thing. They wanted to test their weapon out and send a message to

Trinity at the same time, show them how far along they were. Guy didn't agree. He spoke to me about it."

Ava didn't relax, that wasn't the word, but the tension that wound itself around her nervous system earlier seemed to loosen a little. It seemed strange that Hawkinson would admit such a thing to Samantha. But then, she was that good. If she could get an Iranian hard-liner to give up secrets, a rich American playing soldier would be easy picking.

Still, relief washed over her, knowing that Samantha wasn't part of this Archon insanity.

The mole hunt was a screen for her own activities, Ava knew that now. Samantha had gone too far in that, which would need to be remedied with Colt's people. But at least Ava could rest knowing that whatever Samantha did was for the good of Israel.

"This is all very helpful," Ava said. "So, as far as you know, the weapon is still under development?"

"It is. From what I gather, Archon is highly distributed. Most people working for Archon's causes don't ultimately know what they serve. Probably wouldn't do it if they did. Would make discovering all of their little hives quite difficult. Hawkinson has a bioscience lab in his Geneva facility, but the 'finishing work,' so to speak, is handled elsewhere. Was there anything else that they wanted to know?"

"No," Ava said. "This was tremendously helpful, thank you."

"Of course." Samantha removed her sunglasses and folded them neatly on the table. Then she brushed her left hand over her ear, as if brushing the hair out of place. Her fingers lingered a moment on the lobe.

Almost a...signal?

Ava stared at her aunt for a long, hard moment, regarding her in new light. It would not surprise her to learn that Samantha traveled with a bodyguard, but if so, why would she need to communicate with them now?

Unless...

But Ava dismissed the thought, the doubt. She knew she was jumping at shadows. Inventing phantom signals out of innocuous gestures. That was ridiculous. Worse, it was amateurish.

"I had a question, though," she heard herself say, before she'd even considered the words.

"Anything, Ava," her aunt said.

"I was thinking about my parents."

Samantha's expression both softened and darkened. "Ava, no good can come from this. If you keep ripping off the bandage, the wound will never heal."

"Humor me, please. As you know, the investigation is ongoing. The Institute isn't going to just let this go."

"Well, they should," Samantha said dismissively. "They know it was Hizballah that hired the bomber."

"But not who paid Hizballah to do it. They know, now, it was done through a succession of shell corporations and virtual transactions. Whoever did it covered their tracks incredibly well. Hizballah is not that sophisticated."

Samantha's eyes flicked to something over Ava's right shoulder and then snapped back.

Something had drawn her gaze, and Samantha wanted to cover it.

"Don't go digging in the past, Ava," Samantha said with authority rather than compassion.

Ava held her aunt's gaze, and everything else fell away. All sound muted in her ears; the world outside that mutually held stare didn't exist.

Ava's expression hardened, and she knew.

She *knew*.

Mossad hadn't told Ava that, Trinity had.

Samantha sat back in her seat, considering her niece. One arm moved to her lap, and the other picked up the glass for a deep drink of wine.

Ava slid out of her blazer.

"Go, go, go," Colt said over the radio as he sprang from his chair and bolted up the hill at a dead run.

Samantha Klein's eyes narrowed, and she regarded her niece with a strange countenance, a mixture of appreciation and betrayal.

"So, how long do we have?"

Ava said, "Not long enough."

19

Kavala, Greece

Samantha removed a small tin from her handbag and opened it. She plucked something out of it and turned it to Ava in offering. The tin was split down the center with a collection of tiny pink pellets on one side and aqua ones on the other. "Mint?"

"No," Ava said coldly.

"So, our friends in the Institute wanted a little more than a couple questions, did they?"

Any expression dissolved from Samantha's face. It was blank, hard, and cold. But her eyes, Ava would remember that look for the rest of her life. There was a dark depth to them, and a smoldering anger, like the lingering embers of a charred forest after a wildfire.

Ava shook her head in answer to the question.

"Ahh. CIA, then. Set me up for the boyfriend, did you?" Samantha closed the tin and returned it to her handbag but kept the mint between her thumb and forefinger. She turned it over in her hand, considered it, but didn't put it in her mouth. Some calculus played out in her mind. "Well, I'd hate to meet the Americans with bad breath."

"Did you do it," Ava asked. "Or did you just not stop it?"

"I told you not to go digging about in the past. History holds only pain."

"Answer me, goddamn it."

"Does it bring them back?"

"You're a coward," Ava said through narrow eyes, fighting back tears.

"Closure is myth, love. But, yes. This world is already damaged almost beyond repair. My dear brother believed that the current system might somehow work if we just *believed* in it enough." The cynicism and bitterness in Samantha's voice, that Ava for so long thought was just the hallmark of someone fighting against a system, now had new clarity. She *was* fighting against a system, just not the one Ava believed her to be.

Ava could see a CIA operative approaching without turning her head and giving it away. Not that it mattered now. Ava calculated he was about twenty paces away.

Built before man developed the technology to level ground, the castle followed the natural contours of the hill. There were two different elevations, with the main fortress occupying the upper of the two. The small café sat next to the entrance gate on that upper level and in the shadow of the castle's central tower. The hill behind her descended at a slow grade to the wedge-shaped field below. Ava noted, now, that it was a surprising lapse in tradecraft for Samantha to take a seat that faced the castle's entrance, as she would not be able to see anyone entering behind her.

She saw Colt appear from the shadows of the entry gate, and a wave of relief passed over her.

It would all be over soon.

The plan wasn't to take Samantha in a café.

The CIA team wanted to get her leaving the castle. All things considered, this was a terrible location for a grab, now that Ava could see it with her own eyes. The surrounding streets were so narrow, you couldn't get anything bigger than a small car through without fear of scratching it, and it was all one-way traffic. A fast egress was out of the question.

Ava knew the Americans would adapt. Certainly, they'd done captures in far more challenging environments than a two-thousand-year-old castle, but this extraction would not be easy.

"Since the Americans are coming, I'll remind you of what Thomas Jefferson said. 'A little rebellion every now and then is a good thing. And as necessary as storms.' History is marked by visionaries with the courage to act. It can be violent, but we cannot afford debate. Endless debate is what *got us here*. Change requires a supreme act of will. I do the dirty work necessary so that your children can live in a world of peace."

"Did my parents see it that way?"

"Sadly, no." Samantha popped the mint into her mouth. "I took no pleasure in it. I'm glad you survived Haifa, though it would have been simpler if you hadn't. Hadn't expected you to be there."

Haifa?

Ava's parents died in Haifa.

"What are you talking about? Of course I survived. I was in the back of the restaurant." Ava's voice got small. The day her parents were killed by a terrorist's bomb, Ava was going to introduce them to Colt. When he didn't show up at the restaurant, she'd gotten up and went to call him. She was in the back of the building when the bomb went off, shielding her from the blast.

Calling Colt saved her life.

"I wasn't speaking about the time your parents were killed," Samantha said. "Think more recently when you and the boyfriend were mucking about at the port."

Shapes appeared around them, closing in from the fringes of her field of vision.

"We were there during a terrorist attack," Ava said slowly. "Palestinians attacking an infrastructure project."

Samantha's words from earlier in their conversation echoed in her mind...*Most people working for Archon's causes don't ultimately know what they serve.*

"Ma'am, I'm going to have to ask you to come with us," one of them said with polite dominance.

"Oh, I don't think so. I quite like it here," Samantha Klein said.

The CIA officer that moved in behind her held a tiny syringe that would incapacitate her in seconds.

It would be too late then, Ava knew.

Maybe she knew all along and just didn't stop it.

Samantha's shoulder jerked violently as the convulsions started. Her eyes narrowed, and her face broke into a grim rictus halfway between a haughty smile and a hateful sneer. Blue-tinged foam bubbled up out of the corners of her mouth and then over the lips of that ugly smile.

Samantha collapsed on the table, and the CIA men moved her to the ground to fruitlessly attempt first aid.

Everything that happened next would be frozen forever in her mind, a series of stills rather than a running picture.

Ava stood.

She saw Colt running toward her.

She felt warm sun on her back, heavy air thick with the smell of salt and sea.

Her body jerked, and she fell forward.

Then she heard the gunshot.

And Ava fell.

20

Three Ground Branch officers rushed into action as soon as they heard the gunshot.

Ava was struck from behind, so the shot must have come from the castle's western wall. Unless he was going to jump, the shooter had to descend stairs that were in the towers. That meant he only had two ways down. Easy enough for them to cover.

"It was her, Colt. In Haifa."

"Ava, you need to rest. Let us work on you."

Tony grabbed napkins from the table to fashion a field dressing.

Colt asked someone to call an ambulance. He hoped enough people spoke English here to do it.

"Goddamn it, I'm fine."

"You're shot, Ava."

"Shut up and listen to me. Samantha...Archon...ordered the attack in Haifa."

"About your parents? We know," Colt said calmly, trying to reassure her.

"No! Against *us*."

Colt heard radio chatter that he tried to ignore so he could focus on what Ava was saying. She had her eyes squeezed tight against the pain. The white cloth napkin that Tony pressed against her abdomen was already soaked through.

"Wait, you mean the port attack? That was Archon?"

Ava nodded, and Ikeda told her not to move.

"This isn't fatal," Ikeda said. "But you should try to stay still until help gets here."

Colt looked up, his face drawn to the commotion, the movement around them. A café employee had a first aid kit, which she set next to Tony and hovered nearby in a squat, anxiously looking on. The castle's few patrons were rushing for the exit, mostly screaming. The entry gate was next to the café, so Colt had a solid line of sight to it from where he knelt with Ava. Looked to be about a dozen people pushing each other, all trying to squeeze through the stone archway. He noticed one man, blond with a dark jacket, that somehow maintained his composure in all the chaos.

Good on him, Colt thought. *At least someone has a clear head.*

"Hey—you getting this?" Tony asked him.

"No, I wasn't paying attention," Colt replied.

Tony pointed and Colt turned, following his hand. One of the Ground Branch operatives stood atop the castle wall, waving an arm. Colt couldn't make out exactly what it was due to the distance, but there was a small dark bulge on the battlement near him.

"Alverez, repeat what you found," Tony said.

"It's a rifle, but done up to look like surveillance equipment. Like a security camera. There's a warning placard on the side. Translation app says a bunch of caution and restricted shit. I'm taking video of it now. We got time to break this thing down and take it with us? Guys back home would probably want to check this out."

"I don't think so," Colt said. "Wait. Was it remote operated?"

"Looks that way."

"That means the shooter—"

"Shit!" Colt exclaimed. "The blond guy." He was so focused on Ava, he wasn't paying attention to his surroundings. He looked up at Ikeda. "Tony," he said.

"I'm on it."

"Colt, you have to go," Ava grunted.

"I'm not leaving you."

"We're not doing this again. You're the only one who got a look at him. He's our only link now." Tony had already removed her pistol when he laid her on her back to check the wound. She had it at her side now.

Colt was gone, close on Ikeda's heels.

They throttled their way through the crowd and onto the stone stairs that descended to the surrounding neighborhood. Colt shouted, "There!" when he spotted the blond man.

It had to be Bastian Stager.

They both vaulted the side and dropped to the narrow street of masoned flagstone. Stager heard Colt shout and took off at a run. Ikeda radioed that they were in foot pursuit of the target. Colt drew his weapon and raced down the alley, legs pumping, driving him faster. This ancient street was barely wide enough for a single car. The castle's rocky base sat on one side, and homes lined the other.

Colt saw Stager abruptly shift direction, crashing into someone running away, then he disappeared down an alley. Kavala Castle was at the top of a hill, surrounded by homes and narrow, labyrinthine streets, bisected by even narrower alleys at intervals that likely only made logical sense a thousand years ago when they were laid. If they lost Stager here, they would never find him.

Colt accelerated to close the distance and then slid across the ground to slow himself, shoes skipping on the ground. He looked to the left, where Stager went. It wasn't an alley, it was a steep set of stairs.

Colt aimed his pistol and fired.

Stager's body jolted once, and he crashed forward. He fell onto the steps, but his momentum carried him and he rolled over once and came to a stop in the street at the base of the steps. Colt saw blood smeared on the stone. He ran down the stairs, two at a time, and Stager rolled over.

Colt had just enough time to dive to the side as he saw Stager's gun come up and fire. It was a short burst, a machine pistol of some kind. He launched over the metal handrail and crashed into a leafy green shrub that grew out of what little exposed dirt there was between the stairs and the adjoining house.

"You okay?" Ikeda asked, pulling him out of the shrub. Colt had a multitude of small scrapes on his arms and face. Colt climbed over the railing. Stager was gone, but he was leaking blood and couldn't have gotten far.

Ikeda led the way, and they resumed their hell-bent flight down the stairs. The gray street was stained with blood where Stager landed, and the spotted trail led off to the right. Ikeda peeked around the corner and jerked his head back as the staccato rip of semiautomatic weapons fire split the silence. Bullets impacted the side of the building behind them.

"I'm going to lay down cover fire," Ikeda said. "You duck behind that car." He pointed to a sedan parked on the other side of the alley, maybe twenty feet from them. "Use the car as cover and shoot down the alley. Keep him occupied. Fucker's holed up in a stairwell. I'll move down and get him."

"Rog," Colt said.

Colt moved into position behind Ikeda. Tony popped out of cover and sent four rounds downrange.

Colt sprinted across the gap and dove behind the sedan. The rip of gunfire followed him. The space Colt aimed for, a gap between two parallel parked cars, was just wide enough. Stager was about twenty-five feet in front of him, on another descending stone staircase, using the bridge ledge and metal railing for cover.

In his ear, Colt heard Tony calling instructions over the radio and the team roger back.

One of them stayed with Ava, the others in pursuit.

Another ripping burst of gunfire and then silence.

Tony motioned for Colt to move forward.

If he hugged the car, it'd be hard for Stager to hit him, especially with Ikeda covering. But Colt would still be exposed.

He had an idea. Colt climbed onto the hood and over the roof. Now he could see the stairs over the low brick wall. He slid down the back side of the car, the house shielding him from view, and dropped into the gap between the bumper and the wall. Colt popped up out of cover, leaned over the wall.

Stager was already at the bottom of the stairs. He fired a short burst from his machine pistol to cover his flight and disappeared behind a building to the right. Stager was heading south. Colt vaulted over the railing, missed his landing, and almost tumbled down the entire staircase. He grabbed the railing at the last second to regain his balance. Ikeda appeared next to him, and they pursued.

Ahead of them, they saw a sliver of aqua between the buildings, the Thracian Sea.

They hit the bottom of the stairs and turned right. Colt and Ikeda followed Stager through the mazelike alleys. Never close enough for an unobstructed shot. Colt marveled at the man's stamina. Colt had hit him in the chest and Stager could still move like this. They followed the street as it arced around a large home with ivy falling off the outer walls like emerald water. The alley terminated in a narrow, north-south cross street. Ikeda looked north, Colt the other way. He saw an opening in the building, and cars.

"This way!" Colt took off at a run, chest heaving. He was fatigued, and he knew Stager couldn't take much more.

Maybe he wouldn't have to.

They burst into a small parking lot abutting the water. A line of squat pine trees framed the far side. Stager stood in the center next to a blue Mercedes sedan. Colt could just make out the barrel of Stager's MP-5 sticking through the car's open window, aimed at the terrified driver's head, a middle-aged woman. Using the car as cover, Stager climbed into the back seat.

They heard shouting and screaming, and then the car reversed quickly. The driver turned just before she hit the seawall, angling to leave the parking lot.

Colt raised his weapon, but there was no shot. None that he was comfortable risking. He swore, rage and frustration crashing over him like a dark and angry tide.

"Colt, this way!" Ikeda shouted, pointing to the west. Colt saw he was motioning toward a gap between the two perpendicular lines of trees that framed the outside of the parking lot and the building on the other side of them. Then, he understood. They could cut through. The parking lot looked like it went for a tenth of a mile or so along the water before turning back inland. Colt followed Ikeda, summoning whatever stamina he had left for a sprint. They raced through the trees and around the building, a church with a domed roof by the look of it.

Colt tried to match Ikeda's pace.

They hit the gray brick street at a dead run, leaping down a low set of stairs into a terraced parking lot in the front of the church. Colt didn't have time to slow down, let alone stop, so he just leaped into the air, crashing down on the hood of a car, over the roof, and down the other side. The car's alarm erupted with indignant fury. Ikeda landed on the street next to him and dropped into a crouch behind the line of cars. Colt kept running, crossing the street.

The Mercedes raced toward him.

He saw the driver's eyes, close enough to register their complete terror, probably driving on muscle memory alone. Colt dove behind a parked car, knowing if she slowed to avoid hitting him, Stager was liable to shoot her.

He heard the screeching of tires braking as he dashed across the street —and a single shot.

Then, screaming.

The car stopped with force, a hard brake. Survival instinct overwhelming all sense of reason or rationality, the woman leaped out of her vehicle while it was still moving.

The car rolled, gaining momentum, and crashed into a parked car.

Colt and Ikeda closed on the sedan, pistols aimed at the vehicle's rear window.

Colt approached from the driver's side, so he saw the result first.

The rear driver's-side window was covered in blood. He opened the door while Ikeda covered. Stager, slumped against the door, fell to the street when Colt opened it.

He was dead. Headshot.

Shoulders heaving and legs quickly turning to rubber, Colt sank to the street.

"That," he said between heavy breaths. "Was a hell of a shot."

"You running across the street like that slowed her down just enough that I could do it clean."

Ikeda's two team members screeched onto the street a minute or two later in the van.

When they got out of the van, Tony said, "You missed the good stuff."

They didn't have long to inspect Stager's remote-controlled sniper rifle. The police arrived on scene quickly, confirming Colt's suspicion that they wouldn't have time to disassemble the weapon and take it back to Langley for a detailed analysis. Alverez's video would have to suffice.

The remote-controlled sniper rifle was an ingenious design. The weapon housing was a rectangular box sitting on a squat, gyro-stabilized tripod with articulated legs. These could be folded up and stowed next to the box for easy transport. The box, designed to look like a video camera, housed the rifle and firing mechanism. A barrel extended from the front of the box with two smaller cylinders on either side of it, which they determined to be for sensing and targeting.

Stager had set the weapon up on the end of the battlement where it connected with an adjoining wall, a location that would not see much foot traffic. He'd placed caution tape around it as an additional measure to keep tourists out, but at a casual glance, it was a convincing camera.

It reminded Colt of the device the Russian SVR used to assassinate their officer and his agent, Svetlana, in a San Francisco park.

They watched Ava get loaded into an ambulance from a safe distance via the micro drone and then disappeared into the city.

Ava, who spoke fluent Greek and had a diplomatic passport, told the authorities that she was here as part of a trade mission. She didn't know who attacked her but assumed it was an assassination attempt.

Mossad quietly extracted her from the hospital the next day, once she was stabilized enough for travel, and returned her to Tel Aviv.

Colt and the Ground Branch team were back in Athens that night and went straight to the airport, where the Agency aircraft waited.

There hadn't been time to do anything with Bastian Stager's body. Too many people saw the gunfight. They didn't want to risk putting Stager's corpse in their van and then getting pulled over by Kavala police before they could dispose of it. Colt figured they would have a hard time identifying it, however. At least he was off the board.

Samantha Klein was another story.

The Israeli government would claim her body, and she'd be returned. They would handle any misdirection necessary with Greek officials to keep this quiet. CIA's hand would remain undisclosed.

With Klein dead, they lost any connection to Archon or hope of uncovering any more cyberattacks before they happened. Worse, that was the last option before open war.

Well, maybe there was one last thing to try.

Colt used the aircraft's secure SATCOM link to contact Langley.

21

Geneva, Switzerland

Nadia no-showed to work that day, claiming illness.

She'd been working since before dawn. Nadia couldn't sleep, like that was "news" at this point, but the alert on her COVCOM woke her out of a light, fitful sleep. A two-line message from Langley.

TORRENT KIA
NEED INFO IMMED. HIGHEST PRI.
TORRENT KIA...

They got Samantha Klein. Like, *got* her. Nadia thought they were supposed to capture that bitch.

Rot in hell.

Nadia knew she should feel relief at that; the internal pressure was off her. Except she didn't. Instead, she felt like the only thing standing between her government launching an ICBM into Moscow was whatever she could dig up, right now.

Okay, she allowed, as her fingers hammered the keys, nukes were a stretch. But there *would* be a war if she couldn't do something.

But Washington needed something tangible, something that linked Hawkinson and Archon with the cyberattacks. She'd given them reams of intel on that son of a bitch already, but none of it damning, none of it enough to call off a war.

LONGBOW gave her access to troves of information on Hawkinson's dealings, it showed them everything he did and who he talked to—except for a small number of encrypted comms tools he used that deleted messages after sending. Unless she was watching them when they were sent, she'd have no record.

LONGBOW had a secondary function, though. It contained a limited-use, expert system designed for one purpose—to brute force its way into nearly any existing security protocol. It bombarded the defenses with continual attacks at machine speed, the digital equivalent to the speed of light, and because LONGBOW was already inside that system, prevented it from registering the attack to any intrusion detection software and shutting itself down or alerting its human operators. It just pounded the defenses until it found a way through.

NTCU said they were holding that one in reserve.

Probably for when they needed to take Hawkinson or Archon down in one shot. Take them offline before they could attack again.

If they want to fire me for this, fine, she told herself. She was out of ideas, out of options, and out of time.

Nadia nicknamed the thing "piledriver," though it was closer to a police's battering ram.

She'd tethered her Agency-issued "personal" laptop to the phone with LONGBOW, so she wasn't forced to try this on a small screen. The phone's MAC address, its digital identity, was obfuscated from any external scans; it would just look like a black hole in cyberspace. She'd be safe from even Hawkinson's Eye of Sauron security suite.

The first thing she did was use the piledriver to break into the Hawk-Tech bioscience division's private server.

HawkTech was completely closed off from the public internet, unless Verona—the AI that ran HawkTech's security system—authorized a port. When it did, such as a developer wanting to reference an open-source code repository, those communications were logged and monitored. LONGBOW was designed on the premise that Guy Hawkinson would ignore his own security directives and would never be disconnected from his network.

LONGBOW tunneled into *his* phone and, from there, created a secure portal into the company.

Piledriver was through in seconds.

"Damn," she said. This thing was *fast*. Nadia pored through files as quickly as she could, scanning and dismissing anything irrelevant. Thankfully, the block on conducting rapid, clandestine information searches under incredible, world-ending pressure was one of the classes she actually *had* taken at the Farm.

"Oh, this is interesting," Nadia said. Months ago, she'd talked Tyler Gales into giving her a tour of the lab. He disappeared to help a colleague with something and left his workstation open. Nadia scanned his files and found a list of names the lab called a "client repo." She memorized the names and passed them to Chuck Harmon. NTCU later confirmed each of them were Trinity members. It was a target list.

What she found here wasn't that, exactly.

It was digital transfer records.

Files that the biolab transmitted to a private research institution in...

"Argentina," she said. Nadia copied the name of the firm for her report but also copied the files themselves to her local machine.

She opened a different browser and searched the name of the lab.

Nothing.

Nadia used several search engines to see if they would render different results, but each search produced the same...nothing.

Nadia noted that for her report also, with a recommendation that the Argentina desk investigate this lab.

She opened her COVCOM and prepared a message for Colt, summarizing everything she'd just found. His last message was still there.

NEED INFO IMMED. HIGHEST PRI.

Nadia turned back to her laptop. She used a message with a link to an internal document from HawkTech B.A.'s ops lead, Carlos Aguirre, to access their file directory. Hours dissolved as Nadia scoured the Argentine office's files. Calls and texts on her phone went ignored.

Nadia focused her search on Aguirre. Knowing how Hawkinson compartmentalized, he would delegate work to a trusted lieutenant and no one else. If there was information to find, Aguirre's digital fingerprints would be on it.

It was the IP address that tipped her off.

She found one embedded in a file log that Aguirre created that used a different IP numbering scheme from what HawkTech B.A. used. She followed it and found a heavily secured firewall. Piledriver made short work of that.

This new file store was on a server outside HawkTech. She checked the server's security access controls. There were no user names, just alphanumeric identifiers. This looked like it was little more than a file repository. She found text files with lists of IP addresses and a collection of executable files. Nadia opened those. Everything was written in Cyrillic.

Nadia attempted to trace the IP addresses, but they just reported as virtual boxes on a cloud somewhere. She couldn't do much with it here, but NTCU could.

"This is...," she started to say, "this is it."

Attack files, written in the Cyrillic script a Russian hacker would use, stored on a server linked to HawkTech B.A.

She quickly copied everything over to her machine, compressed and encrypted it, and fired it to Colt via her COVCOM. She grabbed her phone. It would be early there, but he needed to see this. Right now.

"This is a bad idea," Thorpe said as they walked into the holding facility.

"Well, considering it's the only idea left on the table," Ford said dryly, "it doesn't particularly matter if it's good *or* bad."

Ford didn't necessarily disagree with Thorpe's assessment, but they were out of better options, and if they didn't try something bold, something drastic, the situation was going to get a whole lot worse. Basically, no one had the patience for CIA and NTCU to prove that this situation was the work of a murky, global cabal of technocrats. Ford himself wasn't totally certain. He'd seen what Archon could do, but, hell, he didn't *know*.

"For this to even work, Colt is going to have to run him in the field. You really think he can set his feelings aside? You two hunted him for months, and he almost got one of our people killed."

"I remember, Will," Ford said testily. "If I can set the bullet wound aside for the greater good, I'm sure young McShane can shelve any personal animosity. Besides, as you've already said, this is *his* bad idea. It's on him to make it work."

"I'll do the talking," Ford said. "I have practice."

Ford and Thorpe's history was long and checkered. They were once close friends, working out of the US Embassy in Beijing. Ford, the deputy chief of the CIA station and Thorpe the FBI's legal attaché. Then, an asset Ford ran was caught up in a counterintelligence case. Thorpe pushed him to get information, and that got him killed. Thorpe accused Ford of being sloppy. Ford got his tour curtailed, and he was sent home; his CIA career would've been over had it not been for Wilcox's intervention.

The hilarious irony of bureaucratic capriciousness brought them together at NTCU.

Since then, there'd been a thawing. Thorpe recognized Ford was a natural field operative and a damn good, if not unorthodox, spook. Ford acknowledged Thorpe was, for better or worse, a good cop.

They'd never be friends again, but they could at least be in the same room without coming to blows.

Liu sat at the table with a disinterested look on his face.

Ford did not introduce himself.

"My colleague would have liked to have been here himself, but I'm sure you understand. You and I met once," Ford said.

"Is that right?"

"Sort of. I was the guy Denney shot last summer when we tried to arrest you."

Liu's expression darkened. "A regrettable incident."

"Which part?" Ford asked. Thorpe cleared his throat. "When last he met with you, my colleague told you Guy Hawkinson was part of an organization, not quite terrorists, but I suppose that's a reasonable approximation."

"Yes, I found it a little fantastical, but not entirely surprising," Liu said.

"We think this group was responsible for cyberattacks against our country and that they are trying to frame the Russians for it. We also believe they are targeting China but using Hawkinson's corporate activities as their way in."

His mouth twitched into a bemused expression, not quite a smile. "Yes, he told me this," Liu said in a voice that sounded tired and bored.

"We'd like you to work for us. If you agree to help us prove whether this organization is responsible for the cyberattacks, our government will drop the murder charge against you. Once you complete the operation, we'll arrange for your wife to be quietly released from prison and transported to a location outside the United States."

"What happens to me?"

Thorpe ignored the question. "Your espionage with Admiral Denney brought America and China closer to war than anything since the Taiwan Strait Crisis of '54. You can help dial that back a notch by keeping us apprised of current affairs. More importantly, you can help us make sure that this group doesn't try to exploit tensions between our countries and push us into a fight. That only gets bad and gets there fast."

"I'm not going to spy on my country," Liu said.

"Mr. Liu," Thorpe said calmly. "This is an offer that will only be made once. When we leave here today, everything is off the table for good. We're only talking to you now because we think it's the one good chance we have to stop a war."

"What do you think, chief?" Ford said.

"I will ask you the same question I asked Mr. McShane," Liu said. He looked Ford in the eyes. "I know you, Mr. Ford. My service has detailed files on the CIA officers who served in my country. I know your reputation. As one player of the game to another, is Guy Hawkinson as dangerous as you say? This is not hyperbole?"

"He is. These people are serious, and they are very, very good at what they do. Worse, no one believes a group like this could exist, so they can hide in plain sight. Honestly, these people keep me up at night."

Liu was quiet.

Then he said, "What do you need me to do?"

Nadia used LONGBOW to get access to HawkTech B.A., but NTCU's cyber operators couldn't use that to inject any code into Hawkinson's network. They needed a direct connection, not one daisy-chained through a smartphone.

"You haven't earned that trust yet. First, you tell me whether you think you can convince Hawkinson to let you tour his facility in Buenos Aires in the next few days."

"I can," Liu said.

"Okay," Ford said. "Let's start with that."

In his long years of turning people into spies, Fred Ford developed a working knowledge of human psychology few could rival. Leaving that holding facility that cool fall afternoon, Ford couldn't shake the notion that he was being told what he wanted to hear.

22

A day after recruiting Liu Che to spy for the Central Intelligence Agency, Fred Ford flew to Boston to stop an innocent man from getting killed.

I'm getting too old for this shit, Fred Ford thought.

Ford wasn't supposed to be in the field. Not that Boston was Bamako, Karachi, or Beijing or any of the other myriad places where Ford risked his life over the last twenty-five years. Still, he was only eight months or so removed from getting shot. He'd recovered well enough, still had some PT, but the promise he'd made with his wife and the agreement he'd struck with Thorpe was that he would never go into the field again.

Ford couldn't quit *now*, and Hillary knew that. But they'd agreed he would stay out of the field. She didn't know his specific role in the Agency, but she could read a newspaper and knew that Fred Ford wouldn't quit with his nation on the brink of war. And there was no shortage of work to be done. He could only imagine what went through her head when he told her he had to take a trip. Ford told her it would be a short one and he wasn't leaving the country, but his was the profession of lies, and God only knew what she believed.

It wasn't a broken promise, but he was bending the shit out of it.

Archon's last assassination was a killer drone. Ford had no way of knowing what was up their sleeve now.

The man they were here to protect was Dr. Seb Kerensky. Kerensky was a professor emeritus of MIT's Schwarzman College of Computing and former Associate Director for Artificial Intelligence. Dr. Kerensky now headed MIT's Lincoln Labs, a Federally Funded Research and Development Corporation (FFRDC), a kind of advanced technology think tank designed to solve some of the Defense Department's most challenging problems. He also worked with the MIT/Department of the Air Force AI technology accelerator.

Kerensky's name was on the list of targets Nadia smuggled out of Hawkinson's office earlier that year, and he was a member of Trinity. Of their membership, he was the one most directly connected to pure research into Artificial General Intelligence and was believed to be the one most likely to achieve a breakthrough.

As Archon's ideological counterpoint, Dr. Kerensky advocated strongly that AI in general and AGI specifically could be brought to bear on society's toughest challenges—hunger, poverty, education, space exploration, clean energy, the environment. But Kerensky argued that AGI was not the destination but rather a tool to help mankind, *all* mankind, on its journey to better things.

Kerensky was a Russian immigrant. His parents, both physicists, fled the Soviet Union in the 1950s after the government co-opted them into the Kremlin's hydrogen bomb program. Kerensky knew, perhaps better than anyone else in Trinity, the dangers of a despotic government possessing advanced technology. He pursued Trinity's goals with a zeal unmatched in the organization.

NTCU considered him a hard target, or at least a *harder* target because Lincoln Labs was located on Hanscom Air Force Base. Though that only covered him ten to twelve hours out of the day. Kerensky's commute home to nearby Lexington was through wooded back roads. He lived in a modest home with his wife, their kids long since moved out on their own.

The unit assumed any commercial communication—cell phone, email, even apps—was compromised. Though NTCU could message Dr. Kerensky through any of the DoD's classified email systems, that would create an electronic record of the message, and the potential for insider threat was too great to risk. To say nothing of the fact that a message consisting of, "Dr. Kerensky, we're a government agency you've likely never heard of and we believe your life is in danger" wouldn't be received well.

Instead, Wilcox spoke with the professor directly and told him of the Archon plot. He connected Kerensky with NTCU via Trinity's web-based onion router secured by a quantum encryption key.

To his credit, Kerensky was not surprised.

According to Wilcox, the organization took Alana Howe's murder hard.

Maybe this will wake them the hell up, Ford mused.

He didn't put the same stock in this group as Colt seemed to. But then, that kid was an idealist. Ford just hoped that he didn't grant them too much trust. Ava Klein seemed to be swayed by them, and she had a strong hold on young McShane. If she pressed, Ford wasn't sure which way Colt would go.

Ford didn't trust Trinity because they weren't accountable to anything but their own ideals.

Trinity would act in their own self-interest, guided by whatever inscrutable moral compass they possessed.

All Ford could do was hope that it aligned with the Agency's.

Ford had vague notions of what AGI could do and why Archon shouldn't be first to it, but was Trinity better? What did they really know about them?

Still, he trusted Wilcox, and that would have to be enough.

Nine names remained on the Archon target list. Wilcox communicated with each of them. They had no specific intelligence suggesting when or even if Archon would make an attempt. However, when considering the level of tension and instability in the world, it seemed like the opportune moment.

Once they'd established secure communication with Dr. Kerensky, Ford had the NTCU techs use CERBERUS to analyze Kerensky's electronic messages, his personal and business calendars, and his (minor) social media presence to look for anomalies. They even interrogated his utility companies to see if there were scheduled maintenances in or around the professor's home. CERBERUS was tied into nearly every computer network in the federal government, but it could also penetrate commercial systems that had previously granted NSA access for FISA-authorized monitoring.

CERBERUS looked for patterns, sifted through billions of discrete data-points, and made connections. Human analysts would need *years* to produce the results CERBERUS could render in hours.

They found the anomaly.

Dr. Kerensky had a meeting on his calendar to have drinks with MIT's new Associate Director for AI and Data Science. The message came from the AD's assistant's email, which he trusted, and when Kerensky called to confirm, she answered.

As a test, NTCU had Dr. Kerensky call to reconfirm the day of the appointment, but from a different phone. They gave him a Tracfone, fresh out of the package. The AD's assistant said the director did have an hour blocked off to meet Kerensky at the Harvard Club, but she didn't recall setting it. She also didn't recall speaking with Dr. Kerensky. She'd worked in the department for twenty years and had been Dr. Kerensky's assistant at one point, so she would remember a conversation with her old boss. The assistant called back thirty minutes later saying she'd checked with the AD, and he did not schedule the meeting himself.

NTCU surmised Archon placed the appointment on his calendar and intercepted Dr. Kerensky's original phone call to confirm, using a deepfake to impersonate the secretary's voice.

They now had two likely attack vectors.

One: a method similar to how they'd assassinated Alana Howe, which was a suicide drone packed with high explosive.

Two: their bioweapon.

Dr. Kerensky admitted to having given a DNA sample to a private genetics company. His father died of Alzheimer's disease, and the professor wanted to aid the scientific efforts for early detection. Thanks to Nadia's intel, they knew the lab Kerensky used was one of the ones Hawkinson hacked. Ford was glad Wilcox was the one that broke it to the prof.

As long as Archon existed, Dr. Kerensky would never be safe.

He seemed strangely at peace with it.

What happened next? Pattern matching.

"What's happening now?" Dr. Kerensky asked. He sipped tea from a small porcelain cup in his study.

"Right about now," Ford looked down at his watch, "Special Agents Mary Cosgrove and Brent Rowe are arresting one Todd Thackeray for attempted murder," Ford said. "Thackeray, whose real name is Gregory Duval, was looking at twenty years in prison for hacking the IRS. Based on the communications we intercepted, someone promised him fifty thousand dollars and a new identity if he slipped something into your drink."

"Ironic they'd try to use xenobots on me. They were developed here, at MIT."

Even though (or especially because, as far as Ford was concerned) the professor was a member of Trinity and had among the highest clearances the US government would grant, they couldn't tell him exactly how they'd figured out the plot. He hoped Wilcox hadn't either. If word of CERBERUS's existence ever got into the public domain, it would create a shitstorm of such epic proportions that it might just set the Agency back to the gutting that followed the Church Committee.

Taken out of the proper context, CERBERUS would appear to be a surveillance tool that would make ECHELON look like a nosy neighbor in comparison.

Once they knew the meeting was scheduled for the Harvard Club, an exclusive, members-only organization for university alumni and employees, NTCU used CERBERUS to investigate the employees, the delivery companies, and the service providers the club used.

They found Todd Thackeray and zeroed in on him because the young man had only been hired in the last two weeks. Strangely, upon questioning by the FBI, Harvard Club staff didn't recall interviewing the young man; everyone questioned only remembered being told by someone else that he'd been hired.

Thackeray, or rather, Duval, was a decent but troubled kid by all accounts. He was socially isolated, unpopular at school, and had a home life that wasn't much better, so he retreated to the digital world.

Archon grabbed a kid in need, twisted him and made him do something terrible with the promise of a new life.

He wouldn't know who recruited him, wouldn't know what the objective was or who or what he was serving. The kid wouldn't know what he was doing. Surely, they didn't tell him it was murder.

Ford stayed with the professor while a NTCU tech team swept the house and their cars for electronic surveillance or any evidence of a backup plan, should Thackeray have failed. They wouldn't find anything, though, not if Archon could insert themselves into the guy's cell phone traffic. Having a clean phone wouldn't matter if you couldn't trust the network itself.

Ford's phone buzzed.

"Whatcha got?"

"We got him," Special Agent Cosgrove said.

"How is he?"

"Scared shitless," she said evenly. "And very confused."

"Okay. We'll wrap up here."

"What now?" Dr. Kerensky asked.

"You and your wife are safe, for now. As for what's next? I'm sorry, Dr. Kerensky, I can't really say."

"You can't because you're not allowed?"

"I can't because I don't *know*. With your permission, we can conduct digital overwatch over your devices and your home network. If you have a privacy concern, which would be understandable—"

"I was five when my parents fled Soviet Russia. I harbor no illusions about privacy."

"Right, well. You know Archon better than me. I suspect you probably know many of the players. We'd like to debrief you, if you're willing."

"I am."

"All right. I'll set it up."

Could they have uncovered this plot, each of those threads, without CERBERUS? Ford didn't think so. Thackeray, yeah. The Feebs, Agency slang for the FBI, would've pulled that apart, but without the AI, would they have even known where to look? Or the calendar invite?

Ford told Dr. Kerensky he would be in touch and left Lexington. He'd let the Feebs handle Thackeray, wasn't much he could do there. Tech guys were wrapped up and heading back, but they had to drive. Some of the gear in their toolbox they didn't want to let out of their sight, even on an airplane. Ford would be home for a late dinner.

Ford came up in a different world, a human one. He recruited sources, convinced them to betray their governments and give him their secrets. In the nineties, the Clinton people slashed the Directorate of Operations. Satellites and drones could see everything people could—and more, even. Let's get out of the shadows, they said, we're better than this.

Except we aren't. Not if we want the knowledge that the shadows contain.

Bad things happen when we lose the ability to shine daylight on them.

There are no benevolent surprises in intelligence.

People would say, now, just as they did then, that machines can do the work of a human spy. We don't need spooks anymore. Computers could do it.

Maybe this time they were right. Ford didn't know. Probably, it was a little both. He admitted the incongruity of his thoughts.

This was a bad new world, and Ford didn't like it, didn't think he was cut out to operate in it anymore.

In 1984, the Irish Republican Army tried to assassinate Margaret Thatcher by planting a bomb in her Brighton hotel. Thatcher survived the attempt, and after, the IRA released a statement saying, "You have to be lucky all the time. We only have to be lucky once." This felt a lot like that.

Now they faced enemies who were members of friendly governments, if not their own. Their bases of operations were companies and nonprofits, but these were people who could just as easily manipulate evidence with computers to throw law enforcement off track. Christ, they'd impersonated the president of the United States.

Something else bothered him.

Archon had assassinated one Trinity member already and just made an attempt on a second. All this while trying to spark a war between the United States and Russia. What else were they planning while all eyes were watching whether Moscow or Washington would flinch?

23

Geneva, Switzerland

The US Air Force deployed fighters at forward bases in Romania, Poland, and Estonia in movements the service called agile combat employments within hours of Washington declaring DEFCON 2. US F-15s, F-16s, and F-35s as well as other NATO aircraft were now flying Combat Air Patrol (CAP) along the Russian border, with the F-35s providing airborne command and control for the other fighters. The amphibious assault ship USS *Kearsage*, flanked by the destroyers *Donald Cook* and *Forrest Sherman* and already deployed for BALTOPS, shored up the northern quadrant.

Europe was on the edge of panic.

Certainly, things had not been this tense since the end of the Cold War. But even in those nervous and knife-edged days, there was always the hint of stability, the belief that it would never go too far. Except for the exercise ABLE ARCHER 83, when the Soviets mistook a massive NATO wargame for pre-war mobilization and nearly responded in kind, the continent rarely *genuinely* feared for their safety.

Those days were over.

Since the Cold War ended, a president had only declared DEFCON 2 once, briefly, at the start of Operation DESERT STORM. Even on 9/11, the posture only increased the posture to 3.

Layered above that, Europe faced their own energy shortage now that the Russians cut off their traditional natural gas supply. As in the United States, many Europeans worried how they would heat their homes this winter. It wasn't as if relief would be coming from America now. Global instability had been driving markets down for the last year, with Europe bearing the brunt. With the threat of total war, economies reacted as one might expect. Markets crashed.

Nadia received an emergency message from Colt that morning on her COVCOM. She needed to get access to Hawkinson's operation in Argentina immediately to prove whether Archon used that as a staging ground for the cyberattacks against the United States. If not, America could be at war within days.

So, no pressure.

Worse, that asshole Liu knew who she was.

The cable two days ago shocked her to the bone.

Colt *recruited* Liu, and Langley was putting him back in play. They wanted him to get to Buenos Aires, thinking Hawkinson would show Liu his cards. She'd already found evidence of hacks, written in Cyrillic, on servers connected to HawkTech B.A. That was a springboard, but Langley needed to get access to those servers, and they couldn't do it daisy-chaining a hack from Nadia's smartphone.

The mission was now to get Liu to Argentina and buy him as much time as she could.

Nadia was five minutes late to her meeting with Hawkinson and Liu that morning.

Liu messaged Hawkinson as soon as he was out of federal custody, said he'd been held up in Beijing on an urgent matter but was returning to Geneva and wanted to resume their negotiation immediately.

Visibly flustered, she entered the sixth-floor conference room juggling her things and trying to slip out of her jacket. "Sorry I'm late," she said, sheepish, and tried not to meet Guy's stare. Punctuality was a virtue, tardiness a sin, on the order of treason. It was one of the few things he lectured people about.

"Take your time," Hawkinson said casually. "I imagine you were concerned about your sister."

Hawkinson and Matt Kirby sat on one side of the long table, Liu on the other. Liu was alone. Unlike his last visit, where he'd traveled with a staff who were, presumably, also intelligence officers. Ditching them was a smart move, and she was reminded of his tradecraft. Nadia wondered how Liu explained his absence to his service while incarcerated.

"We can talk about that later," she said, staring at the back of Liu's head.

"Yes, of course," Guy said.

She nodded and took a place several down from Liu. Guy instructed her once to never have too many HawkTech employees on one side of the table, as it made the other party feel isolated.

The conversation at the table continued.

"As I was saying," Liu said. "My country is investing heavily in South America, and we have many partnerships."

Yeah, Nadia noted ruefully. Technology wasn't the only thing PRC exported. They were also helping several dictators run more efficient autocracies. The Central Committee had exported "governmental advisors" to numerous countries, including those in South America, to help them centralize their governments, improve surveillance, and exact greater control over their populaces.

"The Americans have neglected this region for so long," Liu said. "We see strategic value in filling that gap with a helping hand. There are also resources there that local economies would benefit from but are largely incapable of utilizing. I am intrigued by your investment in Argentina. This is forward thinking."

"It's a natural fit for us," Guy said. "They have one of the most educated, tech-savvy populations in the region, if not the world. Many tech companies have set up shop there."

"But most of those are simply to take advantage of technical talent. You have made real investment."

"That's true," Guy allowed. "We've invested in some advanced technology, replicating our existing quantum lab here, though on a slightly smaller scale, and a supercomputing array. It gives us an opportunity to try new lines of business."

"That's a lot of power," Liu said.

Nadia watched Guy's eyes flick to her. "It is," he said and said nothing further.

After a moment of silence, as if realizing Guy would not discuss Argentina further, Liu began describing Zhongguancun, the innovation hub outside Beijing that was often likened to China's Silicon Valley. "It would only be proper for me to extend the invitation to you to visit some of our most advanced research centers, to pay you back for your considerable hospitality. Particularly if we are to journey to Argentina together."

The bastard was good, Nadia thought. She had to give him that.

"We would enjoy and appreciate that," Hawkinson said.

Guy and Liu framed a research partnership in broad strokes. Liu suggested several HawkTech products that his government was particularly interested in—the open-source AI and their secure voting tech. Nadia made a note of both of those for her report. Langley would be interested in that. Hawkinson and Liu agreed to a tour of HawkTech B.A. soon, within the next few weeks.

That's not good enough, Nadia wanted to shout. They needed to go *now*. But how to move that along?

Just before they wrapped for the day, Guy asked Nadia if he could have the room. Nadia excused herself and left. She found Guy's executive assistant, Tina, at her desk and chatted her up, keeping a sideways eye on the conversation.

Ten minutes later, Liu, Guy, and Kirby emerged from the conference room. Nadia offered to take Liu to the lobby.

Neither spoke in the elevator.

Maybe if secrets remain unsaid, they stay that way.

The elevator dinged, and the door opened to the lobby. Liu stepped out, and as he did, he accidentally brushed her.

"My apologies," he said smoothly. "These European elevators are so small."

"Have a good day," she said. "Watch the sidewalks. They're a little wet."

"I shall. Thank you."

The elevator door closed, and Nadia noticed something in her hand. She rolled it over, a folded piece of paper.

The son of a bitch brush-passed her and she didn't even know it.

She was so focused on *him*, on avoiding saying *anything*, she didn't notice him putting something in her hand. The fingers just reacted to something touching them and closed around it.

Nadia thumbed her floor and put the paper in her pocket.

This building had eyes everywhere.

So, she went to the one place that didn't.

Nadia closed the bathroom stall door behind her and unfolded the paper.

Chat Noir, 8:30, upstairs

She knew the place. It was a bar in the Carouge neighborhood about two and a half miles from the office—far in the way cities measured distance—that specialized in live music.

It was a good place for a meeting.

Loud, crowded, and upstairs there would be no sight lines to the street.

The music program usually featured jazz acts during the week, which would be less popular with HawkTech's mostly younger talent pool.

So much for keeping secrets.

Nadia had to hand it to him, again. Liu knew his shit.

Nadia arrived at twenty after eight. She took two separate cabs to get here, the last of which she had drop her a mile away and then walked a circuitous path of double-backs to check her six. She'd already verified that she was clear of electronic surveillance devices on her person. Guy was back at his apartment. Or, at least his phone was. Not that he'd be doing the following, that would be Kirby, if anyone. According to their text exchange, Kirby was also back at his own apartment.

Nadia went to the bar and ordered a drink. She didn't even know what it was, it was red-orange in color with a large slice hugging the rim of the glass. She paid cash. Nadia walked up to the club's second floor. A three-piece huddled on the small stage under a purple spotlight: a small drum kit, stand-up bass, and a trumpet.

"You're early," a voice purred from behind her ear.

Nadia turned.

Liu was there in a suit with a glass of whiskey. "Come," he said. He led her to a corner of the room where they could see the stairs. It was crowded, but not so much that they were packed in with people standing over them.

"After Guy asked you to leave, he spoke candidly. Your people's intuition regarding Argentina are correct," Liu said. "There is certainly operational activity there."

"What kind," Nadia said. *I guess we're doing this.*

"He did not say exactly, but he left several hints. He intimated a way to resolve what he termed our 'mutual concern.' He wants to show me what he calls, 'technology demonstrators.' Please tell your people that we will be making a tour of the facility in the next few weeks."

"Why don't you tell them yourself?"

"I suspect you have...better communications tools at your disposal. I do not trust what they provided me."

"A few weeks isn't good enough," Nadia said.

Liu spread his hands in a gesture of mea culpa.

"You have to do better than that."

"How?" Liu asked.

"Figure it out," Nadia said. It was nice to be on the sending end of nebulous objectives.

"Did he say what these 'technology demonstrators' were?"

"No. Just that they were a new growth area for his company and that my ministry would be quite interested in them."

"Is he looking for money?"

"Among other things."

Nadia hadn't expected Hawkinson to admit to attacking the US outright, but she'd hoped for more than this.

"Try to find out which area of mutual concern he's talking about," Nadia said brusquely. "We need specifics."

Liu looked bemused. "I doubt very much he will be so obvious. At least, not until we're in South America."

Nadia felt her face flush. She should have known that.

"Right. Well, that's what we need to know. See what you can find out," she said. "Anything else?"

Liu raised an eyebrow and smiled slightly. He took a drink and considered her a moment.

"I believe that's everything."

"This trip needs to happen within the next few days. Tell him your government is anxious to start."

"Hawkinson is savvy. He will know that nothing in my country moves that quickly."

"Then tell him it'll mean a big promotion for you to bring this deal in. He'll read that as getting more access or being closer to decision-makers. Either way, you need to figure out how to get him to agree to a tour in Buenos Aires in the next couple days."

"I'll see what I can do," Liu said flatly.

Nadia had to buy Liu time to get to South America. She'd told him how vital it was that he get to Argentina as fast as possible, but it still wouldn't happen overnight. They assumed Archon was getting ready to launch another attack, and Nadia needed to shift their focus to something else until Liu was in position.

How do you make days when hours were scarce?

Nadia could think of only one thing. Give them a rabbit to chase.

She checked her watch. It was nearly nine.

Nadia left the bar and found a cab. Instead of taking her home, she had him drop her at Gales's apartment. Nadia didn't text him. While they couldn't have their phones in the building, HawkTech did have a chat client that employees used on their phones, something developed in-house because Guy said that was the most secure. It occurred to her now that was the perfect in for them to have their security system, Verona, snooping on the staff.

Nadia got out of the cab and walked up to Gales's building, hit the buzzer on the door. Like her, he lived in Geneva's Old Town. The buildings were mostly between six and eight stories, with the red-brown tiled roofs typical of central Europe. And they were built so close together, often with little more than a narrow alley—if that—separating them from the neighboring one. There was little spacing on any given block. Old Town made her feel like she was navigating a puzzle.

In the daylight, it was a quaint, historical feeling.

Now, not so much.

"Yeah?" Tyler said through the speaker.

"Hey, it's Nadia. You busy?"

A long pause. "No, not really."

"Great, buzz me up, I'm freezing my ass off." There was another pause, he did, and Nadia entered the building, climbing up to Gales's third-floor apartment.

"What's up?" he said as he let her into his place.

Nadia quickly scanned for signs of someone else—keys on a table, coat, shoes. She could see straight through to the small dining room from the front door. There was a laptop open, a bottle of wine, and one glass, a quarter full. He was alone.

Nadia stepped in and closed the door behind her.

"Tyler, I need you to listen to me very carefully. You need to leave."

"Nadia, what the hell are you talking about? It's ten o'clock at night. I've got a demo tomorrow."

"No, you don't. You need to pack a bag, whatever you can carry, and you have to go. Now."

"Do you...know something I don't?"

Don't ask questions you don't want to know the answer to, she thought. Then she realized he was talking about her sister. Gales knew Nadia's sister was an Air Force intelligence officer. He was thinking about Russia.

"Guy Hawkinson isn't who you think he is. He's turned your work into some kind of a weapon. He's got an off-the-books research facility in Buenos Aires, and they figured out how to weaponize it. He's already used it to kill someone. They're using DNA to target it, which he's pulling from labs that they are hacking into."

"This is...there's no way that's happening." Gales looked behind him to something deeper in his apartment. "Look, this is pretty weird, Nadia. I think you should go."

Nadia pulled her phone out, and the quickness of the motion startled him. She opened LONGBOW, tunneled into HawkTech B.A., and then pulled up a file transfer record.

"Is this your xenobot data?" She turned the phone to face him. Nadia watched his eyes scan it, straining to see the small screen.

"Yes, but how are you on a work system on your phone?"

"Everything I just told you and *that's* what you're focusing on? Look at the file path."

He did. "This looks like a different directory structure."

"That's because it's not here in Geneva. This is in Buenos Aires. Hawkinson is having other scientists finish your work, then weaponize it. The man they used it on, they had the xenobots swarm his arteries and cause a heart attack. Only, they did it before it was ready, and apparently it got his kids too."

"How do you know all this?"

"Again, you're focusing on the wrong part of this story."

"Jesus Christ." Gales sank back into his apartment. Nadia guided him to the couch. She walked back over to the table, refilled his wineglass, and gave it to him.

"This will help," she said. Gales took a deep drink. "American authorities are onto him. You need to leave now or you'll be arrested as an accomplice."

"Accomplice? I didn't goddamn *do* anything! I...just...I just created. I didn't do anything wrong. I didn't—"

"Tyler, it doesn't matter. If you are caught with him, they'll think you're involved."

Gales looked up at her with pleading, anxious eyes. His entire world was crashing around him.

"There's an overnight train to Paris that leaves in just over an hour. That's plenty of time to get packed. You're going to ride to Paris and then take a direct flight to Dulles. I will have friends meet you. They will take you somewhere safe. Tell them what you know, tell them everything."

"Who are these friends?"

"They'll be with the FBI."

"Oh shit oh shit oh shit oh shit." Gales kept repeating that, a panic mantra.

He needed to get moving, he needed something to concentrate on. Nadia pulled him to a stand and walked him into his bedroom. She instructed him to pack, but pack lightly. Assume he wasn't coming back here, take what he couldn't replace.

When Gales had a bag together, Nadia closed up his laptop and handed it to him. He numbly put it in the appropriate slot in his travel ruck.

"Why are you doing this?" he asked.

"I don't want to see anything bad happen to you," Nadia told him. "You don't deserve it."

She got him into a jacket, and they went back out to the street. Nadia flagged a cab. It took a few minutes, but there were enough of them out, even late on a weeknight. They rode to the train station, just two miles away.

"This is really important," she said. "Assume Hawkinson can look at your phone."

"How?"

"HawkChat," she said.

Gales swore, so obvious now.

"Don't tell *anyone* you're leaving. Is your credit card loaded on your phone?"

He said it was.

"Use a different one to buy the train ticket and your flight home. Don't use that other card for anything. If it's on your phone, assume they can see the transactions. In fact, they can probably track you with it." Nadia held out her hand.

"I'm not giving you my phone," Gales said, incredulous.

"How far do you want to make it?" After a moment of some internal debate, Gales handed his phone over. Nadia walked with him to the ticket kiosk and watched him complete the transaction. They waited inside until it was time for him to board. "My friends will meet you at Dulles."

"How will they know?"

"That's what they do."

"Nadia...what are you?"

"Right now, I'm the only friend you have." Nadia leaned forward and kissed him.

She waited until the train departed to make sure he didn't get off.

Once Gales was away, Nadia returned to her apartment and fired up the laptop/LONGBOW tether. Then, she set about digitally framing Tyler Gales as a spy.

24

Washington, DC

Will Thorpe and Jason Wilcox sat in the National Security Advisor's office in the West Wing at a round mahogany table not far from the man's desk. An aide poured them both coffee from a carafe, which he set on the table next to a water pitcher.

"Gentlemen, will there be anything else?"

"No, thank you," Wilcox said, and the aide departed.

It was a large office. The National Security Advisor's desk sat in the center, flanked by two floor-to-ceiling windows. The ivory-colored curtains were drawn, allowing the gray morning light to accentuate an already dismal occasion.

They'd gotten a twelve-minute slot on Jamie Richter's schedule as he moved between crises.

The president was meeting with select cabinet members, the Director of Central Intelligence, and the Joint Chiefs. Thorpe wasn't cleared to know the subject of the meeting, but he could guess.

Hoskins was in that meeting as well, as a backbencher. One of the few places in Washington that the head of the National Clandestine Service would be relegated to a wall seat.

The office door opened, and an argument entered, followed by Richter and Hoskins.

"Jamie, you cannot seriously be considering this," Hoskins said.

This meeting was an odd grouping, the kind of weird political alchemy that only Washington could produce. Jason Wilcox was the last DNCS, forced out of the role largely due to Senator Preston Hawkinson's demand for accountability following a perceived intelligence failure. The CIA Director tapped Dwight Hoskins to replace Wilcox. Hoskins was seen as a safe bet, a headquarters mainstay with tours on the Office of the Director of National Intelligence staff and having run the national counterproliferation fusion center. His appointment was as much to mollify the sharks surrounding the Agency as it was to fill the vacancy. Hoskins wasn't well loved within the clandestine service. He hadn't seen the field in fifteen years.

Wilcox was here because he'd led the Agency's initial hunt for the mysterious entity known as Archon and their suspected ties to the Hawkinson family. Though forced into an early retirement, Wilcox now contracted with the Agency, providing the kind of expert counsel that only someone with his experience could. Thorpe suspected there was another reason. The CIA Director wasn't a spook himself, but he was also no fool. He knew what he was getting when he elevated Hoskins. Having Wilcox as an advisor checked some of Hoskins's more political instincts, pushed him to consider riskier options. Wilcox was no longer cleared for all of the intelligence he had access to as DNCS, but he was granted access to anything pertaining to Archon and select other operations he had expertise on.

"What do you want me to say?" Richter pleaded, voice tired and hoarse. Weary eyes tracked across the office to where Thorpe and Wilcox sat. "Gentlemen, I'm sorry that we're late. Please don't get up." Another aide followed Richter in with a folded piece of paper, presumably the latest iteration of a constantly evolving schedule. He gave some instructions in a voice too low for Thorpe to hear and asked for them to have the room. Richter sat at the table, then Hoskins joined. "I'm afraid I wasted your time in coming here," Richter said.

"Is this about the *Times*?" Wilcox asked.

That morning, the *New York Times*'s cybersecurity column broke a story attributing the pipeline attack to the same Russian military intelligence unit that took control of Folsom Dam. The columnist referenced a source with direct knowledge of the matter, speaking off the record because they weren't authorized to discuss it. Thorpe had his suspicions.

Leaking to the press was one of Washington's darker traditions, and in recent years it was as much a policy tool as a position paper or an official speech. There was a dedicated faction of the senior staff that did not believe the Agency's theory that a third party executed the two subsequent cyberattacks. Thorpe understood this. If he didn't see the intelligence every day, he wouldn't believe it either.

When they were here last, Lieutenant General Burgess, the National Security Agency Director, argued China's military intelligence cyber units attacked our air traffic control system. Hit an America still reeling from the Folsom Dam, her people scared. Colt shut that argument down in front of the president, and Burgess hadn't forgotten it.

When the next one hit, temporarily crippling America's fuel production and distribution, then subsequently attacking supply chain systems, the National Security Agency seemingly reversed course and focused all of their efforts on Russia. Thorpe believed Burgess, or one of his inner circle, was the leaker. Get their side into the media and turn it into the official version. What better source could confirm that the Russians did this than the nation's chief cyber operator?

"The president met with the Joint Chiefs and leaders of the intelligence community," Richter said, by way of introduction. Whatever his argument with Hoskins was, the National Security Advisor intended to leave it in the hallway. "General Burgess shared convincing intelligence that the GRU attacked our oil infrastructure and the supply chain system used by many of our retailers and distributors."

"Jamie, with all due respect, I have people in the field. Burgess does not."

"I understand that, but—"

"Do you? One of our officers, at considerable personal risk, found executable files matching the operating systems known to be in use by the GRU. The owners had a way to deploy them on a Russian military server. You know where those files were found? Argen-fucking-tina."

"But you admitted that it could've been anything."

"No, I said it appeared to be the attack vector for a third strike, but it clearly showed it was *not* the Russians."

"Haven't you been saying all along that any number of actors could use these events as a target of opportunity? We're saying the same thing here, Dwight."

"Goddamnit, we aren't—"

"Deputy Hoskins, if I may," Thorpe said. He feared these two would just keep circling their old points and they'd burn the eight minutes they had left. "Sir, my unit uncovered the intelligence Deputy Hoskins is referencing. Our analysts as well as our expert systems conclude the attacks are almost identical to the ATC and pipeline strikes. We have high confidence that they were indeed launched *from* Russian servers but not *by* the Russians themselves. The files were planted there."

The National Security Advisor shook his head. "I'm afraid that I have to side with General Burgess on this one. I just don't...I can't get there."

"Jamie," Wilcox said, voice even. "The threat landscape today is unlike anything we've ever seen before. We have to reorient our thinking. In many ways, it's a lot like the nineties when we didn't give terrorism any real credence. I've listened to your lectures on this," he said, smiling slightly. After positions with the State Department in previous administrations, Richter had returned to academia to teach foreign policy at Georgetown University before the president tapped him to be his National Security Advisor. "We didn't think terrorists could project power. We didn't take them seriously, and it cost us. We live in a world now where it isn't just nations or rogue states that we have to worry about. A single hacker could do a hell of a lot of damage. Non-state actors, individuals, even corporations can be a threat."

"The attacks we're talking about were found on a virtual server belonging to a 'research institute' in Buenos Aires," Thorpe said. "We're still trying to figure out exactly who and what they are. Right now, it looks like a Russian nesting doll of shell corporations. But that server address came from HawkTech's new Buenos Aires office. Guy Hawkinson's company."

Richter put his hands on the table. "Gentlemen, the president of the

United States is considering the most consequential military action since the Cold War, maybe even World War Two. We've never directly attacked the Russian Federation or the Soviet Union. This will have global implications."

"And what if you're wrong?" Hoskins challenged.

"They *did* attack us, Dwight. Folsom Dam was them. It's the only part of this you and the NSA do agree on. I will remind you, that attack took a hundred and fifteen lives and caused billions in damage. Even if they didn't do anything else, that alone necessitates a response. One we are long overdue for."

"We could take Moscow offline tomorrow," Hoskins said. "Respond in kind."

"In kind? The president is going to give the appropriate, proportional response, but one that visibly communicates America's resolve."

The subtext was that it would be an unmissable, physical show of strength for an embittered administration under incredible challenge.

It also brought into crystal focus for Thorpe how murky and dangerous this situation was.

The Russians had attacked America. Archon, if it was indeed them, used that as impetus for one or two strikes of their own and painted a convincing picture that the GRU was responsible for all three.

The president would have to respond to the first, but what about the other two?

If America struck back with its full force, it could very well signal the start of World War Three. If they did not, but could not convince the American people and their allies that another entity was responsible for the ATC and the fuel supply chain disruptions, the administration would look weak and incapable.

They were in an impossible position.

"Jason," Richter said after a long and tense silence. "You're the resident expert on this Archon group. That's why you're here." Archon had been mentioned in the President's Daily Brief, but the Hawkinson connection was not. Too many entities in Washington received the briefing packet, in addition to POTUS, including the Senate Intelligence Committee. "What's your assessment?"

"I agree with Dwight," he said. "This evidence shows capability, beyond the shadow of a doubt, that Archon can hack into Russian military networks and suborn them for their own ends."

"But we don't *know* that Hawkinson is part of that group."

"Yes, Jamie, we do," Wilcox said. "NTCU's intelligence confirmed that when I was at the Agency. This latest find backs that up. These people are real, and they are dangerous. The actions playing out right now appear very much to be by design. NTCU believes Archon is trying to provoke a war with Russia. I concur with that assessment."

"This is a situation entirely without precedent," Richter said. "I agree with you that the information your operative uncovered is compelling. But please understand where this puts the administration. Unless there is damning and irrefutable proof that Guy Hawkinson personally ordered this, if we were to use US government resources to investigate—let alone anything more severe—the family member of a political rival, it would make Watergate look like an after-school special. It would undo this presidency and cause irreparable damage to our country, possibly forever."

"Jamie," Hoskins said slowly. "I know the position—"

Richter held up a hand. "The president issued a finding several weeks ago, authorizing you to investigate Archon's involvement and to give him options. Where are they?" Richter wasn't going to say it outright. He'd already admonished them that officially, the president could take no actions against Hawkinson. But in reminding them of the prior finding authorizing an operation to uncover evidence of Archon, he'd effectively green-lighted covert action.

Richter said, "We're going to respond to Russia's attack on us. The level of restraint we show will largely be up to you."

25

Geneva, Switzerland

Frankly, after what happened to Samantha, Guy would feel safer in Argentina. Buenos Aires was long at odds with the United States and the United Kingdom. Intelligence operations for both countries were severely curtailed. His "donations" ensured access where he needed it, the considerable money he invested in the local economy earned him favor.

He would be protected in Argentina.

But he needed to be here. If Guy left, his employees might think he was fleeing in fear of war, and they would panic, operations would shut down. They couldn't afford that, not now. Kirby would go in his stead and escort Liu Che.

Guy would make the follow-on trip to Beijing as a show of respect and contrition.

By then, Liu would be with them.

Guy had concerns with Kirby making the offer. He had little experience in diplomacy, whereas Liu was a spymaster of considerable experience and talent. Kirby was a soldier, and direct. Still, he was a dutiful acolyte and a deft student. Most importantly, Guy trusted him.

Liu would respond favorably to their partnership. Guy was sure. He didn't make a habit of proposing ventures when he wasn't already certain of the outcome.

Kirby wouldn't leave for another day, and their morning was blocked off to prep for the trip. The important thing was to ink the tech collaboration with Liu's government and lock in the follow-on trip to Beijing. Well, Guy mused wryly, that wasn't the *only* important thing.

Guy finished dressing and stared at the sky outside his windows, gradually brightening, though it would be some time yet before the sun cleared the mountains at the far end of the lake.

He turned his head at a sound downstairs. It was 7:12. His driver shouldn't arrive for another eighteen minutes, and anyway, even if he was early, *Guy* wouldn't be outside for another eighteen minutes. He traveled with a detail, heavies from Hawk Security Group's Executive Protection Division, though they met him at the building's front door and ushered him to the vehicle.

The detail waited outside in the Land Rover, always.

Was this O'Neill, the new guy, trying to shine on the boss? If it was, Guy was going to have his ass.

Guy descended from the penthouse suite to the living area, ready to confront his overly ambitious security guard.

It was not O'Neill.

There were three of them.

Two were clearly security, they just weren't *his*.

Their boss was tall, Guy put him at six foot one, hair gray at the temples and darkening by gradient to a salty brown on top. He had dark brown eyes and was clean-shaven. He wore a double-breasted blue suit, light blue shirt, and navy tie beneath an open camel-colored topcoat. A pair of imposing men with hard stares and short haircuts flanked him. Guy knew the type by the look in their eyes.

"Who the hell are you?" Guy said. "What are you doing in my apartment?"

The man regarded him with a look that was at once condescending and pitying.

"I should think that obvious," he said.

Italian, Guy concluded from the accent.

"Humor me."

"You can call me *Il Doge*," he said. "For now. If I decide you can be trusted, I will tell you more. Please, make us an espresso, and we can discuss business."

What in the hell is this man talking about?

"You don't get to barge into my home and just order a goddamn coffee. Who are you and why the fuck do you think that gives you authority? My security team is going to be here in two minutes and—"

Il Doge held up his free hand. "Archon's chief problem is that they are known to the opposition," he said. "This is the risk with splitting off from an organization. It robs one of anonymity. And my men could cause you considerable pain in two minutes, even if your security team were coming, which they aren't."

"You're not a member of the board. I've met them."

"Correct. I am not a member of the board, and no, you have not met all of them. Stop making assumptions. I am here to help you." This Doge... character...waited for Guy to move, and when he did not, the man said, "Espresso?"

Everything else he just said aside, the question that continued to ring in Guy's mind, however illogical it was, was how did he know Guy owned an espresso machine?

There were times in Iraq, walking through the streets on a patrol, when they *knew* the insurgents' eyes were on them. You couldn't check every door, every window, couldn't jump into every shadow, but be there long enough and you just knew when you were being watched. Call it a sixth sense.

This felt like that.

Guy walked into the kitchen. Son of a bitch wanted a coffee, fine. Better come with answers. He ground the beans, packed the grounds into the silver handle, and slid that into the maker. The machine hissed as it heated the water and shot it into the grounds. The pungent aroma filled his kitchen. Guy placed the espresso cup on a small saucer, then went to the fridge and pulled a lemon out. He used a knife to slice a thin edge of lemon peel off and placed it on the saucer. This felt like a test, and attention to detail mattered.

Guy turned and placed the espresso on the counter between himself and the Doge.

Doge—Guy knew that word from somewhere but couldn't place it.

"Myself, and others, followed Trinity with much interest over the years. I agree with the belief that technology can usher in a new era of human achievement. I also know, far better than most, that few are truly qualified to lead. Or destined. I saw the schism and subsequent founding of Archon as an opportunity and brought a small number of trusted, like-minded believers with me. We provide counsel."

"So you're part of the organization?"

"You are a businessman, Mr. Hawkinson. When starting a new venture, it is wise to have senior advisors to your board of directors, yes? Mentors. People of experience and wisdom."

"Then why have I never heard of you?"

"Because you have had no cause to. You are a *soldato*. A capable and valuable one, true, and with potential. But you have been told what you need to know in order to serve the organization best."

"If that's true, why am I hearing from you now?"

Again, the man ignored Guy's question. "You have done well for the group, and we are grateful for your efforts. You suffered a considerable setback with the destruction of your island and weathered that commendably. You have also advanced our research cause markedly. Truly, I doubt anyone else could have accomplished as much in as short a time, Guy."

The man, this *Doge*, was well informed. Guy knew better than to suggest that in conversation in hopes that it would get the man to reveal his sources.

Rather, it would just invite another look of condescending scorn.

"You will not take this case of yours to the board. We do not need any additional attention. Nor do you, or your family. And I have plans for you."

"Additional attention? One of the board was killed by—" and he bit back the words, deciding not to speak it aloud. Why, he didn't know. "The board rushed the deployment of my...research project. It wasn't ready, and there were consequences. Innocents were killed."

"This is not a job for the squeamish," the Doge said curtly.

No one died when the air traffic control system went down. Tens of thousands were at risk, true, but there were contingency plans to get them safely on the ground. It was one of the reasons they chose that particular system. But they'd murdered two children, collateral damage, his sister called them, and Guy verbally lacerated her for it.

"What happened to Archie Chalcroft's family was regrettable, and we agree with you. Which is why I am having this conversation with you and not with the board. Your wise objection is noted. There will be consequences for poor decision making. Their strategy is foolish. You cannot remake a hostile world."

"If you're trying to avoid attention, why the rush to continue escalating with the Russians? I can't keep launching attacks from their servers. Eventually, they will notice. Or the NSA will."

"Indeed," the Doge said. "We've already accounted for this. The American government has all the proof they require. As do the Russians. The Russians will not acknowledge this publicly, but their integrated air defense network has recently experienced some...challenges. They have concluded that the Americans are conducting test runs to lay the groundwork for more substantial strikes."

Now, Guy couldn't help himself. "But I haven't done anything. Who is executing these attacks?"

"You are not our only asset, Mr. Hawkinson. Bear that in mind." The Doge turned and walked from the kitchen to the front door. When he reached it, he turned and said, "Have a good day, Guy. We will speak again."

26

Buenos Aires, Argentina

Colt arrived at Argentina's Ministro Pistarini International Airport under a commercial cover, traveling as the vice president of an American IT firm called "Quantum Solutions." Colt hoped fronting as a businessman would slip some of the scrutiny.

He'd used this cover before, so there was a verifiable history, and the legend was intact.

The same thoughts that plagued him entering Israel those months ago hounded him again now. Records existed of entering other countries under a slew of different identities, connected by a single common denominator —his picture. How long before one of those was matched to a photo with a different name? Argentina was a modern nation with a tech-savvy popu- lace. Their foreign intelligence service was formidable and dangerous. Despite the country's physical size, there were few border control points or airports. If one of Colt's identities were compromised (or any intelligence officer's, for that matter) and Argentine intelligence learned about it, there would be a short feedback loop with border control. It was much different than America's sprawling and overlapping national security bureaucracy.

Of course, the danger wasn't just at the border. As developing nations rolled out domestic surveillance capability, such as pervasive video coverage, the threat of discovery extended to anywhere with a camera. Those video feeds could be linked to centralized image recognition software, which could search the internet, that country's law enforcement or intelligence databases, or even those of partner nations to match faces. The Chinese had been using this technology to surveil their own people for years. If an intelligence officer was burned in one country, they might be burned in many more, depending on who identified them.

This was one of the most prescient and subtle dangers the Chinese government represented. They exported what American analysts jokingly referred to as an "anti-democracy tool kit." The Chinese taught other governments how to conduct surveillance and sold them the tools to do so. This was another of the Agency's concerns with Belt and Road. The data collection and dissemination potential was unlike anything the world had ever seen. Not only would partner nations (likely unwittingly) contribute to this massive intelligence gathering effort, but clients to Chinese tactics might gain information-sharing benefits, like the identities of suspected intelligence officers.

China had, today, the capability to log every foreigner entering their country, associating a photo with a passport. That could easily be exported to partner nations for verification. As Colt slowly trudged through the passport control and faced the downturned frown of the customs official upon seeing his American papers, he wondered when would be the time the man asked, "This says Walter Keane, but *this* says Colt McShane."

It was not this time.

Colt made it through passport control and took a broken chain of taxis, split by double-back walks of several blocks each time, to the safe house in barrio Villa Crespo.

Villa Crespo was an artsy, cosmopolitan neighborhood on Buenos Aires's western side. The safe house was a second-floor apartment in a two-story building, above a café on a treelined street. The building's architecture dated back to the 1950s. It was off-white brick with wrought iron balconies and occupied a quarter of the block.

Before Colt left, Ford asked him if he'd wanted to reconsider. He said there was something about Liu he didn't trust. Ford said he understood the stakes and knew they were short on options but, after meeting and pitching him, felt like Liu was a mistake. It was the only time Colt could recall Ford speaking without a trace of his signature acerbic sarcasm.

Yet here they were.

Has Ford seen something I missed, he wondered often on his flight down.

Tony flew in two days prior for reconnaissance and was at the safe house when Colt arrived. As was local Chief of Station. Their mission was off the books, and only the CoS knew they were in country. Luckily, he was a friend.

Alfonso Lopez, Jr., was the son of Cuban immigrants with a mixture of Latin and African heritage. Al spent most of his career in the Latin American Division—with a stint in Angola screwing with Castro's efforts there—but he'd been pulled up to Vancouver for a short tour because there was an Agency initiative to broaden officers' careers by giving them exposure to other regions. Colt met him when Al was a case officer assigned to Vancouver Station and Colt was working on his eight-year undercover operation collecting economic and technical intelligence in the global IT sector. They'd become fast friends.

The talk was Al's next assignment would be the Chief of Havana Station, the Agency's largest and highest-profile operational offices.

They shook hands when Colt entered, exchanged short pleasantries, and then Al excused himself to get their food from the café downstairs. While he did, Tony pulled three bottles of Quilmes beer out of the small fridge and popped the caps. It was a little stuffy in the apartment. It was early summer in the Southern Hemisphere and nearly eighty degrees outside, and they would have to make do with fans.

Al returned a few minutes later with two plastic bags. He removed the Styrofoam containers and handed one to each of them while Tony handed Al a beer.

"What've we got?" Colt asked.

"*Choripán,*" Al said. "It's like a kind of sausage made with beef and pork. Here." He handed Colt a small container of chimichurri sauce to drizzle on the meat. Colt closed the crusty bread around the sausage and took a test bite. It reminded him of chorizo, and it was delicious.

"I assume you didn't have a chance to get a country brief before you headed out," Al said.

"They don't know we're here," Colt confirmed.

"Cool. So, the long and short of it is that we have few friends here, officially. At one point, Argentina had the distinction of being labeled the 'most anti-American country in Latin America.' The US has never been popular here, but we backed a particularly awful junta in the seventies out of anticommunist pragmatism that killed some thirty thousand civilians. Then, we backed the Brits over the Falklands in '82. They held that against us. The Argentines didn't join the Second World War, harbored Nazis after it. We held that against *them*. The populace is about split. You won't find anyone overtly hostile to you, and they welcome foreign investment. America had a lot of tech companies here, primarily outsourcing software development. Their government moved close to China and Russia in the early 2000s, and that continued until Macri was elected in 2015. Thawed a bit. Fernández is more of a hard-liner and tracks closer to the anti-American sentiment."

"What's the opposition like?" Ikeda asked.

"First, there's the PFA, Argentine Federal Police. Easiest analogy is most of our federal law enforcement agencies rolled into one—FBI, DEA, and ATF, counterterrorism. The PFA has their own intelligence agency, called the Inteligencia de la Policía Federal Argentina. Up until 2017, they were also responsible for policing Buenos Aires, when the government established a provincial police force to govern the city. That'll be important in a minute," Al said with a wink and took a sip of his beer. "Their Federal Intelligence Agency is our equivalent. They handle counterintel. Used to have a decent working relationship, but that all dissolved in the 2000s. You should have freedom of action as long as you're off their radar."

"You mentioned the provincial police?" Colt asked.

"Yeah, so those are equivalent to our state police, and they handle local law enforcement. We've got a support asset inside the B.A. Provincial Police. He got me these." He turned in his chair, reached for a backpack just inside arm's length, and handed it to Colt. "Argentine version of a Browning Hi-Power nine millimeter and a Bersa Thunder, .45 caliber. Both were reported missing by the PFA and recovered in a sting by the B.A. Police. They were ordered destroyed by a judge and, according to their records, have been. If you need to use them, they can't get traced back to the station or our asset."

"That's good to know."

"The rest of your gear came by dip pouch, and Tony picked it up yesterday."

"I checked everything this morning. It all works."

"The Argentines are great people and very friendly," Lopez said. "There is the amount of street crime you'd expect, but they've come a long way since the junta in the seventies. I'd phrase it like this, they have no love for America but little problem with Americ*ans*." Lopez put a heavy emphasis on the last syllable of the word. "Buenos Aires is an international city and about as diverse as you'll ever find. Did you know half of the city is actually Italian descent?"

Colt said he didn't, and Ikeda just smiled.

"Neither of you will stand out. Any other questions for me?"

Colt looked to Ikeda, who shook a negative.

"I think we're good," Colt said.

"Then I'll leave you to it," Al said and stood. "Great seeing you, Colt. You've got my direct line if you get into hot water. Good hunting."

"Thanks, brother," Colt said and hugged his friend.

After Lopez left, they inspected their gear. Colt had a micro drone like the one he'd used in Israel. Next, he removed a heavy case of impact plastic with ballistic nylon over it. Colt opened the case, and inside was a pair of thick-framed eyeglasses in a style similar to what Liu wore. Colt pulled one of the bridge pads off, revealing a small port. He connected that to his Agency laptop, pairing them and starting the file transfer.

The glasses contained an optical sensor in the bridge that worked the same way the LONGBOW device did. In fact, the glasses were a kind of extension of it, the next iteration of the technology. Their mission here was simple. Liu would wear the glasses into the building and needed to connect with a camera or infrared optical sensor on any computer connected to the HawkTech network. Once the device completed the electronic handshake, Langley could open a secure, undetectable port enabling them to tunnel into Hawkinson's network here. Once inside, they had to validate the intel Nadia found. She'd discovered evidence of an impending attack; their analysts and expert systems would break that network open and prove Archon directed the shutdown of the air traffic control system.

They just needed to get Liu to make eye contact with an optical sensor without telling him why.

───────────

Liu Che arrived shortly after Colt on his flight from Geneva. He checked in to his room, and Colt gave instructions to meet at the Café de las Luces in the InterContinental Hotel. Monserrat barrio, near the city center and ocean, held many of the city's higher-end hotels and businesses. Colt ran a two-hour surveillance detection route before arriving at a bar themed for Buenos Aires of the 1920s. Colt arrived early and found a booth in the back with an eye on each of the entrances.

Liu went to the bar, ordered a whiskey, and then casually made his way to Colt.

"How was your flight," Colt said.

Liu shrugged.

"I've got two pieces of equipment for you," he said and handed Liu a small glasses case, trying to banish his bleak thoughts. Liu opened it. Inside were a pair of glasses and a lapel pin. "The pin will map and geotag everything you see inside. The glasses will allow me to see what you see." They'd do a lot more than that, but Colt wouldn't admit it to Liu.

"Out of the question."

"This isn't up for discussion," Colt said in low tones. "Thorpe explained the terms of your release."

"You expect me to wear something that can transmit into their building? Are you actually a fool, or is this just your first time?"

"I'm not going to threaten you, Che, because I don't need to. You already know the stakes, and the consequences."

"Maybe I decide to just return home. Let the cards fall as they may."

Colt motioned to the bar. Liu turned and saw Tony Ikeda sitting behind a beer, perpendicular to them, wearing a black polo and jeans. Tony ran his own SDR using a different route than Colt, arriving a few minutes later. "I think you remember my colleague from Switzerland. He might have a say in that. The glasses match your prescription. We had a good look when you were in custody. As for leaving, there are few places on this earth you could hide if you really piss us off."

Liu said nothing for a long moment, occasionally sipping his whiskey.

"I have an early morning." He slid out of the booth, taking the glasses case with him. "What do I need to do with these?"

"Just put them on. I'll do the rest."

Matthew Kirby met Liu in the lobby.

HawkTech B.A. was an impressive structure of red brick and mirrored glass in the Puerto Madero neighborhood along the Río Darsena Sur canal. Kirby explained that the building was once a university, which had relocated. HawkTech leased a quarter of the building but had an option on the rest of it. Signs of construction were everywhere.

"Guy wishes me to express his regrets at not being here in person. He hopes that with the situation in Europe, you understand why he feels he cannot leave headquarters at this time."

"Of course," Liu said. "It is the sign of a good leader. Also, for him to send such a trusted advisor speaks highly of your qualifications. I anticipate fruitful discussions," Liu said.

Kirby smiled. "Shall I give you a tour?"

"I would like that very much."

Kirby wore a light gray suit over a midnight-blue shirt with a slightly metallic sheen and an open collar.

Kirby explained the ground floor was primarily offices and administration. They *could* automate most of this but employed a larger staff than they likely needed as a show of good faith to the local government. The second floor, which required badge access, housed the software developers. Engineers were organized in squads, each one working on specific features for their assigned product line.

"Our focus here is cybersecurity and pure AI research," Kirby said. "Whereas our European business is geared toward tools to support the international community."

Liu noted security cameras in the corners of each room behind their black bubbles. He also observed oblong black boxes with a matte finish around each of the doors. Motion sensors, perhaps.

Kirby badged them into a room that also required a secondary authentication with a biometric hand scanner. There was a small table next to it with a bottle of hand sanitizer, which Kirby used after. He led them into the room. Once inside, Liu realized that this room occupied most of this floor. It was organized into wide aisles of floor-to-ceiling metal cabinets with glass cases. Within them were stacks of computing equipment. If there were overhead lights, none were used, because the room was lit in an ambient blue glow from the display panels.

"Cray built these just for us to our specification. It's called Paragon. We pull in water from the canal and pipe it through the floor to cool the machines. The quantum array is on the floor above."

"You have a supercomputing and a quantum array?"

"Yeah," Kirby said.

Liu held off on any deeper technical questions, knowing that Kirby would not be able to answer them. Instead, he said, "Could I speak with some of your engineers? I would be fascinated to know how this works."

"Of course," Kirby said confidently.

Liu walked up to one of the cabinets and gave it an up-and-down look, being sure to let his eyes fall over each component. He wasn't sure where the camera was on these glasses, but Colt had said, *I'll see what you see.*

Kirby then took him to see the quantum array. He explained that the combination of the two types of systems allowed their AI to have the incredible computational power that supercomputers afforded, with the quantum array reserved for the kinds of problems the supercomputer couldn't solve.

Liu believed that was an artful explanation, at best, if not wholly incorrect.

Their tour eventually brought them to the top floor and Hawkinson's office of brick and glass. It was a corner office in the rear of the building, which meant it faced the canal. Kirby pulled two sparkling waters out of a small fridge and indicated for Liu to sit. Liu took one of the large, cream-colored chairs. Kirby continued his lecture on their projects here, which he termed as more "pure R&D" than their Swiss team.

He talks too much, Liu thought. Kirby had already revealed more information that Liu would have deemed confidential.

"So, what do you think so far?" Kirby said.

"Most impressive. I'm most intrigued by your combination of supercomputing and quantum. As you know, my government is one of the world's leading developers of both technologies. Though, we are not pairing them in such a way. This is interesting."

"As you know, data is the key to this game," Kirby said.

"Yes, of course." *You are a fool, and you know nothing of which you speak.*

"Guy wants to explore a collaborative partnership with you. Or rather, your ministry. He thinks that—"

"Yes, I'm sure the Ministry of Technical Cooperation would be—"

"Not *that* one," Kirby said, smiling wolfishly.

Liu had to fight back the urge to inform Kirby that he would eat him alive.

"We think a partnership with your country would be highly beneficial and lucrative for both of us. Guy is prepared to open a Beijing office and is interested in pursuing a joint research corporation with your government. We call them FFRDCs in the US."

"I know the term," Liu said.

"Right, well, something like that. We would contribute some of our AI and quantum technology. Your government would do the same. We'd both reap the benefits of the research output."

"Why us?"

"The US government is shortsighted. China outspends America thirteen to one on quantum computing. We want to work where the breakthroughs will be."

"To achieve AGI?" Liu suggested.

Kirby nodded. "That's one of them, yes. Guy is also concerned with more direct problems."

"Such as?"

"We think quantum could disrupt biosciences, pharmaceuticals, and the financial services industry. As it is, economists aren't good at predicting macro trends in the global markets. They are simply too dynamic to reason over."

He has no idea what he's talking about, Liu thought as Kirby droned on. *Curious that Guy would send someone to pitch me with the depth of talking points. Unless he believes that I'm not interested in the conversation and have already decided to carry the proposal forward.*

"What *exactly* are you proposing, Matthew?"

"Well, for starters, we know who you really work for, Mr. Liu, and that's who we're interested in speaking with. We have a mutual adversary, and we think that, together, we can cause them a considerable amount of trouble. In the long run, that buys us both the space we need to explore our interests."

Colt had to restrain himself from shouting out in surprise.

He posted at an outdoor café on the other side of the canal. He was connected to Liu's feed via a secure satellite uplink.

Kirby all but proposed they jointly attack the United States.

The FBI might be able to make something of that, but it didn't bring them any closer to proving Archon launched cyberattacks at the United States and framed the Russians for it.

Colt hadn't really expected Kirby to come out and say that. Had he?

He opened his phone and navigated to the COVCOM.

He typed: **Did you get the shot?**

The response from the NTCU ops center was immediate. **Neg. No angle. LIU needs to hit an optical reader.**

Shit.

At least they'd gotten an excellent map of the facility, including passive detection of surveillance and security equipment. They had visual verification of Hawkinson's hardware. The computers were iMacs, and most did not have the privacy shield over the integrated camera.

Colt and NTCU followed Liu's facility tour via the glasses feed and saw several viable attack vectors. Liu had a follow-up meeting tomorrow, which they'd just scheduled. Presumably so Liu could communicate with his superiors in Beijing and discuss Hawkinson's pitch. Liu would have to sell the quick turnaround, but Kirby would not know any better.

Colt's attention went to someone seated at the café next to his.

Colt had a tablet on his table with a digital copy of the *Financial Times* open and a small window overlaid showing the feed from Liu's glasses. The screen had a privacy coating so that someone next to him couldn't see what was on it. Colt looked up every few minutes to refresh the mental map of his surroundings, making note of who came and went.

There was a man at the coffee shop next door sitting outside with a newspaper. Colt put him in his late twenties or early thirties, average height, and in good physical shape. He wore a light blue polo, tan pants, and wraparound sunglasses.

The paper was the giveaway.

Colt remembered lectures at the Farm during the covert surveillance block. Milt Farrington was an old-school spook and field legend. Had his choice of any job in the clandestine service. He didn't want to advance, he wanted to teach. He taught this class on how to properly surveil people. "Newspaper is a good prop," he'd told them. "You can hold it like this and look over the top, fold it in half. People looking at someone with a newspaper naturally look to the object and not the owner's eyes. Here's the thing, though," Milt told them, holding a newspaper. "You have to make progress on the paper. Turn the pages. Fold it over. Give it a good shake. Two hours on the front page is a dead giveaway. Not even the FSB is that slow, and most of them can't read."

Two hours on the front page.

Colt was being watched.

27

Geneva, Switzerland

"And this is outside my building, Guillermo?"

"Yes, it is." The other voice spoke with Spanish-accented English. "On the other side of the canal."

"He couldn't observe anything from there, not without technical means."

"My man noted he had an iPad."

"Yes, I see that in the photo," Guy said. "There could be a camera on the front of my building. He doesn't have a listening device inside. I'd have detected it."

"Do you know this man?"

"Not yet," Guy said, studying the photo and the inconclusive results of the facial recognition software on his screen. He assumed CIA would attempt to plant something on Liu, a listening or tracking device. If they'd guessed Liu would go to Argentina and so soon, what else did they know, Guy wondered. And how?

"This man works for the Central Intelligence Agency." Guy paused.

"How can you be sure?"

"Those glasses, and I suspect the baseball cap as well, are emitting signals that are scrambling visual recognition. A tourist wouldn't have that. We suspected CIA would intervene. I would be most grateful if this problem went away. Quietly."

"It will be done."

Guy disconnected the call and dialed Matthew Kirby, using the same encryption program.

"Hey, boss."

"Matt, CIA is in Buenos Aires."

"No shit."

"Our friends in FIA are going to handle it, but I wanted you to be aware. I'm sending you a photo now to be on the lookout for. Make sure he doesn't see you with Liu before our friends can take care of him."

"When are they going to move?"

"Quickly, is my expectation. How did it go with Liu today?"

"He seems receptive, but I didn't pitch him on specifics. We'll get into that tomorrow."

"Good. Agree to whatever they ask. I don't care about cost. I doubt there will be any actual negotiation tomorrow, we just need to know that Beijing is interested."

"Roger that."

Hawkinson disconnected the call.

The question remained how CIA managed to get a listening device on Liu.

They might have recruited Gales as an agent, but he was no intelligence operative. Guy vetted him exhaustively before hiring. Interviewed people that he'd studied under at MIT going back a decade. An asset could certainly plant something, that was done all the time...but Gales never had contact with Liu.

The only people who had were Guy, Matt, his assistant Tina, and Nadia.

———

Nadia, listening in on the conversation from LONGBOW, waited to see if he contacted anyone else, but he did not. She'd spent the entire evening huddled in her apartment just watching Hawkinson's phone, following his contacts, his messages as he typed them. It was the only way she had to view the apps that auto-deleted messages. Langley told her LONGBOW was invisible to the device it was on, that there was no way it could detect monitoring.

She desperately hoped that was true.

Nadia opened her COVCOM and fired an urgent message to Langley, warning them. She also activated her exfiltration plan.

She'd leave in the morning. It was snowing now and expected to continue through to tomorrow, a rare early winter storm.

Good cover to leave.

28

Buenos Aires, Argentina

Between the jagged route Liu took to ensure he wasn't being followed to his meet with Colt and their own subsequent to that, it was early evening by time they arrived at the safe house.

Colt was edgy and forced himself not to pace.

Another day down.

Thorpe's words echoed in his mind. *Hours, not days. This comes from the president.*

Frustration welled up in him. The administration had yet to take action against the Russians for their crime, swirling in a miasma of "investigation" in the intervening months trying to prove complicity in the two subsequent attacks. Rather than respond to the sure threat, they waited to get proof on the other two. Now that NTCU was hot on Archon's tail and had finally taken decisive action against them and, for better or worse, caused the death of a key member of Archon's leadership, bureaucratic expediency forced Colt into an ill-conceived operation. A mission like this should take months to plan, not hours.

Some things you can't force, Colt knew, but he did recognize they were also out of time.

He'd already had three pings from Langley asking for a SITREP.

Colt was going to have to go back and say, "Need more time."

That'd go over well.

"We need to go back to HawkTech tonight," Colt said. Though, the odds of a computer they could access being on after hours were slimmer. "What if you said you'd heard back from Beijing already?"

"To what end?" Liu asked.

"I need a better look at their computers," was all Colt said.

"We will appear too eager."

"I think that works in our favor. Kirby isn't an intelligence officer, and he isn't that savvy. He won't recognize the play. He'll just think you can't wait to jump into bed. He's desperate to impress his boss, show that he can play on a bigger stage."

"Is that your professional assessment?"

"We've been watching him up close for some time now," Colt said. Then he added, "As you know."

"You Americans are too aggressive."

"We don't have a lot of time to screw around, Liu," Colt snapped. "We need to do this, tonight." He softened his tone. "Tell him that Beijing is interested, but they want to see a demonstration. They need to know that Hawkinson is on their level."

Liu considered this for a moment. "That may work," he said softly. "But I need to know why if I'm going to do it. This is out of character for me, and my government. We are known for our...patience."

"You know why."

"No. Why do you want another look at his computers? Under normal conditions, that would appear a reasonable request, but these are not normal conditions. Why do you want to see Hawkinson's computer?"

"Out of the question," Colt said. What game was Liu playing? *Is he trying to work me right now?* Colt wondered.

"Then we are at a stalemate. You want me to take a risk, I want to know what it is."

"Did you tell Denney about his risks?"

"Hey," Ikeda broke in. "This is really fun to watch, but we do have a ticking clock here."

"Liu, we may only have hours before the US and Russia are at war. How many dominoes fall after that?"

"I understand the grand strategy, Colt," Liu said. "I want to know the risk *I* am taking to avert it." Liu held up the glasses, now folded. "This doesn't just record video, does it?"

Colt looked at him for a long, slow time. Liu was as fearsome an opponent as Colt had ever met. He was responsible for the most damaging espionage case in American history. He'd also nearly gotten Nadia killed. Liu belonged in a cell, or worse.

He remembered something Wilcox told him once about how the job will wear you down. You join the clandestine service to make a difference, to do a job most people would never be able to handle. To serve your country in a unique way. As the years drag on, spooks are forced to make tougher, harder decisions under increasingly nebulous conditions. Sometimes it's recruiting and running an asset that is truly reprehensible yet necessary. Sometimes it's forcing a good person to do a terrible thing and get ruined because of it, but that's what the job requires, and the stakes won't let you walk away. Eventually, it wears at your soul, grinds you down bit by bit. The good ones figure out how to compartmentalize, to anchor on the greater good. Most decide they are tired of deciding life and death in the gray world and leave, or maybe they rationalize staying in by staying out of the field. It occurred to Colt that he may have judged Hoskins too harshly. Perhaps he'd been forced to make an impossible choice once in his career and decided that was the last one.

Something like trusting a Chinese intelligence officer to set up a hack of a closed Archon network.

"No, it does not just record. I need you to get a good look at one of their computers, one with a camera. Satisfied?"

There was an RF antenna in the left arm and a micro-battery in the right. The charging port was beneath one of the nose pads, accessed by pulling the pad out. The glasses tethered to the phone they'd issued him, which the Agency also heavily modified (and could remotely destroy if necessary). The glasses and phone communicated via an encrypted radio frequency, transmitted at a different bandwidth that would hopefully not be picked up by any sensors in the HawkTech office. It was good up to a hundred yards and should (the techs emphasized the "should") transmit through walls, but it wouldn't penetrate a SCIF if Hawkinson had one. The phone would handle the satellite uplink and transmission back to Langley.

Once connected, the system would transmit specialized computer code into the HawkTech computer by establishing a data link through the optical sensor. The software would secretly worm its way through the network and open a covert port to the internet, hidden from the system's digital watchdogs. This gave NTCU hackers back at Langley a back door into the system that HawkTech would know nothing about.

"Enough, for now." Liu picked up his phone and dialed Kirby.

"I will admit," Liu said, "that this strategy perplexes me."

Kirby agreed to the meet but said he needed to clear the demonstration with Hawkinson first. They hoped Kirby was savvy enough to intuit the double meaning. They wanted him to show HawkTech—or whatever proxy they were using—could successfully hack the US.

"What part?" Colt asked, voice sounding more sarcastic than he intended.

"The pitch. It doesn't make sense to me. If their intent is to undermine governments, then why pitch mine?"

"Early on, they were looking to the Russians for investment," Colt said.

"Protection?" Tony offered. Liu shook his head. "If they're operating inside China, they're almost untouchable by the West."

"For any company to do business in China, they must agree to give the government access to all of their data *and* their technology. Western businesses are now setting up their own data enclaves in China, entirely separate from the rest of their enterprises. It doesn't seem like Hawkinson would allow this, not if what you say about him is true."

"They wouldn't grant him an exception?" Colt asked.

"I've never known the CCP to grant exceptions."

"I think he wants the data and access. Your government is collecting economic and commercial intel on countries throughout Asia, the Middle East, Africa, and now Europe." That was true, Colt believed, but *why now*?

Why would Hawkinson try to push that while his group tried to get America and Russia to square off?

There had to be another angle here.

"So you say."

Colt gave Liu a hard stare and then continued. "If Archon had access to that information, or if they could somehow co-opt those networks for themselves?"

"They would control the information flow to many, many countries."

It was a staggering admission for Liu.

Was this a break in the armor, or something else?

"This certainly lends weight to the idea that Hawkinson would open an office in China. Giving the government access to all of his technology, even what he limited to just that site, would be an opportunity to deploy a Trojan horse under the guise of an AI. As sophisticated as we are, we might not see it."

Colt's phone vibrated. He looked down and saw a notification on one of his apps. In and of itself, the app was nothing. It was a social media reader, or a close approximation of one, designed by NTCU's tech team. Its purpose was to notify him of a message on his COVCOM. Colt opened that app, also designed to look like something else. The app confirmed his identity, and he opened the message.

No form of communication was impermeable, no encryption unbreakable. Ultimately, covert communication was about risk tolerance. With this new messaging system, the Agency was field testing quantum encryption. In this model, the sender and receiver each had a randomly generated, secret key or encryption and decryption algorithm, transmitted in a quantum state. Because the keys were created using the properties of quantum mechanics, they were inherently unpredictable and theoretically impossible to break. An additional benefit to this method was that the message's creator would be able to detect anomalies in the transmission stream, indicating whether a user was eavesdropping.

Its one believed vulnerability was attempted decryption by an expert system AI, enabled by quantum computing of its own.

Which Hawkinson possessed.

URGENT//YELLOWCARD reports your mission compromised. Positive ID by ARG FIA. Y/C reports FIA officer working for HAWK. Imminent danger. Advise immediate EXFIL.

Colt glanced up from his phone and traded a fast look with Tony. Ikeda wouldn't know exactly what the message contained, but he could gauge from Colt's eyes that it wasn't good.

"We good, Colt?"

"We're fine," he said.

"We should get moving if we're going to make it there on time," Tony said.

"Let's roll," Colt replied.

When the three of them reached the car, Colt opened the rear door for Liu, closed it, and crossed over to Tony and said, "Message from the unit. I'm burned. Nadia intercepted a communication on Hawkinson's phone. Apparently, he's got people in Argentine intelligence on his payroll. HQ ordered us to bug out."

Tony said, "What do you want to do?"

"We don't get another shot at this, so I'm going forward with the op. But you don't have to be here."

Tony gave a half laugh. "This is what we do. You telling him?"

Colt shook his head.

Liu was an asset.

When this was all over, he was still going to answer for what he'd done.

Before they left, Colt messaged Langley and said they had one more chance for the LONGBOW shot but they had to take it in the next few hours. He believed Liu's cover was intact and said they needed to take this chance. He told the ops center to be ready.

Langley rogered.

There wasn't time for a proper SDR, but they did the best they could under the circumstances.

In fact, to get Liu into position in time, they had to travel almost directly to his hotel, with a few double-backs to check for tails. Liu would be dropped off a few miles from it and catch a taxi to take him the rest of the way. He'd go to his room to change and then walk the eight blocks to HawkTech.

Colt would post nearby, though at a different location than where he'd been before. Tony would orbit around Colt, conducting counter-surveillance.

As soon as Langley confirmed a positive connection, Colt would figure out how he would get them all the hell out of Argentina.

29

Buenos Aires, Argentina

Liu stepped out of his hotel onto the evening streets of Buenos Aires. It was a city beginning to awaken. The sky was still pale blue, though moving to darkness quickly.

Under other circumstances, he would have enjoyed his time here.

Liu changed into a fresh suit and tie, not one of his Savile Row numbers, unfortunately. This was a light gray tropical weight from Singapore, which still had excellent tailors, though not British.

The cab driver seemed perturbed by the short fare. Liu ignored him, occupied with his thoughts.

He wondered what would happen if McShane was correct. If they failed here and America went to war with Russia.

China's president was a tyrant and not a benevolent one; he just had an exceptional public relations machine. And he didn't look the part, unlike his opposite number in Russia, who resembled a leering reptile. But the Chinese Communist Party their president led was corrupt beyond measure, cancerous with patronage and a tradition of guaranteeing loyalty through bribes dating back to the days of Mao. The generals of the People's Liberation Army were dirty to a man and inexperienced in warfare. While the

PLA had numerical—and in some cases, technical—superiority over their American adversaries, they had none of the warfighting experience America first built squaring off against the Soviet Union and later honed during their War on Terror.

Would mass be enough?

Because Liu worried that might be all they had. He'd *seen* America's war plans, and he knew of the coalition they built from Japan to Australia. While far short of the NATO alliance, these were countries that feared Chinese expansion and committed to going to war if China invaded Taiwan, fearing they would be next. Japan, Singapore, Thailand, the Philippines, and, Liu noted with no shortage of irony, Vietnam.

Already, members of his service infiltrated the Taiwan as sleepers, ready to be activated. They quietly monitored preparations and defensive fortifications. They mapped the places the Americans would stage. The PLA's special forces would send in sappers and saboteurs to damage infrastructure and assault the power grid, the cell phone towers. And to conduct targeted assassinations of key military and governmental leaders.

America and NATO would make short work of Russia, providing that conflict stayed conventional.

Could an America bloodied in Russia stand against the People's Liberation Army?

Liu did not know the answer to that question. But the president believed *he* did. And that made him dangerous.

This was not even Liu's only concern. If America and its allies engaged the People's Republic in Taiwan, that insane, flat-topped, chubby goblin in Pyongyang might decide that was the opportune moment for him to take the Korean Peninsula.

That would break all hell actually loose.

The Ministry's assessment of Kim was that he'd unmoored himself from reality some time ago. Their analysts didn't believe Kim was capable of understanding the consequences of his actions, and that made him far more dangerous than his predecessors. He'd also stopped taking...guidance...from Beijing. America's response would be total, as would that of their allies. A regional war would almost certainly become a global one as other countries became engaged.

Even if the war was short, the economic impact to China would be devastating and generational.

Now, to learn that there was another actor pulling at the very strings that would push America and China to war, it made all those terrible things possible, if not probable.

McShane told him very little, as was to be expected.

He used the name "Archon" once.

He said they wanted to be the first to achieve AGI and that doing so would enable them to upend the world order, to remake it in their image. Hawkinson was a member.

Tumblers fell into place for Liu, slowly at first, like watching someone assemble a puzzle from a distance. What terrible things could Hawkinson and his backers accomplish if they gained access to China's quantum computing facilities, its AI research labs? What could this Archon do with technology at scale?

While China's president and his party cronies believed it was they who manipulated Hawkinson, tricked *him* into sharing *his* secrets, Archon would actually be tunneling into Chinese networks and subverting control.

Is that what this was about? A massive feint? While the world looked to conflict in Europe, Archon secretly tunneled their way into China?

Liu considered his options.

The Chinese Embassy was not far from here. He could be at its gates within minutes, and safe. The Americans would still have his wife in custody, though hers was a much lesser charge. If McShane and Ford were to be believed, Beijing might be able to exert some political influence to free her.

But what if the Americans were right?

What if this Archon existed and was as capable as McShane alleged? Liu would not have believed it if he were not *here*, now. The CIA would not have attempted this operation were it not connected to the looming crisis with Moscow.

He had no love for the Americans, but they could be counted on to be rational.

To a point.

And they could deal with the Americans in time. But not if China was at war with them.

Liu exited the cab and strode across the sidewalk to the red brick and blue-windowed building, backlit brightly against the darkening sky. Even through the mirrored glass, he could see Kirby waiting for him in the lobby.

Liu adjusted the glasses on his face.

If he stepped through those doors, there was no turning back.

He would be an American spy. Perhaps he would help avert a war.

But Liu Che would become what he had always controlled—an asset.

Per McShane's instructions, he needed at least sixty seconds at the optical sensor for the connection.

Liu pulled his phone out of his pocket to surrender to their security people.

We have visual link, Langley informed him.

Colt rogered.

Should I be risking my life for this guy? Would he do it for me?

Colt knew the answer to that already. Maybe Liu didn't kill Denney himself, but he could've told the admiral his car wasn't safe. Colt didn't buy the story that Liu didn't know.

Colt had no idea how they'd found him. It didn't seem possible that Archon could tap into Argentine passport control and run his photo against their recognition software. Even for them that seemed like a stretch.

Maybe it was just old-fashioned spy craft.

Hawkinson had people in the Argentine intelligence service. It could be as simple as giving them Colt's photo and saying to be on the lookout. Canvass the area around the HawkTech office.

Even still, Colt didn't exactly stick out among the local populace, which was highly diverse to begin with.

No, something was off.

"Clean so far," Tony said in his ear.

"Copy," Colt said.

Colt reviewed their exfiltration options.

The airport was almost certainly covered, and they did not have a disguise kit with them. Uruguay was an hour away by ferry, but they'd missed the day's last crossing in order to come here. It'd take a day or two for Al Lopez and the B.A. Station team to fabricate new passports, which Langley wouldn't go for. That meant leaving by land; however, given Argentina's interesting geography, it was a complicated proposition. Argentina had few internal highways connecting its major cities. Neighboring Chile was hours away by car. Frustratingly, even Uruguay, which they could see from the coast, was three or four hours by car because there were no bridges to cross the Uruguay River near Buenos Aires.

So, he and Tony would drive.

And if something went wrong tonight, they'd have to decide whether to take Liu with them.

"We're glad to see Beijing so interested," Kirby said, leading Liu back to the offices.

"To use one of your idioms, we believe in striking while the iron is hot. My government also recognizes the, shall we say, *strategic opportunity* to be had in such a bargain, given world events."

"I'm happy to know you see things as we do."

Kirby was a man trying to sound smarter than he was.

"I will still need to see a demonstration of efficacy. And," Liu added with a shrewd smile, "your commitment."

Kirby led him back into the offices. The computer pods were still half full of developers, most wearing headphones, cranking out code.

"Many night owls," Liu said.

"That's tech," Kirby replied, as though he knew. "People kind of work when they want. We don't force hours, just set expectations of productivity."

Kirby guided Liu to a glass-walled conference room. There were programming problems drawn out on the glass from the last meeting.

"What exactly does your government want to see, Mr. Liu?"

"Matthew, respectfully, you're dancing around the subject. You're speaking in generalities, and I need specifics. Your boss has made an enemy of the Russian government, which puts my own in a precarious position. You've talked about opposing a mutual adversary, but you haven't told me anything. Do you mean Taiwan? Japan? Or am I to assume that Guy Hawkinson is going to take a stand against the tyranny of his own government? A nation he once served in the military? A government his uncle is part of?"

Kirby said nothing, searching for words.

He's nervous, Liu assessed. *And is unsure of how to proceed. He doesn't want to fail before his boss but is worried about exceeding his authority.*

"Guy believes that our government has failed us. It's no longer accountable. So, he's acting." Kirby narrowed his eyes to look serious. Liu found it comical. "That work isn't done on-site, you understand."

"Then why am I here, Matthew? Why did I fly halfway across the earth to have a tour of your offices?" Liu turned on his heel and opened the door. There was a small cluster of developers working about ten feet from him. Each of them had a large iMac workstation, and not one of them had a privacy shield up over the built-in camera.

Liu walked over to the developer and declined his head, as if looking over his shoulder. Sensing the presence, the engineer turned around.

"I'm just curious what you're working on."

"It's okay," Kirby said from behind Liu. "Mr. Liu is a potential investor. Why don't you tell him what you're working on..."

"Paolo," the dev said.

"Paolo, right."

Liu listened as the engineer explained in slightly irritated tones what his team's project was about. Liu asked a few questions to keep the man talking.

He felt a hand on his back. "I think we can let Paolo get back to work, yeah?"

"Of course," Liu said. Kirby took them up to Hawkinson's office. The silence between them thick.

Liu didn't know how long he'd been gazing over the man's shoulder but hoped it was enough.

Kirby poured two scotches from a bottle on Hawkinson's bar and handed one tumbler to Liu.

"Most of the work here supports our new infosec practice, which is where the vulnerability research comes from," Kirby said, mouth behind the glass. "That's amplified by our existing open-source intel project in Geneva. Most of the devs here are white hats," he said, referencing the term information security personnel used to describe people who identified vulnerabilities for the sake of closing them. "We have a black hat team, but they're not on the books and don't work out of this office. The facility is here in B.A., it's in a nearby industrial park. We lease warehouse space in a shipyard through a series of shell companies. It's totally untraceable. As far as anyone knows, our hackers are dockworkers."

"Who knows?"

"About the operation? Me, Hawk, and Carlos Aguirre, our head of ops. We recruited him out of Argentine intelligence. He headed up Argentina's version of the National Security Agency. That is the team we used to hack the GRU. So, is that good enough?"

Liu gave Matthew Kirby a wry smile and lifted his glass. "Yes, it is quite good. Now, what is the real reason you want this alliance with the People's Republic?"

"America and Russia are corrupt. Russia invaded a sovereign country for no reason, conscripted hundreds of thousands, and sent them to their deaths. My own country invented a war, one that Guy and I both fought in, and kept sending men in like it was a meat grinder. And it wasn't even for something as noble as oil. They just wanted to settle a score. They aren't fit to govern," Kirby said, seething.

"I understand that, but how does China help you achieve that goal?"

"We thought the prospect of winning a war without firing a shot would be attractive to you," Kirby said. "If we can take your only real opponent out for you, what can China accomplish?"

He's lying, Liu thought. *Or at least he's not telling the whole truth. They want us distracted.*

Jesus Christ, Colt said to himself. He was walking along the canal, not far from the HawkTech building. He wanted to be close, in case Liu needed him, but didn't want to give any potential surveillance the advantage of him sitting alone at a nearby restaurant at the height of the dinner rush.

He messaged the NTCU ops center. **Tell me you're getting this.**

Langley replied immediately: **5x5.**

Colt typed: **Did you get uplink?**

Colt looked up from his phone. A feeling, a tingle on the back of his neck, sixth sense, whatever it was, it was that feeling you get after years on the street where you just *know*.

That you're being watched.

"I'll offer you something else," Kirby said, bolder now. He'd taken his second deep drink and refilled his glass.

Liu pantomimed several sips but had only taken the one.

"We can protect our friends."

Liu said nothing. Instead, he waited for Kirby to continue speaking. An old interrogator's trick was to simply not speak and let the subject fill the uncomfortable silence with words.

"We know how important the Belt and Road Initiative is to your government. Particularly in light of certain...setbacks. HawkTech could be a valuable distribution partner here, opening you back up to some Western markets that recently closed their doors. But that's not really what I'm talking about. We know that CIA is actively working against you. They tried to disrupt one of your installations, drive a wedge between you and the Israelis. As a show of good faith, we put a stop to that. Thanks to us, your operation at the Port of Haifa is secure."

"Those were Palestinian terrorists."

Kirby flashed a toothy, predatory smile. "We protect our friends," Kirby said in a dry voice.

He drew a piece of paper from his pocket and handed it to Liu. Liu unfolded the paper and read it. It contained a name.

"Who is this?"

"The name of Mossad's agent in your Tel Aviv Embassy. The one who sold you out to the Americans."

30

Buenos Aires, Argentina

Colt was on the move.

He messaged Tony: **ORANGE.**

The bug-out signal.

Colt hastened beneath the skyline, a mixture of neocolonial and techno-modern architecture. The air was dark and warm, patchily lit by streetlights and storefronts, full of salt tang. He moved north along the water, several buildings up from the HawkTech offices. The Argentine Ministry of Defense sat on the other side of the row of structures. Colt thought it wise to keep buildings between it and himself. There would be cameras and security.

If Hawkinson had assets inside Argentine intelligence, he might within the MoD as well.

His phone vibrated, the other phone, the burner smartphone he carried with him with the Trinity-designed secure comms app.

"Now is not the best time," Colt said hurriedly.

"Afraid it can't be helped," Ann said. There was something in her voice. She was scared. "That little favor you did for us last year?"

"What about it?"

The "favor"...would be the Trinity-designed hack that Nadia deployed onto HawkTech's network. Ava slipped it to her and Nadia took it, thinking it was from Langley and that Colt was using Ava as an intermediary. Once Colt decided to cooperate, Ann acknowledged that it would allow Trinity to secretly monitor everything that transited Hawkinson's network and, if they needed, burn the thing down to the bare metal.

"It's gone, Colt." There was a cold and hard finality in her voice.

"What do you mean it's gone?"

"I mean, it's not there anymore. We have no access. It's...just gone."

I'm burned. They found Trinity's bug. Colt knew two things immediately. One: Hawkinson's AI was far more advanced than they'd given him credit for. Two: Nadia was in immediate danger.

"I have to go," he said and hung up the phone. He got out his other one, stopped, and looked around to see if he was being followed. Assumed he was.

He typed: **UMPIRE believes exploit discovered / removed. YELLOW-CARD in grave danger. IMMEDIATE EXFIL.**

Colt took the bridge across the canal to the Hilton, entered, and worked his way through the hotel, ducking out a service entrance on Juana Manso. There, he picked up a cab and took it back across the canal to the Hotel 8 de Octubre in barrio San Nicolás. Colt walked briskly to the Carlos Pellegrini subway station and rode several stops west. Once streetside, he turned south, sawtoothing the city blocks so he could check behind him for tails. He took this four blocks to a small park, Plaza Miserere.

Colt compartmentalized. Nadia was on her own. There was nothing he could do for her here.

And he was still trying to process what he'd heard Kirby say, what he'd admitted to.

Archon, not Hizballah, attacked them in Haifa. But Kirby said *they* put a stop to it. He spun a fiction for Liu, claiming that the operatives who foiled the attack—in reality, CIA and Mossad—were actually Archon agents that were protecting a potential partner?

Tony waited for him on the southern edge of the park with their black sedan.

"What about Liu?" Tony asked as they started to roll.

What about Liu? Colt wondered.

He had no idea that the operation was compromised. Colt assumed Hawkinson knew about Nadia and the Trinity hack and he knew Colt was here; it wasn't an impossible leap to think he *could* make a connection to Liu.

If Colt and Ikeda left right now, they could be out of the city and on the road, heading for the border crossing outside of Gualeguaychú, three hours north of here.

Or they could wait for Liu, costing precious time and possibly jeopardizing their escape.

"Go to the B site," Colt said. "We can't leave him."

Liu had knowledge of CIA's operation against Hawkinson. They couldn't let the Argentines capture and interrogate him.

Colt sent a message to Liu's phone via their COVCOM with the code word to abort their primary location. The secondary was a sandwich shop in the barrio Chino subsection of Belgrano, about ten blocks from the Buenos Aires city airport. Though it only had regional flights, any pursuers might immediately think they were using that to hop across to neighboring Uruguay or Chile.

"Well, clearly this calls for a celebration," Kirby said. "I've got us reservations at Aramburu."

"I'm not familiar."

"It's one of the finest steak houses in the city, and Buenos Aires is the steak capital of the world, so..."

Kirby picked up his phone and called down for a car. Clearly, senior staff weren't checking *their* phones into security.

They rode the elevator down to the main floor, and Liu retrieved his phone. "Let me just check messages a moment," he said.

Kirby said, "Yeah," while looking at his own and stepped outside to make a call.

Liu opened his CIA-issued phone and scrolled to the COVCOM app, musing that the CIA apparently did not learn from past mistakes. The decade before, the Ministry of State Security uncovered the allegedly "secure" web portal the Agency used to communicate with their Chinese assets. It was rolled up in an operation that made the Night of the Long Knives look passive by comparison. Just like that, America lost every spy in the People's Republic.

There was a single-word message from Colt.

His emergency exfiltration signal.

Something was wrong.

Liu stepped outside into the warm, early summer evening. "I'm sorry, Matthew, but I must reschedule our celebration. I'm afraid I have a working dinner with some of my colleagues from the embassy. My country has many interests in this part of the world. I'm sure you understand."

"No worries," he said. "At least let me offer you a ride."

"Thank you, no. I wouldn't want to inconvenience you."

"But it's really not a problem. I'd hate to be a poor host."

Colt and Tony drove through the sluggish evening traffic, slowly wending their way north through the eastern barrios. The bright city was packed with life; an orchestra of car horns rang out constantly.

He tried messaging Nadia while they moved but got no response.

"Any word from back home?" Tony asked.

Colt scanned the COVCOM app.

There was a terse message from the ops center: **Access confirmed.**

"They're in."

"Thank God for small miracles," Tony said.

Colt rogered and informed them he and Tony were proceeding with the backup exfiltration plan. They wished him luck.

Something told Colt they would need it.

At least Liu's LONGBOW shot worked.

It took them a half an hour to crawl through traffic the few short miles to barrio Belgrano.

This neighborhood was home to Buenos Aires's Chinatown, which was Liu's pickup location. If Liu were followed or tracked somehow, he would have an obvious reason for visiting this part of town and could easily blend in. Belgrano was a mixture of high-rise apartments and commercial buildings. The Chinese government donated a large arch, called a *paifang*, that marked the entrance to barrio Chino, which enraged the significant Taiwanese population who didn't recognize the CCP as their government.

Pickups along the main north/south roads were difficult because the sidewalks had waist-high iron fences to protect pedestrians.

They turned right on Avenue Juramento. There was a sandwich shop on the corner of Juramento and Cabildo, with entrances on each street. Liu was to enter one and exit the other. The car would slow, and he'd get in. The landmark was, hilariously, a Kentucky Fried Chicken across the street.

The only problem was Liu wasn't here.

Tony slowed, and Colt looked through the open window for their pickup. The sidewalks were filled with commuters leaving work and people heading out to dinner. Barrio Chino was one of Buenos Aires's more ethnically diverse neighborhoods, sporting a large East Asian population.

A driver honked behind them.

"I'll circle," Tony said. Colt nodded in agreement. Even if there were no traffic, they still couldn't loiter on a major street like this. It would be too obvious to anyone watching.

These are the times you second-guess yourself, he remembered Wilcox telling him once, early on. Like Nadia, Colt was pulled from the clandestine service school surreptitiously for a highly classified assignment. His classmates thought he'd washed out. Many didn't learn the truth until he'd reentered the mainstream service after eight years under nonofficial cover. Like his experience with Nadia, Colt felt that sometimes his own training was rushed, hastily done, and that there were simply things about being a spook he didn't *know*. So much of this job was OJT in those critical field assignments, supervised by more experienced spooks.

Colt had none of that.

He just disappeared into a different world.

Tony looped slowly around the block, not hard given the heavy traffic. Unfortunately, it wasn't a single-block loop, as the side streets were mostly one-way. A full route was more like four blocks round trip.

When they got back to their original position, he slowed, and Colt again looked for signs of Liu.

Nothing.

"How long do we want to give him?" Tony asked.

That was a great question.

"Let's just take another loop."

They did.

By the fourth pass, Liu was twenty minutes late.

"Is there anywhere we can park?" Colt asked.

"That is not a good idea. If he's burned, we could be too." Colt glanced over and saw a grim smile on Ikeda's lips. "I mean, more than we are already. Look, I know you don't want to leave him behind, but there will come a point where we have to make that call. It's probably, now, a four-and-a-half-hour drive to the border crossing. Every minute we loiter here is more time for Hawkinson's people in Argentine intelligence to contact the border guards."

"I hear you," Colt said. "You thinking we should try the airport?"

Tony shrugged. "There's a flight to Lima tonight. Takeoff is in about seventy minutes, so if we're going to do this, we need to call it now. As South America goes, Peru is about the best place for us to bolt to."

Tony's voice was perfectly calm and analytical. He wasn't panicking, he was simply telling Colt the options.

"Let's do one more loop," Colt said. "If he's not here by then, we'll assume he was picked up."

"He's a pro," Tony said. "Dude knows the game."

"Yes," Colt said. "He does."

Tony made one more slow orbit around the block. Darker now, there was an iodine-yellow corona around the streetlights.

No messages from Liu on the COVCOM.

They turned onto Avenue Juramento.

A form appeared in the store, backlit, a contrast to the dark street, a man in a business suit.

Liu.

"There he is!"

Ikeda slowed the car, and the driver behind them laid on the horn. Liu saw them. He moved quickly to the car, opened the door, and climbed in. Ikeda accelerated and made a right turn, then a left, heading east to the airport.

"What happened?" Colt said.

"Kirby insisted on giving me a ride. I couldn't message you for obvious reasons. I had to make up a location where I was allegedly meeting counterparts from my embassy. Were we successful?"

We?

"We were," was all Colt said.

"Well, that's good, at least. Were you listening in on the conversation?"

"I was."

"I have fewer qualms about helping you than when I started," Liu said in an icy voice. "He's trying to get us to pay him protection money like some kind of gangster. But that speech about 'revolution'...I think they are just trying to separate their adversaries to be handled in turn."

Liu seemed convinced. Colt pressed. "What do you think they could do if Archon had access to China's digital infrastructure?"

"Connection to six hundred and fifty million users, and that's just in China. Once they were in our telecommunications network, they could connect with every node in the Belt and Road."

AI required data to learn. *Was this how Archon accelerated their path to AGI?*

Tony made a succession of turns, stair-stepping his way east.

"Che, we're going to try and fly out of here tonight," Colt said. "Our original plan was to drive to the border with Uruguay, but given the geography and traffic, that's about four hours away. The flight is risky, but it's doable. We do not have evidence that you are compromised."

"I don't believe Kirby suspects me," Liu agreed.

Escorting Liu back would be tricky, and every leg they added, every additional complexity would be one more opportunity for him to break and run.

But he wouldn't, because Liu's wife was still in federal custody.

Colt was counting on that.

Tony made another turn.

"Gents, I think we're being followed."

"You should get down," Colt said, and Liu lay across the back seat. If they were being tailed, maybe the opposition hadn't seen Liu get in or discovered the car's additional occupant. It was dark, but they shouldn't take chances.

"How long?"

"They've been on us since we grabbed Liu."

Colt looked at his watch. About ten minutes. Tony had them on a staggered, looping, illogical route.

"How'd you pick up the tail?"

"Looks like it's just the one car."

When tailing a subject, the pursuers would ideally have four to five cars, coordinated by radio. They would trade off intermittently so that their target would not get wise to the tail. If it was only one car, that would be the FIA men Hawkinson bought off.

Tony turned right onto Avenue del Libertador, one of Buenos Aires's major roads. Colt followed along with a map on his phone. There was a large golf course a few blocks to the right and beyond that, the airport.

They could not be caught with Liu. Or rather, Liu couldn't be caught with them.

If they were, Hawkinson would suspect his network penetrated and would shut everything down—here *and* in Geneva.

"Che, we need to separate. There's a shopping center south of here called Alcorta. We'll pick you up again in twenty minutes on the Jerónimo Salguero and from there go to the airport."

The opposite side from the federal police headquarters, Colt thought but didn't say.

They had enough to worry about.

"Get ready," Tony said.

Liu asked, "Ready for what?"

"When's the last time you jumped out of a moving vehicle?"

"I'm sure I was in my twenties," Liu said sardonically.

"I'm making the turn. Ten seconds."

"We're going to slow, and you're going to hop out on the turn."

"Is this safe?"

"It'll be sporty," Ikeda said. "Go!" He pulled left across the street and slowed to a few miles an hour. Liu opened the door and stepped out, tripping on his exit, and braced himself on a parked car to stop.

There was an Audi dealership on the corner, and Colt saw Liu stepping into that as they drove off. Smart. It would have multiple exits, and, hell, he might even be able to talk his way into a test drive.

That kind of split-second decision making, using intuition to turn around a potentially fatal situation, reminded Colt how good his opponent-cum-asset was.

Tony accelerated down the street.

"Oh, that's not good," Ikeda said.

"What?"

"They're not following *us*."

31

Geneva, Switzerland

It was nearing midnight, and Nadia already stayed here too long.

She had to make sure that Gales got away and, then, needed to stand digital overwatch for Colt.

She'd signaled Chuck Harmon a few minutes ago and said she was leaving, sending a single code word over their secure chat: BANTAM. Their plan, put in place months ago, designed to be executed on a moment's notice.

Still, it was the middle of the night, and she hoped he wouldn't be too upset.

It burned her that she'd have to drive all the way through the night and a snowstorm for a clean getaway when there was an international airport three miles from her apartment, and she'd missed the last flight of the day.

The train station, too, was a mile from her apartment in Geneva's Old Town. It wasn't like they'd murder her on the train or anything, this wasn't a Hitchcock movie. But she'd missed the last train by thirty minutes by the time she got the exfiltration order.

Langley also worried about Nadia's safety using verifiable travel within Switzerland.

They knew Archon had a man inside the Swiss Federal Intelligence Service and had access to their ONYX electronic surveillance platform. Modeled after America's own ECHELON system, ONYX monitored all source communication traffic in the country—phones, internet, satellites, even faxes. The risk was that Archon knew the alias Nadia entered Switzerland under and flagged the record. Between ONYX and their own open-source AI aggregator, they would know if that alias bought any kind of a ticket.

Instead, she'd meet Harmon an hour outside of Geneva, halfway between here and Bern. He'd have a fresh passport, food, and coffee.

Harmon would drive her to Zurich, just in time to catch a ten a.m. flight to Dulles.

Nadia closed and locked her apartment for a final time. She would miss this place. The last months were frenetic, at times panicked, but she loved Geneva. Such a vibrant, amazing city. "Melting pot" got thrown around too much, but here it was true.

She had a black duffel and her computer bag. Enough for a quick trip, a weekend away.

Anything tying her to her life here remained inside the apartment. She carried only clothes, a passport (to surrender to Harmon), and her Agency-issued gear, which looked mundane, anyway. And a Glock G26 in a concealed holster under her shirt.

Harmon helped her get it after the incident with that Archon agent, Bastian Stager, earlier that year.

Nadia walked through the cold, deserted streets. The night looked like a black-and-white photo. Nadia wore a puffer jacket and a white knit beanie. No scarves, no clothing with toggles, straps, or cords. Anything she wore could be dropped in an instant.

Nadia rented an Audi A3 the day before. The car was parked three blocks from her apartment. As she stepped out into the bitter, wet cold, she wondered if that was a wise decision. There wasn't parking near her apartment, anyway—this was a part of the city built long before cars, and available spaces were harder to find than diamonds.

Snow fell at a rapid clip—there was an inch on the ground already and more coming. It was a rare storm this early in the season, and Geneva did not typically experience that many.

There was a yellow glow from the streetlights, matted by white motes of snow. Snow crunched under her feet, and she declined her head against the cold. She wasn't walking an SDR at this time of night.

Nadia was glad she'd spent so much time walking these streets in her spare time, committing them to memory. She'd learned that one lesson the hard way, when she'd planned a surveillance detection route but not thoroughly enough and ended up with Bastian Stager on her heels.

Tonight would be faster than that.

She replayed the route in her mind, mostly to keep herself occupied and not to think about the cold.

She would drive Rue de Lausanne, running along the shores of Lake Geneva, until it connected with the A1 Autobahn. As long as the weather held, she'd have a smooth trip to Lausanne, on the opposite side of the lake. There, she'd ditch the car where it would officially become someone else's problem, meet up with Harmon, and her Swiss assignment would end.

As she fled Geneva, the one thought that never left her was that she hoped she did it right.

The raced training, inserting her into an undercover role before she'd even finished at the Farm. Jesus...spy school on nights and weekends. Her peers, they all had probationary assignments supervised by senior officers, and some of them didn't even cut it. The washout rate even after graduating from the Farm was high enough to be respected and feared.

Those people who'd *been* trained, who'd been mentored, hadn't cut it.

Here Nadia was, undercover for the last eighteen months.

She second-guessed every move she made. She didn't know better, didn't have experience to rely on. All she had were the periodic check-ins with Harmon, her only real flesh-and-blood link to the Agency. Communication with NTCU became more sporadic, especially as shit went sideways back home. It's not that they were ignoring her, she knew that much, but they had enough bandwidth to read her reports and issue instructions.

Nadia hoped Colt was proud of the work she did.

He was like her big brother. They shared a common bond of rushed training and a job without an instruction manual.

She wondered what Colt would think of her decision to frame an inno-cent man as a mole to take the blame for her snooping around. Would he rationalize it, as Harmon had, arguing that the most moral action was to the greater good? Or would Colt see it through his typical idealistic lens. She always thought his personality wasn't wired for espionage, how someone could see things so clearly as "right" or "wrong" and still do this job.

Maybe the Agency needed more of that, she didn't know.

Nadia wasn't sure she was going to stay in the Agency once she got back home. Maybe they could find a role for her in Sci-Tech, designing gadgets for her to condescendingly explain to people like Colt. Or perhaps one of NTCU's hackers.

Nadia was pretty sure she was done in the field, though.

She cut across a parking lot reserved for official vehicles of some type and squeezed through a darkened alley that gave her the creeps. Nadia emerged on the street, recognizing Place du Bourg-de-Four, which had the distinction of being Geneva's oldest town square. It was a wide (for Old Town, anyway), triangular plaza with barren trees now outlined in white. There was a good restaurant on the corner. Her car wasn't far from here, just another couple blocks. She'd snagged a spot outside the French Consulate General. Not technically city parking, but she'd learned the local police infrequently ticketed and never towed there.

Nadia was crossing the small plaza when she heard footfalls behind her, muted by the snow.

Then she heard the roar of an engine and saw headlights track across the far wall.

She was turning her head when hard hands grabbed her from behind. An unseen attacker jerked Nadia backward and enveloped her in thick arms. He couldn't get a solid grip because of her backpack, and she broke free, using the gap between them as leverage. The attacker grabbed her backpack as she twisted, but she corked her body around and kneed him in the groin. The man grunted in pain, fell back a few steps, and Nadia snap-kicked him again in the crotch.

Her attacker recovered quickly, or, at least, he was trained to fight through the pain. She sized him up—average height, lean and wiry. She'd spent most of her military career around Air Force special operators and knew the type. This guy had military training, probably one of Hawkinson's pet attack dogs.

Nadia had hand-to-hand training, but this guy was a trained killer.

She was dimly aware that a vehicle was also in the mix.

Nadia heard car doors open.

If they weren't the police, she was outnumbered and badly.

Her attacker landed a hard kick on her right side.

The force of the blow knocked her a few inches, and her body arced, collapsing in with the blow.

She whipped her head around to see two more men approaching from the vehicle.

Nadia pulled the pistol and fired two shots at close range. Her attacker stood frozen a moment, a dumb look on his face. He fell, comically on his backside, still seemingly surprised.

There were no shouts behind her, no frantic commands to "get her." They just knew what to do, and they acted. She turned and snapped off a shot, missing, but they both dove for the ground. Nadia took off, pumping her legs, driving herself forward as fast as she could go. She wore sneakers rather than boots, and it was hard to grip on the unplowed street. She hooked around a corner, momentarily breaking up their line of sight. She ducked into an alley.

The two of them rounded the corner and immediately saw where she went from the tracks. One of the attackers turned and plunged into the alley.

Nadia fired from the shadows.

In the narrow space, it was impossible to miss. His head jerked back, and he fell to the ground. She faded further into the background. The third attacker didn't enter the alley, knowing it was a kill box. He disappeared to the right. Nadia knew he was trying to flank her, to get around the building faster.

But she knew these streets.

She turned and ran deeper into the alley, picking up the cross street on the other side. Nadia looked to her left. The route her would-be killer took was going to buy her at least three minutes. These old, unevenly spaced blocks were deceptive, especially at night.

Nadia turned south and ran hard.

She looped back to where they'd ambushed her and grabbed her things. Their vehicle was where they'd parked it in the center of the plaza. One of them would have the fob, and she didn't know which. Instead, Nadia used two of her remaining three rounds in the driver's-side tires.

The last attacker might hear that, he might not. Sound played strangely in these streets.

Nadia stashed the gun in its holster and ran to her car along the street at the French consulate. She threw her things in the back seat, checked to make sure that her remaining pursuer hadn't figured out where she was, and opened the phone. There was one last thing to do.

Guy's phone beeped.

He looked down at the message app. This was an anonymous one, not designed by HawkTech.

It's done. She put up a fight. We lost two. Need cleanup.

So, his instincts were right all along. Nadia *was* the CIA mole, Gales was her agent. At least the problem was dealt with.

He mobilized a cleanup team and then messaged Kirby. If she'd recruited Gales, was it possible she'd turned Liu as well?

32

Buenos Aires, Argentina

Colt flipped open another app, this one showing him Liu's location. He was moving south along Avenue del Libertador. The dot changed position quickly, indicating he was in a vehicle or public transit. The city had a light rail that ran along that road. It would be a sound choice to lose vehicular surveillance.

"South, back to Libertador," he said.

"What are you doing?"

"We're going to intercept."

"I don't need to tell you this is a bad idea," Ikeda said. He didn't. These would be Argentine intelligence officers. Colt knew the FIA by reputation, and they were good.

"Tony, he knows we're after Hawkinson. He knows about Archon. We're not...we're not losing him."

"Roger that," Tony said.

That was the thing about Ikeda, Colt noted. He didn't debate. Once action was decided, he committed. Colt was certain that if Tony thought something couldn't be done, he'd say so. But, in his mind, as long as it was possible, hell, even plausible, he would try.

"Okay," Colt said, looking at the map. "He's definitely on the light rail. It's going to split off this road in another half mile."

They stayed on Libertador when the train curved to the left, toward the water.

"No sign of a tail behind us," Tony said.

Even through the sludge of evening traffic, they were roughly parallel with Liu's rail because of the long curve it took. Colt's map showed a rail station close by.

"He's slowed, I think he's on foot now," Colt said.

He typed a message to Liu: **Status? You are being followed.**

Liu replied: **I know. In cab to Hospital Rivadavia.**

Colt pulled the hospital up on the map. That was a smart move. It would be busy this time of night, well populated with multiple modes of transportation available. Colt relayed the directions to Tony, who turned right at his first opportunity.

A few minutes later, they approached the hospital. "Oh shit," Colt said.

It was a hospital all right, about a hundred and fifty years ago. Something you couldn't tell looking at a map. Hastily planning a place to run to, Liu would just see the red cross symbol and assume it was a working hospital, not a historic landmark.

"He's on foot, about four blocks from here," Colt said. He sent another message asking for status but received no reply. That most likely meant he couldn't.

Colt and Ikeda were now on Avenue General Las Heras in barrio Recoleta. This looked like a residential neighborhood of townhouses, leafy trees, and narrow streets. It reminded Colt of Paris. "Turn here!" Colt said, and Ikeda prepared to make a left onto Avenue Pueyrredón. "I think I know what he's doing."

"What?"

"He's trying to lose them in a cemetery. One block east."

Tony made the turns. But when they reached it, they found a twenty-foot stone wall with anti-climb bars atop it.

"Is there a Plan B?" Tony asked.

"We're a lot deeper into the alphabet than that," Colt said.

Ikeda's head snapped to the side. Colt saw it too, something moving fast on the left side of the car.

Ikeda had just enough time to belt out a curse before the speeding car rammed them.

Street craft wasn't part of the usual MSS tool kit, as the service tended to outsource things like breaking and entering. Liu, however, had come up in a different time, his early days as an intelligence officer spent in a country that lagged far behind their Western competitors in technological means. As a result, they had to rely on old-fashioned methods.

In short, Liu Che knew how to pick a lock.

Liu learned a long time ago that there were a few items of equipment he was never without. One was a good set of lockpicks, the other was a knife.

His cab driver was a little surprised that Liu asked to be dropped at Hospital Rivadavia, and when he arrived, Liu understood why. It hadn't been in operation for some time. He decided to bail from the cab and cut his way across to the next logical landmark, the Recoleta Cemetery. He knew from studies of Buenos Aires this was more a city-within-a-city of mausoleums and tombs where Argentina's wealthiest and most famous were entombed. He also knew it closed at sundown, but that suited him perfectly. He needed a place where he could easily lose his pursuers.

Liu picked them up as he boarded the light rail, and they'd followed him the entire trip. He lost them, for a time, in the cab ride to the hospital, but they'd picked him up again. He'd only managed to get this far because a traffic accident jammed up the roads, allowing him to make up time on foot.

They were tracking him somehow. What Liu needed was a quiet place to hide so he could figure out how.

"Go!" Tony shouted.

A car T-boned them in the intersection, racing in from a cross street and slamming into them with purpose. The car smashed into theirs just in front of the driver's-side wheel, pinning Ikeda's door shut.

Colt opened his door, rolled out onto the street, and yanked his backpack from where it sat on the floor.

Gunshots erupted and spiderweb cracks shot out like lightning on water across the car's windshields.

Colt drew his weapon and crouched behind the rear passenger door. He popped out and fired three rounds over the roof into the other vehicle, giving Ikeda cover to scramble out of the car.

Doors opened, and people piled out of the other vehicle.

Tony crouched next to their vehicle, drawing his own pistol.

Gunshots peppered their car.

Tony rose in the corner between door and the car, firing across the front windshield. He put three rounds through the car's window, driver's side. Colt stood and fired, aiming for the passenger side.

The other car's back doors were open now with shooters using them for cover. Their return fire was hasty and disorganized.

"Colt, you have to go get Liu," Tony said.

"I'm not leaving you here."

"I've got this." Tony leaned out of cover, fired three more rounds at the rear shooter on his side, and Colt dashed for the sidewalk behind them. The intersection was the kind that existed in the older cities of the world, designed before automobiles were a consideration. A fast count showed seven entry points into the intersection, with a small section in the center holding a large, irregular sidewalk and a tree. The other car had hit them as they were making a left to pull around the tree, the third exit from the intersection.

Colt ducked behind a city bus and took a disgusting mouthful of diesel exhaust. The car crash caused a minor pileup and forced the bus to stop. Its passengers now bolted, screaming for the exits, desperate to escape the gunfire. It gave Colt the cover he needed to move. He cinched the straps on his backpack and ran down Avenue General Las Heras two more blocks, the combat sounds fading behind him.

Colt turned left on a cross street and saw the cemetery's looming dark walls on the next block. They looked twenty feet high. How in the hell did Liu get in there?

He ran up the block and crossed over to the cemetery, heedless of traffic and earning some angry horns in the process. He spotted a massive gate of black iron as tall as the walls it connected to. It was halfway down the block, so he ran the length of the wall until he reached the gate. It was open a crack.

Colt pushed the bars and slid inside.

He knew a little of Recoleta Cemetery. The size of several city blocks, with ornate structures of marble and stone, fifteen to twenty feet high of weather-beaten and streaked grays, whites, and blacks, stood on either side of wide flagstone paths with cross streets that bisected them.

It was a city of the dead.

Colt crouched down and dropped his ruck onto the ground. He unzipped it and removed the small, shock-proof box, which he then opened, revealing the micro drone he'd used in Israel. Colt activated it and sent it aloft. Then he pulled up the control app on his phone.

Night vision was never as good as Hollywood depicted, but these optics were better than most. The lowlight camera rendered images on Colt's phone that resembled photos taken on a phone—bright objects in the foreground against a darker backdrop. Flying high over the cemetery to give it a wider aperture, the drone used an onboard infrared sensor to locate anyone moving through the dark grid.

The good news—Colt believed he found Liu. There was a single heat signature about three "blocks" over. It stood upright and was not moving.

The bad news—he wasn't alone.

Two shapes moved quickly toward what Colt believed was Liu's location.

Colt set the drone to hover and ran toward them, phone and video feed in one hand, pistol in the other.

———

"You can raise your hands now, Mr. Liu, slowly," Matthew Kirby said, flanked by a pair of inky shapes. There were no lights in the cemetery, it was a dark stain on the bright skyline. The sky above was long at the end of twilight, casting long shadows below. There was just enough light to see, though Liu didn't need it to know the three men were armed.

Liu held his arms out, but not quite up, showing he was not.

"Is this wise, Matthew?"

He laughed. "I should ask you the same question."

"You know who I work for. Perhaps this isn't the move you want to make."

Kirby gave an ugly smile. In the darkness it looked ghoulish. "I *do* know who you work for. You see, we picked up on an encrypted RF transmission inside the building. We haven't cracked it yet, but we will. We assumed you'd be recording everything you saw. That was the point of the tour. We *wanted* them to see. Our mistake was that we assumed you were recording for Beijing, not Langley."

"I don't know what you're talking about," Liu said, stalling. For what, he didn't exactly know. McShane would be going to the new pickup point. Liu was unarmed, save his pocketknife, not that it would do him any good. Kirby was a former soldier with extensive combat experience. The two men with him were either Hawk Security Group mercenaries or Argentine intelligence.

"We thought you were recruiting Ms. Blackmon, not the other way around," Kirby said. The two men with him took up positions around Liu, closing off his escape. "But it was getting into a car with a CIA officer that sealed the deal."

Liu didn't carry his MSS-issued phone, only the one McShane gave him with the CIA COVCOM protocol. Kirby's people couldn't have cracked that and injected something in the time he was inside the office, could they?

They had a quantum computing array here, and Kirby acknowledged this was a cybersecurity-focused office. Still, it didn't seem likely they could hack into a CIA-modified phone without McShane's people knowing about it.

"We placed a tracking device on you. It's about half the size of a postage stamp and fit very nicely underneath the collar of your suit. Or did you think my pat on the back tonight was because we were friends?"

Liu gave a condescending chuckle. "This is a despicable betrayal of trust, Matthew. I wonder what Guy would think of this. How unfortunate that you weren't up to the task. I had high hopes for this partnership, as did Beijing."

"Whose idea do you think it was to track you?" Kirby said.

"Ahh, I see. So, you are just a lackey. That's unfortunate. Though, I suppose, not surprising. A hive will be mostly drones, after all. I wonder, did Guy authorize you to disclose as much as you did, or were you just trying to impress me with your inside knowledge? Admitting your organization tried to sabotage our project in Haifa was a mistake, though not as stupid as the attempt itself. Were you trying to get us to pay protection money to you? Is that what this was about?"

Liu saw the two heads behind Kirby turn to face each other, clearly confused.

"I was only trying to show that we protect our allies. Everyone else is fair game."

"I doubt that was the message Guy asked you to convey. I suspect he'd have wanted that part hidden. If I'd joined your little band, I'd have figured it out, and there would be consequences. The smarter play would be to blame it on the actual terrorists you impersonated. I gather that was Guy's plan and whatever you said was some ill-advised improvisation."

"Okay, I've heard enough of this bullshit. "

Kirby closed the distanced between them, raised his weapon, and jabbed it into Liu's chest.

Colt sprinted past the houses of the dead.

Colt saw Kirby and two others—presumably FIA or HSG heavies—close around Liu on the drone feed and swore under his breath.

He didn't know where Ikeda was, what his status was.

He did know that if he didn't do something, Liu was a dead man.

Colt stopped long enough to beacon his location to Tony's phone and dove into action.

The drone hovered approximately thirty feet to Kirby's right. Colt was creeping around the tomb and now had them in view. He was just a little too far away. Colt drew his pistol. There was no way he was risking a shot at this distance, not with Kirby and Liu so close together.

Instead, he sent in the drone, ordered it to descend.

He issued instructions and then put the phone away. Kirby's voice was elevated now, angry, losing his cool. Colt knew those tones, it was reaction speech.

Using the tombs as cover, Colt moved fast through the shadows. He crouched and walked quickly, nearly invisible.

"What the fuck?" Kirby half shouted.

Colt saw the frantic dancing and hand-waving, Kirby trying to bat something away from his face.

Liu backpedaled, reacting to whatever just interposed itself between him and Kirby.

"What the hell is the matter with you?" one of the Argentines barked at Kirby. Colt guessed they couldn't see the drone but could probably hear its tiny whine. Kirby juked and jived like an inelegant drunk shadowboxing.

Kirby distracted, Colt sighted one of the Argentines and fired.

He hadn't wanted to hit him, necessarily, just get them to dive for cover and hope Liu picked up on it. Liu did. They stood in an intersection. Liu lunged past Kirby and out of Colt's limited field of vision before the FIA officers recovered. Colt sent three more shots downrange to give Liu time to get some distance.

The Argentines found cover of their own. One behind a marble column in front of a mausoleum and the other inside a recessed doorway to the tomb next to it.

Kirby backed away from the drone, which, acting without instructions, simply hovered.

The three of them could now cover each other and work their way down to Colt's position. The mausoleums on this block were smaller, less impressive, and therefore had some space between them. He could fade back, though he didn't know if it connected to the next "street" or just deadened at the back of another tomb. If so, he'd be cornered, but he'd be in the dark and would have tactical advantage.

Colt heard footsteps shuffling on the brick pathways. They were moving.

He chanced a look at the phone. Colt commanded the drone to rotate and watch their backs. Kirby was giving the FIA officers infantry signals, which they probably didn't understand. One moved forward to another tomb, crouched next to the doorway because there was nowhere for him to go, weapon out, and Kirby stepped into the street to move.

Colt would be pinned in a matter of seconds.

There was nowhere to run.

He hoped Liu got away in the confusion.

Colt set his phone on a ledge next to him so he could watch their movements with free hands.

Colt ejected his magazine and hammered a fresh one in, racked the slide to load a round in the chamber.

33

Buenos Aires, Argentina

Watching Kirby and his two paid goons on the video feed, Colt saw they'd already passed the intersection. Kirby sent one of the FIA men after Liu and kept the other with him. That changed things. Liu wasn't armed. Maybe he'd figure out a way to loop back and get to the entrance, but chances were that he'd get lost in this maze. The agent was probably from here and likely familiar with the cemetery, more so than Liu, anyway.

"I see every move you make, Kirby," Colt shouted. He aimed his head up, rather than forward, to change the direction of his voice. "I can see you scratching your ass."

"Nice try. Is that McShane? Why don't you give up now? Sorry to say, your girl didn't make it. They're probably stuffing her into a body bag as we speak."

Colt grabbed his phone, eyes on the camera, and backed up to the adjoining wall. This tomb didn't take up the entire plot, so he could slide around the back of it. It was a smallish block of yellowed marble, the corners streaked dark with weather. There was a heavy, wet smell here, and it was damp and cool. It was not the thick, tropical air of the city. This was something else.

Colt slid along the back wall.

"You're outnumbered, and you're trapped," Kirby said. Colt froze, watching Kirby and the agent with him cover themselves and move down the next set of tombs. They passed right by where Colt now crouched, separated only by a hundred-year-old marble box. Watching Kirby move on camera through an area just outside of where Colt stood was disorienting, and his brain had trouble processing it. Cognitive dissonance.

Colt stepped through the gap between this mausoleum and the next. This was the last one in this row before the intersection Liu and the other agent ran down. It was late dusk, the sky above fading to indigo, and the shadows where Colt now lurked were a liquid black.

"The longer I have to play hide-and-seek, the more this is going to hurt when I find you," Kirby said.

He was past Colt now. There was a stone wall, about five feet high, that marked the end of this street. Colt was wedged behind a tomb, larger than the one he'd just left, and the wall in the back corner. He put the phone in his pocket and holstered his pistol, then used the wall and back of the tomb to boost himself up to the top of the wall. Colt slid over it, looking first down the dark avenue. There was a murky form in the distance. He lowered himself onto the stone bench below the wall and silently dropped to the ground.

Colt drew his pistol and padded down the dark street of the dead, keeping close to the taller crypts and long shadows on the left side.

Kirby shouted something in the distance, but Colt was too far away and there was too much obstruction to make out what it was.

Weird things happened to sound here.

There were no birds and no wind. Even the traffic noise was distant and distorted.

The crypts here were much larger, so Colt guessed he was on a main path. These were ten, maybe fifteen feet, perhaps higher, it was hard to tell in the dark. Small houses. Some had angels, cherubs, or other statuary atop them. Some, massive crosses. The roofs alternated between flat and steepled. The colors alternated as well. Colt noted more black marble here. Those appeared newer. The street widened to accommodate tombs in the center.

There was a light at the end of this row, a tall, gothic streetlamp on the corner of the next intersection. Old, orange light drifted down.

A form shifted in front of him, coalescing out of the darkness. Colt strained his eyes to see, wishing he had the drone. With his phone in his pocket, Colt couldn't see the feed and couldn't issue it any new commands. The figure moved from one side to the other at the far end of the row.

He could not hear Kirby and the other agent behind him.

Colt held his pistol in a low, two-handed grip and took long, careful strides to close the distance between himself and that inky shape ahead.

Distance was difficult to judge in the dark, harder when contrasted against dim light, but this was something he'd learned at the Farm. And later put into practice in the brackish swamps of the Virginia Tidewater, where clandestine service trainees stalked through the murk on night navigation exercises.

Twenty yards.

The form stepped into the light and turned, listening for a sound.

Gun.

Colt raised the pistol, sighted, and fired twice.

He struck the man, and he fell.

Colt ran.

Shouts in the distance. He heard those.

He reached the end of the row and kicked the gun away from the agent's hand. Colt rolled the man over to inspect the wound. A hand flew up and connected with Colt's jaw.

McShane swore, his head snapping to the side with the impact. He fell back on his haunches, steadying himself with one hand, trying to regain his balance. The FIA agent kicked and landed a strike in the center of Colt's thigh. Sharp pain shot through his leg.

The agent rolled over, looking for his weapon. Colt pushed himself to stand and used the momentum to drive himself forward, kicking his opponent in the gut. The agent crumbled with the blow.

There was blood on the yellowed bricks but not much. Colt obviously hadn't hit him anywhere vital.

Shots rang out behind him.

"McShane!" Liu called from somewhere.

Colt jumped to the side, out of line of sight and behind one of the tombs in the center of the wide avenue. The agent scrabbled on the stones, reaching for his pistol. Colt kicked it farther away, the pistol clattered into the darkness. The agent swore at him in Spanish. Colt didn't know what he said but recognized the word "mother." He could fill in the rest.

Colt saw Liu in the shadows, hidden on the other side of the lane, crouched behind a monument in the shape of a large, leaning cross.

"I was trapped back here," Liu said.

"We don't have a lot of time. Let's go," Colt said.

He pulled Liu out of his hiding spot and ran to the far side of the inter- section. They found a thin row at what looked to be a forty-five-degree angle with the street. It was barely wide enough to walk down and utterly dark. "Here," Colt said and pushed Liu in. "Go as far as you can," he said. And he followed behind, walking backward, pistol up.

Kirby and the other agent reached the one Colt shot.

Colt turned and followed Liu down the narrow corridor and practically ran into him.

"What are you doing?" Colt hissed.

"Dead end," Liu said.

Not a great choice of words, Colt thought. For a number of reasons.

Colt turned and slowly crept back down the row to the street. Their only chance was to catch Kirby and the agent off guard, take them one at a time.

Tall order.

Colt sneaked nearly to the end and stopped. He could hear them moving now, shoes scraping along pavement.

A form passed across the end of Colt's row, ten feet from him, tops.

Kirby.

Colt raised his pistol.

Kirby turned.

There was a loud, sharp crack, thunder echoing off the stone canyons of the dead city.

Kirby's head snapped to one side and burst. His body fell to the ground.

Colt saw red beams trace along in the darkness.

"We've got four long guns on you right now," a voice growled from the far shadows. Colt saw a brief flash of red and then another. "Drop your weapons, interlace your hands above your heads."

Ikeda.

"Do it now," Ikeda repeated.

"Tony," Colt shouted. "I'm stepping out of cover."

"I got you," Ikeda said, sounding closer.

Colt slid out of his row and found himself standing next to Tony.

"Hey," he said amiably. "What's up?"

Colt looked to his left and saw the two FIA agents standing dumbfounded. One armed, the other, the injured one, not. Colt saw red dots on their chests.

No one moved. No one breathed.

Then the sounds of distant sirens broke the night.

The FIA men didn't take any action, but the one who still had his weapon didn't lower it either.

"You're in trouble now, American," one of them said in accented English, turning his head to face Colt. "You have no friends here."

"No, but you do, and that's going to be a problem for you."

"What the hell are you talking about? We just saw you commit murder," the Argentine said.

"Did you?" he said. Then, "There's ways this plays out. One, we keep up this standoff like some stupid Tarantino movie. We get arrested, and you have to explain what you're doing with intelligence officers from two different countries and him." Colt looked down at Kirby's body. "Once we're in questioning, we're going to have to say what *we* know about Mr. Kirby there. And that's going to raise some questions about you two. Probably they start looking at bank accounts. I don't imagine that ends well for you. We have diplomatic status. It'll be a pain in the ass, but we'll get cleared. Will you?"

Colt and Ikeda absolutely did not have diplomatic status. This was an unacknowledged mission. If they were arrested, the US government would not recognize them as lawful agents. Colt's only hope was that the bluff held.

"I think we broke up a foreign espionage operation," the Argentine said, looking from Colt to Liu.

"That's until we show your government proof that Hawkinson paid you off," Colt said. "How do you think we knew? We followed the money."

"That's not possible."

"One thing my country has gotten very, very good at in the last twenty years is following dirty money."

"And then," Ikeda said, "there's the car full of assholes that you paid to kill us. Two of them didn't make it, sorry to say. The other two, once they got on the 'answering questions' end of my pistol, had a lot to say. Like how you paid them off. Used cell phones to tell them where to be, where we'd be. Now, maybe that's fine in your government, but they probably wouldn't want you to have hired goons shooting up a city street."

"What's the other option?" the other Argentine asked.

"We leave now. You leave now. No one speaks a word about Kirby. You keep whatever Hawkinson paid you."

His partner was not convinced. "I don't think so," he said. "I think we turn you in, and I think they don't believe whatever is this bullshit you're talking."

The sirens got louder.

"Gentlemen, we are running out of time," Liu said, appearing behind Colt. "This argument is not productive."

Ikeda said, "Fellas, the police that roll up here are going to ask a lot of questions that I don't think any of us particularly want to answer. Maybe you dodge the bullet, but like he said," Ikeda nodded to Colt, though in the darkness it was a barely perceptible move, "we'll burn you with the money trail. Either way, we're looking at a three-way international incident, and I don't think that's good for any of us."

"Where are the others?" the first Argentine said. "You said you had four guns on us?"

Tony stepped into the light, a slight smirk on his face. He held his left hand out, revealing two black pens. "Laser pointers," he said.

The Argentine shook his head slowly and swore.

Regardless of whatever side they fell on, most professionals recognized a good play when they saw one. There were few zealots in intelligence. Their world was too bleak, too gray, and too real for fanatic loyalty to anything. There were a lot of stories from the early nineties, in the initial thawing after the Cold War, where CIA and former KGB officers met in Europe or elsewhere over drinks and swapped stories about shared operations. Two teams meeting on the field after a championship. One of them won, the other one lost, but they could both recognize the opponent's game.

"That's a good one," the Argentine said. "There is a street exit on Junín, opposite side of the cemetery from where you came in. It will be locked, but I suspect that won't be a problem for you."

Colt nodded and motioned to Liu, and they started moving in that direction.

Ikeda stayed. "What about him?" he said, pointing at Kirby.

"A cemetery is a good place to hide a body, no?"

"Need any help?"

"It would be better if you were not here. The police force is new, and they're still trying to get their feet under them. We have some...influence, yet. Try to stay away from the west side of town. We'll make sure the pursuit is focused that way."

Colt said, "Thank you," and was gone.

Tony caught up to him.

"I've got another job to do," Ikeda said.

"What?" Colt asked, genuinely confused.

"Sorry, pal." Tony flicked his eyes over to Liu. Colt understood, or at least understood why Tony couldn't say anything more.

"You'll get out okay?"

He gave a sly smile. "Yeah, I've done this before."

And Tony Ikeda disappeared into the night.

Colt and Liu moved quickly and silently through the avenues of the dead.

The large marble and stone structures, weather-beaten and dark, loomed over them. Colt turned right onto a wider...street? He didn't even know what to call this. They strode past the tombs, sirens building and adding to the unease. Colt hoped the Argentine intelligence officers kept their word. He hadn't expected them to buy his bluff about the money trail and wondered if the flip wasn't driven by something else, like perhaps Hawkinson hadn't been entirely honest with them about who they'd be following.

They reached the gate.

It was a massive, foreboding thing of black wrought iron set into a wall twenty feet high. It looked more like the gate to a medieval dungeon.

Liu said, "Allow me." He pulled a thin sleeve out of his jacket pocket and set to work on the lock.

"You never cease to surprise," Colt said.

"In my experience, it is best to be prepared for any eventuality."

Liu opened the lock, and it took both of them to pull the massive gate. They opened it just enough to slip through and into the deeper darkness beneath the trees. There were few lights on this side of the street.

Colt pulled his phone out, sent a message, and then turned north on the sidewalk.

"What's the plan?" Liu asked, and Colt could hear the nerves in his voice.

"Well, we're not flying out by plane. The last flight that would've gotten us anywhere good is taking off in a few minutes. But I'm still getting you out of here," Colt said, resolute.

"How?"

"We're going to steal a boat."

Without the car, they'd need to chance it with taxis. Colt guided them away from the cemetery, turned east toward the high-rises there. He saw many restaurants on the ground floors and people on the streets. That would mean both good cover and plenty of loitering taxis.

"Thank you," Liu said as they walked. "You saved my life." After another few moments, Liu said, "This is a bitter game, is it not? Friends become enemies, enemies friends. Or, at least, something less than enemies. That men like you and me could find ourselves on the same side, however fleeting. I know the lengths your colleagues went through to get their agents out of my country when we burned your covert communication network." Colt flicked a glance to the side and saw Liu holding the phone the Agency issued him, considering it. "My service would not have gone to those lengths." Liu sounded wistful. "I told you this once before, though I suspected you did not believe me. I did not order Glen's death. I was quite angry with my superiors when I learned of it. Though, there was little I could do."

Was Liu telling the truth? Colt didn't know. Liu was a master spy, a master manipulator. He was one of the best at this game Colt had ever seen. Perhaps he was being sincere, now, or maybe this was just another move in the bitter game.

Colt hailed a cab and took the risk of going to Aeroparque Buenos Aires, the smaller, regional airport they'd hoped to fly out of tonight. The airport was a long, low building with a glass front that followed the contour of the river behind it. It reminded Colt of a Latin American Reagan National. They entered, walked down to the baggage claim and then back out on the lower level, where they grabbed a different cab.

Colt gave the driver the name and address of a restaurant in barrio Vicente López.

The buildings melted into smaller structures as they moved north, mostly two- and three-story residences with the odd apartment tower, but nothing like the massive structures of the city center. As elsewhere in the city, the buildings on the corners of the blocks tended to be rounded and more decorative. Thick, leafy trees lined each of the streets, giving it an older-world feel.

"So, what we're going to do now is improvise," Colt said after they got out of their cab. They'd been dropped on a residential side street with a couple neighborhood restaurants on it.

They worked their way east toward the water. Colt doubled back several times but detected no one following them. This told him that if Hawkinson had any other FIA agents on his payroll, they weren't in on this operation. Or the other two directed them to wave off. True to their word, there didn't seem to be any police here.

Colt and Liu left the line of buildings and crossed to a large park that ran along the length of shoreline. They took the sidewalk north, Colt consulting his map one last time. The park abutted the brackish waters of the Río de la Plata, which then mixed with the South Atlantic in a wide delta that connected Argentina and Uruguay by water. They walked past a succession of traffic circles on an otherwise deserted road until they came to the final one, which terminated the road. There was a tall concrete-and-wire fence separating a thick, low forest from the grass beyond the end of the street.

Colt led a highly dubious Liu down a path through the trees. They could hear the river lapping against the shore.

"Where are we going?" Liu asked.

"This path leads to the river, and there's another trail we'll pick up along the shoreline. We're right next to a marina, maybe a quarter mile. We can access the harbor from this side. We'll steal a rowboat, they have rentals there, or kayaks if we can find them. Paddle around the shore to Uruguay."

"You're joking," Liu said, looking down at his expensive tailored suit.

"I hope you keep in shape."

They moved down the path for a tenth of a mile, the sounds of the river becoming more pronounced.

Colt cleared the trees. It was a clear night and warm, there was no moon, so it was quite dark. There were no city lights. Ahead of them, they could see the running lights of several ships out at sea.

A flashlight hit them, and a voice said, "That's far enough."

34

The man on the shoreline was dressed in black, held an MP-5 in one hand and a flashlight in the other. He wore dark face paint, streaked in wavy lines.

Colt swore under his breath.

"Move, now," the man growled. It sounded like British-accented English. He pointed with the pistol barrel toward the beach. There were two other men there, similarly dressed, next to a black inflatable raft with a power motor. Colt recognized the type. It was similar to what Ikeda's colleagues in the Special Activities Center's Maritime Branch used.

The man with the gun fell in step behind them.

The man on shore frisked Colt and Liu, removing Colt's pistol and backpack, Liu's knife, lockpicks, and all of their phones.

"Get in," he directed, and they did. He followed. One of his fellows climbed in, went to the motor, and powered it on while the third one pushed them off from shore.

"Anyone speaks and they get shot."

The driver opened up the throttle when the third man climbed in, and the little raft took them out to sea.

No one spoke.

Liu's shoulders deflated, though.

Colt knew how he felt.

It's hard to tell time in the dark, but there are ways, things spooks use to gauge how much of it has passed when it's not safe to look at a watch. Colt judged the trip was about twenty-five minutes.

The destination became clear in the last few minutes as they angled toward some running lights bobbing in the dark waters.

The accents made sense now.

Hawkinson wouldn't only source his security personnel from the American military, especially if he was going up against the Agency, where some of those boys would have connections.

All this way to be drilled twice in the head and dumped a few miles offshore.

At least they'd been successful. Colt could take some grim consolation in that.

The raft pulled up alongside the boat, which looked like a fishing trawler. "Out," their captor said.

Colt and then Liu climbed up the ladder and onto the boat. Someone emerged from the dark, grabbed Liu, and separated them. They guided Liu belowdecks while their captor, still the only one of the opposition to speak, said, "You first," to Colt before Liu was out of earshot.

He guided Colt up to the pilot house.

The boat started to move.

"How are we doing, Eduardo?" he asked, his tone now light and friendly.

"Right on schedule, sir," the pilot replied.

"Best speed, then, and don't spare the diesel." He turned to Colt. "Good evening, Mr. McShane. Ethan Dunning." He then poured something into a tin cup, and handed it to Colt.

"You're not..."

"Ann sends her regards," Dunning said by way of explanation, "and told me to tell you, 'message received.' Said this is her way of saying she's 'in the fight.'" Dunning chuckled. "No idea what she means, of course." Dunning smiled in the dim light. "Well, some idea."

Colt took a drink from the offered cup, coughed, and looked at the contents. "This is scotch. I thought it was water."

"Thought you might be thirsty," Dunning said, smiling beneath the makeup.

"You MI6?" Colt asked.

"Probably."

"So, what was with all of this?"

"Let's go back here." Dunning poured a cup for himself and gave Colt another splash, then walked back to a small navigation room. There was a small table and bench seating there, charts on the walls. They sat. "As you guessed, we have a friend in common. Like you, I know what Trinity is and help them where I can. Still work for king and country, though. They were monitoring the situation here and thought you'd need help getting out. Ann talked with a friend of yours back home, Fred Ford, and he gave her some insight on your exfiltration plans, so we knew about where you'd be. Once we knew your A and B plans were scrubbed, we moved in. Apologies for the scare. Wasn't sure what to make of that MSS chap."

Colt took a drink and then asked, "So, what now?"

"Well, we'll take you to Montevideo. Bit friendlier there. You can meet up with your people." He smiled knowingly. "Or not. Either way, you can get out safely."

Colt finished his drink and asked where he could find Liu. Colt went belowdecks to the boat's small dining area, where Liu was seated at a table, face drawn. The other two British Secret Intelligence Service men stood a few feet from him in guarded stances.

"Thanks, guys," Colt said. "I'll take it from here." The darkly clothed Brits walked up the stairs to topside.

He sat at the table and saw that Liu Che was very confused.

"They're friendlies," Colt said.

"Did you know?"

Colt ignored the question. "Let's talk about what happens next. They're taking us to Montevideo. Your service knows you went to Buenos Aires, right?"

Liu nodded. "They did. I was to observe everything I could on his technical efforts and try to get him to come to Beijing. I think you can surmise the rest."

"Okay, so, it won't raise any flags for you to fly back from Uruguay."

"Nothing I can't handle. You're...letting me go?"

"We're letting you return to your service," Colt said heavily. "We're going to honor our agreement to release your wife from prison. It will be done quietly, and it may take some time, but she will go free, as we agreed."

"I understand. Thank you for honoring your word." Liu's eyes tracked over to the galley. "You saved my life. That was...unexpected. What is next for our...arrangement."

"You will continue to work for us. I'll give you intelligence requirements, and you'll satisfy them. If we think you're lying or playing us in any way, we'll burn you to your government. For now, our immediate goals are to figure out what Archon's next move is. I don't expect they're going to give up because we won today. Archon wants us to fight each other. You and I are among a select few in the world who understand that, and we have to do everything in our power to prevent it."

"Our president is corrupt," Liu said. "As are the communist party and the PLA. My service is little different. Archon will have many avenues to exploit. We've heard of them, of course. Though, I should warn you my service does not consider them to be a threat. And they're content to watch the West carve itself up."

"I don't think they're going to get that chance," Colt said.

"No," Liu agreed. "It would seem not."

"Are you willing to work with me, Che? You've seen what we're up against."

Liu Che was silent for a long time.

"Perhaps we have an understanding," Liu said.

"Perhaps we do."

"As I understand the politics of your country, there is little your government can do against Guy Hawkinson without it seeming like a political attack on his uncle, the senator and presidential candidate."

Colt nodded. "Yeah, we'd pretty much need video of him murdering someone while claiming allegiance to ISIS."

"What if the news was broken by someone else?"

"What do you mean?"

"Hypothetically, if, say, British intelligence discovered information that Guy was forging an alliance with my government, what would happen?"

Colt scratched at his chin, thinking. "FBI would have enough to open a case against him, at least." He thought it better than to acknowledge the FBI had done so already. In fact, before they'd inserted Nadia into Hawk-Tech, the Bureau managed to get one of their people in undercover in the company's finance department. Unfortunately, they hadn't been able to uncover anything substantive, and the Bureau pulled the plug when Hawkinson moved his operation to Switzerland.

Liu gave a cold, dark smile. "MI6 still has assets in my country, mostly left over from the Hong Kong transition. I know of an information channel within the People's Liberation Army Intelligence that the British have compromised." The derision Liu poured on the PLA was unmistakable. "They would certainly relay this to their old friends in the CIA."

"Why would you do this?"

"You saved my life, Colt. You didn't have to." Liu smirked. "My service is fiercely competitive with the PLA's intelligence directorate. I might take a professional hit for losing the Hawkinson case, but my superiors will enjoy the bad publicity for their political opponents in Department Two far more."

Colt wondered for a moment if Dunning was listening in on their conversation, what he'd think of it if he were.

It was nearing midnight when they left the boat, and Montevideo was quiet, but bright orange-yellow streetlamps illuminated the roads beneath the blue-white glow of the modern buildings. Intermixed were the eighteenth-century colonial structures and palm trees.

Dunning, now cleaned and in street clothes, let them off on a pier on the city's eastern side. He said they had an arrangement here and did not offer further details. Colt and Liu hopped off the boat. Dunning explained that he and his men would be dropped elsewhere. He never explained whether the fishing vessel (if that's what it truly was) belonged to the

British government or was actually a trawler that they'd used for this mission.

"Glad I could help out," Dunning said before Colt left the boat.

"So am I."

"Godspeed and all that."

Colt had more questions about Dunning, his relationship with Ann and Trinity, but decided to let them lie.

He'd seen the looks Dunning made toward Liu and suspected he had questions of his own.

Colt and Liu stood on the pier as the boat departed and then walked up to the long seawall erected to protect the harbor from the ocean.

"You'll head back to Geneva, then?" Colt asked.

"Yes. I suspect the operation against Hawkinson will be terminated."

"What will you tell them?"

"Kirby attempted to bribe me, recruit me into working for them to circumvent our regulations. They will believe that story. It validates what they already believe about Western businesses," Liu said, without a hint of irony.

"I'll be in touch. Do you have a way to keep that phone?"

"I am not inspected at customs," Liu said dryly.

35

Washington, DC

It took Colt two days to get back to Washington.

Colt cooled his heels in Montevideo until eleven the following morning, buying a travel bag, change of clothes, and toiletries. He'd kept his passport with him, in a concealed pocket in the ruck. His new friends in SIS were able to affix a Uruguayan customs stamp so Colt wouldn't raise any eyebrows when he left. The pistol went over the side of the boat last night. He took a one o'clock flight to Santiago, Chile, with a six-and-a-half-hour layover before another to Atlanta, landing at five forty the next morning.

He'd still heard nothing from Tony Ikeda.

Colt was exhausted, suffering from an adrenaline crash and just wanting to be home. This would be a long day. He messaged Ford to let him know that he was back in-country. Ford told him to "get his ass in the office faster than whatever passed for 'Colt McShane ASAP.'"

Colt took a cab home when he'd landed at Dulles, a gray, blustery December morning. Showered, changed, had real food before driving into Langley, arriving just before noon.

Colt found Ford, Thorpe, and the other senior officers in the unit's conference room, which they'd converted into a de facto war room.

"YELLOWCARD is safe," Thorpe said as soon as Colt entered.

"Also, welcome home, glad you're safe, and good job not causing World War Three," Ford said.

"Let's go to the ops center," Thorpe said, and led Ford and Colt out of the war room. "You might as well get to see what you risked your neck for."

"What's going on?"

"We're walking *and* chewing gum," Ford quipped.

They entered the ops center. "Why does this place seem half full to me?" Colt asked.

"Because it is," Thorpe said. "The NSA recalled all of their people."

"They did *what?*"

"Said current operational requirements dictated returning them to operational billets at Fort Meade."

Ford said, "What it really means is General Burgess is a spiteful prick."

"I feel like I'm a few conversations behind."

"What my old friend is saying," Thorpe said, "is that we think General Burgess didn't appreciate getting embarrassed in front of the president during our little meeting in the Oval a few weeks ago. He's recalled all of the people NSA loaned us."

"That's a third of our staff!"

"Yep. The director is taking it up with him. Burgess isn't going to come out of this looking very good, but there's little we can do. They're his people, this isn't a congressionally funded unit, so we don't have any actual end strength to maintain. But, one crisis at a time." Thorpe pointed at the wall screens in the ops center. "Fred?"

Ford folded his arms across his chest. He addressed the other two but didn't take his eyes off the wall monitors. "We've got a SIGINT intercept between the GRU and the Russian General Staff, as you know. To put it in technical terms, they are currently shitting egg rolls. The General Staff didn't order the ATC and pipeline cyberattacks. Intercepts suggest about a sixty-forty split between thinking it was someone else and they're being blamed for it and a rogue element acting on their own. Leading theory in Moscow is that one of the 'contractors' they use in Bulgaria or Hungary decided to act out of turn. We're getting so much intel on Russian proxy hackers right now because of all the people the Russians are panic-calling to see who's doing what. When this is all over, we're going to take a lot of assholes off the board. KOSCHEI is furious. He's called the head of the GRU in about four times in the last week to demand answers."

"We know the substance of those conversations?"

"Some," Ford said.

A few years ago, CIA recruited a senior staff officer in the Russian Eighth Army. The Eighth Army was assigned to the Southern Military District, which oversaw Russia's operations in Georgia and the Caucasus. However, as a result of the incredible casualties they'd sustained in their invasion of Ukraine, particularly among general officers, the asset, code-named GT-PARABLE, now found himself as a deputy on the staff of Main Command–Ground Forces.

PARABLE supplied his Agency handlers with context from the inner-most meetings of the General Staff which he received, unfiltered, from the Chief of Ground Forces, Colonel General Galkin.

"KOSCHEI is convinced that our president is planning for his removal based on that goddamned doctored video. They are moving their interme-diate rocket forces into position on the Ukrainian border."

"Nukes?"

Thorpe nodded grimly.

Ford said, "The General Staff is in a panic. About a third of them are newly promoted into the job because of the GO losses they've sustained in Ukraine and a few, ah, 'ballistic retirements' courtesy of KOSCHEI thinking CIA has an assassin lurking in the Kremlin. They aren't as hard-line about the war as their president, and no one wants to tussle with the West. The line officers all knew what shape their forces were in and assumed their bosses were telling KOSCHEI. The part we don't know is if KOSCHEI ordered a strike, would their troops carry it out. I mean, ultimately, *someone* would." Ford exhaled. "It's a shitshow."

"So, what's our next move?"

"There's a response, but we aren't briefed on it. Nor are we involved," Thorpe said.

That means it's kinetic, Colt thought. *Shit. This is getting out of hand fast.*

"Which brings us to now."

"ATTILA is ready to go, sir," one of the operators said.

"You may proceed," Thorpe said.

"ATTILA?" Colt asked.

A network map appeared on screen. Thorpe narrated as the actions played out. "This is HawkTech B.A. Thanks to the work you and Mr. Liu did, we are now inside their network, and there's nothing they can do about it. Our analysts have been poring over every bit of data for the last two days and, thanks to pattern analysis and data reconstruction done by CERBERUS, we can trace a direct line from HawkTech to that off-the-books server farm in a B.A. industrial park to the GRU. We've got source files showing the exploits they would've needed in both the ATC and pipeline attacks. Those red indicators on the screen, by the way, show admins and super-admins being locked out and taken offline. We're doing this while they watch, so they know what it feels like," Thorpe noted ruefully.

A few seconds later, the operator said, "We have control."

"Good," Thorpe said. To Colt, "We now control HawkTech B.A."

"But if we can prove that they're responsible, why isn't Hawkinson being arrested?"

"Next step is we're going to disable the water-cooling for their super-computer array and are giving it a rather hairy computational problem to solve. This is mostly for spite. We've already copied over everything they had stored. This should overheat and melt down in time. We have other malware that's attacking the rest of their systems. There won't be much left. As to your question, this is what we were directed to do. He's got too much political cover from his uncle. The only people who know about this operation are in this room."

Ford picked up the thread from there. "So, we've stolen all of the AI research, trade secrets, concepts in progress from HawkTech—B.A. and Geneva, right?"

Colt said, "Yeah?"

"Well, now we're going to start scatting it all over the internet. Dark web, open-source research forums, freaking Reddit. All courtesy of one Matthew Kirby."

Color appeared around the edges, and Colt gathered the plot. With Kirby missing, they were leaving breadcrumbs to look like an inside job.

"We've got all of Kirby's electronic and text correspondence going back years, courtesy of LONGBOW," Ford said, with a hand flourish to Colt. "Our techs are using CERBERUS to construct messages that will sound authentically drafted by Kirby. This will give us attribution. It's not going to be a manifesto or anything, just enough conversational text to convince Hawkinson it is Kirby's hand."

"I'll say this, Colt," Thorpe said dryly. "Buenos Aires was a complete fiasco, but it's working out as a fiasco in our favor."

"Once this stuff hits the internet, Jeff Kim is going to be able to prove that Hawkinson stole from him. Even if the Justice Department can't do anything to him, the civil suit will bankrupt him."

Thorpe nodded, and Ford just said, "Yep." Ford's face broke into a dark smile. "I think Hawk Actual is going to bounce off the deck, hard."

That night, Colt lit a fire and poured a bottle of Old Rasputin imperial black ale into a Naval Academy pint glass.

Colt lived in a small, midcentury home in Falls Church, about twenty minutes from Langley. His decor reflected his vagabond years traipsing across the globe with nothing to anchor him to any one place. From his Navy years, Colt had mostly framed photos and local art from the places he made port calls—Toulon in France, Rota in Spain, Sicily, Crete, Cyprus, Marmaris, and, of course, Haifa. Colt took a photography elective at the Academy and found he had an eye for it. Some of the pictures weren't bad, a couple good enough to sell.

The souvenirs from his Agency time were a little more circumspect. His eight years undercover as a corporate technology investor got him small sculptures and more photos from places like Tokyo, Singapore, and Taipei.

If someone were to walk through Colt's home—and few ever had— they'd notice most of the pictures were of subjects, there was no one in them. Certainly, the earlier photos of port calls had shipmates and classmates, but the moments of the latter years didn't even include himself. There were no selfies on Mount Fuji or shots of him by a helpful tourist.

It was a random collection.

His life felt that way sometimes. Honestly, most times, when he was somewhere long enough to contemplate it.

Colt messaged Ava with the Trinity message app. The rules governing communication with officers from other intelligence services were clear, and this was entirely outside official channels. Though, when Colt considered the lines he now traveled between the Agency, NTCU, and Trinity and Archon, no sane person would begrudge him a few words with one of the only people on earth that understood what he was going through.

There would be hell to pay if he was ever caught communicating with Ava outside the process again. Though, that was sort of the point using Trinity's messaging system.

He wanted to know if she was recovering.

From her wounds, from the loss of her aunt and last connection she had with her parents.

From learning her aunt was a prime mover in Archon.

Colt didn't hear back from her. He still hadn't heard from Ikeda, so he fired up a clean laptop and surfed news sites in Buenos Aires. It was still early for there to be any real revelation in the media about Hawkinson yet, that wouldn't come for a few days, maybe a week, though the unit had a few tactics to speed that along.

He did find one interesting thing, however. There was one story, a follow-up on a piece from three days before about a strange explosion that leveled a building in an industrial park in Puerto Madero. The building was unoccupied, and the police speculated the building was used to store computing equipment.

The next morning, Colt posted to the NTCU conference room for his formal debrief with Ford and Thorpe. The war room had been cleared, or at least temporarily relocated. There was still no word on Nadia.

To his great relief, there was Tony Ikeda. He wore chinos, a dress shirt, and a blazer and seemed hilariously overdressed.

"I read last night that a building exploded," Colt said.

"Gentlemen, can we save this for the debriefing?" Thorpe said.

Tony only shrugged and smirked.

They were joined shortly by Ikeda's team lead in Ground Branch and the head of the Special Activities Center. Thorpe admonished Colt and Tony for allowing a firefight inside a cemetery. At least they hadn't shot up Eva Perón's tomb.

CIA kept their operations heavily compartmented, even within its ranks. Often, an individual case officer might risk their life on a mission and wouldn't know how it fit into the larger part. So, it was rare for Thorpe and the Ground Branch boss to acknowledge that Ikeda's additional mission was to sabotage Archon's covert server farm in the Buenos Aires industrial park. In classic Agency fashion, the Ground Branch chief didn't know what "Archon" was or why that building full of computer equipment had to go.

NTCU watched the revelations about Guy Hawkinson slowly unfold on television over the next several days. It was one of the few stories able to slip into the news cycle in between segments on the continually escalating tensions with Russia.

News outlets swarmed on the story.

Four days after Colt returned from Argentina, Deputy Director Hoskins appeared in NTCU. Thorpe gathered Colt and Ford, and the four of them crammed into Thorpe's small office.

"We just received an emergency cable from London Station," Hoskins said the second the door clicked shut. "MI6 has a source in the PLA's Intelligence Division. They're reporting the PLA is working with Guy Hawkinson."

36

Somewhere Over Western Russia

The B-21 Raider slid into Russian airspace like a thief from the Barents Sea.

The aircraft, call sign "FAIRLANE One-One," took off from Edwards Air Force Base in California under cover of darkness and flew northwest, fleeing the dawn.

The aircraft skirted Murmansk, then the White Sea, and came within two hundred nautical miles of Arkhangelsk without detection.

It was a ghost.

The aircraft, first unveiled to the world in a ceremony held at Edwards the year before, was the most advanced ever designed. There were six in existence, currently in operational trials at the Air Force Test Center. Though the Air Force had not yet designated the Raider as Fully Operationally Capable (FOC), and it wasn't expected in the Air Force inventory until the end of the decade, the service deemed it the only one capable of executing this mission.

The aircrew, a pilot and copilot, were selected from the top aviators in the 509th Bomb Wing. The 509th, which traced its lineage back to the Second World War and the *Enola Gay*, operated the B-2A Spirit, the so-called "stealth bomber." The pilot, Lt Col Wade Hall, and his copilot, Lt Col

Paul Wheeler, began training for the operation four months before. Given the risk involved, both men were given the opportunity to decline. They did not.

Initially, the Air Force planned the mission with B-2s but rejected it as too high risk. The B-2's mission profile evolved as radar technology advanced. Now, it was more akin to the door-kicker on a SWAT team than a thief in the night. The B-2 would approach at stand-off range and destroy enemy air defenses before it could be identified, opening a secure corridor for other aircraft to fly in and wreak havoc.

For this operation, they needed something more.

They would need to sneak in, deliver a payload, and then sneak out with no trace left behind. A mission the B-2 could have pulled off when it was first designed, but likely not now. It was the Air Force's Rapid Capability Office (RCO) that suggested the B-21. The Air Force established the RCO in 2003 to fast-track advanced technology into the service, acting as the USAF corollary to DARPA. RCO led the B-21's selection and development, rather than the traditional arms of the service's acquisition command. RCO argued the jet could do the job, and they'd already tested it against captured Russian radar systems, so they believed it would work. As they watched the Chinese military's meteoric advancement, RCO suspected they might need the B-21 sooner than its development timeline allowed. They began training combat pilots in secret, working with the test pilots to fully understand and operationally vet the jet's astounding capabilities and to develop the tactics, techniques, and procedures (TTPs) they would use to guide it in combat.

Hall narrated each of their actions for the flight recorder.

The jet slipped past Petrozavodsk on the shores of the massive Lake Onega, with no indications of detection.

The land below was lightless, a bleak no-man's-land.

Their target was preprogrammed. They were approximately five hundred miles away, well within the weapon's operational range.

"Target acquired," Hall said. Then, "Launching." He activated the launch mechanism. The forward munitions bay opened and ejected four YAGM-181 Long Range Standoff (LRSO) weapons and closed. Like the aircraft that launched it, LRSO was still a prototype, intended to replace the venerable AGM-86 Air Launched Cruise Missile (ALCM). The LRSO could maneuver around enemy air defenses and was, itself, stealthy, a fiery sliver in the darkness.

Hall said, "Fox One, Fox Two," as the first two missiles fired. Then, "Fox Three, Fox Four." Four streaks lanced off into the night.

Hall banked the aircraft to the west.

There would be a momentary blip on Russia's air defense radar; likely they wouldn't even notice.

The four missiles streaked toward their target, accelerating up to a speed just shy of Mach 1. Each took a varied route and altitude to increase survivability. While two were deemed sufficient to destroy the target, they'd launched four to be certain.

Wheeler watched the missiles' progress on one of his display screens while Hall flew. Forty-five minutes after launch, they were over Lake Ladoga, approaching St. Petersburg and, more importantly, the Gulf of Finland and safety. The original mission profile was to launch from outside Russian airspace, but the White House wanted to send a message. This mission was as much about future deterrence as it was retribution.

"Missiles approaching target," Wheeler said.

At 3:42 Moscow time, all four YAGM-181s struck a nondescript, hulking square building in the Moscow suburb of Khimki. The first hit the building's outer wall with devastating force. The second and third flew through the hole made by the first and angled down, impacting on the floor, seconds apart, detonating on the first floor and basement, respectively. The fourth and final missile struck the building's uppermost floor, just seconds after the first blast. The building was consumed in overlapping explosions.

Seconds later, there was little left but fire and smoke.

The GRU's elite hacking group, Unit 74455, was gone.

––––––––

Aircraft scrambled throughout Russia, though the Air Defense Army had no idea what happened.

The Russians flew continual CAPs along their border with Estonia and Latvia and coerced Belarus to do the same, so some aircraft were already in the air. Eight MiG-31s, NATO reporting name "Foxhound," of the 180th Guards Fighter Aviation Regiment launched from the air base at Gromovo, outside St. Petersburg. The MiG-31 was an advanced version of the original MiG-25 Foxbat, a Mach 3 fighter the Soviets designed to catch the SR-71 Blackbird.

The Foxhound carried an active electronically scanned array radar, which gave it the ability to detect and track up to twenty-four targets in a one-hundred-and-twenty-nautical-mile range, steered by a computer. Once locked on, the MiG-31 would typically fire R-33 Vympel air-to-air missiles (NATO reporting name AA-9 "AMOS"). A MiG-31's radar suite could also detect and intercept cruise missiles in-flight.

Though not today, it would seem.

The aircraft formed a tight net around St. Petersburg. Su-27s were now up over Petrozavodsk, and the air over Moscow looked like a hornet's nest had been kicked over.

The Russians closed their airspace to all traffic and ordered every non-military aircraft in the air to the ground immediately.

"Tracking eight bandits," Wheeler said calmly.

Though they could bank right and escape over Finland, the flight plan called for them to head straight for the international waters of the Gulf of Finland. First, the US had not advised the other NATO members of this strike in order to maintain secrecy and also didn't want them drawn into a conflict unnecessarily. Second, the Air Force had a squadron of F-35s deployed outside Tallinn, Estonia. Those aircraft were conveniently on a nighttime patrol over the gulf and established an airborne picket line. If any Russian aircraft crossed that line, they would be splashed immediately.

There was a third reason as well.

Another valuable lesson and a warning to the Russians—and some farther east—on how far US aircraft technology had come.

The B-21 sneaked past the MiG-31 patrol as though the Russians flew with blindfolds on and randomly batted at a piñata.

The MiG-31 AESA radars doubtless detected a single blip fifteen miles northwest of St. Petersburg before it quickly vanished.

Then they saw eight more.

These did not vanish.

"FAIRLANE One-Two: Fox One, Fox Two, Fox Three, Fox Four," and on until all eight AIM-260 Joint Advanced Tactical Missiles ejected from the aircraft's munitions bay and fired. This would serve as an operational test for one of the B-21's secondary mission, what some in the Air Force were calling a "super fighter." The mission parameters were for a stealth aircraft to carry large numbers of air-to-air weapons and fire from behind enemy lines or at standoff range.

Hall and Wheeler watched as the bandit indicators disappeared from their screens one by one. The AIM-260 was incredibly fast with one of the most accurate targeting systems ever designed, created to take out fifth-generation fighters. The MiGs didn't stand a chance.

FAIRLANE One-Two was entirely a backup, originally intended to open an air corridor if, for some reason, Russian air defenses detected the first B-21. But, as with the missile strike, Washington wanted to send a message.

There were times when you hid your capabilities from the enemy, and there were times when you showed them exactly what you could do.

The president sat in the White House Situation Room watching a multi-picture feed on the screen at the far end of the long mahogany table. The images came from the Global Strike Operations Center at Barksdale Air Force Base.

The Secretary of Defense, Chairman of the Joint Chiefs, and Air Force Chief of Staff sat at the table. As did the chairman and chairwoman of the Senate and House Armed Services Committees. The Commander of US Strategic Command and Commander of Air Force Global Strike Command joined by secure videoconference.

The vice president, Speaker of the House, and Secretary of State had been sent to the government's doomsday bunker at Mount Weather, Maryland, as a precaution, in case the Russians foolishly decided to respond.

The Commander of Global Strike stated impassively, "Mr. President, we report target destroyed."

The president turned to the SECDEF. "Make the call, Walt," he said.

The Secretary of Defense stepped out of the situation room to a secure anteroom where a phone had been set up for him. The Secretary of Defense called his opposite number in the Russian Federation. The White House Communication Service opened the line. Instead of going to the MoD, they patched SECDEF in directly to the Minister's residence in Moscow.

"General Dragunov, Walt Hughes here," the Secretary said, conversationally. The Minister of Defense knew damned well who it was; the call passed several hands before he picked up.

"You have attacked the Russian Federation, Mr. Secretary. This is an act of war!" Dragunov growled.

"You murdered a hundred innocent civilians and caused us billions in property damage attacking Folsom Dam," Hughes countered. "So, spare me the righteous indignation. You attacked us and didn't think you'd get caught. Unfortunately for you, we're better at this. We exercised extraordinary restraint by limiting our response to a military target. It can stop here, Evgeni. What you and I decide to do next may well be the most consequential decision of the next fifty years." Hughes had practiced this speech. He and the president worked on the exact phrasing. It was also being broadcast in the Situation Room. Hughes assumed the Russians were recording it as well. If KOSCHEI wasn't listening in now, he would hear this soon enough.

"Now, we know that you didn't shut down our air traffic control system, and we know you didn't mess with our pipeline. We know who did, and they've been dealt with. What happened just now, we deemed an appropriate, if not disproportionate, response to your attack on our dam. Don't bother denying it, we have the logs to show the GRU launched it. I'm sure your president will be angry. He will want to show strength. It's vitally important that you don't let him do that."

"You cannot expect me to let you violate our sovereignty and attack us."

That was posturing for the inevitable reviews later. If he capitulated over the phone, Dragunov was probably a dead man given the state of things in Russia, but Hughes knew the minister was listening.

"I'm here to urge you to exercise caution, General. We've shown a little of what we're capable of, what we're *willing* to do. If there is any reprisal, if there is talk of retaliation with your nuclear arsenal, if we feel threatened in any way, we will not hesitate to act. And NATO will act with us. By any objective measure, Evgeni, you have performed poorly against a much smaller, ill-equipped force. How well do you think you'd fare against the combined forces of the West?"

The phone was silent save for the crackle of static from the poor telephone lines in Moscow and the God-only-knew-how-many additional taps on them.

After a minute, Secretary Hughes said, "Do you understand me, Evgeni?"

"I understand," he said.

"Good. Then I wish you a pleasant day."

The Secretary of Defense hung up.

37

Geneva, Switzerland

To put it succinctly, Guy Hawkinson wanted to murder the first person he saw.

The Buenos Aires operation was a total loss. The physical space he could give two shits about, that amounted to petty cash, but the supercomputing array and the quantum lab represented an investment of hundreds of millions of dollars.

And they were not *his* dollars.

That was money from an Archon-directed capital investment firm, and it would need to be paid back. And Guy did not have the money to do it. Kirby stripped them, laid them bare, he put their secrets on the fucking internet! R&D projects, trade secrets, source code, development notes... Christ, he'd put the original files from Pax AI out there.

HawkTech was ruined.

There would be enough for the DoJ to prosecute him for industrial espionage now. Not even Uncle Preston could shut that down.

Guy couldn't understand it. Betrayal, yes, but not from Matt. They'd fought together. Matt *bled* for him, withstood unimaginable torture at the hands of Russian mercenaries, and he didn't give up a thing.

So why now?

It just didn't make sense that Matt would take everything they'd done and just give it away.

Had Liu flipped him? That didn't seem likely either. Guy still had a few sources at CIA, but no one could—or would—find out anything more.

He thought of Nadia Blackmon. Guy intentionally put her next to Liu to see if one would recruit the other. If she turned Liu, that would mean Liu couldn't trust her and Guy could dispatch them both. If Liu turned her, then it didn't matter and CIA was taken off the board. Only, it seemed Liu must have been working with Langley, because how else could they have gotten access to his network?

Not only that, they (whichever "they" it was) found the server farm in Puerto Madero that Archon's operatives used to hack the GRU.

Fireballs in an industrial park didn't seem to be the Ministry of State Security's style.

Guy's phone rang.

He turned from the window overlooking Lake Geneva to his desk. The HawkTech offices were sparsely populated. A quarter of his workforce quit when they learned what happened in Argentina. Between the Russians attacking their island and whatever this was, many did not want to be associated with HawkTech any longer. It was too risky.

Guy held an all-hands, told people that one of their own had betrayed them, sold their secrets, when their work began appearing on the internet. That seemed to mollify some. People were understandably furious that their work was stolen and given away. Then, quiet words began popping up online suggesting some of what was released was Pax AI source code. That was the final straw for many. Most didn't even bother to resign, they just *left*. He told them it was bullshit, something Matt made up to cover his tracks. He did not get the sense that people believed him.

Whether people believed Hawkinson's story or not, there was something going on they didn't want to be part of. They didn't want to be collateral damage in whatever fight Hawkinson started with some very powerful enemies.

The resignations grew to fifty percent of his employees by the end of that first week. The ones who held out, mostly the senior staff, were loyal to him. Either they believed his story or they simply didn't care.

The phone continued to ring.

His long serving exec assistant, Tina, was one of the ones who left. That one hurt.

When Guy wasn't in all-hands or damage control meetings or war rooms or whatever the hell else they were calling them, he was on the phone with investors, practically begging them not to pull out. He urged patience, pleaded grace.

Some hung on, most did not.

He called his sister and asked her to do damage control, to call their backers (the public ones) and get them to reconsider.

Sheryl had the gall to call him "goddamn Icarus."

Say what you will about pretentious boarding schools, that upbringing did net a higher quality of insult.

The phone kept up its noise.

Guy had also heard nothing from their *other* backers.

Nothing from "the Doge."

Sheryl had never heard of him either. The implications, of course, were far reaching. The Doge, which Guy knew now was Italian for "duke," the head of a city-state and most often attributed to the nobility of the Republic of Venice. So, not a disaffected computer scientist.

He'd told Guy at their meeting he was a kind of chairman of the board for Archon, someone who sat above the organization, advised and perhaps directed. So why had Guy never heard of him before?

Of course, he and Sheryl were still outsiders to the organization, after a fashion. Guy thought of himself as Archon's J3, the head of operations, the executive arm but detached from decision making.

The goddamn phone still wouldn't stop. Whoever it was, was persistent.

Guy stalked over to his desk, grabbed it, and thumbed the phone icon.

"What," he said.

"Listen carefully, Guy, you do not have much time."

He knew that voice. The lilting, almost musical intonation of Italian-accented English.

"What do you want?"

"I am trying to save your skin. The FBI has a warrant for your arrest. United States Marshals and the FBI Legal Attaché for Switzerland are on their way to you now, with the Swiss Federal Police."

"How long do I have?"

"Ten minutes. Perhaps nine. Now, do exactly as I tell you. Once we hang up, you will get in your car and drive to Vevey. Do not take longer than one hundred and twenty minutes. There is a hotel two blocks from the ferry terminal, the Guest House Le Charlot. There will be a bag waiting for a Mr. Neils Perry. They will not ask for identification. Inside you will find a clean passport, credit cards, and sufficient euro to last you several weeks. There will be a few items to reduce discoverability. You will also find a telephone in the bag. It contains the number of someone who can get you a clean vehicle. You will then drive to Maribor, Slovenia. Take no more than three days to get there."

"Why am—"

"You talking wastes time," the Doge said. "Go there. You'll receive further instructions when you arrive. Go alone. We *will* be in touch."

The line went dead.

Guy had a choice to make. Trust this man who referred to himself in the third person as an Italian duke, or chance it that the FBI would arrest him for espionage within minutes.

Little choice at all.

Guy told his security detail to get his car but park it about two blocks from here so it was off the quay. Said he wouldn't need a driver. When he walked out of the building to go to his car, a light snow drifting down from gray skies, Guy told his detail that some people might be asking about him. Stall them.

Guy Hawkinson found his Mercedes G-Wagon with one of his security detail idling with the vehicle so it wasn't towed. He left the man on the corner.

With the weather, it took him a few minutes shy of two hours to get to Vevey, on the far side of the lake. He found the hotel and asked for a package for Mr. Perry. The man at the small check-in counter handed him a black bag of ballistic nylon. Guy asked for a room. The man checked him in.

Upstairs, Guy opened the bag and found the contents as described. There was comb-in hair dye, black, and contacts, blue. Guy applied the hair dye and put the contacts in. He found the passport in the bag, Swiss, with a modified photo of himself showing black hair and blue eyes and bearing the name "Hans Reichert." There were two credit cards in the Hans Reichert name and five thousand euro in cash.

Guy used the phone and spoke to a man with an accent more German sounding than Swiss-German, who told him there was a vehicle waiting for him in the parking lot of the ferry terminal. He gave Guy the row and spot number. Guy asked about his Mercedes, and the man said, "Not my problem."

Guy left the hotel through a back entrance so the clerk didn't see him with the dye job.

He found the car, a black BMW 330i xDrive. The keys were in the glove box. A step down from the hundred-and-fifty-thousand-dollar SUV he'd just abandoned.

Guy thought a day like this might come eventually, so he kept a bug-out bag with him. It was little more than a few days' worth of clothes, money, an unused cell phone, and a clean laptop still in the factory seal. He brought that with him, along with the black duffel, and climbed into the BMW.

And Guy Hawkinson disappeared.

38

"My fellow Americans, earlier today, I directed elements of the United States military to strike specific targets belonging to Russian military intelligence. This group was responsible for flooding the Folsom Dam, which resulted in the deaths of a hundred and fifteen of our fellow citizens and caused billions of dollars in damage. I also delivered a warning to the Russian president that the United States will not tolerate any more aggression. Such would be met with decisive and tremendous force. Furthermore—"

The video reduced to a box that appeared over the newscaster's shoulder, above the banner, "Special Report: America Strikes Targets in Russian Federation."

The anchor delivered the network's post-speech analysis, joined by their foreign policy and national security correspondents, as well as a retired Army general who was now a contributor.

And former Director of the National Clandestine Service, Jason Wilcox.

"This speech, delivered by the president just minutes ago, detailed America's response to cyberattacks carried out by Russian military intelligence units. I'm joined by our national security team to break down each part of the president's speech, but first, I'd like to bring in Jason Wilcox. Mr. Wilcox is a career CIA operations officer and the former Director of the National Clandestine Service."

"Thank you, Grace, it's good to be with you. The post–Cold War Russian intelligence apparatus is largely defined by three groups. The SVR and FSB, which consist of the remnants of the old KGB, and the GRU, their military intelligence arm. And that's who we're talking about here. The GRU is responsible for most of the Russians' operational work abroad. It is also their lead agency for cyber warfare. The group we're talking about is Unit 74455, and they have been linked to the 2015 Ukrainian power grid attack as well as the 2016 hack of the Democratic National Committee email server and subsequent release to WikiLeaks. They're believed to have interfered with the French presidential election in 2017, social engineering activities during the Brexit campaign, and to have interfered in our own presidential elections in 2016 and 2020. The building that was destroyed in a Moscow suburb was their headquarters."

"What do we know about—"

Ford muted the television and leaned back in his chair. He and Colt were both still at the unit, sitting in the common area watching the television mounted on the wall. It didn't seem right to go anywhere else.

"Boss looks good on camera," Ford said.

A sidebar appeared on the screen next to the anchor's face, listing locations in Romania and Hungary where additional arrests took place.

The Romanians were staunch US allies, and they had a strong tradition of organized crime all too common in countries freed from Soviet rule. Drawing on Romania's highly educated and tech-savvy population, those groups turned to cybercrime and several became favorite proxies of the GRU. Acting on intelligence provided by CIA, the Romanian General Directorate for Countering Organized Crime executed raids in Bucharest and Cluj-Napoca. The Hungarian government, which had recently edged closer to Russia's orbit, was initially less willing to act. Until a direct call from POTUS reminding them of their NATO obligation facilitated a reconsideration. Then, their federal police raided two suspected hacker groups in Budapest. The groups in Belarus were a little harder to get at, but the Agency's Minsk Station had that assignment.

"Oh, this is the part I wanted to see," Ford said, almost giddy, and thumbed the volume back on.

The anchor showed a picture of a frog-faced man with a ruddy complexion and blond stubble haircut in a green uniform with a ridiculous amount ornamentation.

The anchor said, "In a stunning turn of events, General Valery Koskov, the head of Russian military intelligence, fell to his death today…"

Ford chuckled. "Man, no one is going to be safe in that country until they build balcony railings higher than FSB agents are tall."

39

Langley, Virginia

Nadia escaped Switzerland and returned to the United States. She was awarded an Intelligence Commendation Medal for her undercover work in HawkTech. In particular, during her final days there, she risked discovery and nearly certain death if exposed. Nadia continued to work, ensuring that Hawkinson did not discover a CIA officer in his midst. This gave Colt critical hours to execute his mission, which did grave harm to Archon.

Tyler Gales was not so lucky.

French police discovered his body in a field several miles outside of Paris. Despite her best efforts, Hawkinson's men caught him anyway and killed him before he could board his flight for the United States.

Nadia was devastated.

Colt tried to console her, saying that if she hadn't shifted suspicion to him, the operation would certainly have been discovered, Colt and Ikeda likely killed. Colt knew better than to reiterate the unit's belief that few in key roles at HawkTech didn't know what was actually going on.

It was cold comfort to ease her conscience. Nadia believed she'd gotten a man killed, whether he was guilty or not.

She was not permitted to contact Gales's family.

Liu Che returned to Beijing shortly after the new year, and he'd stayed in touch with Colt. Colt made good on his promise, and the US government eventually released Liu's wife, quietly. She was flown on an Agency aircraft to Vancouver, where she was released from custody.

Liu thanked Colt via the COVCOM when his wife repatriated.

Colt would continue to handle Liu directly but would coordinate closely with the China Mission Center. He was currently the only asset the Agency had within the Ministry of State Security and, as the geopolitical tides continued to shift in China's direction, was expected to become one of the most important assets CIA had.

They agreed he would keep a low profile initially, and there was little expectation of reporting for the first few months. Did they trust him? No. Did they trust him to keep up his end of the bargain? That jury was still out. Possible Liu could flip, double-agent them and feed them false information. That was a risky move for him. It was a lot of initiative for a service that liked to make all the decisions at the top. Colt believed Liu didn't want to see America and China at war, and he might just do as he'd promised to prevent that.

Time, and intelligence, would tell.

KOSCHEI did not heed Secretary Hughes's warning and back off his rhetoric of brinksmanship, but he took no further action. The Russian foreign minister delivered a speech to the UN General Assembly demanding the United States be "held accountable for violating the territorial sovereignty of the Russian people." Most in attendance considered the speech to be bad comedy.

The US government, borrowing a term from its Taiwan policy, chose "strategic ambiguity" when referencing the air traffic control and petroleum supply chain cyberattacks. They would not reference Archon publicly (indeed, that organization was not mentioned outside of select offices in CIA and the Oval), nor would they specifically blame Russia for them. They let the GRU bombing standing on its own as retribution. While the move was popular with most Americans, the president received criticism from his party and the opposition for taking so long to retaliate.

Recovery efforts in Sacramento would last years. Thousands of homes were completely wiped away, whole communities decimated. It would go down as one of the costliest disasters in US history. The head of the Bureau of Land Management was called before Congress for the usual post-crisis punitive hearings over their inability to protect the dam's operating systems. Some remarked that this would be the first time most Americans knew there *was* such a thing as the Bureau of Land Management. A bill called the Critical Infrastructure Protection Act, designed to create stricter security standards and mandates for software management, which had strong bipartisan support, died in the Senate, blocked by a small but powerful coalition of senators led by Preston Hawkinson. Senator Hawkinson argued that "Big Government overreach would not keep Americans safe."

Fearing Congressional intransigence, the president used a series of executive orders to enact a plan conceived of by his National Security Advisor, Jamie Richter, to elevate cyber defense. First, they reestablished the Office of Technology Defense within the National Security Council, the position previously held by Admiral Glen Denney, whose head would be known as the "Cyber Czar." The administration called for the creation of a new Information Security Agency within the Department of Homeland Security to "unify the government's cybersecurity protection efforts." In typical Washington fashion, it created new and confusing reporting relationships and duplicated the responsibilities of several existing agencies, the National Security Agency chief among them.

CIA established a new Technology Mission Center designed to analyze and assess foreign technological developments. This, too, seemed duplicative of what NTCU already attempted to do, and it was little surprise when they learned NTCU would be moved under the TMC.

That was the last straw for Fred Ford.

Ford broke the news of his retirement to Colt that spring once he learned about the reorganization. He would stay on until the summer as they dealt with the continued fallout, but he was done. "This is too stupid for words," he said of the change. Since they'd already lost the staff loaned out from the National Security Agency, Ford said this would be just one more step closer to shutting the unit down and returning to the bad old days of siloed intelligence work. They'd also lose their direct line to the head of the National Clandestine Service; being buried deeper in the

Agency bureaucracy would make it much harder for them to operate decisively in the field. Ford said retiring was the right thing to do, even though it would mean he'd probably have to get the kind of job that required a tie. Colt understood. Ford had a lot to lose. If their two years together combatting Archon was any indicator, things would get more dangerous, not less. Still, he would miss the acerbic wit, the fearlessness, and the too-much-bull-for-too-close-china. People like Ford were exactly what the Agency needed, intelligence officers that didn't play politics, didn't care about advancement, and would *only* tell leadership what they needed to hear, consequences be damned.

Colt would miss him.

The one thing they got right in this move, in Colt's estimation, was to establish technology counterintelligence portfolios at select CIA stations worldwide. Those stations would have their own technology portfolio, the same way they had local programs for counterterrorism, counterproliferation, or narcotics. Technical counterintelligence officers would receive training from NTCU and the new TMC prior to assignment.

Nadia was being inserted back into the Clandestine Service School at the point where she was pulled out the year before to complete her training. Her classmates were told that she'd been selected for an operational assignment, run through an accelerated program, and deployed to the field because of unique qualifications. And that was the actual truth, she was just forbidden from telling them what she'd done. Nadia was likely the first person to ever graduate from the Farm with an intelligence commendation medal.

When she reentered the Clandestine Service, Nadia was going to an overseas station and given the local technical counterintelligence program. Colt and Ford convinced her to stay operational.

Colt would be promoted to the NTCU deputy role upon Ford's retirement. Though, with the move to the Technology Mission Center, Colt wasn't sure he would stay with the unit. He wanted to get back into the field and carry on the hunt for Archon.

Guy Hawkinson had not been seen since December when the FBI and Swiss Federal Police attempted to arrest him at his office in Geneva. Colt believed he'd either been tipped off by one of his many contacts in the government or, more likely, Archon had technical surveillance on the Justice Department and knew it was coming.

Hawkinson was only listed as a "person of interest" in connection with a Chinese espionage case. There was no active warrant for his arrest that Thorpe could find. The FBI did not put him on the Most Wanted List, nor did they issue an INTERPOL Red Notice. Thorpe could not get a straight answer from the Bureau. Everyone at NTCU suspected his uncle's hand.

The Russians did not retaliate against the missile strike against the GRU cyber unit. It was a tense, dangerous time in Moscow. After the "accidental falling death" of General Koskov, the rest of the Russian General Staff quietly panicked. Everyone wondered who would be next.

GT-PARABLE reported that there were soft rumors circulating about a potential coup. He didn't think it was serious but said it was worth noting that there were enough deaths in the senior ranks of the Russian military over the last two years that the replacements were officers that only recently advanced through the ranks, were new to the role, and therefore didn't have direct connection to the Russian president.

Colt didn't hear from Ava...

...until he did.

She called him on the encryption app they used. Outside of official channels.

"I've left Mossad," she said. "After Samantha, I...I just couldn't do that job anymore."

He understood that too.

"I guess I lost my faith."

"What are you going to do now?"

"I'm in London, Colt."

What she said next would stay with him for a long, long time and would alter the course of Colt McShane's life in ways he could never predict.

"I've joined Trinity," she said. "And I want you to come with me."

All Secrets Die
Book 5 of The Firewall Spies

When a techno-terrorist group threatens to break encryptions on a global scale, a CIA officer must take matters into his own hands to save a world held hostage.

A massive security breach in China. CIA operations compromised in Turkey. Undercover ops breaking down the world over. A techno-terrorist group dubbed "Archon" has unleashed a terrifying new technology that can break any encryption. Humanity's secrets are about to be laid bare, and global order tilts toward chaos.

Up against a doomsday clock, CIA officer Colt McShane hatches a desperate plan: infiltrate Archon, capture one of the terrorist group's leaders, and force them to divulge the kill switch. But when Colt arrives just in time to see his target assassinated, he realizes that the stakes have been raised. Someone else is killing the terrorists and targeting their technology. And the question is: are they friends, or a new, and even more dangerous, enemy?

Aided by the beautiful and mysterious Ava Klein—an operator in a covert organization known only as Trinity—Colt must stay one step ahead of all who want him dead: international terrorists, government agents, police. Even those he once called friends can no longer be trusted.
Because in a world where power is built on a foundation of secrets, unlimited truth is the most destructive force of all...

Get your copy today at
severnriverbooks.com/series/the-firewall-spies

ABOUT ANDREW WATTS

Andrew Watts graduated from the US Naval Academy in 2003 and served as a naval officer and helicopter pilot until 2013. During that time, he flew counter-narcotic missions in the Eastern Pacific and counter-piracy missions off the Horn of Africa. He was a flight instructor in Pensacola, FL, and helped to run ship and flight operations while embarked on a nuclear aircraft carrier deployed in the Middle East. Today, he lives with his family in Virginia.

Sign up for the reader list at
severnriverbooks.com/series/the-firewall-spies

ABOUT DALE M. NELSON

Dale M. Nelson grew up outside of Tampa, Florida. He graduated from the University of Florida's College of Journalism and Communications and went on to serve as an officer in the United States Air Force. Following his military service, Dale worked in the defense, technology and telecommunications sectors before starting his writing career. He currently lives in Washington D.C. with his wife and daughters.

Sign up for the reader list at
severnriverbooks.com/series/the-firewall-spies

Printed in the United States
by Baker & Taylor Publisher Services